Happy Miles Publishing

Long Island City, New York

This is a work of fiction. Names, characters, businesses, places, events, locales, and incidents are either the products of the author's imagination or used in a fictitious manner. Any resemblance to actual persons, living or dead, or actual events is purely coincidental.

For information about special discounts available for bulk purchases, sales promotions, fund-raising and educational needs, contact Happy Miles Publishing Company Sales : Novel@haniselim.com

Cover Art by: Jennifer Lopez

Cover Art Digital Editing: Kaylin Wittmeyer

Editing by: Gina Heiserman

ISBN: 978-1-733

D1044342

i

DEDICATION

This book is dedicated to my grandmother, Etidal, and my uncle Abd El Rahman Selim. May you rest in peace!

Our common humanity

The innocent victims, everywhere!

And the love of writing and art.

11/11/2016

Dear Journal,

Today, and to my own surprise, I stopped by the Barnes & Noble on Court Street; it was Baba's favorite for some reason. He always had an affinity for Brooklyn and its Arab-filled neighborhoods. On my way home from work, the navigation's recalculations led me away from the BQE's traffic and right onto Atlantic Avenue.

There was something about seeing the Arabic writings on store fronts. It triggered childhood memories of walking up and down the avenue with Baba from store to mosque to car. Baba liked the mosque there, and its imam.

Everything slowed down, and the memories kept on coming one after the other. I saw my parents running to the car with bags of halal groceries on a rainy Ramadan night—long-gone memories, locked away with many others. They were buried one by one as I grew in years.

I had to stop the car. I couldn't breathe. I needed to fill my lungs with cold air. It felt like death in the car—a feeling I would have welcomed not too long ago—and I had to stop, for everyone's safety. I did it for Adam.

I got out of the car and walked around until I found myself purchasing a journal. I felt the urge to jot down those memories—they felt like a long-lost treasure. I spent much of my life running away from the family, and in doing so, I erased a lot of the memories. They returned, and I don't want to lose them, ever again. They were full of love and warmth; they were full of Baba.

I never had the desire to write anything before. I am not one to share my secrets with anyone, and definitely not on paper where others can read it. I didn't invest in a fancy journal; I opted for the most basic one, neon green and white.

I don't know if it was the color that caught my eyes—since green is for *go* in traffic lights, I felt like it was my green light to unravel on paper. It seemed like the universe was leading me to this notebook. My watch read 7:11 p.m. and the date was 11/11, which according to Asmaa is a great number because it is her birthday. I thought about buying her something, but I wasn't sure if we were supposed to celebrate birthdays with a death in the family just three days ago.

I also needed a place to put Baba's letter, which had been in the glove compartment for two days. It needed a better and warmer home.

I don't even know what I am supposed to write, or how to write a journal entry. Must I address the journal every time I put pen to paper?

It has been three days since Baba passed, and I really don't know what to do with the pain, anger, regret, and whirlpool of other emotions that I can't contain any longer.

Baba has, supposedly, trained me for this day, to be the man of the family.

Am I allowed to break down at my age? Am I allowed to cry out of nowhere because I remember that I can no longer hug my baba? Seriously, what is the etiquette of the mourning process? I don't think I can burden anyone but lines on a paper with my scrambled thoughts. A journal seems like a good place to do so—after all, green is good, green is Mother Nature, green is heaven. Maybe I will find some heavenly solace in writing, since it seems like everyone else loves writing letters right before their death.

Why didn't he tell me to my face everything he wrote?
Why did I have to find out this way?
Why couldn't he confront me all those years?
When did he find out?

Why couldn't he say something the last hours I spent with him in the hospital?

I sat there by his bedside the whole time as he talked about everything else but the one thing we both hid for so long. He spent his last waking hours telling me to take care of everyone else and listing all the things that should be done in case of his death. He knew he was dying. Mama knew he was dying—I saw it in the way she held and kissed him before she went home to rest. I knew my worst nightmare was about to unfold.

But why did he waste his last few breaths on telling me where he wanted to be buried and what he should be buried in?

I already knew all of this. I knew he wanted to be buried in New York, close to us, I knew he wanted to be buried in the same ihram cloth he wore to hajj. He even included all of that in his will. He could have talked to me like he used to when I was a little kid, he could have hinted or something. It would have been so much better to hear those words uttered by him rather than reading them in a letter from a lawyer.

I've never felt this lost and empty before. I have been running away from him all these years and avoiding any confrontation when all I wanted to do was run into his arms like I did when I was a child.

I feel like a total idiot for hiding all this time, but I didn't want to disappoint him. I didn't want to hurt him, the one man who has been there for me, within his capacity, every step of the way since my birth.

I always thought it was better to keep some things hidden from him, but why didn't he tell me that he knew? Why didn't he say something before it was too late?

Or did he try, and I didn't pay attention? Or maybe he couldn't try.

Maybe, he didn't know how to do it.

In the name of God, the Most Gracious, the Most Merciful

Dear Osama,

If you are reading this letter, it means only one thing: that I have passed from this world and moved on to the next. I am sorry that I couldn't keep my promise to always be there for you, but that is just the way life works—nothing lasts forever.

I am positive that I have not written a letter of such significance since I won your mother's heart ages ago. Therefore, you must pardon my poor attempt to write you a heartfelt letter at a time like this. After all, I am only a surgeon.

As a surgeon, I delivered tragic news more times than I would have liked. My line of work somewhat desensitized me to death, which I learned to accept as an integral part of life's cycle. Delivering such news to any of my patients and their families was the worst part of the job. Telling someone that their heart would expire in a few months exposed me to the vulnerability of human existence. I witnessed those who fell into the traps of depression upon receiving the news. I also experienced those who welcomed it, decided to accept the challenge, and marveled in the beauty of life. The latter taught me a great lesson; it taught me to appreciate every second I was given with my loved ones, doing the things I love.

With all the discoveries we made over the centuries that allowed us to control nearly every variable in life, we never came close to controlling the end of life. We, as scientists and doctors, try to prolong it, but we can't alter *el maktoob*. Our moment of departure was written long ago, and we all must depart upon reaching the end of our book.

Do you remember when you came to Egypt a few years ago and I was in the hospital?

I knew back then of the severity of my condition as I came to. I knew that my days with you and the family would be cut short.

I became one of my own patients who had an expiration date.

Writing this letter is taking me back to the moment when I saw the worry on your face. It was the look I saw many times on the faces of families who would do just about anything to appease their loved ones in their moment of weakness. It was a look of pure unconditional love. It also made me think of how selfish I was then. I made you do things that I thought would make me happy. I was not thinking of your happiness. It was not fair of me to push you into doing things against your own will, knowing that you wouldn't refuse your dying father's wish.

Yes, Habibi, that was the reason I made my wish right there and then. The urgency of the condition called for extreme action. It triggered every fear a parent feels for a child from the moment we are informed of the pregnancy. It is something which I am sure you felt when you heard of your own son's arrival. As a parent, you will find yourself

worrying about the smallest of details. You
will think of all the ways to protect that
little piece of you from the world. We go
above and beyond to protect our own
offspring from external factors, but we
forget to protect them from ourselves.

And in our case, it is very true. I tried to
do right by you, and in doing so, I failed you.

Like my father before me, I thought I knew
what was best for you. I failed you when I
didn't accept you for who you are and the
choices you make. I imposed my own choices
on you, knowing very well that you would
comply. I didn't trust you to make the right
choices for yourself. It is never an easy task
for a parent to admit fault to their own
kids, it rarely happens. Yet here I am
admitting mine in hopes that you can
forgive me. I was wrong when I found out
about your biggest struggle in life and didn't
broach the subject with you. I wanted to fix
your broken pieces, but I wasn't there for
you as a father or as the friend I promised

myself to be. I guess it is right what Egyptians say: When your son gets older, treat him like a brother. I didn't do that.

I failed you in life, and I refuse to do so in death. I know the last few years were rough, and we kept some distance between us—a distance which was an act of love, respect, and fear. I feared losing you to many things, but I never thought I would lose you because of life choices. I didn't want things between us to have the same fate as they did many years ago with my father. I knew of your struggles ever since Nora passed; I knew of your relationship with her. I knew many things, but I didn't have a clue how to deal with the whole situation. I didn't know how to be there for you without losing you. I let my own views and beliefs come between us. In my mind, you were wrong. You were at fault for everything that unfolded then. I was ashamed, angry, hurt, and confused. I let all of that stop me from being there for you when you needed me most, and I am truly sorry. I just didn't know how to react to any of it. I couldn't believe that my only son, dear to me above all else, would be the cause of the deepest of wounds to my heart. I did attempt a few times to approach you, but I failed miserably. I let my pride and cultural barriers stand between us every time.

I know that I made you do things against your will, because I knew how much you cared for your mother and for me. I knew that you would do anything to placate us; I knew that you would do anything to keep your secret safe. I knew which buttons to press to get you to do the things I wanted you to do. I just knew you too well, and I want to say I am sorry for each and every time I forced you to do something against your will. I wish I can take it all back. I wish I could do it all over again and be there for you every step of the way as a supportive friend rather than a father who did nothing while his only son was hurting the most.

It is a parent's duty to provide the kids with a safe and loving environment where they can openly express their thoughts, emotions, and fears. It was a duty that I unsuccessfully fulfilled. You didn't feel safe talking to me, just as your sister didn't in her time of trouble. In case you are wondering if I wrote Asmaa a letter too, the answer is no. I didn't write her one. Asmaa and I made amends years ago. She was the one who pushed for a closure. She never appreciated the fact that I exiled the two of you to solve the conundrum we faced. She demanded both my forgiveness for her wrongdoing, and an apology for my own wrongdoing.

I did as I was programmed to do. I did my best to shelter my kids. I thought controlling them would keep them safe. Like most parents, I spent my time telling you and your sisters what to do or not to do. I tried to pass my knowledge on to you. I think we are the only creatures who try to control their own offspring. I can't imagine a bird doing more than providing a nest, food, and flying lessons to its young. I can't imagine a bird, or any other animal for that matter, forcing their young to marry a lighter-color bird instead of a darker one. Animals teach their offspring the basic survival skills then set them free to learn through trial and error. You will never see a bird carrying its young on its back to teach it how to fly. A cat gives its kittens a nudge to help them stand, and that is all. Yet we push our babies in carriages until they are five years old.

In a way, I think we cripple ourselves. There was a time when kids weren't so sheltered. With indigenous tribes and their rite-of-passage celebrations, the young are welcomed as functional members of the tribe at a much earlier age. In our modern society, we don't trust our young until they are well into their 20s. We overload them with cultural and religious rules, and we add some more legal rules to mold them into something out of a catalogue. We are told to be unique and free, but we are taught to fit in.

I know that I taught you much throughout your life, but you managed somehow to teach me the ultimate lesson of my life. You taught me how to love someone unconditionally. Yes, Osama, you taught me that lesson, but I was never able to express it or show it in the way you might have wanted me to. I hope that you can find it in that big heart of yours to forgive me for failing to give and show you my unconditional love and support. I hope that you can forgive me for making you do things that I saw as best for you but, in reality, were only to satisfy my selfish desire to turn you into what I wanted you to be, rather than giving you the tools to be you.

Last, but not least, I want you to know that I always loved you, from the moment the doctor placed you in my arms and I welcomed you into this world, to the moment my body is lowered into the ground. I also want you to know that I was always proud of you and your accomplishments. I am proud of the man you turned out to be. I hope that one day your son makes you as proud as you made me. I hope that he loves you just as much as you love me. Teach him everything you know, teach him everything I once taught you, and let him fly high and soar freely.

I love you,

Baba

11/12/2016

Dear Journal,

Hi, it is me, again.

I rudely forgot to introduce myself to you. My name is Osama, and I am not telling you more than what I shared with you the other night; you are a dangerous place. I told you, it is that green color.

I don't know why I chose you of all places to keep Baba's letter.

I don't know why I keep reading it over and over again, as if he will resurrect through his words or something. I feel myself slipping into a gloomy abyss once again. I have been there before, and it is not a place I wish to visit again.

Does it ever get any easier?

I feel like a nutcase, talking to a notebook. Why is it so hard to cry in front of others? I don't even remember the last time my eyes allowed a tear to escape their barbed lashes. Lashes look like the bars in a jail cell when you squint your eyes. I am seeing everything like a jail— even Adam's crib looks like a jail or a cage.

You know, when I was a kid, Baba never interrupted me when I sat by the car window and gazed at the world around me. He was thoughtful and encouraging like that. I loved how trees looked when we drove by them fast. Now that I think about it, those trees look like the columns to a high wall of some natural jail.

I am sorry my face is leaking all over you; it has been quite a while since I cried this much. I feel the bones crushing my heart, or the muscles of my heart tightening up and strangling one another. I really believed that mourning got easier as we got older. This is far worse.

I miss you, Baba.

Now you've got me talking to him.

Is this what others do when they write in their journals? Do they let it all out? Do they talk to anyone they wish to talk to?

I should google this; I should ask Laila if she keeps a journal. It is weird that I don't know if my wife keeps a journal or not. I know she did as a little girl for a bit, and she stopped.

Maybe I shouldn't ask her. If I do, she will want to know what I am writing. Humans are curious by nature. Some things are meant to be private, maybe.

So yeah, I am married, and we have the most adorable son, Adam. He is my world, and he is the beat of my heart. He was the angel that rescued me from my previous torturous life sentence; he snatched me out of some really dark stuff. His first cry was my wake-up call. He is the only reason I am still holding it together.

I feel like a shitty father—I haven't spent much time around him. He isn't even two years old, but I don't want him to see this shallow shell of human I have been the past few days.

I was moving forward, accepting death as part of life's cycle, but that letter was some curveball—and the man hated baseball. Each word that made up the letter felt like a sharp knife cutting open my old weak stitches, slashing them wide open again and then some. Why, Baba? Why did you have to do it like that? Was there any wisdom to your choice?

Journal, you are dangerous!

11/13/ 2016

I am still trying to accept the fact that he's gone. I know death is a part of life, as he mentioned in the letter, yet I can't explain the void I feel. I won't get any more phone calls from him. I won't get to roll my eyes at the phone when I get his daily texts. It annoyed me how involved he tried to be, but I also loved it. It was weird; I knew that was his way of showing us love. Sometimes I wished he'd stop, and when he did, something was missing. Just like it feels right now. This time, it is permanent.

It's painful. My tears fail me; I can't write anymore.

11/14/2016

Why did God have to take him right now?

We were starting to get close again. I was starting to learn to be myself around him again. I could have used some more time with him. He knew how to do the fatherhood thing better than I could, ever. I needed him around to ask the tough questions about fatherhood and how to answer all the tough questions Adam may ask one day. He would have been the perfect guide and mentor. I was finally starting to see things from his point of view, the view of a father who loved his family wholly.

11/18/2016

"Can we blame Trump for Baba's passing?"

Asmaa, my middle sister, sent this today in our group message on WhatsApp. We've had this group for a while to make sure that Baba and Mama were well looked after, without them knowing that we are always scheduling visits among ourselves. Now, we are going to discuss Mama and her needs. There is no more Baba. We also have a group with all the in-laws.

I don't know why I am explaining the groups to you. You are a journal, and I should know these things when and if I read you later. Anyway, Asmaa sent that message, and I laughed. Baba did have impeccable timing; he escaped Trump, though I don't think Trump had it in him to shake my old man. But Baba did end up in the hospital that night right after they announced the results. Many went to sleep in fearful tears for America and her future; I didn't have a restful night of sleep since that night.

It was late Tuesday when my phone rang. It was Mama. It was unusual for either set of parents to call at such a late hour. My parents are usually in bed before ten. I picked up the phone, worried. Mama was crying on the other end of the line and I couldn't make out much of what she was saying except that I knew it was something really bad.

"Mama, please calm down and tell me what's wrong. Did something happen to Baba?" I kept on repeating myself.

After several attempts to calm her down, she finally spoke in an understandable tone and said, "Osama, the ambulance came and picked up Baba. He was with Uncle Said in the dining room and he just collapsed. I want to go see him, come pick me up right now."

I ran to my room to change and to get the car keys. Laila was up and heard the rushing noises and came running to find out what was happening. I told her exactly what my mother told me over the phone. As I ran down the stairs, Laila called out, "Osama, please call me once you get to the hospital and find out anything. I hope it is nothing but him reacting to the news the whole country just received."

I got into the car and a feeling of heaviness and fear hit me all at once. I realized the possibility of losing him. It was my second time visiting him as a patient in the hospital. I didn't like the feeling one bit. I began driving to my parents' house and I couldn't shake my fears away. Baba was invincible, and for his age, he was in great shape. It had to be something so strong that did that to him. I thought of every possible scenario and reason that could have led to Baba's collapse. Old age was a thought that crossed my mind, and the bullet that penetrated his chest years ago was another. He hadn't shown any signs of weakness when we saw him last.

I arrived at my parents' house. Mama was already waiting outside and got into the car quickly.

"Mama, why didn't you go with him?"

"Habibi, I was in my nightgown when the ambulance arrived. I performed some CPR on him when he collapsed, and by the time the ambulance showed up, he was conscious enough to tell me to stay home. He asked me to call you to come pick him up."

"Even in times like this, he is still stubborn. Why would you even listen to him?" I asked.

"Osama, you know how Baba gets, plus I didn't want to aggravate or argue with him. I figured it would be easier this way. And as soon as the ambulance drove away, I called you."

Mama seemed so calm, but I knew deep down she was more worried than I could ever be. Baba was everything to her and she was everything to him.

I tried to distract both of us by asking if she had called any of my sisters to inform them of what had happened. We kept on making small talk throughout the drive; neither of us wanted to think about what might happen.

Within an hour of our arrival, everyone we knew had managed to call or arrive at the emergency room of the hospital. All three of my sisters made it with their husbands. It was one big family reunion, or so it seemed. I instructed my sisters to keep a close eye on Mama and comfort her as much as possible while we waited for news from any of the passing nurses.

After four hours of waiting, we were finally told of Baba's condition. He had suffered a minor heart attack and they had to keep him under observation for a day or two before they could release him.

We were all thankful that he was fine and still with us. Although the doctor advised us to leave, most refused to go home until they got to see him, even if it was for only a second. One of the nurses kindly sneaked each one of the family members into the room to glance at Baba quickly while I stood in the far corner of the room watching the whole thing unfold.

I am not sure what it was that I felt at that moment and I am not sure why I felt it, but for some reason I knew that this was the last time we would have Baba in the same room with any of us. It was an overwhelming feeling and it reached its peak when Mama entered the room to say goodbye before she headed home with Fatma.

There was something about the way Mama held him and kissed his forehead as he laid there motionless, hooked up to all these machines. She did it in a way as if she, too, knew that she was saying goodbye for the very last time—she did it in such a loving, accepting way. It is so Mama, she is so at peace with life and herself.

I spent the rest of the night by his bedside praying that he would wake in the morning healthy and sound. It was hard to sit there watching him lie helpless, and it was even harder picturing life without his presence, without his phone calls, without his random visits to play with Adam. It was impossible to hold back my tears. I kneeled next to his bed drowning into my own grief. It was a repeat of a past experience. I had been by his hospital bedside before, praying and bargaining for his life.

Baba woke up in the middle of the night. He looked so frail, but nevertheless he was still alive, and my fears and worries were nothing but that. He instructed the nurse to wake me up.

I must have dozed off in my chair as I sat with him. I jumped off my seat and hurried to his bed. I grabbed his left hand and kissed it as he reached over with his other arm to pat my head, my tears of joy soaking the back of his hand. He struggled to get the words out as he asked me about everyone else. He even joked and smiled and said, "Can you believe this guy won the election? That should teach the Democrats not to rig the elections again. I was ready to vote for the Jewish guy."

He was too tired; he went back to sleep, and he never woke up again.

I really fucking miss him. I hate that my last memory of him is his lifeless body. He was my hero; he was my superman; he lifted me up high. I soared because of him. We all did.

12 /18/ 2016

Dear Journal,

It has been a month since the last time I have written a word. It hasn't been an easy month, but I am managing. I am trying to put the pieces together. I am doing my best to be strong, at least for Adam's sake. I returned to work about two weeks ago, and I hate everything about being there. I hate people asking me about Baba and how I am feeling. I am positive they can see it in my face. I see it in my face when I look in the mirror. I avoid mirrors to avoid seeing that blank look, and today of all days, I made sure I avoided everything but the phone call from Mama.

She called because today marked the fortieth day since Baba passed. It is something similar to a memorial or a remembrance day of the deceased. It is a practice which the ancient Egyptians started, as far as I know, and it made its way into other religions and cultures in some form. I am so full of these random facts about random things, I will probably fill you up with them if I continue writing. It took the ancient Egyptians forty days to mummify the body, and once they were done, the soul was free to go. There is something about the number forty; it is mentioned in every religion. It keeps on appearing everywhere in the Torah, Bible, and Quran. What is so magical about that number that even the ancient Egyptians knew it before everyone else?

While I was on the phone talking to Mama, Adam managed to get himself all the way across the living room. It was as if he felt the gloominess and heaviness of the phone call. He crawled his way to me and stood up shored by my legs. His little hands hugged two of my fingers. He had this smile on his face, and he yelled out "Babaaaaa." His playful scream and radiant smile lightened the load; the clouds were fanned away—even Mama laughed.

She asked to see his face, and we switched over to facetime—it's a feature I wish we had available growing up, and I am not sure it will still be available by the time Adam is a teenager. I am sure something else will take its place. Hologram phone calls are next, maybe. I don't know, we're a bit slow when it comes to innovations—we don't have flying cars yet. Flying magic carpets had to be a thing at some point. I remember sitting on Baba's lap and watching Aladdin flying around on his magic carpet. Baba was so good to me; he gave me everything I needed as a child. I was such a fucking idiot for wasting so much time away from him. We could have done so much more together. I can't think of him and not think of all the things we did together when I was a child. I have albums upon albums of pictures with him and the family. He gave us great memories that will last us a lifetime. I really hope this regret doesn't last a lifetime; I hope it is nothing but mourning. I need to keep focusing on tomorrow, on Adam.

Adam's presence in the room altered the energy. He traveled through the air with the radio frequencies and changed the mood of a mourning elderly lady. It is one of the many gifts given to us since his birth. He adds so much joy to our lives and the lives of both sets of grandparents. And today is one of the days when I am beyond thankful to have him as my son, and I hope one day to have him as a friend.

His eyes smiled in a way identical to Baba's. It was the perfect reminder of the letter and Baba's will to share and teach Adam the lessons he once taught me as well as the ones I learned on my own.

But how will I do it?

Baba would have been the perfect person to answer this question. He would have known what to say to soothe my current anxieties. I really worry for Adam. I worry that he won't have the same kind of parenting I had. His mom and I are both beyond damaged, and I am scared we will end up ruining him. I also worry about the day he must leave this house and go out into this crazy world.

Adam, if by any chance this journal falls into your hands, I want you to know I love you more than I have ever loved anything in this world. You are the lighthouse that rescued my lost boat. And Laila, if you are reading this, put it down! It is not for you; it is father-son talk.

Journal, you are brilliant. But maybe I should address Adam rather than addressing you. I think it is a good idea to share the family story with him. I know I will forget a lot of it by the time he is old enough to comprehend it all. It is one of the pitfalls of becoming a father in my late thirties. Baba got married young, and he had me in his early forties. I always felt that gap with Baba; I felt like there was a lot we couldn't connect on. Plus, I didn't get to enjoy him for as long as Aisha and Fatma did. Sometimes I wish I was the eldest, and not them.

I am going to start creating memories with Adam from now on. I am going to spend my nights in his room writing, and I will address him instead of you. I will tell him about our family history and the things Baba did and taught us. In a way, it's the third chance for our family to have a normal father-son relationship. I heard that infants and babies can feel our presence at all times, even in their sleep, and the closeness calms the trauma of being on this side of life. I watched him scream his way into the world, and he continues to scream and cry sometimes. It is understandable; no one wants to come into this life only to die.

I miss you, Baba.

Fuck you, death!!!!

12/19/2016

Hi, Journal,

I made it into Adam's room as I mentioned last night. We can't wake him up; we have to be very quiet. He looks like an angel in his sleep. I spent half an hour watching his lips and hands move—I think he was having a fun dream. I hope we are not making any noise. You may lose me for good if he ends up waking because of us.

It is odd—now that I am here, I don't know what to write to him. Last night I had a lot that I wished to share. Now I am just imagining how this journal could end up in Adam's hands one day. Do I want to give it to him some day as a present, so he knows it all? Do I want to be a bit more creative and leave it in a time capsule with a treasure map? Or do I just address him but never give it to him?

I don't know why, but everything feels so real now without Baba; I have to do things differently. I must be an adult, and I am feeling a new sense of responsibility. I felt it the first time I saw Adam's heart beat on the screen when the doctor scanned Laila's belly. There was a sense of curiosity, because it was all new and exciting. I was struck then by the responsibilities of fatherhood to come, but I didn't feel like an adult then; I felt like a boy who was just handed his most precious toy, and I was told to take care of it and be watchful. Tonight, it feels different. I feel like everything about me can be a part of Adam. I feel like a real baba who has to pass down the best of his knowledge to his offspring. I am really responsible for the well-being of another life, and I have to make decisions that will impact him for his eternity. I am giving myself some serious anxiety thinking of all the possibilities and all the things that I went through with and without my own baba.

I spent the last month realizing how numb I was for most of my life. The flashbacks have been my guide into the past, and they have all revolved around something or other that I did with Baba. For so long, I didn't care to acknowledge his efforts, and I was blinded by my anger and guilt.

Adam deserves to know the same things Baba taught us. They were the foundation that kept me somewhat grounded, even in my troubles.

"Osama, it is about The God, not me and not anyone else. It is the relationship that matters most. Pray to your creator and your prayers will be answered; he is your closest ally." Baba drilled those things into our minds.

I will never forget the day he came home and found me walking on a rope I had laid on the floor. "Osama, what are you doing?"

"I am practicing walking on the Straight Path. The imam said it's as thin as a hair strand."

He laughed, sat me on his lap, and began teaching me these fundamental Quranic verses, "Say, come, I will recite what your Lord has prohibited to you. He commands that you not associate anything with Him, and to parents, good treatment, and do not kill your children out of poverty; We will provide for you and them. And do not approach immoralities—what is apparent of them and what is concealed. And do not kill the soul which Allah has forbidden to be killed except by legal right. This has He instructed you that you may use reason.

"And do not approach the orphan's property except in a way that is best until he reaches maturity. And give full measure and weight in justice. We do not charge any soul except with that within] its capacity. And when you testify, be just, even if it concerns a near relative. And the covenant of Allah fulfill. This has He instructed you that you may remember.

"And, moreover, this is My path, which is straight, so follow it; and do not follow other ways, for you will be separated from His way. This has He instructed you that you may become righteous."

The next morning, he called the imam and gave him an earful about the things he should and shouldn't teach us as children. Thanks to Baba, my straight path was never a strand of hair.

There is so much that could have been averted if it wasn't for the family's decision. Life could have been so different based on one or two decisions based on very limited knowledge. Anything I do can send Adam into a hell like mine or Laila's. I wonder if I suddenly feel this way because my own protector is gone, and now I have to step up and be the "man" for the entire family. I need to focus on something else before I give myself a panic attack. I should go back to the reason I am sitting here. I am going to write to Adam.

Hi, Adam,

It's me, your father.(That sounded like a scene from *Star Wars*.) If you couldn't tell, I am not having the easiest of times right now realizing that I have to do this fatherhood thing all alone, without my baba's guidance. I didn't think this day would come so fast, and I am freaking out. I seriously don't remember any of what I wanted to write down. I know I wanted to tell you all about the family and the lessons Baba taught us, and hopefully we don't fall into the same trap as previous generations. The letter you read upon opening this journal was from your gedo; he left it behind with his lawyer, and I received it a couple of days after his death.

Baba was the one constant in my life who never failed me, though, according to his letter, he thought otherwise. In many ways, I felt like I was the one who failed him. I did a lot to meet his expectations of me as a son. I put so much pressure on myself throughout the years to be somebody I thought he wanted me to be. I feared that if he ever knew my truth, we would cease to exist to one another. I discriminated against my own father and my whole family. I didn't give them the benefit of the doubt. I thought the worst of them. I saw them as simple- and narrow-minded people. I projected the ignorant and intolerant image of every Arab and Muslim onto them. I *was* them.

Even in his death, your gedo was selfless and thought of me before himself. In his final moments, he chose to teach one more lesson about humility and openness—he chose my peace of mind, he chose to give me the perfect ending to my torment. He understood my need for closure.

It was his will for me to teach you the lessons he taught me, and that is exactly what I shall do. I shall let you in on all of the moments that made the letter significant. I shall share with you the family's history

27

and why things are the way they are today. I shall keep no secrets from you. You shall learn all the things that matter, so you may never feel the need to fear those closest to you.

Adam, if you made it this far into my journal, don't put it down. Please read this with a nonjudgmental mind and an open heart. This is my journey through life, and all the things that brought us to this very moment. I am going to share with you all that I can, because I want you to see things clearly. Most people talk about the greatness of their parents, unless that parent was a bad one. For those of us who were blessed with what we conceive as a normal family, we tend to hold our parents in such high regard, almost as untouchable as God. I knew there was a point in my life where I couldn't go to Baba for much; I had to hide a lot from him, and it wasn't because he wouldn't have listened. He lost my trust somewhere along the line because I didn't think he would be able to handle my life, because it was so different from his own. I want you to know both the good and bad; I want you to see me as your fellow human, and not a God. I want you to see me as your friend one day and to not fear approaching me.

Equipped with lessons learned from the failures of my father and his father before him, I hope to lay a new foundation starting today. I will share with you the stories of the family, my own personal stories, and those of how you became a part of our lives. I plan to share with you openly and without censorship. I plan to share stories that most fathers—especially those of conservative roots—wouldn't share willingly. Your gedo always said, "When your son gets older, treat him like a brother." I always loved that saying, but I never really practiced it. I don't know if it was his fault or mine that we didn't meet halfway; I feel like we never quite saw eye to eye ever since he sent us to Egypt.

The letter is my only validation that he saw me as an adult, and it was the letter that made me buy this journal.

First things first. As you well know, I go by the name Osama. The name was chosen by Baba. No, I was not named after you-know-who. Wait, you wouldn't know who I am talking about. Anyway, *he* wasn't part of the international scene as yet. Maybe I should tell you about Osama bin Laden—by the time you find this journal, I am hoping his name will not be as recognized as it is today. He was considered the most dangerous criminal on the planet for quite some time, and in many ways, he was part of my struggles in life. His mega-status as a criminal brought unwanted attention to me and my name. I could write books about the dirty looks I received at airports and any place where my name was called out loud, and it started before the horror of September 11, 2001. He was already notorious in the 90s throughout the Middle East and Africa, and anyone who followed the news knew the name. I absolutely hated the man, but loved the name because it was mine. I will tell you more about the name when I tell you about my birth. I will say this much: My name is one of many synonyms for *lion* in Arabic.

I was born into an Egyptian Sunni Muslim family on American soil. You see, we already have something in common. At first, the family consisted of your late grandfather, Issa, your grandmother, Hannan, me, and your aunts, my sisters Aisha, Fatma, and Asmaa.

You will know more about each one of us; you will learn the circumstance of each life lesson we endured. However, I am making my request once again—don't be too quick and hasty to judge. I am so nervous thinking of you reading this journal in the future.

And now, since you know how the story ends and what made me write it, let me tell you how it all unfolded.

I feel like Shahrazad and Shahryar in an episode of *A Thousand and One Nights* we watched as kids in Egypt. I definitely watched a lot of television growing up. I am not repeating the same mistake with you; I am limiting your television access, young man. You are going to learn the things that really matter, and the first of those things is our family's story.

Baba Issa was born on the 23rd of July, 1936. His roots originate from Upper Egypt and he belonged to a wealthy family in Asyut. Unlike the rest of his siblings, he excelled in his schoolwork. He wanted to continue with his education and obtain a degree in medicine. I always understood that Baba's upbringing impacted his philosophy of raising us. He did everything within his power to be nothing like my gedo. It was why he used to always tell us, "You could lose your money, your house, your job, you could lose it all, but with an education, you can rebuild and regain it all."

He taught us much by telling us about his upbringing, hoping we would appreciate all that he gave us. "You know, Osama, things weren't always as accessible as they are today. And back when I was young, parents didn't encourage studying or schooling that much." Baba paused. "You know how your mama and I always encourage you kids to do better in school. I didn't have that. Your gedo was all about the land and agriculture. I had to push myself to study as much as I could while fulfilling my duties and chores."

"Did you have to throw out the trash and mow the lawn in Asyut?" Asmaa asked, smirking.

"No, we definitely didn't have those kinds of chores in Egypt. We had maids and servants in the house taking care of that stuff. I am talking about helping your gedo with his dealings. I sometimes had to oversee the farmers working the field, and since I was the only one who continued his education, I had to work in the office, though I think I was also there as a spy."

"Are you serious? You were the only one who finished his education?" I asked. That seemed like common knowledge to everyone in the room. I was the youngest, and there was a lot that I didn't know. My sisters had heard some of the stories over the years, but I loved hearing them every time we were together for our mandatory Sunday dinners.

"Yes, your uncles didn't go beyond grade school."

"How about Gedo?" I asked.

"He was illiterate. He didn't read or write. He had his own stamp which he carried around everywhere—he always had it in the inside pocket of his vest." He pointed to his chest. "I used to read a lot of the contracts and agreements to him. Growing up, I used to read him the newspaper."

"You two were really close!"

"We were, and we weren't." He drew a deep breath. "We were close when he needed my help, but he was never an affectionate man. He never expressed his feelings towards any of us. We were his kids, and we had to do as we were told; unlike you kids, we didn't have much of an option. And if we didn't do as we were told, we were punished immediately."

"What kind of punishments are we talking about? Did you get grounded?" I asked.

"Grounded!" Baba laughed hard. "Yes, and we got time-outs too."

"Really?"

"Your Gedo was far more creative with his punishments. I remember this one time when he tied my eldest brother, Ibrahim, to a tree trunk, and he whipped him with one of those things you use when riding a horse, what do you call that?"

"He used a whip?" I asked.

"He whipped him, and he didn't stop until the whip tore apart."

"Do you remember what he was punished for?" Asmaa asked.

"Someone told him that they saw Ibrahim following a girl with some friends of his, and they were bothering her." Baba laughed. "It wasn't even him. He got punished for nothing, but in a way, he did deserve it for all the other things he got away with by blaming them on the rest of us."

"Baba, did you ever get punished like that?"

"Yes, Osama, I got a few beatings growing up, but I don't think your gedo had the energy to beat me up the way he did my older siblings. They thought I was his favorite because I didn't get punished as much, but I had a different theory. He had wasted a lot of energy beating up my older brothers all the time, and by the time he got to me, he had run out of gas."

"Did you get in a lot of trouble growing up?" my questioning continued.

"No."

"I don't believe that one bit," Asmaa said.

"I was more focused on school. I didn't have much of a support system at home. Your gedo, his friends, and relatives used to get together every day. They used to sit on the verandah talking and laughing loudly throughout the evening and into the night. There were many nights when I took my books along with a gas lamp to the barn. It was the only place where I was able to study and have some privacy and quiet."

"*Ewwww.*" Asmaa produced a sound of disgust and fanned her right hand by her nose. "Did it stink in there? I am sure it did."

"I don't even remember." Baba paused. "I was accustomed to the odor. The barn was the place where I found silence. Unlike you kids, I didn't have my own private room until I moved to Cairo for college. I shared a room with your uncle Saleh. And your gedo, he didn't like closed doors at all. All hell broke loose if he saw one of our doors closed for more than ten minutes."

It wasn't easy for Baba to get his father's consent to move to Cairo on his own. My grandfather wanted his youngest son to join the others, managing his business. He thought a college degree was unnecessary, since the family was well-established financially.

I never met my grandfather, Reda, but saw many black and white photographs of him in Baba's albums, standing with his four sons in what looked more like a military lineup than a family photo. He stood 6'2" with a dark, olive complexion, a narrow face, and a tough demeanor accentuated by his very thick mustache. I don't think I ever saw a picture of him smiling. He looked both serious and mysterious in those photos. I always imagined that there was a smiley child hiding behind the bushy, thick mustache of his or somewhere within the folds of his oversized *galabia*. He owned a substantial amount of land on which he cultivated vegetables and fruit to be distributed throughout Egypt. Each of my three uncles—Ibrahim, Saleh, and Moussa—handled a part of the family business. The eldest, Ibrahim, took care of the cultivation of the land and dealing with the farmers, while the other two dealt mainly with merchants in various parts of Egypt.

Since Baba was the youngest son, and the one who received the most attention from my then-aging grandparents, he was able to convince his parents to allow him to continue his education in Cairo. The opportunity was granted on condition that he would promise to never forget his roots.

"You have to come back every holiday. And once you are done, you will work here in Asyut," grandfather said. "That is the only way I am allowing this to happen."

"Let him do what he wants to do. You have everyone else helping you here." My grandmother, who never expressed her opinion while others were in the room, did so for Baba's sake. "I am sure Issa will not stray; you raised him well." Baba always believed it was his mother who swayed Gedo Reda's opinion.

The first couple of years Baba spent in Cairo went exactly as promised—he kept in constant contact with the family. He wrote letters, sent telegraphs, and visited them every holiday. During such visits, my grandfather displayed a great sense of pride. He was so proud of his youngest son—the only college student in the family, and soon to be the first college graduate—but that sense of pride ultimately pushed him away, little by little. He overwhelmed Baba with all the plans he had for his future. He wanted to live Baba's life and make the decisions based on his own ideas of the world around him, rather than those of his own kid.

Baba went on. "He had determined where I'd work and live upon graduation; he had even chosen the woman whom I would marry. That was how he showed his love and support to all of us," Baba once told me, when I asked him about my grandfather. "I didn't see it that way; I didn't see it as love. I felt that he was suffocating and controlling me, but I didn't dare voice any objection to these plans."

"How come you never told him what you wanted for yourself?" I asked.

"I didn't know what I wanted, but I knew I didn't want him planning my whole future. That was the way things were done in that part of the country; that was the only way most people operated," Baba explained. "Before moving to Cairo, I never saw a future outside of Asyut, but when I moved it was a whole new world. Everyone was dressed in pants, shirts, suits, dresses, skirts, and blouses. I didn't see much of those things in Upper

Egypt; I got glimpses of them on TV and in newspapers, but they weren't part of my daily life."

"Your baba didn't own a pair of pants until he moved to Cairo," Mama added.

"And it wasn't until I moved to Cairo that I started to realize that life outside of the countryside had more to offer."

"Really? Was Cairo the real reason?" Mama sarcastically asked. "That wasn't how you told the twins and Asmaa the story."

"Yeah, Baba, you said it was when you met Mama," Aisha commented.

"Do you tell a story the same way every time?" Baba laughed. "I was getting to the good part."

"What is the good part? I want to know too," I said.

"My life began the day I saw your mother. It was love at first sight."

It was Baba's fourth year in medical school. He saw her for the first time as she was entering a building in the neighborhood with her mother. "I was on my way back from one of the lectures. I was struck by her beauty—her long, dark, wavy hair reaching right down her back. I couldn't get the image of her smile or her honey-colored eyes out of my mind for days, and then I saw her in the neighborhood again."

Baba, who at that time always had his nose in a book, began to look forward to catching sight of her in their Giza neighborhood. Once he realized that his Cinderella lived right across the street from him, he moved the study desk in his apartment from the living room to the balcony.

He would sit on the balcony for hours, leafing through his books and hoping to catch a glimpse of her going out for a walk or opening the door onto her balcony. And when she did, he sat out on his balcony, admiring her beauty and thinking of ways to introduce himself to her, but almost a year went by and the two remained total strangers to each other.

"I didn't know how to approach her. I had never tried to pick up a woman before. And no other woman made me feel the way I felt watching her from afar."

During that year, Baba went back to his home village for the summer break, and that was the summer when he knew in his heart that he couldn't live the same way his parents and siblings did. He knew that he wanted more for himself; he wanted to pave his own way rather than live off his father and his wealth. He was finally sure that he belonged elsewhere but, again, he said nothing of this to anyone in the family then, because he had not yet formed an alternative plan.

In the fall, he returned to Giza. Upon entering his apartment, he ran to the balcony and saw her standing at the window of her room. At that moment, he felt something he couldn't explain, but he knew that she was the woman he wanted to spend the rest of his life with. "I knew she was the one for me; I knew that we would get married one day, but I just didn't know how or when. It was that smile that melted my heart," Baba always said.

Growing up, I never understood how he could have felt so strongly about someone he had never spoken to. It was puzzling and silly. He didn't even know her name. He knew nothing about her and had never even dared to ask about her in the neighborhood, but I was able to relate to it once I experienced the same thing myself in my teen years with the girl next door, Nora.

"It was a warm winter day, too warm for winter. I was on the bus heading home and there she was right in front of me, sitting by herself, looking out the window. She looked like an angel disguised as a human. She had on this long, purple dress with flowers on it, a light grey coat, and her long hair braided. The whole ride, I tried to muster the nerve to talk to her. I was imagining how I could initiate the conversation when I got so lost in my own thoughts, I didn't even realize that I missed my stop," Baba reminisced. "I really wanted to talk to her then. It was the perfect opportunity. There weren't many people on the bus; we were practically the only ones. I closed my eyes for a few minutes to imagine how the conversation would go. I wanted to be ready, and in the process, I didn't realize that the bus had stopped, and she had gotten off."

For weeks, he walked to the bus station and waited for her to show up, but she did not appear. Another term went by and nothing changed. They were still complete strangers to each other. Fate certainly had plans for these two, but on its own terms.

Baba was very studious and had been something of a loner up to that point in his college career. He had made scarcely any friends, except for one or two study partners of the same disposition. Much of his time was spent attending lectures or reading required texts in the library or in the lab. What spare time he had, he would often spend reading medical journals and other books he thought important. All of this intellectual activity came to an almost complete halt when he came across his princess in the hallways of Cairo University.

He always defined that instant as his moment of rebirth. He felt his heart totally stop for a minute; indeed, he felt as if the whole world stopped—there was no one else in it, just the two of them.

Whenever my parents told us their story, Mama would always tease him. "Your baba used to ride the bus and stare at me from afar. His gaze was always fixed on me, but he never approached me, and I was just waiting for him to say hello or something." Mama continued, "Although your father followed me for months around campus and on buses, I always felt safe when I saw him near. I saw the love in his eyes, which he wasn't able to express.

"Even the first time I saw him, I could tell right away how he felt," Mama would always say. "There was something different about your father, and I felt it."

Being the shy and bookish person he was, Baba had to undergo a complete metamorphosis to get closer to his dream princess. He started spending more time on campus, but he didn't spend it in the library. He began socializing with people he wouldn't spend time with under normal circumstances. However, those weren't normal circumstances; it was all about getting closer to the girl and then getting the girl. He developed new habits. He began to hang out with new friends on the south lawn of Cairo University's campus, which was over a mile away from El Kasr El Aini, the medical school facilities.

"She used to cross Al Gamaa Bridge to the main campus. Your aunt Afaf went to the college of commerce and that was where they both spent their free time. They used to sit at the cafeteria, then they would take the bus home together. I started spending a lot of time on the main campus myself. That walk was one of the best parts of my day."

His plans seemed to be working; with every passing day he felt closer to achieving his goal. He was spending his time with large groups of medical students in the hope that his princess would pass by and join one of the groups, and that it would be his "in" to her world, her kingdom. With a little bit of help from fate, the two found themselves part of the same large circle of students who used their free time between lectures to discuss the political situation in Egypt.

"You do what you must in the name of love, especially if your heart tells you that she is the one," Baba always said.

Dr. Issa had never been interested in politics, but he changed his ways and actively participated in the discussions in order to catch her attention. He was willing to do anything for that one chance to speak to her, hear her voice, and find out her name. He became an avid reader of political books and newspapers; he learned about socialism, Marxism, nationalism, and capitalism. He did it all in the name of love.

He was finally successful—he did manage to speak to her, but the first time he did, he was nervous and awkward, the total opposite of how he appeared to be when he spoke of the political situation in Egypt. Nevertheless, he learned her name, Hannan, which means *compassion*; to him, she was full of it, even in her very words. Without knowing too much about her, he was deeply in love with Hannan.

Months passed before the two would speak again, but the second time wasn't on campus—it was at the bus stop on their way home. The two talked for the entire ride. There was something in the air, which guaranteed that more was in store for them.

Their love story was an inspiration for us growing up, an epic romance unfolding before our eyes.

"We both knew there was something, but neither of us dared to admit it or to say it aloud to the other. We became friends who were secretly in love with each other," my parents always said. "My favorite part of the day was meeting her after lectures and walking over the bridge. The walk lasted hours sometimes; we strolled along El Cornish overlooking the Nile. The Nile witnessed our love blossom; it watered our love."

"I don't even remember what we used to talk about then. I know we talked about everything, but it is all a blur now. I just remember the butterflies in my stomach walking next to your baba." Mama adds laughingly, "And we used to walk a lot—we walked everywhere. We had the whole Garden City area memorized and the downtown area by Tahrir Square."

"You are making it sound like it was the only thing we did."

"It's true, we did a lot of that, and whenever you wanted to splurge, we went to that café you loved."

"Groppi!!"

"Yes, that one. You used to love their ice cream. I don't think I ever saw anyone devour an ice cream the way you did then. And the other one right on the Nile where you told me you loved me for the first time."

"No, that wasn't there. I remember we were sitting at gnent El Orman, and we were right next to the orchids. I can still smell it, now that you mentioned it."

"You are right. I hate that you remember those things better than I do," Mama would say every time he recollected something of their past. "Kids, Issa was always the romantic one. He always had a song to dedicate to me. He did simple things, which meant the world to me."

Baba used to go home and listen to Abd Elhalim and Om Kalthoum songs. As most Egyptians and Arabs would say, "You know it is love the minute you start listening to Abd Elhalim."

Their love story was as intense as those you see in a chick flick, and it had its ups and downs. Their biggest challenge was religion, which almost put an end to the whole thing.

12/20/2016

Dear Journal,

I can't believe how much I ended up writing last night, and I thought I didn't have much to share. It's crazy that I still remember all those stories Baba told us over the years. And by the way, I ended up ordering one of those reading light clips to keep the lighting to a minimum for Prince Adam to get his solid 16 hours of sleep. This kid can sleep. He takes after his aunt, Asmaa. She was the deep sleeper of the family.

I remember she used to kick anyone who tried to wake her up—she got Aisha's face once while we were away for our summer vacation in Egypt. She was most certainly the ass in the family, and it was in her name, Ass-maa. Baba would probably strike me down for writing her name like this, because he never liked any of us teasing one another. It was bullying to him.

I really like starting off by talking to you about random things; it gets the writing flow going.

I will go back to telling Adam the story.

Hi, Adam,

We left off with how your grandparents fell in love with one another, not knowing that the ambiguity of their names would cause a chain reaction that is still felt two generations later. It was a piece of their story that I never fully understood until I lived in Egypt and saw it for myself. (I will tell you more about that later.) I learned firsthand how people can judge you based on your name or looks. After September 11, 2001, the stares I got whenever someone called my name out loud in a public place were hurtful and brutal. In a way, the fact that we named you Adam, which is an endearing name to many cultures and religions, is similar to what my maternal grandparents did when they named Mama Hannan. Minorities do things to adapt and survive in communities where they can be easily targeted.

"Her name is Hannan Kareem," Baba said, "and religious differences never crossed my mind. Back then, Muslims and Christians got along just fine, as one family. No one ever bothered to ask if you were Muslim, Christian, or Jewish. Things were different then."

"And your name didn't sound like a Muslim name either; it wasn't a given," Mama would say whenever he made that statement. "Who names their child Issa, *Jesus*? And I always assumed that we were the same. But I guess it was meant to be this way. And *Alhamdulillah* it was."

In Egypt, a name can reveal a person's religion. To avoid the masked discrimination, many Christian families pick ambiguous names for their children that can pass for both religions.

You know what, that reminds me of something I witnessed myself. I remember a conversation Mama had with one of my sisters.

"Mama, who chose your name?" Asmaa asked

"Your gedo, *Allah Yerhamo*. (God be merciful on him.)"

"And who picked my name?" she asked.

"It was your baba."

Asmaa pouted. "I wish you had named me yourself. I wish I had a name as pretty as yours."

"Why don't you like your name? It's as beautiful—I think it's more beautiful than mine."

"That's not true. No one can pronounce it right, ever."

"Asmaa, Asmaa, Asmaa, the princess of my heart," Mama playfully replied. "You see, I got it right."

"You can, but no one in my school can; none of my friends can either. Is it possible to change my name?"

"It is, but it will hurt both your Baba and me."

"Why? It is my name."

"Look, *Habibti*, in a few years, you will be eighteen. You can do whatever you want then. Try to embrace your uniqueness, instead of trying to be like everyone else."

"Mama, I hate my name. It sounds funny when non-Arabs say it, and I can never find anything with my name on it," Asmaa protested.

"Baba better not hear you say these things. Our family was never about fitting in. We gave you Arabic and Muslim names because that's where we come from. And we are in America, we don't have to hide who or what we are," Mama stated firmly.

"Mama, you are not even a Muslim. Why do you care?" Asmaa rudely shouted as she got ready to walk out of the living room. Silence filled the room. As the only spectator, I expected mama to lash back at her with one of her screams that signaled the beginning of a war—they weren't many.

"Asmaa, stay put, "Mama ordered, and moved closer to her on the couch wrapping her arms around her. "Habibti, I understand your frustration, it is something every Coptic kid in Egypt with a Muslim-sounding name feels. You see, there are people in the world who feel the need to hide their identity to evade unwanted attention or conflict, and it is not here or in Egypt alone, people all over the world do similar things out of fear."

Mama went on telling Asmaa all about Egypt and its once-openness to diversity, and how religious differences never played a role in the way people interacted with one another.

"For the longest time, Egypt was known as a place of tolerance and openness. Unlike today, people never questioned others' religious beliefs or ideologies—everyone was accepted. Somewhere along the line, things changed. Egypt shifted to a religion-driven society. Whatever was once the norm turned into a sin; whatever was once fashionable turned into a sin. Teach your friends how to say your name the right way. Don't change who you are for anyone else's sake."

Though I wasn't part of the conversation, I knew that some of it was directed at me. Mama sounded like a patriotic nationalist who was on a mission to liberate and educate. I think it was that speech that talked me out of changing my name, many times. I didn't enjoy the unwanted attention, but Mama's words rang in my ears.

Noticing that the rebellious Asmaa wasn't pacified, Mama found a clever solution. "How about we make a bet? As soon as Baba gets home, we will ask him to pronounce "pepper," and if he gets it right, I will get you whatever you want next time we go to the mall." It was Mama's way of defusing the tension and protecting her other half from any hurt. She knew that our names were dear to him. But Adam, your gedo had a problem pronouncing the letter p; he pronounced it b. It is the Egyptian curse. "A large bizza bie" was our go-to meal when Mama didn't feel like cooking.

Unlike Baba's family and upbringing, Mama grew up in a very liberal environment and attended French private schools her whole life, which you can hear in her accent and her use of French words here and there, especially when she is mad. I pray that she lives many years and watches you grow up and enriches your life as she did mine. And remember this, her favorite word is "*d'accord*," and if she says it, it means you are in trouble or she is being dismissive of something.

I'm going to ask Mama for all the old photo albums to scan them. I think everyone will appreciate it, and those pictures will be a part of our collective digital family history. All your aunts, uncles, and cousins will have access to them. I think it will be a good thing for the whole family to remember the happy moments with Baba.

I remember some of the old photos in my parents' album showed a different side of Egypt—they showed a more modern form of living. Some of the pictures looked like they were taken somewhere in Europe. Women wore short skirts, their hair uncovered.

"We didn't have to worry about anyone bothering us on the street. The men were chivalrous and respectful. We weren't treated like streetwalkers. Cairo was a safe place for a woman, unlike today," Mama would say.

Mama came from a Catholic family, which is the minority of the Christian minority within Egypt. She was an only child, raised by my grandparents, whom I never met. They lived in Alexandria until my grandfather, Kareem Gamal, suddenly died of a heart attack at the age of 42. He was very socially and politically active, which was a trait that his only daughter inherited and developed during her college years. After the passing of her father, she moved with my grandmother, Mary, to Giza, near one of their few living relatives. Baba had moved there a couple of years earlier.

It is amazing how events unfold. Baba, who had lived all his life in the southern part of Egypt, ended up meeting Mama, who had lived her whole life in the northern part of the country. Fate, destiny, or whatever you wish to call it worked in mysterious ways for sure. Issa, who once made promises to return to his family after college and improving his own life, was in for a date with fate and a completely new life—one that would take him well beyond the borders of Egypt. He gave up the comforts of home; he gave up pretty much his whole past, his childhood, and family. He did it all for love.

My grandfather Reda opposed the idea of Baba living anywhere else but Asyut and threatened to disown his youngest son if he married the girl he loved. Your gedo defied my gedo and gave up the known for the unknown. He gave up the certain for the uncertain.

It saddens me that stories like theirs still exist in every part of the globe. There are people who still believe that their way is better than all others. But, in my own world, love won. Issa didn't care about Gedo's threats.

"How come we don't see any cousins or any kind of family when we are in Egypt?" I asked when I was around six or seven years old.

"Baba's family doesn't talk to him, because he married Mama," Asmaa whispered.

"Why?"

"Gedo had a bride in mind for Baba, and he didn't like the idea of his son marrying a Christian woman. He told him she wouldn't raise him good kids."

"Was Mama a bad person before?"

"No, but Gedo wanted Baba to marry a Muslim woman to give him Muslim kids, not mixed kids like us."

"You're lying. We are not mixed. We are all Muslims."

"Why do you think we celebrate Christmas, smarty pants?"

"You are right. We do it for Mama" I said, laughing. "But why can't we see our cousins? What does that have to do with Baba and Mama getting married?"

"Gedo kicked Baba out of the family for marrying Mama, and he threatened to do the same to any of our uncles and their families if they didn't kick him out too."

It was much easier for Tayta Hannan. Your great-grandmother, Mary, passed away during Mama's final year in college. Mama had no other family, and so Baba became her family. The two got married in the spring of 1961, while Mama was still finishing her schooling. They lived together in Baba's small Giza apartment.

Love conquers all if you let it.

12/21/2016

Hi, Adam,

Insomnia is such a horrible thing to endure. Here I am up at 12:30 a.m. in your room, watching you sleep while your mama snores the night away. Don't tell her that I told you this; she swears that she doesn't snore at all.

I read last night's journal entry and realized that I was all over the place. You are going to have to understand that most of these stories happened before my birth, so most of my knowledge is based on the bits and pieces I collected from conversations I heard from my parents and your aunts. Plus, I am too excited sharing all those stories with you.

Tonight, I am going to tell you about how our Egyptian family became an American one.

Your grandparents got married March 9, 1961. It was a small wedding; they were surrounded by only their college friends. From the pictures, it looked more like a dinner than a wedding. I remember counting about eleven people in total. Mama had on a simple white dress, and Baba wore a weird suit with huge lapels.

It goes without saying that no one from Baba's family dared to attend. They all gave in to Gedo Reda's threats, which were more than just threats. He stuck to his guns; the man didn't budge. Baba thought he would budge after the birth of your aunts Fatma and Aisha, in 1966, but that wasn't the case. Baba didn't stop trying for a while. He used to send letters and cards to the family in Asyut. Every now and then he sent them pictures of the family, but no one ever wrote back.

Remember how Gedo Issa had to get into politics to get closer to Tayta Hannan? Well, I think we had to pay the price for that shift of interests and hobbies. Baba had a history lesson for every story, and some of them we had to hear over and over again. And guess what? I am my father's son, and I am going to share some of those history lessons with you too. You never know, history books may burn one day, and this may become your only reference.

The family was made up of four people at that point. The late 1960s saw the devastating Six-Day War and led Egypt to a very dark place as it made its way into the 1970s. The country was defeated; the leadership had exhausted its resources and betrayed the people. As the 1970s dawned, Egypt lost its president, Gamal Abdel Nasser, and the whole region mourned the death of a man whom most people saw as a great and charismatic leader. Tayta Hannan was never a fan of his though. According to some of her Baba's old friends, Abdel Nasser's regime had something to do with my grandfather's death.

Anwar Sadat became president after the death of Nasser, and a couple of years into the job, he did the unthinkable—he launched a full-scale attack against the state of Israel in the early fall of 1973. He embarked on a war against a state that was still protected by the greatest power in the world; he embarked on a war that was almost won through the backing of other Arab states. Somehow, Arabs found a way to unite, but their victory didn't last long. The United States became involved in the conflict and assisted the Israelis until a ceasefire was ordered by the United Nations, which was eventually respected by all parties. The ceasefire was the first of many agreements reached among the parties during the 1970s. Egypt was at the forefront of the political arena. I had to hear this story numerous times, because it did have a happy ending for Baba.

As Egypt underwent its changes throughout the 1970s, so did the family. The first of those changes was the move from Egypt to the United States at the end of the summer of 1971, two years before the war. At that time, my parents moved to New York City, accompanied by my older twin sisters, Aisha and Fatma. They moved into a small two-bedroom apartment on the Upper West Side of Manhattan, according to Mama, and Harlem, according to the zoning of the city.

It was late August, just before the start of the school year at Columbia University, where Baba was due to begin his classes. My sisters were also due to start their schooling in a foreign school, far away from home and from everything they had grown to know and love. They often spoke of that period of their life with bitterness, which they always wished to forget and erase from their memories.

"You and Asmaa are so lucky—you two never had to go through what we went through when we moved here. We got teased so much. We hardly spoke English then, and when we did, people made fun of us," Aisha said once when we were looking at pictures from the family's first year in the US. "I hated everything about living here. I hated the school, the people; I even hated Baba then. Outside of school, we lived like prisoners. We couldn't go anywhere without Baba, but he was always busy with work or school. He had no time for anything when we first moved."

The transition was hardest on the twins and Mama. They had never wanted to leave Egypt; they had never wanted to move away, especially not as far as New York, and not to a place where they couldn't communicate with anyone but one another.

I think it was Mama's sacrifice for Baba. She understood that he wanted more out of life, and Egypt was no longer the place to give him that. The family had to move for Baba to fulfill his dreams and goals, and there was no way on earth that he was going to leave his family alone in a turbulent and occupied country on the brink of war. Plus, things were changing in Egypt drastically. The once-tolerant city of Cairo wasn't so anymore. My parents' mixed marriage and way of living raised brows wherever they went.

"The looks we got whenever I went to church with Hannan—they were suspicious of me," Baba recalled. "They thought I was there to spy on them."

"It was really bad for all of us," Mama said. "People were becoming more nationalistic, and more religious. Everyone was scared, and when you are scared and thinking of your death, survival instinct kicks in and the afterlife becomes a haunting reality. We were infidels to everyone." Mama paused. "We wanted something different for you kids."

It is funny how they wanted something different for us in a new country, but they forgot to leave some of their old ways behind. Baba had all girls then. It was a house full of women, something that bothered him greatly. He wanted a boy to carry on his name and continue his bloodline.

I remember Mama teasing him about how closed-minded he was.

"You wanted a boy so badly. You should have seen your face after Asmaa was born." Mama had this way of looking at Baba; it was a look of love and total contentment. "I had Osama in my late thirties. Yes, I was the idiot who was willing to risk her life to give you everything you wanted in life. I knew that deep down, you were like any other man, or every other Arab, wanting a boy as his prize."

"You are my only prize; the kids are a bonus." Baba had a way of reassuring Mama of how much she meant to him. Their love story inspired all of us; they exemplified everything that was beautiful about a marriage. They worked together as a team, they complemented one another. The sacrifices were many, but they never kept count.

I have pictured Baba begging Mama for another child. I have also pictured him trying to give Asmaa back to the doctor after her delivery or looking between her legs and asking for the rest of her. But knowing Baba, I always found it hard to see him as this close-minded man who wanted a boy rather than a girl. He never seemed like the type.

Back to the history lesson. The 70s were a very emotional time for the family. They went through an emotional rollercoaster as they witnessed the war between Egypt and Israel, the Camp David peace deal, and Sadat's famous visit to the Knesset. Baba loved his country greatly. He fully supported Sadat's policies and actions, regardless of the disapproval of other Arabs who viewed the peace deal as an act of treason.

I heard so many stories about that period from both my parents, and how Baba lost many of his Arab friends in New York because of their conflicting political views. On the other hand, he made many other non-Arab friends who viewed Egypt as the new up-and-coming democracy of the Middle East. The year of my birth was the year Jimmy Carter became president, and that was when Egypt became the number one item on the foreign policy agenda. Egypt and Israel worked together on a peace agreement the year of my birth, and it was signed before I turned a year old. It was one of the happiest years for the family, and especially for my Baba, who had waited so long to have a son.

When it came to naming me, he was at a loss. Choosing a newborn's name is usually a huge deal for any family. Expecting parents, nowadays, buy books, browse sites, and ask family members for ideas in search for the perfect name—we did all of that trying to pick a name for you. Some families have their own tradition when it comes to names. Some will pick names that have the same initial; some will pick names because it reminds them of someone special or dear to their heart. Then there are people who will pick a certain pattern or theme like both Baba and my grandfather did. Your great-grandfather named all of his kids after the prophets, while Baba picked names of those who were close to Prophet Muhammed.

He wanted to name me after someone he really admired. "He had a whole list of names ready," Mama told me. He wanted to name me Omar, after the Second Khalifa (successor of the Prophet) of the Islamic empire. There was also Hamza, after the Prophet's uncle, or Khaled as in Khaled Ibn El Waleed, who was one of the greatest Muslim commanders. The list also included Moustafa, after Moustafa Kamel of Egypt, and Saad, as in Saad Zaghloul, who was one of the main figures in the establishment of Egypt's Wafd party. Names such as Gamal, Sadat, Anwar, Abd El Wahab, and Abd El Halim—and many others—were on that list. He finally picked Osama, after one of his favorite Islamic historical figures, as well as one of the closest people to the Prophet, who many referred to as the beloved son of the beloved. Osama was the son of Zayd Ibn Haritha—the adopted son of the Prophet. I was named after one of the youngest appointed generals of the Muslim army—I was named Osama after Osama Ibn Zayd.

Your aunts were named after women who were dear to Prophet Muhammed. Aisha was named after one of the wives of the Prophet, and the daughter of his closest companion, Abu Bakr. She was the one who supposedly got married to the prophet at the age of seven, and their marriage consummated at the age of nine. Most people tend to overlook the other narrative, which clearly states she was 17. I think it is sick individuals who are into kiddie porn who hold onto that narrative.

Fatma was named after the daughter of the Prophet and his first wife, Khadija, and who went on to marry Ali Ibn

Abi Talib. Ali was the fourth Khalifa, and the cousin of
the prophet. Aisha is highly regarded by Sunni Muslims,
because she was considered the ultimate source of
prophetic saying. On the other hand, she is not liked
much by Shia'a Muslims who opposed transmitting the
saying of the Prophet, and they loved Fatma. Shia'a hold
Ali in such high regard, along with his wife and their
offspring, we almost named you Ali.

Your aunt Asmaa was named after another daughter of
Abu Bakr. She was known as one of the very first people
to accept Islam, and she was a crucial part of the
Prophet's migration from Makkah to Madinah. She was
one of a few who knew of the plan and would disappear
into the desert to deliver food to the two men hiding in
the cave.

12/24/2016

Hello, my dear baby boy,

Sorry I haven't spent much time in your room writing the past few days. Things have been a bit hectic at work and with the family. I had to go to bed early and skip our nightly chats.

Tomorrow is Christmas, and for some reason, people lose all sense. I miss the days when we used to celebrate it at home for Tayta Hannan's sake. We used to celebrate it twice, once on December 25, and again on January 7. It took me a while to understand why we had two different celebrations for the same holiday. I didn't get it until I was old enough to learn that Christianity had a few different sects with their own sets of beliefs. So, Catholics celebrate the birth of Christ in December, while Orthodox Christians celebrate in January.

Baba used to take us to buy a tree and gifts for Mama. She got two gifts from each one of us, paid for by Baba. "Hannan deserves the moon and every star in this universe; you will never understand until you find that person who completes, supports, loves, and gives unconditionally. She gave me all four of you. She is my home and has been so since our college days," Baba said when your forever-complaining Tant Aisha once asked him why he made us do it every year.

You are a half and half like Tayta Hannan; you are half Sunni and half Shia'a. And the two of them don't agree on everything either. And I am half and half too. Focus on commonalities.

So, I was telling you all about our names, and the reasons they were picked. Today, I am going to tell you a bit more about my birth and childhood. My birth marked the arrival of the long-awaited prince who would one day carry on and rule the kingdom, or so I was told. The year of my birth also marked other changes. The family moved from the two-bedroom Manhattan apartment to a two-family house in Astoria, Queens. It was also the year Baba earned his PhD and began teaching. It was a happy time all around for many different reasons.

I was born into a family who showered me with love and attention. Throughout my childhood, I was the spoiled one of the children. Baba rushed home from work to play with me. The older I got, our time together was more related to education—he taught me Arabic and told me stories about his youth in Egypt. He used to always tell me these stories about my gedo and how tough he was with all his children.

Baba told me stories of the Islamic empires of the past and of their glory. He used to tell me about Muslim heroes and how it was their strong faith in God that guided them to spread his word throughout Africa, Asia, and Europe. Religion was a big part of his life—he believed in it strongly and had most of the Quran memorized, though he never talked publicly of his religious knowledge, and he avoided all controversial debates. It was one of the many qualities I loved about Baba; he was humble to a fault. He told me stories of the Prophet and his companions, and tales of every prophet, starting with Adam, Noah, and Abraham.

The bond we had was one every boy or girl wishes to have with a parent or both parents. In his company, I entered a different dimension, a whole different world. That bond was my happy place for many years. I remember waiting for him to come home from work to finish the story from the day before or start a new one. He was a great storyteller; he knew exactly what to say to hold my attention.

I was very much attached to Baba, and I always tried to imitate everything he did. I used to stand next to him as he prayed, trying to follow his every move. At times, I would climb onto his back as he knelt in prayer. He would wait until I got off to carry on with his prayer. As I grew older, we joked about the mark on his forehead from praying. Mama would joke that my rides on his back forced him to keep his head on the floor much longer, which imprinted that mark.

Baba and Mama were very affectionate and very involved in our lives. They wanted to provide us with the best things in life to the best of their abilities. We had our family rituals, outings, and habits, which were observed religiously. Every Sunday, Baba took all four of us to our Sunday school at the Islamic Centre on the Upper West Side of Manhattan to learn both Arabic and the Quran. Those classes weren't the most fun thing to do on a Sunday—they stood between me and watching wrestling. Yet I always looked forward to the outings with the family afterward, and I enjoyed the Sundays I did skip school and sat on the couch watching wrestling next to Baba.

They used to drop us off at 9 a.m. every Sunday. While we were in our classes, they ran their errands and did the weekly grocery shopping at one of the Arabic shops in Brooklyn. Baba was very keen about eating halal meat only, which was available at only a handful of places throughout the city. Things then were not as they are today—halal food carts were not on every corner. They always timed it so they would be back at the school before our classes ended. Afterward, all six of us would pick a place to go for the evening. Sometimes other families joined us, especially when we decided to have a picnic at the park during the warmer months. I think people definitely came for Mama's *kofta*. She makes the best *kofta* I ever tasted.

I think I had a childhood that any other child would want or envy another child for having. Baba worked very hard to ensure that he was nothing like his father. He provided us with an abundance of love, affection, and endless encouragement to excel and stand out as individuals. He did his best to treat us all the same but, no matter how hard he tried, his favoritism for me showed at times. It was something that both Fatma and Aisha picked up on very early, and they used it to their advantage. Fatma, surely, didn't forget about it.

A couple of days ago on our way to the Costco to pick up a few items for our traditional Christmas dinner, your aunt Fatma reminded me.

"Osama, you know that Baba did truly love you more than anything in the world," she said.

"I know. It is the one thing I remember clearly from our childhood. You and Aisha reminded me of it every time I got away with something."

"We were just teasing you. We knew it got to you when we called you Baba's little boy."

"Yea, you two were mean about it, and smart too. You knew how to use that to your advantage."

"In our defense, things were more fun once you were born. Baba became a more involved parent; he was around more often, and we loved you and him for it." She lowered the visor to look at her reflection. I am pretty sure she was checking for tears in her eyes. I was tearing up myself as we talked about Baba.

"You know, we started this tradition after you were born. It was then that Baba took more interest in assimilating and allowing us to be a part of the new world."

"What do you mean?"

"Baba was all about his work and studies. And in all the time he had for us, he was more focused on cementing our Egyptian and Muslim identities. He had no interest in Thanksgiving, Halloween, or Labor Day. Before you were born, we never had any candy in the house to give out on Halloween; we were the only household in the building that didn't give out candy."

"I think I knew that. I heard that story before, when we were looking through our childhood photo albums. I think it was you who told me then. You were dressed as a witch, Aisha was a fairy, Asmaa was a ghost, and I had the Superman outfit."

"No, I had the fairy outfit, and Aisha was the witch." She laughed. "God, I can't believe it has been that long."

"But Aisha, are you telling me that he loved me that much? Why now?"

"Call it woman's intuition; I just felt like you needed to hear this. I know he meant the *donya* to you, and I wanted you to know and always remember that you were his *donya*, his world."

"I know this though. I know that I was the son he was dying to have; I know he wanted a boy to carry on his name more than anything else. I have heard that story many times. And I know you well too, and there is more that you are not saying."

"Selfishly, I want you to always remember it, so that you take on the role he had planned for you all along. I want you to keep his memory alive. Our family should continue to live the way he wanted—the family gatherings on holidays, our Sunday dinners. You are now the man of the family. You are the loving force that will keep his memory living for all of us."

Fatma was right; I needed to hear that more than anything else. Her words tore through me.

Every year, on the weekend before Christmas, we cook a feast and take it over to the church in our town to feed those who can't afford a home-cooked meal. It was something Baba started years ago, and we continued to do it every year since.

I miss Baba so much, and I wish there was some way to bring him back. I wish I could go back to being your age and enjoy that time with him all over again.

I do miss the simplicity and innocence of childhood. Things were a lot easier then. There wasn't much to worry about, and there was a lot more to enjoy. I didn't have to worry about what people thought of me or what their looks meant. Back then, when kids in my classes heard my name, they didn't think much of it, and when they found out I was Egyptian, they thought it was the coolest thing ever. Every kid was infatuated with Egypt and the pyramids. They would ask me whether I had ever been to Egypt and whether I'd been inside the pyramids. The curiosity of a child's mind is one of the greatest things, but it is somehow suppressed by society as we age. They call it growing up and maturing.

I remember that back in school we used to always tell one another stories and ask anything and everything without passing any kind of judgment. Even when they laughed when the substitute teacher butchered my name during roll call, there was no malice; it was nothing like the looks like I get today. It was kids making fun of the adults for not knowing how to pronounce the names we had all mastered. I never felt left out among my friends, except at Christmas time. I felt like an outsider among my peers in school, especially when they talked about the gifts Santa gave them for Christmas. Deep down inside, I envied them for receiving gifts. I was envious of Mama, too; she was the only one who got gifts for Christmas. I definitely didn't think it was fair, just as it was unfair for my classmates to get gifts, and not me. I felt like an outsider; I felt left out when someone would ask me what I got for Christmas. It was not the easiest thing to explain that I didn't really celebrate Christmas the same exact way they did, and how I didn't believe in Santa Claus. But I believed in Jesus.

That wasn't a conversation a seven- or eight-year-old boy can have with his friends. I was clever enough to find a way to avoid the awkwardness and fit right in with the rest. Since my birthday wasn't far from Christmas time, I used to keep a couple of my birthday gifts secret from them. Then I would tell my friends that those were the gifts Santa had brought me.

Aside from religious holidays, things were pretty simple then. My friends and I enjoyed the same shows on TV. We all loved *Knight Rider*, *Diff'rent Strokes*, *The Cosby Show*, and *MacGyver*. Everyone wanted to be like MacGyver and defuse a bomb with a paperclip! We all loved the Mets in the 80s. The things we had in common as friends were far grander than those we didn't, and that was what mattered. On the other hand, that was not the case with my parents. The older I got, the more our taste in things and our preferences clashed. As Americanized as they were, they weren't really Americans. They were physically here, but they were mentally and emotionally Egyptians. Baba loved soccer, I loved football and baseball. Both mom and Baba loved old-school Arabic music and movies, I loved my MTV. The same applied to my sisters, who were as Americanized as it gets. Fatma and Aisha held on a bit tighter to their Egyptian roots; Asmaa was the only one who experienced New York in a similar fashion as I did.

12/25/2016

Earlier today, we were at your grandparent's house in Long Island. I told you earlier that we had lived in two homes. The first was the one in Queens, which we moved into right after my birth. A two-bedroom apartment in Harlem wasn't enough for all six of us. Astoria, Queens, was our first house, but we didn't last there long. Arabs and Muslims were slowly moving into Astoria, and with that came the ignorance and intolerance of that part of the world. Arabs and Muslims weren't accepting of my parents' union. Their tribal way of thinking trumped the openness of their new home, New York. They viewed my parents as an odd couple. Muslims offered unsolicited advice and schemes to Baba; they thought he would be better off if Mama converted. On the other hand, Christian Arabs advised Mama to leave Baba for a Jesus-loving man. We ended up selling that house in 1983, and we moved out to Long Island, away from any unwanted meddling.

Baba didn't go through the bank to purchase the house. He actually agreed on the selling price with the previous owner, and the monthly payment needed. He didn't care to be in debt or to pay interest for anything. "It's forbidden for us, and no one should make money because they lend you money. That encourages a lazy society." Baba and Mama had fallen in love with the house as soon as they saw it, and luckily for them, the previous owner was receptive to Baba's argument against the banking system. I am sure the 80s' financial crisis and the greed of Wall Street made it easy for him to make a good argument. We shared so many memories as a family in that house.

And today was our first Christmas and Sunday dinner at the house without Baba. We gave out food at the church earlier without him; people who didn't know of his death asked for him by name. Those who knew offered us their condolences and prayers. It was an emotional day, and it was great to see and hear how Baba was loved by all those lives he touched. I bet my gedo would turn in his grave if he found out that a church offered a service in his son's honor. Imagine if he found out that his grandkids were cooking and distributing food in a church during Christmas. Baba instilled in us a strong sense of community, and he wanted us to always give to those who didn't have. "You don't give the money to the church, mosque, government, or anyone else for that matter; you give it to the needy yourself. Don't always count on the middle man. The money you are spending in God's name is the money that benefits those in need."

I never got how some Muslims talk so highly of the Prophet and preach that Islam is a religion of peace, but the minute they have to engage with someone different, they withdraw into their shells. Didn't my gedo know that the Prophet married a Christian woman? Didn't he know the Quran encourages us to treat others with love and respect? I often wondered: Did he oppose the marriage because of religion? Or was it because Baba defied his plan for him? I should try to get more information out of Mama. Here I go again, rambling about something else.

After the church service, we all went back to our homes to change, to return to the house for our Sunday dinner ritual. And for some reason, I didn't want to go. You and I and your mama were the last ones to show up.

"You have to make a grand entrance, don't you?" Aisha said. "Prince Osama is always late to the party."

"The traffic was bad. You know how the streets in NYC get around this time of year."

"We all got here on time, and we have been waiting for you." Aisha continued her friendly attack while the rest enjoyed our bickering. "You are the man of the house now, you should be here before everyone else. Come on," she continued, "you know I have always counted on you to play the role of the man of the family; you've always done it well."

"Osama! And Aisha! Stop your bickering. I swear you kids never change," Mama called from the kitchen. "Help me set up the table."

Mama gave the order, and everyone complied. Everyone, including your cousins, made their way into the kitchen and grabbed a tray of food, plates, and cups. The table was set and ready under five minutes. It was a record time in comparison to all previous Sundays, but this wasn't a regular Sunday dinner with the family. As well as being Christmas, it was our first Sunday dinner in your grandparents' home after Gedo had passed. There was a lurking sadness. I don't think any of us knew what to do, and it became inescapable once we proceeded to sit down. We didn't play our usual musical chairs.

The sadness settled in once Mama placed a plate in front of Baba's empty chair at the top of the table. We looked at one another, not sure how to react to Mama's action. An awkward silence took over.

"He will always have a place at this table. He built everything in this house from scratch for all of us to sit together as a family, and we will go on as if he is still with us." Mama made her way to the other end of the table. "Osama and Laila, you go first since you were late."

Your grandparents had this weekly ritual—we had to go around the table and tell about something that stood out during the week. Everyone had to participate. It was their way of keeping up with all of us and keeping us involved in each other's lives. It was brilliant and intrusive. It was brilliant because I got to know so much about your cousins growing up. I got to know their first words, and when they took their first steps. And I got to know about my brothers-in-law and their jobs, and their lives outside of the family. It was intrusive because I didn't always have something to share, or there were things I wished to share and couldn't. I made up so many stories over the years.

"We booked Adam his first speech therapy session," Laila blurted out. "He will have his session on Tuesday, *Inshallah*."

"You don't need to take him to a therapist. He shouldn't be watching so much TV and all these games on the tablet. It is all because of the YouTube. He needs to interact with the world and people, not electronics," Mama commented, and we all looked at each other, trying not to laugh at the YouTube remark.

"Mama, it doesn't hurt to have a professional opinion. He is two years old and still can't say more than a few words," Laila replied. "But I agree, kids nowadays are glued to their tablets or their parents' phones to play games. A lot of my girlfriends tell me they have the same problem with their kids' speech abilities. I blame Osama for it—he is always the one getting him into these games and spoiling him rotten."

"Like father like son." Asmaa giggled.

"What is this? Is it roast Osama day? First Mama, and now my wife and Asmaa. I miss Baba."

Everyone muttered "Me too."

It is still hard to accept the fact that he's gone. The finality of death provides comfort to no one but the departed. He has been a part of my everyday life; he has been an integral part of all our lives. The hardest part of it all has been watching Mama suffer in silence. She has been the mountain on which we all lean; she has been the source of strength in our family.

I will openly admit it: I was Baba's boy, but Mama is the human I aspire to be.

At dinner, I watched her across the table hold back her tears. I knew she was ready to break down. I knew she wanted nothing more than to go to her room and cry herself to sleep the way she did every time she heard Baba's voice on the phone those years when she and I and Asmaa lived in Cairo without him. That was really rough on Mama.

Watching her across the table awakened something within me. I walked up to her and kissed both her forehead and her hand then gave her a big hug, saying, "Thank you." Her reaction was totally unexpected, or maybe it wasn't. I got up knowing she was holding back her tears, but I didn't think she would let it out all at once. It was as if she had been waiting for that hug all along. I wanted to let go too; I wanted to drown in that same ocean of tears with her, but I didn't allow myself to do so. It was her moment; she needed it more than anyone else. Ever since Baba passed, she was the one comforting all of us. The way her body shook in my arms, and the way she drew deep breaths as she let the tears out of their prison reminded me of one of the worst summers our families had to endure. It reminded me of the first time I saw Mama cry. It was the first and only fight I witnessed Mama and Baba have.

I am sorry, baby boy; I have to say goodnight now. It is getting too emotional for me, and I need to let my tears free too. I will tell you the rest tomorrow, *Inshallah*.

12/26/2016

Every family consists of individuals who possess different traits—even identical twins who have the same genetic makeup are different. "Your fingers are not all the same," Baba used to say. And within our family, we each had our own traits. Aisha was always the intellectual and argumentative one, Fatma was the stubborn and silly one, Asmaa was the rebel, while I was the quiet loner, or at least that became the case as I got older.

The sister closest to me, Asmaa, had a knack for always getting into trouble. She was the typical middle child who was desperate for attention. Regardless of how much she tried to hide her wild side from our parents, her dirty laundry ended up being aired in many of our family discussions. In early August of 1989, Mama received a phone call from a hospital in Florida. Asmaa had fainted while working as a waitress in a local restaurant and was taken to the hospital.

I will never forget the blank, uncomprehending look on Mama's face as she talked to the hospital. She was somewhere between crying, screaming, and fainting. Still, she managed to hold herself together enough to take down the details of the hospital and call Baba at work, crying, "Issa, you need to be home now; we are losing our kids."

That day went down in the history of our family as one of the hardest. I had never seen my parents fight before that day. They were in Baba's office behind closed doors, but they could be heard clearly, each blaming the other for something my sister had done.

"It's all your fault, you didn't pay attention to her! You didn't do a good job raising her!" Baba yelled.

"You can't put all the blame on me, you're just as much a part of this, and you're to blame too," Mama yelled back at him. "You are her father!"

"I am the one to blame? It's not my job to sit at home and teach them right from wrong—that's your duty. I'm out all day working, busting my ass, and you expect me to sit here and follow their every move!" Baba roared back.

I was sitting in my room hearing them going back and forth until, all of a sudden, it went quiet. Now I could hear my mother crying in a way I had never heard before. I tiptoed my way down the stairs and watched her walk out of the office with a tearful face.

It was all a puzzle to me. I knew it had something to do with my sister, yet I didn't know any details. Hearing and seeing my mother cry the way she did made me fear the worst. I really thought Asmaa was dead. I sat in my room that night thinking that I had lost my sister for good. Although we always fought with each other, she was my closest sibling.

I was very much forgotten for the rest of the day as my parents were consumed with arguing and finger-pointing. They were doing some serious planning while I was drowning in fearful thoughts in my room.

Based on my parents' behavior, I believed Asmaa really was dead and my parents were making the burial arrangements.

They were fighting over where they should take her. Mama was demanding Egypt as the best option. Baba, on the other hand, was against the idea. He wanted to have her close to him; he wanted to have a close eye on her at all times.

I was beyond lost. Nothing became clear until they came to my room and asked me to be on my best behavior with my older sisters while they went to bring back Asmaa from Florida.

It is weird how I can remember so much of that day yet block out the twins. I don't remember anything about them except for the fact that they had to watch over me the next few days while our parents flew to Florida. All we knew was that Asmaa was in big trouble and our parents had gone to rescue her.

We didn't have a clue for a very long time either. Asmaa held on to her secret tightly; she kept it hidden in the same darkness where she was lost. And since I didn't get to find out the details right away, I will keep you waiting for a bit longer and tell you only this much: The story took a very interesting turn. It somehow ended up impacting my life too. It was Asmaa's action that set into motion the waves that carved my life for years to come.

Newton's third law of motion—you will learn all about that, my dear boy, in a physics class—states that when one body exerts a force on a second body, the second body simultaneously exerts a force equal in magnitude, and opposite in direction, on the first body. And it was my favorite sister's careless action that forced Mama to react in such a fashion as she deemed appropriate. The two together, along with their actions and reactions, broke the family apart. Asmaa's actions led to one of the toughest decisions Mama ever made. Three of us—Mama, Asmaa, and I—had to move to Egypt. It was the first and only time our family unit was broken in half.

"Osama, you are the man of the family while in Egypt. Don't cause any trouble there," Baba said, holding my face in the palms of his hands. "You aren't a little boy anymore."

"But Baba, I don't want to go," I protested. "Why aren't you coming with us?"

"I have to work, plus I have to stay with your older sisters."

"How come they get to stay? I want to stay too."

"Osama!" Baba yelled, only to hug me once he saw the tears stream down my face. "I promise to call you every day and come see you every chance I get. But for now, I need you to be a man and take care of your mom and sister. And don't forget the straight path."

"*Hader,* Baba."

I was both sad and happy at the same time. I blamed my sister and her troubles for such a drastic move. Egypt was always nothing more than a vacation destination, but this was totally different—there was no telling how long we would stay in Egypt. I packed all my belongings for what seemed to be more of a permanent move.

But in a way, I was very excited about experiencing living in Egypt and getting acquainted with its culture and our extended family there. I figured I would have as much fun in Egypt as I always did every summer. On the other hand, I wasn't sure how I would survive; I wasn't sure if I would be able to fit in, or how I would manage in the school system with my level of Arabic. As good as my Arabic was for someone born and raised abroad, I knew it wasn't perfect. I knew that I would suffer the same fate as fresh off-the-boat immigrants, such as when we made fun of their accents and pronunciation in their first few weeks at school. I panicked every time I thought of it. I didn't want anyone to make fun of me. And I certainly didn't want to say goodbye to my home, New York. I didn't want to go from the popular kid in school to the new nobody in a new school across the Atlantic. I loved Egypt, but it wasn't New York. It wasn't the place where I grew to know and love everything around me.

Within the first week of our arrival in Egypt, Mama turned into super woman—she managed to take care of everything on her own. She enrolled us in a private school with an American curriculum. After a week, we were already shopping for the new school uniforms, which for me were grey pants, light blue shirts, grey sweaters, grey ties with navy blue stripes, and grey jackets. I so hated the idea of wearing a uniform to school. I also hated the idea of waiting for a school bus every morning. I never had to do it in New York. I hated everything; I didn't want to be there. Within the first few weeks there, I learned the meaning of the word anxiety. I tossed and turned thinking of every possible embarrassing situation and how others could make fun of me.

"Can't I just go back home? Why am I even here?" I asked Mama.

"Because it is best for you and your sister. You two need to learn everything there is to know about your roots and your country," Mama calmly answered. "Stop complaining."

"That is not true! We're here because of *Asmaa*. I don't want to be here. I want to be back home with my friends and Baba." I threw a tantrum, screaming and crying.

"*Simsim*, stop acting like a little baby. I know you are terrified, but you will be fine. Remember your promise to Baba?"

"I don't care. I hate it here."

"You are just making it worse for yourself." She held my hands. "Whoever fears the monster will actually see it."

And that was how it was for me. I did see my fears and insecurities come true within days of joining the new school in Egypt. I was hoping my efforts to go unnoticed in all of my classes for the first week would continue to be the case for the duration of my stay in the school. I remember one of my very first days. My Arabic teacher, Mrs. Houda, called on me to answer a question from the homework assignment. The second I opened my mouth to answer it, all of my classmates burst into laughter. Their teasing made me hate the whole experience even more. I didn't want to go to school for days. I hated everything and everyone there.

School was a bit harder than it was in New York; the curriculum was far more advanced, but I got by. The most difficult challenge was having to take some courses in Arabic. For those courses, Mama found private tutors to help me and my sister. The whole business of private tutoring is big in Egypt; everyone was taking private lessons.

The feeling of hate didn't last too long. It all came to an end once the other kids found out that I had just moved there from New York. I redeemed myself in English class. I made it a point to correct the pronunciations of others, including the teacher. I went from being the victim of their silly jokes and teasing to being the superstar of the school. My New York accent gained me respect, and everyone wanted to hear about what it was like to grow up in the Big Apple. The boys wanted to hear all about American girls, while the girls wanted to get close to the new cool American kid in school.

The first friend I made in school was Mahmoud, who was a couple of months older than I. He was as Egyptian as it gets—his features screamed out Egyptian—yet everything else about him was very much American. He attended American schools his whole life in both Kuwait and Egypt. He had joined the school a year earlier and he too suffered the teasing of others when first enrolled. "Don't worry, Osama, they do it to everyone. They did it to me and I grew up in an Arab country, but since I didn't know the latest slang, I was their target for a few weeks."

Mahmoud later introduced me to a few of his friends— Sameh, Amr, and Michael—and I became a part of a new circle. I was no longer surrounded by childhood friends like Peter Ruffus or Michael Johnson. I didn't

have to attend a Sunday school with the many
Mohameds or Ahmeds in the Manhattan Islamic Center.

1/1/2017

Happy New Year, Prince Adam Osama Issa Reda Mohamed!

I made a few New Year's resolutions, which is something I have never done before. And those resolutions are:

1- Be the best father I can be

2- Get closer to the family; be a better son and brother

3- Go back to the gym to satisfy numero uno.

I am taking baby steps—I don't want to shoot for the moon, just yet. However, as I look around at everyone else, I realize that I can't afford to let myself go like I did in the past. You brought me back from that very dark place, you were that savior.

I am hoping you can revive me once again. I still have that blank look on my face since Baba's death; it won't dissipate. Life doesn't return to me until I am playing with you during your waking hours, or when you fall asleep on my chest while we're watching cartoons together. Your mama has tons of pictures of us sleeping on the couch.

I promise to do better; I am going to keep trying. If time travel were possible, I would go back to that night before we were shipped off to Egypt, and I would run away to change the course of my life.

But would I have you as my son if I did that?

Let's stick to the positive since it is a new year. I am going to tell you about the new experiences I had in Egypt.

It was a whirlwind of excitement. Every sink and faucet was an all-day pass to the Nile's water—I showered in the Nile's water for years. I shared that water source with the ancient Egyptians who once stood on its sands and built the Great Pyramids. Egypt was every kid's infatuation. We were mesmerized by its ancient beauty and magical spells.

I was thirteen; it was easy to love and hate things, and others, at that age. So it didn't take much to disappoint thirteen-year-old me who was used to having everything his way, and it didn't take much to win him back. I went from hating Egypt and all that came with the experience to falling deeply in love with it. I made new friends in a short period of time. I was enchanted with my new life. I was learning new things about Egypt that I had never known or experienced during my short summer visits. I finally saw Egypt as an Egyptian. I was an Egyptian teenager.

Sometimes I wish I could go back in time and enjoy again the little things I enjoyed growing up. The beauty of childhood is never appreciated until we are much older, looking back at things. You should never rush growing up. Enjoy every second of every single minute you are breathing and alive—embrace it all.

As kids, things we learn become engraved in our souls. Our love for certain things, things we learn or do as kids, is similar to the love for our mothers that inhabits our souls the second we suckle on their breasts. And one of those things, which I loved dearly, was Ramadan. The first time I fasted the month of Ramadan was at the age of six. Everyone else in the family was fasting and I wanted to do it with them. I was too young to fast the entire time, so I fasted until the late afternoon. It was Baba's excitement when Ramadan came around each year that made me want to observe it too, and to start fasting at such a young age.

My first remembered Ramadan happened to fall during a very hot New York summer. Fasting Ramadan in the summer is one of the hardest challenges faced by Muslims. The days are very long, bearing in mind that the dawn prayer, when the fast begins, takes place at around 3 or 4 a.m. and ends at 8 p.m. or so, when the sun goes down. Waking up in the middle of the night at around 3 a.m. to eat *Suhoor* with the rest of the family was the most thrilling part about fasting when I was a little kid. I felt like an adult, a part of an elite, cool group, since not many kids my age got to be awake at such an hour. I will not lie—sometimes I did wake up feeling grumpy and lazy, but I still enjoyed it very much and I also enjoyed the attention and praise I received from Baba. He was always encouraging when it came to anything that was related to religion or culture. He wanted to make sure that we didn't lose our identities as Egyptians, Arabs and, most importantly, Muslims. And Ramadan was the perfect setting for him to do so for thirty days every year.

On the eve of the first day of every Ramadan, Baba had this ritual. He would sit us all down after praying together and we would recite from the Quran together. Once the recitation was over, he would tell us of the importance of Ramadan and fasting.

"Fasting is one of the Five Pillars of Islam and it is the one act that you do for the sake of God and God alone. There is no one there to watch you all day to see if you eat or drink when you aren't supposed to. You are your own watcher. Fasting teaches you self-discipline and how to control your instincts and desires. Fasting is not just about food and drink, it is about controlling your mouth and your words; it is about controlling your eyes and the things you look at. It is also a great opportunity to feel what the less fortunate go through." Along with praying, reading of the Quran, and enjoying a very delicious meal every day at *Iftar* to break our fast, there was the part when Baba, Mama, and the twins reminisced about spending Ramadan in Egypt. Every Ramadan, I had to hear their stories and remarks.

"There is nothing like fasting in Egypt, where everyone else is enjoying it with you." They all agreed on that fact. They would go around the table, telling tales of how the neighborhood kids decorated the streets to welcome Ramadan. "Ramadan was the time for families to visit and invite one another to break the fast together," Baba used to say. They used to talk of the simplest things that everyone experienced in Egypt, and they made them sound so grand. Something as simple as the *Athan* that marked the five daily prayers was one of those things—one they missed dearly. I always felt both jealous and left out for not knowing about or having experienced what the rest of the family had enjoyed at one time. Those feelings stayed with me until I came to experience them myself when we moved to Egypt. My excitement at fasting my first Ramadan in Egypt was greater than my excitement over anything else in my life. I was finally able to experience what I had heard so many stories about. From the moment the *mufti* announced the beginning of Ramadan after the new moon's sighting, I was able to feel the Ramadan spirit in the air. The excitement was so contagious, I felt it right to the core of my being. It was very similar to the excitement of my friends back in New York when it was time for them to open their Christmas presents.

It is impossible to explain or describe people's excitement as they welcome Ramadan in Egypt. The celebratory mood would amaze an outsider who may know nothing about the religion or the culture. I never imagined that people would be this excited about fasting for thirty days from sunup until sundown. That first Ramadan in Egypt was vastly different from any Ramadan I had ever fasted through before. For the first time, I felt a sense of unity and belonging during that month. I didn't need to explain why I was fasting or what Ramadan was all about. Everyone around me was doing the exact same thing, or at least most were. Even the Christians in Egypt were both understanding and respectful of the holy month, unlike my non-Muslim New York friends, who would ask me a million and one questions about fasting while holding a sandwich in their hands. Many of our Coptic friends in Egypt fasted with us while in public.

One of the great perks of spending Ramadan in Egypt was the fact that my school schedule changed. Every school and business in the country amends their schedule to shorter hours during the holy month to accommodate all of us who are fasting. As much as I had enjoyed fasting with the whole family in New York, that first Ramadan in Egypt was the first time that I wanted Ramadan to last longer than thirty days. School was not a burden; our school workload was much lighter. After school, we got together and played soccer for hours to keep our minds and bodies busy or, as the Egyptian locals would say, to "entertain our fasting."

Everything in Egypt got better during that month. TV programs were much better, though the choices were limited then. Everyone watched roughly the same things during Ramadan and we would all talk about it the following day when we saw one another. There was always something for everyone: kids' shows, soap operas, and the famous *Thousand and One Nights* series.

As that first Ramadan in the land of my ancestors came to an end, I was saddened by the fact that I didn't know whether or not I would actually be there the following year. However, the sadness didn't last for long. It was time for Eid, and it was my first in Egypt. That was also an overwhelming experience. The literal translation of the word Eid is "feast," which is something I never understood until I spent it in Egypt. Prior to that, I always associated Eid with buying new clothes, saying the Eid prayer at the mosque, and being with the family if, and only if, it fell on a weekend day.

In Egypt, it was totally different. It was definitely a celebration—the whole country was off for all three days of Eid. We did buy new clothes to wear on the first day as we visited Mama's best friend, Tant Affaf, who gave us money. Kids do get money for Eid, at least that was the custom then. Most kids used that money to buy fireworks. But the most overwhelming experience of all was the Eid prayer. It was the first time I found myself among thousands of my own kind, all heading in the same direction, repeating the prayers out loud. I couldn't help it—I couldn't do anything but cry tears of joy. It was the first time in my life that I had felt that I really belonged somewhere as a Muslim. There was something about the unison of thousands repeating the same prayers. The echo of millions can be heard throughout the city and the country; the vibrations of the sound travel through the air and into the eardrums. Close your eyes and imagine your favorite band playing your favorite song to an audience of one—you.

1/2/2017

"I remember the first time I scraped my knee."

"I remember my first bike ride."

"I remember the first time I went to a game."

"I remember my first dance."

"I remember my first crush."

"I remember my first kiss."

We all remember our first time doing something or other. We all experience many firsts in life—both good and bad. I will never forget the first time you mumbled something close to "Baba" or "Dada"; it was such a surreal feeling. In a way, that was the most love I have felt since Nora said, "I love you, Osama." She was my first love. I will tell you all about her as I tell you more about my stay in Egypt and the firsts I experienced. I witnessed many things that were very foreign to me. I was there during the 1990 World Cup, which was the second time the national team made it into the soccer championship. "*Gohary! Gohary!*" In the streets of Egypt citizens chanted the coach's name as they would that of a returning conquering hero. The same applied for Hossam Hassan, the best striker in both the *El-Ahly* soccer team and the national team. You can't live in Egypt and not fall in love with soccer. You can't live in Egypt and not support one of two teams—*El Ahly* or *El Zamalek*—who dominate the field and collect trophies. It is impossible not to give in to the soccer fever that sweeps the country whenever there is a big game. I finally understood Baba's love for the sport and the many things he loved as an Egyptian. I was becoming more aware of his reality. I remember hating him when the World Cup was hosted here in '94—I wanted to be here and not Egypt, I wanted to be at the stadium. I don't think he realized then how much I had grown to love the sport.

In my young mind, I remember wanting to *be* Baba; I wanted to love the things he loved. I was his greatest imitator.

Here in New York, you know when there is a big game, but life doesn't come to a complete halt. If the Yankees or the Mets are playing in the World Series, all New Yorkers will pretend to care, but in reality, only a relatively small percentage are diehard fans of the sport or the clubs. The rest are riding the bandwagon. The same goes for almost every other sport played across the US—you never feel the awesome togetherness of a whole city or a country, unless you live in one of the small towns across the US or are a Green Bay Packers fan. I am not exaggerating when I tell you this: Life in Egypt stops for a soccer game. The streets are empty and everyone is glued to a TV set at home or in a café. Even those who can't watch it are listening to the radio. In Egypt, everyone is a soccer player, a fan, and a coach. That was when I first fell in love with soccer; that was when I first fell in love with a sport other than football, baseball, and basketball. Game time in Egypt was also Mama's favorite time to run her errands. "Osama, *yalla*, come help carry the meat back from the butcher. *Yalla*, hurry before the game ends; I want to get it done while everyone is mesmerized by the game."

The intensity of Egyptians doesn't apply to just soccer alone, but it also applies to politics and political discussions. As young as I was then, I managed to grasp the meaning of many things because they were discussed wherever you turned. I witnessed the fall of communism and the Russian empire, which was talked about by all the adults around me. However, that didn't compare to the amount of talk and coverage the war against Iraq received. I still remember the images on TV as the news covered the first strike of the coalition forces against the Iraqi army. I remember feeling scared and terrified; to

my young mind, Egypt wasn't too far from Iraq, and
Saddam Hussein was portrayed as a ruthless monster
who would stop at nothing to inflict suffering on those
who stood against him. Egypt was part of the coalition
forces sent to liberate Kuwait from Saddam and his
army. "Kuwaitis are everywhere; they are looking for
apartments to rent," Abdo, the doorman, would tell
Mama, trying to convince her to rent out one of the
apartments. (We owned the whole building. Baba had
never planned to stay so long in NY; he was always
planning to go back.) There was a flood of people—
Egyptian workers from both Kuwait and Iraq returned,
and the Kuwaitis were refugees.

In the early 1990s, Saddam became one of the most
hated men on the face of the planet. As kids, we had this
drawing of a pig which transformed into Saddam's face
when it was folded in a certain way. There were also
rumors of Saddam creating a list of ninety-nine names
for himself, as though he thought he were God. The
number of jokes and rumors about that one man was
ridiculous. They spread faster once large numbers of
Egyptian workers returned home from Iraq and Kuwait
after losing everything they had spent decades working
and saving for. They certainly hated the man.

It was scary. I knew what war meant; I knew about all
the wars fought throughout history. It is different reading
about a war in a book and experiencing the fear of an
actual war that is not too far away and can easily spread
throughout the whole region. "This Saddam is a menace,
he has rockets that can reach us." Or, "He has the biggest
army in the region, he will soon retaliate against
everyone." Those were the things we heard from adults
around us.

I remember every detail of that war, and I am surprised
I still remember the pig drawing thing. I didn't
understand its purpose then, but now I see how it was

used to persuade Muslims to go to war against other Muslims; that was very smart. They used religion to manipulate the masses to move toward a single purpose. Changing Saddam's face to that of a pig, which is the foulest of animals to a Muslim, and spreading rumors of his attempts to imitate God by creating ninety-nine names for himself, were very clever ways to achieve the devious plan. As I grew older and learned more, I learned not to believe everything I see and hear through the media, and you shouldn't either. I learned that I must make my own journey of *jihad* to find the truth in everything. The divide-and-conquer tactics are endless.

In the course of a couple of years in Egypt, I experienced a war. It was terrifying yet enlightening. However, that didn't come anywhere close to how petrified I was when terrorists began randomly bombing various parts of Cairo. After the first couple of terrorist attacks, which targeted a school in Heliopolis and a café in Tahrir Square, a cloud of fear and terror overshadowed everything in Egypt. I suddenly feared for my life and the lives of those dear and close to me. I feared leaving the house. They were attacking little kids like me; I saw kids like me on television shaking in their boots as they interviewed the parents. I didn't want to fall victim to a random terror plot—so much for those who thought terrorism started by targeting non-Muslims. It is like terrorism followed me everywhere from that point on; it was a part of my life in NYC when I moved back a few years later.

Another first that I experienced while in Egypt was the earthquake that happened on October 12, 1992. The country was hit by a strong one in the late afternoon. That was definitely one of my most bewildering and startling experiences ever. I had read about earthquakes in my schoolbooks, I had seen images of their aftermath on the news before, but I had never experienced one, and

I did not really think I ever would. It was bewildering because I actually didn't know what was happening when our building swayed and things in our apartment fell to the floor. It didn't register in my head until much later, when I was safe on the streets of our neighborhood.

That natural phenomenon showed me a side of Egypt that reflected its beauty and magic. It was one of the few experiences I had that made me understand the sense of pride and belonging that is instilled in every Egyptian. I saw total strangers rushing to aid one another; I saw neighbors offering to share their own dwelling with others. You felt the sense of warmth and closeness among neighbors, family, friends, and even total strangers. Another memorable part of this earthquake experience was the number of naked people who had rushed out of their homes in their birthday suits. It was definitely an unforgettable experience.

1/4/2017

Baba was never the kind of parent to hit any of us, at least I never witnessed it. If he was mad, he called us *"Ibn elkalb"* or *"Bent elkalb"* (son or daughter of a dog). I can't believe that I did the same thing to you earlier today, when you spilled soup all over my pants and the couch. It was one of those bittersweet moments. It brought back so many memories of your gedo and him calling himself a dog. I guess it has come full circle now; I am a dog too. There are so many memories of Baba that your presence triggers, and writing in this journal and remembering the old stories is making me miss him even more. I feel connected to both of you when I write.

Speaking of dogs, I can't get myself to trust most animals. I always feel like their animal nature can emerge at any moment. I guess it all started when a street dog chased me down the streets of Cairo. I remember the crippling fear that took over when I ran for my life, and I have never trusted dogs since.

My stay there shaped my life in many ways; it impacted every aspect of my being. Yes, I did get in touch with my Egyptian and Muslim roots in ways that I wouldn't haven't been able to do in NY. My Arabic improved tremendously, and my knowledge of Islam did, too. I learned how to drive while I was there when I was only fourteen, when one of the guys took his parents' car one day. I learned how to tie a necktie thanks to Mama.

Believe it or not, Baba was no longer my favorite. After seeing Mom turn into Super Woman on many occasions, she took that spot in my heart and my life. The absence of Baba during that time allowed her to shine. Or maybe she always did shine, but I was never able to see it because Baba was always the one showering me with love and affection. I was finally able to see all that she was capable of doing. She just knew how to handle all situations. She also knew how to pacify our worries and fears.

Those years and experiences in Egypt shaped the rest of my life, and one in particular was the changing force that turned my life upside down.

On the eve of my fourteenth birthday, there was a lot of ruckus outside of our building. Movers were loud as they carried furniture up and down the stairs. The noise got to Mama, and she called for Abdo, the doorman, to inquire.

"The new tenants arrived with their belongings; it should be over soon. They are almost done."

"They couldn't move in during the day like normal people do?" Mama asked. "Tell the movers to keep their voices down. The kids are studying for their exams."

"Yes, ma'am." Abdo left and returned a few minutes later with some strangers. "This is Madam Hannan," he said, gesturing to Mama. "She is the owner of the building. This is Mr. Mohamed Abd El Salam, and his family. They are the family moving into the third-floor apartment. They insisted on coming up to apologize for the noise."

"Salam, Madam Hannan, I am very sorry about all the commotion we are causing. We would have waited until the morning, but we had no place to store the furniture or park the trucks. Plus, the drivers are in a rush to return to the borders," Amo Mohamed said.

"Abdo told me that a Palestinian family was moving in, but he didn't tell me you were moving from Palestine."

"We are truly sorry." I heard another's woman voice in the background as I listened to everything while sitting in the living room finishing my geometry homework.

"Where are my manners? This is my wife, Shadia, and our daughter, Nora," said Amo Mohamed.

"Welcome to your new home," Mama said, "and your second home country. Please, come in; you must be exhausted from traveling all day." Mama pushed the door open. "*Ya Allah*, you must be tired. Please come in."

"Thank you so much, but we wouldn't want to impose on you at such hour," Amo Mohamed said.

"Nonsense; come in for a few minutes and have some coffee or tea," Mama insisted. "Abdo, go and stay with the movers and keep a watchful eye on them."

"Let's leave it for another time when we are not covered in dust and tired," Amo Mohamed rebutted. "Plus, you know how those movers are; you have to be watching their every move, otherwise, they will take forever."

"Just come in and have some tea. You can leave the women here to rest. And don't worry, there is a man in the house." As Mama called my name, I walked over to the door and joined her. I offered the usual greetings a bit reluctantly, without paying any attention to the faces. I was a kid; all I wanted to do was to get back to finishing my homework and finally watch *Terminator 2*.

Despite Mama's attempts to invite our new neighbors in, Amo Mohamed insisted on going back to direct the movers, taking his daughter Nora with him. Tant Shadia, however, joined Mama for tea. Little did I know then, but Mama had just made a new friend in the building, and my life was about to take a completely new turn: my falling in love with young Nora. Thinking back, I knew then that my first crush and my first love would last a lifetime, but not in the way I expected at all.

Tayta Hannan well understood how important it was to make immigrants feel welcome in their new surroundings. It was one of the lessons she learned from her own experience when the family moved to New York. For a couple of months, while she did her best to make our new neighbors feel at home, I knew nothing about them except the basic facts. That all changed one afternoon.

A few weeks after the new family had moved in, Mama called me from the kitchen. "Simsim, wait. Don't leave yet."

"You are about to ask me for something if you are calling me Simsim."

"Yes, just wait for a few minutes. I am finishing this rice pudding for Tant Shadia."

"Why don't you have Asmaa drop it off? I have to meet the guys in ten minutes and it's a long walk. I am already late."

"Osama, the world isn't going to end if you wait a couple of minutes."

"Fine, I will wait," I said, sighing loudly. "Can I at least have some to go for myself?"

"No, you can't," she said, and slapped my reaching hand. "I will have one ready for us when you get back."

I took the bowl to Tant Shadia, thinking only about how late I was to meet the boys. But when I rang the doorbell, time stopped, and none of this mattered anymore. My whole world stopped spinning, my own thoughts came to a halt. I could not think, I could not breathe. That very moment I was struck by the light of an angel opening the door. I gasped and stuttered and my face turned red as our eyes met for the first time. I handed her the bowl of Mama's famous rice pudding, and not without difficulty managed to babble that it was a gift from Mom for her family. The rest is a blur. I vaguely remember Nora thanking me, but then I was outside, somehow finding my way to my friends, lost in a daze. The moment was altogether so awkward and so uniquely wonderful as nothing ever before. For the rest of that night and the following days and weeks, I couldn't get her out of my mind. I had heard of love at first sight in movies and songs, but to experience it firsthand was totally unexpected and so different—it was raw, intense, it was consuming. Was it really the same girl that stood next to Tant Shadia that very first time I met the family? I could not believe it. How could I have not noticed such an angel then?

"Osama, where did you go? You are not here with us at all," Mahmoud teasingly asked.

"Nowhere, I'm right here."

"You haven't said a word in forever. We are talking about the soccer game and you didn't have any input. It is so not like you."

"I just saw the neighbor's daughter. You know the ones who are renting one of our apartments? Now I can't get her out of my mind."

"Sounds like someone is in *looooooove*." He laughed. "But Osama … really? The neighbor's daughter, how cliché."

"If you saw her, you'd understand. She is an angel, she is perfect. She is intoxicating, and I want to see her again so badly, to look at her some more. I need to figure out a way to talk to her or something."

"That is the easiest part, your moms are friends already, so get closer to her mom or something and take it from there," he suggested.

I couldn't get the girl out of my mind for days after that, and not being able to see her was consuming me. It felt like torture. I began to show interest in Mama's talk when she mentioned the family, as discreetly as I could. I had met an angel, and I wanted to be with that angel forever. That angel's name was Nora, and she was a ray of light that was to brighten life for me in a way I could not have possibly imagined.

I spent the following days and weeks thinking of her. I couldn't make myself think of anything else but her. Nora. My angel. It only got worse as time passed. I would scribble her name next to mine in my books and my notebooks. I spent my time thinking of ways to approach her, miserably failing to find a plan that would work. At times, I couldn't help but remember my parents recounting the beginning of their own perfect love story, which made me feel as if I were living my parents' love story all over again, standing on the balcony or in front of our building, hoping to finally get a glimpse of her. I needed to find the right moment to approach her and express my burning love for her.

I waited and waited what felt like an eternity. But nothing happened. There was no way to climb into the castle to reach my princess; she hardly left the house without one of her parents accompanying her. The walls of the castle where my princess resided were too high and well-guarded, but I didn't plan on giving up on my quest to win her heart—I am my father's son.

I started nagging Mama to spend more time with Tant Shadia and to invite them all over for lunch or dinner. Of all possible plans I could think of, I figured it was probably best to follow Mahmoud's advice: "If your families spent time together, then you wouldn't be considered an outside threat and you could at least be in the same room as her."

Eventually, the plan did work. The two mothers were slowly getting closer, spending more time with each other. They also scheduled their shopping trips to the market together. However, I was becoming desperate and very concerned that my plan would never work, as I still didn't get to see much of Nora. The two mothers spent most of their time together while I was in school, which really wasn't part of the plan I had made. Again, I found myself back where I started, consumed by my burning love for my angel, whom I could not approach. I just had to find another way to solve the puzzle to win the princess.

And so, I did just that. I had no choice but to involve
Asmaa in my master plan. I told her the whole story; I
confessed to my liking Nora from the first time I laid
eyes on her, and I begged her to help me out. She did
come to my aid after teasing me about it for a while.

From there on, Asmaa made a point of asking about
Nora every time her mother came over.

"Tant, where is Nora? How come she doesn't come up
with you?" Asmaa would ask.

"She is always busy with her schoolwork or reading
one of her books. She loves reading so much, it is hard to
tear her away to do anything else."

"Maybe you could bring her with you some time. I
hardly have any friends here and it would be so nice to
have someone around my age, living in the same
building, to spend time with."

Tant Shadia accepted the suggestion without much
difficulty, seemingly relieved that her daughter may have
found a new friend.

"I will bring her with me next time, *Inshallah*, and you
are more than welcome to come over any time. Our
house is your house, you are not a stranger."

**A lover must be scintillating and must find frothy
ways to win the beloved—something new and
different to stand out. Like peacocks showing off their
feathers, all to attain the attention of the beloved.**

1/5/2017

Sometimes I wish I had never gotten rid of the small passport photo of Nora. That picture was in my wallet for years, and it was the only one that I had. We didn't have cell phones then, and we didn't take selfies. We used to exchange photos with those we loved and cared for. I remember everything about her, but I feel like I am forgetting, too. To this day, she appears in my dreams, but not as the beautiful girl she was. She appears as this ghostly figure that haunts my existence. I see a silhouette of her, and I know it is her. If there was ever a boogie man, she was it for me.

In case you are wondering, yes, I did get the girl. It was your Tant Asmaa who helped me. She laid the groundwork, but I had to put in the final touches myself. It wasn't an easy mission. Nora was resistant and unapproachable. She was living in her own world, isolated. She was homeschooled and seemed to have no interest in the outside world. At first, I thought I had imagined her and she wasn't real. If Baba's year and a half seemed like a lot of time to win someone's attention, the months I spent trying to win Nora's favor felt like years and an impossible mission.

Asmaa was the first one to break through Nora's walls; she was able to infiltrate her world.

"You know I liked you ever since that first time you opened the door," I told Nora once, as we sat next to each other on the rooftop of the building.

"I liked you too," she said.

"I don't believe you at all. It took forever to get you to talk to me. You wouldn't even look at me."

"I didn't look because I thought you were cute, and I really liked you. I was shy. I also knew that Asmaa wanted to be my friend for you; she told me right away."

"That traitor . . ."

"She is not a traitor." Nora didn't let me finish the sentence. "She was honest with me, and that was why she became like a sister to me."

"She knew how much I liked you, and she didn't tell me a thing. For months, I asked her for information, and she didn't have anything to share."

"Yeah, because I asked her not share anything with you." She held the palm of my hand close to her cheek. "I was going through my own issues. I had just moved here and I was trying to accept my new reality."

"I know; I went through the same thing when I moved here from New York. I was terrified."

"It is something like that. I don't know if I can explain what I was going through."

I wonder now if she was referring to her secret then, and if she and Asmaa traded secrets. The two of them did get close to one another, and both were dealing with their own issues. Their personal problems were different in nature, but they were somewhat similar. Neither could openly discuss the things that consumed them; they couldn't share them with those closest to them.

I guess this is a good place to tell you about Asmaa's secret and the reason we were uprooted to Egypt. You should keep this one to yourself; we never discussed it after that day, and I never heard a word of it within the family. It is as if it never happened.

Asmaa and I were always close, but things weren't the same after she returned from Florida with my parents. She behaved strangely with all of us. She closed herself off to the world; she spent most of her time alone in her room. She hardly spoke. Something inside her had died—she was no longer the energetic, crazy, and funny girl she had been. She remained sad and depressed. She had always been the free-spirited rebel in the family, but in Egypt she became more of a quiet loner who only spoke when spoken to and, even then, said little. It was rare to see her cheerful and giggly as before. Her feelings of guilt, shame, and grief took her to a very dark place for a very long time.

Mama was not the worrying type—she almost always had things under control—but she worried constantly about Asmaa. She wanted to bring her baby girl back into the light, but without seeming to be too soft on her. After all, our presence in Egypt was more of a punishment of Asmaa than anything else. I remember overhearing Mama on the phone with Baba back in New York, complaining about Asmaa's state of mind and how she didn't know what to do with her.

"I don't know how to get to her, she just listens and doesn't say anything, and then she goes into her room and sits for hours by herself. Sometimes I hear her crying in there and it breaks my heart that I can't do anything for her. Issa, I feel like we're losing her."

Asmaa's low state persisted throughout the first couple of years of our stay in Egypt. She lived in her own little bubble and hardly stepped out of it. One of those few times was when she helped me talk to Nora. It was as if Nora's presence in our lives was the starting point; it brought us closer once again.

I knew nothing of her secret for a couple of years, then one day and out of nowhere, she finally told me about all that had happened before, during, and after that Florida trip. She had been in love with a Latino college student who was once a student at the same high school as hers. She gave herself to him—she gave him her virginity. He was her first love, and everything was going really well between them until she got pregnant.

They were both pretty much against the idea of abortion and there was no way she could tell our parents. She knew that something like that would kill one of them, if not both. And if it didn't kill them, they would end up killing her for the sake of the family's honor. She and her boyfriend decided it was best to run away together, as far away as possible, from the family and everyone else.

However, things didn't go as planned. They began fighting constantly shortly after they arrived in Florida. Asmaa, who had always been a spoiled little princess, took a job as a waitress to survive, instead of living her romantic fairy tale. It wasn't long before the adventure was brought to a close by the stress and exhaustion of working long hours, fighting with her boyfriend, and the burden of guilt.

"I will never forget it. It was a very hot summer day. I fainted while working at the restaurant, and I was rushed to the hospital. While there I learned that the pregnancy was causing health difficulties and that they needed to operate to save my life." Asmaa wept. "They should have let me die in that operating room. I was ready to have my own baby; I wanted to be a mother. I had names picked—everything was planned."

She was still a minor, and the hospital needed to call one of her legal guardians. This was the reason for the distressing phone call Mama received. It was the reason my parents fought; it was the reason Asmaa's secret was revealed; it was the reason the three of us had to move to Egypt.

"That explains a lot," I said, struggling to process all that information.

"Osama, I had never seen Baba the way he was that day. I knew it would be bad, but the look on his face was unbearable."

"What look was that?" I asked.

"It was the look of a dead man walking, an empty shell of a man. And, knowing I was the cause, I wished I had died instead of my unborn child."

"I can only imagine."

"No, Osama, you can't imagine the amount of pain I saw in his eyes, and Mama did nothing but cry hysterically."

"So, whose idea was it to move to Egypt? And what happened to your boyfriend?" I asked. "Please don't tell me that Baba did anything to him."

"The boyfriend was at the hospital when Mama and Baba arrived. He was there for a while until the doctors said I was fine, but I had lost the baby in the process. Baba approached him and told him to stay as far away as possible from me or he would call the cops because I was still a minor and he was over eighteen."

"How did you find out about all of this?" This was my way of asking if she was still in contact with the guy or not.

"I overheard Mama and Baba discussing the whole thing while I was going in and out of sleep on the hospital bed. I also overheard Mama suggesting the move to Egypt to avoid any confrontations between Baba and me for a while. She convinced him it was the best solution to take me to Egypt away from the craziness of New York and my bad friends."

In my own selfish way, I wish Asmaa had never shared her secret. The way she spoke of Baba and Mama's pain made it impossible for me to want to talk to them about any of my own troubles, and I was about to have plenty. I didn't want to be the cause of their hurt, and I didn't want to be sent far away ever again.

1/7/2017

Earlier today, I was thinking of what I should share next, and I realized that I have been stalling this whole time. I am not sure how to tell you about Nora and her role in my life. I kept thinking of all the things that unfolded ever since I met her, and how much of it to disclose in my notes. I guess I am not proud of many of the things that I did then and what I did thereafter.

The whole thing got me thinking of how the Arabs treat dating as this major sin. The rule is very simple: Remain virtuous until your wedding night. Boys become girl crazy, and girls become boy crazy, but the rules and traditions are meant to keep them apart. Contrary to widespread beliefs and stereotypes, Egyptians do date during their high school years. Some start as early as junior high school. They are very secretive about it, especially the girls' families. It is nearly impossible to find a girl who openly discusses her romantic life with her mother or anyone in the household, unless she has a close sister, who would automatically become the designated secret keeper and scapegoat if needed. I definitely didn't follow the rules.

This is making me think of how I will, one day, talk to you about dating, love, and sex. Will I be a hypocrite and preach abstinence? Will I apply a rule similar to Baba's no-dating rule that he had us all follow? Will I not care, because you are a boy and I'll let you do whatever?

You are not even two, and I am thinking of how I am going to talk to you about things that won't happen for another thirteen years, give or take!

Anyway, I did come up with some answers to those questions that have haunted me all day.

And the most important thing I wish for you to know is this: Love is the soul of this life. I would say it is the fuel of life, but fuel runs out, and love doesn't. It is the mysterious force that has kept us going for centuries. It was someone's love for another person that helped us evolve and become who we are today. Love shapes who we are in many ways. Its presence or absence in our youth impacts our adulthood, which impacts our future generations; the cycle has to be restarted somewhere. And that is why I want you to experience love in all its aspects; I want you to flourish in love and to be one with love itself. I wish for you to love and be loved. And unlike Baba, I won't enforce any anti-dating rules. However, I will enforce rules that teach you all about chivalry and being a fair lover. I want you to do better than I did, and better than your gedo. I wish for you to be a good listener like Baba and do both the small and big things for your partner—he exemplified just that with Mama, every day. I wish for you to be able to express yourself openly, freely, and, most importantly, with respect for those on the receiving end. I guess good manners is another one. Love is a double-edged sword; it can make you or break you. It can be your lighthouse in a storm, and Nora was both my lighthouse *and* storm.

I don't recall how the two of us became an item, or how our relationship really started. I remember Tant Shadia and Nora coming over to spend time with us, almost daily. Nora used to disappear into Asmaa's room, while Mama and Tant Shadia watched some series on TV or played cards. They had their small coffee cups with them—coffee was their drug. Asmaa and Nora played dress up. Nora never looked the same entering the room. Your aunt Asmaa had a knack for makeup—she was the diva among the three sisters. She enjoyed changing her looks and trying new things. Nora became her latest guinea pig, and Asmaa had her try on all kinds of outfits—imagine 1990s' looks and everything that was wrong in that era. She did her makeup too. I wish we had smart phones taking pics; I would have had the biggest collection of funny selfies with Asmaa and Nora. They always came to ask for my opinion—well, not really always; there was a time when Nora wouldn't speak a word to anyone but Asmaa. "Go ask Osama; we have to get his nod of approval," Asmaa used to say upon finishing her masterpiece. I didn't have the heart to tell them how ridiculous some of it looked.

At first, I used to stay at home hoping that I'd get closer to Nora. For months, nothing happened. If anything, I felt more alone. Mama and Tant Shadia got closer, more like best friends. The absence of Baba and the absence of Amo Mohamed provided the optimum conditions for all kinds of strong female bonds to form, so I was left to my own devices. I could have had any of my friends over, but there is a long list of unspoken rules in Egyptian households, and the main rule is: The house is the women's kingdom; it is their realm. It wasn't done in a sexist way. It was understood that women were safer and freer at home, and if a household was full of women, the men excused themselves and found their way to the nearest coffee shop.

So, after a few months of zero progress with Nora, I resumed my social life with the guys. I tried to keep myself busy rather than going crazy watching the girl I loved walk through the same hallways, and not being able to utter a word to her. I couldn't say anything, thanks to my shyness—it was my first crush. And I couldn't say anything out of respect. Nora wasn't just the girl next door—she was the neighbor, the sister's friend, and her mom was a dear friend of Mama. And if that wasn't enough, the fathers became acquainted, and they spent time together when the two happened to be in Cairo at the same time.

Amo Mohamed owned a small clothing store in Gaza, and most of the products he sold were made of Egyptian cotton, so he was in Egypt frequently. We got to see him at least once a month. He was intensely political. His views were very much pro-Palestine, yet he was also realistic. He didn't care much about whether or not the Israelis lived in the region, but he wished to see a day when his people would be treated with respect and dignity. I remember our very last encounter; it was on November 5, 1995, a day after Yitzhak Rabin was assassinated. Once he heard what happened, Amo Mohamed went off about the Arab-Israeli conflict. He referred to it as the enigma of the late nineteenth and twentieth centuries, which remains one today. "They can lick my ass if they solve it anytime this century or the next." The man knew his stuff. He listed every peace talk and its respective result. He labeled most of them as total failures and disappointments for his people, as well as for those Israelis who wished only to live a peaceful life.

"The international community has failed to find a solution to end the conflict once and for all, mainly because of extremists on both sides who view the conflict as a holy war over the holy Promised Land." Baba triggered Amo Mohamed some more with his comment.

"Come on, Abu Osama, you should know better than this. No one wants this thing to end," he said, interrupting Baba. "Look, they just killed their own prime minister to stop the peace process."

Amo Mohamed was utterly convinced that the governments on each side of the conflict, although forever announcing initiatives aimed at ending it, were not really interested in rallying public support for peace. Their main goals were to gain support for their political campaigns and to win the sympathy of the international community. Their speeches did not focus on change and progress; they were about maintaining the status quo. Thus, little changed. He continued:

"If we were to conduct a simple opinion survey of those trapped within the walls of the conflict on both sides, I am sure that the results would be in favor of peace and cooperation. The average citizen has no wish to live in a state of constant fear and terror, but their governments don't mind so as long as they are well guarded in their castles, living off their offshore bank accounts."

"But Amo, it is a holy war," Asmaa protested.

"It is a holy war that is not so holy; it's a war that is run by the unholiest of men on both sides. There is more profit to be had in war than in peace, and there are those on both sides who will never allow a peaceful resolution to emerge. It is very easy for them to manipulate the facts and the minds of ordinary people; they will use religion, history, money—whatever it takes to achieve their ends."

"How does anyone in Palestine benefit from the thousands who die every year?" Asmaa persisted.

"You know why those Arab leaders won't settle for anything? It could end the career of their winning race horse. Every Arab leader in the region plays the Palestine card to get the public on their side. It's the one issue that unites all Arabs, yet it's also the one issue that distracts the citizens of Arab states from their real internal issues. Arabs will rally in support of Palestine; they will direct their anger, sadness, pain, or whatever you wish to call it, toward the external 'enemy.' They will totally forget about the corruption of their own governments and their own misery, and rally in support of Palestine."

"And why wouldn't Israel want peace?"

"The Israeli government can't allow a peaceful solution, because the flow of billions of dollars in donations from devout Jews across the globe would dry up. It would also mean the creation of another neighboring state that could easily overwhelm it one day, based on annual mortality rates."

He paused and took a sip of his tea. "The excuses are endless and complex on both sides.

Both sides refuse to accept any solution put to them. Any solution involving concession is a defeat in the eyes of those who run this idiotic puppet show. They have brainwashed those involved in the decision-making process, as well as the general public, into believing this foolishness. The Arab-Israeli conflict is not a product of religion—it's a product of nationalism, it's a product of Arab nationalism, it's a product of Zionism. The Arab-Israeli conflict isn't a holy war; it is simply a matter of pride and selfishness. It's a matter of corruption and incompetence." That was how he ended the discussion, leaving all of us in total silence and bewilderment.

1/8/2017

I can't believe I ended up straying away from the story once again. It is as if the story refuses to be told. I did have to tell you what Amo Mohamed had to say about the conflict since it is still very much a part of our lives. If anything, it was a big part of why things happened the way they did. If Israel had used our tax money that was meant as aid for humanitarian efforts, Nora and I wouldn't have met. A decent medical facility could have saved her a trip to Egypt and in turn save us.

It is almost impossible to understand the circumstances of a life event unless you know all sides to the story. But looking back and connecting the dots, it makes sense that Asmaa and Nora communicated on a much deeper level than I understood. Both knew what it was to be young, wounded, away from home, and holding on to some dark secret. Nora connected with me on another level that reminded her of the greater part of her life. I reminded her of younger years when she roamed freely among the boys.

Those are the things we really seek in one another: As kids, we seek those who enjoy the same games and define fun the same way as we do. As we get a bit older and our childhoods are robbed—all childhoods are robbed or broken; it is usually a sudden, violent transformation—we seek out those who relate to our transition. As teenagers, we rebel and we attempt to create a new reality. As young adults, we look to recapture it all and find the person who can relate to all of it, and we add a shade of shallowness to it. As adults, we come to the realization that we have been trying to recapture the simplicity of the purest form of love— happy love. We look for someone who can pull us out of the darkness of adulthood and ignite the simple, childish joys of life.

As Nora and Asmaa got closer, Nora stepped out of hiding. She started spending more time with our family; her mom did too. The two families leaned on one another. Asmaa held on to her girly ways, and Nora was curious; she wanted to learn everything about makeup and fashion from her. And that was how Asmaa brought Nora closer to me. We got closer every time they asked for my opinion. The three of us laughed together. We went to El-Nadi, social club, together as a family.

I am going to share a quick story with you that sort of summarizes my relationship with Nora.

A few years ago, I was walking home from work and I saw a pigeon lying on the sidewalk, helpless and powerless—it had broken its left wing. It was crying out for help as it attempted to fly and failed. People paused, took pictures, and continued walking. I stopped. I looked at it, and I saw a look of mistrust. It is an animal's innate instinct not to trust a human because we are seen as predators. The pigeon's eyes told me so, and I understood. A broken body on the concrete was a trigger for me; it was a reminder of Nora. I wanted to help the bird. I went into the corner store, asked for a box, and bought a bottle of water. I poured some water into its cap, placed it close to the grounded frequent flyer, and stepped back. The bird drank all it could, and the look of distrust was dwindling. I stood there for some time before I placed it into the box. I had to earn the bird's trust; I had to wait for that look to dissipate. All living creatures have a recollection or a memory of a time when they were neither a prey nor a predator, and I waited for the bird to recognize it.

Nora had to learn how to trust those around her. She had to go through her own process to become a part of anything. I really wish I'd noticed that then—there is so much we fail to see, though the signs are there. I have always wondered what my reaction would have been if I had known Nora's truth from the start. Would I have treated her like everyone else? Would I have led a rescue mission to save her rather than win her heart? I will answer these questions later, once I finish telling you the story—it is easier when you know the whole story.

"So, when did you know you were into me?" I asked Nora.

Her fingers went to her lips, she pulled them slightly and gazed down to recall her first memory. After a moment, a smile crept onto her face and her cheeks filled with color.

"That time I was in Asmaa's room ... when she stormed out and left the door open while I was beginning to get undressed." She looked up. "Do you remember how our eyes met?"

I nodded, and felt the warmth take over my face. "How could I forget?" I said. "Is that it?"

"No," Nora said, almost in a whisper. "It's because—" she looked carefully for the words— "you didn't stare at me. I saw you blush, and you immediately lowered your eyes. And I should have been embarrassed, ashamed ... but I, I just felt safe, and I stood there unafraid." She closed her eyes, taking in all the feelings of gratitude she had for that moment. "That's when I knew I could trust you in a way that I didn't know was possible."

There is an indescribable feeling that accompanies love. It is as if you are entering a different dimension and everything transforms. Our brain, while in love, operates on a constant high, and love is the drug. It is a feeling, the very first time we fall in love, that we continue to chase in our adulthood. That was how everything felt then, and Nora became my best friend. She simply understood me, and I felt whole whenever we were near. She wasn't just any girl. She was the girl who kept up with soccer news and discussed it with me. She watched the same games; she understood the game. She liked it when I explained football and its many rules. She asked me to show her how players tackled one another, and that was when we became more than friends.

Nora became my world. She was my light at the very end of the tunnel. Her absence was felt whenever I couldn't see her for days, and that happened quite often. I lived for the time we were able to steal for ourselves, and in between, I lived on the memories we created on those days.

"Once you meet your love, you forget all about your friends." Mahmoud used to tease me with that old Egyptian saying whenever I had to cancel plans with the guys to spend time with Nora. She was my priority.

We would spend hours talking on the phone about anything and everything. She was definitely the reason I came to love Arabic music even more than I already did. We would listen to songs on the radio together and over the phone. She was the reason I started listening to Amr Diab and Mohamed Fouad. We also managed to steal some time together in person. She used to come watch me playing soccer with the guys whenever our families went to El-Nadi, which we did once a week.

Sometimes we waited until everyone fell asleep and met on the roof of our apartment building. We would hide up there for hours, looking up at the stars, talking nonstop. We had our perfect spot on the roof where no one could ever see us. We used to lie there counting the stars and connecting them to make shapes or words.

We were in love but, as with most loving relationships at such an age in Egypt, we had to keep it a secret—it was my first secret. No one could know anything about what we had. The only one who knew the true nature of our relationship was Asmaa, and she didn't know much. To the rest of the world, we were just neighbors and family friends.

Falling in love with Nora was the best thing about living in Egypt. It made the whole experience more exciting—Egypt was beginning to feel more like a permanent home. It was the place where I found my first love.

She was my first love, and I was hers. Having to keep it secret from everyone was both exciting and sad. Growing up, I had always imagined my first encounter to be a little different. I thought it would be more public; I thought I would be able to shout it from the mountaintops and confess my love in front of the whole world. I thought we would be able to go anywhere and everywhere among friends, holding hands and exchanging public displays of affection. I really thought my first encounter with love would be as grand and public as those I saw in Hollywood movies or Disney fairy tales. I feel like I am describing a scene from *Grease* (it is a good movie). Instead, it was the foundation for a life full of secrets.

The love Nora and I shared was certainly grand. We built our own fantasy worlds. We would sometimes role-play. At times, she was the captive and I was the rescuer who traveled the world and swam the seven seas to save her. Other times, she was the nurse who attended to my needs as I recovered from a deadly unknown disease, which was miraculously cured by love and a soft kiss from her luscious lips.

We shared everything with each other. We found happiness, we found comfort, we found security, and we found love. Together, we would let our imaginations soar beyond the heavens. We imagined what our wedding would be like, and the songs we would dance to. We named our future kids.

"I love your name." I paused. "If we have a daughter, we are naming her Nora; if we have a boy, we are naming him Nour."

"Why?" Nora asked.

"What is not to love about it? It means light; it is one of the ninety-nine names of God. It is beautiful in every way. Plus, you are the *nour* in my life."

"You have been watching a lot of romantic movies, haven't you?"

"And you can't take a compliment," I teased her, wrapping my arm around her shoulders. "You don't like it when I tell you how beautiful you are, but you have no problem complimenting me all the time."

"Osama, you don't understand what you have done to me, and for me. You are like the gift I have been waiting to receive all these years. I always felt out of place until you looked at me like you really *saw* me. You didn't stop trying to win me over, and you still amaze me every day."

"And how do I look at you, Ms. Evasive?"

"I am not evading anything, *Wallah*! You should see how you are looking at me now. It is like you are studying my every micro-detail, and you are learning something new about me, every time. It is the way your eyes light up; I feel your soul smiling and floating. Please, don't ever change. You give me reason to hold on, and hope." She paused for a few seconds waiting for me to say something. "Now, who is the one who can't take compliments? Your face is as red as a monkey's ass." Laughter filled the space above us.

"And I am the one who has been watching romantic movies. I think you have been watching a lot of romantic comedies."

For a year and a half, we shared an amazing love story; we shared our very innocent and simple feelings with each other. Every now and then we shared an embrace, or a kiss that sent chills down my spine and launched me on a flight to the moon. The slightest touch or caress of her hands against mine did wonderful things. It was just amazing. It was intoxicating.

My parents, and all other Arab parents, have a very well-known saying, which is one of the most over-used phrases ever: "Whenever a man and a woman meet alone, the third person is the devil." It is a saying that is derived from a *Hadith*, or so we were told. Growing up, I often heard it from my parents when they lectured us about how boys and girls should not be left alone in a private setting, unattended by adults, to avoid temptation.

I really didn't understand it then, and I used to ask if that applied if I was left alone with any of my sisters. "Does that mean the devil was there with us when I was home alone with Aisha the other day?"

I didn't really get it, until the innocence of our love began to wane. A couple of months shy of our two-year anniversary, Nora and I began stealing more than one or two random kisses.

Kissing, hugging, and groping were becoming the norm for us whenever we were alone in one of the apartments while everyone else was out and about. As things became more intense, she used to let me explore her upper body—everything from the face to the waistline was my playground—with my hands and lips, but I was never allowed to wander below her waist. I never placed any restrictions on *her* wandering hands. The stolen hugs and kisses turned into lingering embraces. The lingering embraces turned into long and passionate make-out sessions. The make-out session awakened the burning desires, lust, and love. And as the desire for each other grew, the innocence of our young puppy love took a major dive down below.

On the night of our second anniversary, and as both families got together for dinner at her parents' place, we managed to sneak back to our apartment, making our way to my room. It was there on my bed that our bodies laid pressed against each other. It was on my bed that she undressed me and kissed every part of my body before placing her soft, full lips on my manhood. It was at that moment that I lost all control. I was seduced by an angel in the presence of an invisible devil.

Things continued to move forward between the two of us. However, what was once so pure and innocent had changed in nature. It was like a drug that I couldn't get enough of. We continued to meet on the roof of our building. Sometimes we managed to sneak into her apartment or mine when no one else was there. Although we recreated that night on my bed many times, I was never allowed to explore beyond her upper body and we kept on doing the same thing over and over again. But I wanted more; it was no longer enough to satisfy my appetite. Nora felt it, too.

"Osama, you are becoming more aggressive. We need to slow down before we do something else that we would both regret." She would hold my face with both hands and look me in the eye.

"Why would we regret it? We love each other."

"But we have already crossed so many lines and, if we cross any more, there will be no going back."

"What do you mean 'no going back'? I thought our love was forever, that we would be together forever."

"That is not what I am talking about. I know we love each other, and we talked about forever, but if we go any further than we already have, the damage will be permanent. We are still too young—we might do something we won't be able to undo."

Nora was the mature and logical one for the most part. Her argument made a lot of sense, but my thirst and hunger for more didn't let my mind take it in. The sexual beast within me had been wakened and it had to be satisfied. I wanted more and I wasn't about to give up. I wanted my first time to be with my first love. I wanted my first time to be with Nora.

Needless to say, I was able to convince Nora to take our relationship to the next level by using the tried and tested line, "If you really loved me, you would."

I abused that line and nagged until her defenses were destroyed. She agreed to give me more, but with some conditions of her own. We agreed to do everything but vaginal sex.

"Osama, a girl's virtue is like a match, you can only light it once."

Those words could have had the effect of an ice-cold shower under any other circumstances. Those words were repeated so many times in our household full of women. I was raised to always respect and protect a woman's honor and virtue. And to most Arabs and Muslims, a woman's honor means her virginity, followed by her reputation.

Things were different between Nora and me. We were deeply in love and we had promised each other an everlasting love. Plus, my hormones and puberty had total control over me. Once again, we made use of my room while everyone else was out. Mom and Asmaa had to go to visit one of mom's friends in downtown Cairo. Nora told her parents that she was coming over to spend time with Asmaa. We had the whole place to ourselves. We were together in my room, enjoying the comfort of my soft bed instead of the usual cold floor of the roof. Our bodies found their way to the bed, nervously. We knew what was about to happen, but we certainly didn't know what to do about it. Nora was far more nervous— she was lying there shaking and breathing loudly as if she had run a marathon. As our bodies met in the middle of the bed, she asked me to turn off the lights so she could feel more comfortable.

Looking back at that moment, I was far more nervous than Nora. I was about to lose my virginity, I didn't know what I was doing at all, and I was about to commit a sinful act. Actually, there was more than one sinful act—premarital sex and anal sex. As nervous as I was, I pretended to be very calm about it. One of us had to be calm, and it sure wasn't going to be her. Things were moving smoothly between the two of us until I attempted to penetrate her from behind. She let out a loud scream, which worried me. I really thought I had hurt her. We kept on trying but every attempt failed. She then suggested that I should use something to make it easier to penetrate her tightness.

Our lack of experience and knowledge led us to using soap to lubricate the shaft. I ran into the bathroom and lathered my shaft with soap, and then I ran back to the room with a bucket of water and a bar of soap. Once I was back in the bed, she took the lead as she bent over in front of me. She reached back and guided my slow entrance inside of her. The whole thing felt both weird and amazing. I didn't know how to react or act. I was in a state of shock and ecstasy, which didn't last more than couple of minutes.

As soon as we finished, I threw myself on the bed right next to Nora who, for her part, jumped off the bed and ran out to the bathroom. She spent over an hour in the bathroom, crying her eyes out, while I sat on the floor outside of the bathroom door trying to convince her to come out.

"Nora, open the door, please. Stop crying, please."

"Nora, I am not going anywhere, I will not leave you, and I will never leave you. I will fix everything. I will marry you."

I was there by that door, begging her to stop crying. I was begging her to open the door and let me in. All of my begging and pleading failed miserably. She kept

repeating the same words, "You don't understand, you won't understand. You will leave me once you find out."
  She was right.

1/10/2017

Dear Journal,

I really hope no one finds you anytime soon, not even Adam. I am sharing way too much. There should be some limits to what a father or a mother can share with their kids about their previous lives. But why did Baba always say that he would treat me like a brother when I got older? He didn't do that; instead, he ended up shipping me off to a different part of the world. I look at Adam, and I don't think there is anything in the world that could take him away from me; I would never choose to spend a day away from him, much less years. I know Baba lost me in Egypt. He had refused to leave Mama and the twins in Egypt when the whole family immigrated, but he had no problem breaking us apart when Asmaa was in trouble.

Nora wouldn't have been one of my causalities if it wasn't for that move and my ignorance.

I really want to treat Adam like I would a brother or a best friend. I don't want to just say powerful proverbs because they sound good. I want to apply them to our lives. Adam can't continue in the same cycle; he should have a head start and know more about everything. It will help him make better decisions and become a better human. Horses' eyes are covered with blinders to keep them unaware of their surroundings and focused on the race or pulling a wagon. Horses without blinders are horses who can be themselves. I want Adam to be himself, without any blinders, which only means I must continue telling him the story.

I hope no one else but him finds you. Asmaa would probably kill me if she reads it.

So, Prince Adam,

The next part is a bit of a slippery topic to discuss, so I will do my best to tell you about it without getting too graphic. But before I begin, I want you to promise me to stop whenever a woman asks you to stop. Rather than taking it as a challenge to get her to let down her guard, try to understand her reasoning. I didn't know that Nora's pleas were meant to stop me from opening the door to unfamiliar grounds until I broke my promise to her. Her determination only piqued my curiosity; it made me want to know more. I wanted to understand why we were limited to one position. Why couldn't we try others, some of those that I saw in the magazines my friends showed me? Why did she have the quick reflexes of a cat protecting her kittens whenever I attempted to reach around and explore her promised land? Why did she think I wouldn't understand? Why did she think I would leave her if I found out the truth? It was a mystery, and I was determined to solve it. But it was a mystery that should have remained so, and I wish I had never attempted to solve it. The truth was too much to bear. The truth sent me spiraling into the abyss; the truth ripped us apart.

Nora wasn't fully a woman. She had a penis.

As I look back on that day, I wish I had never forced my way past her defenses in a bid to conquer that last citadel of her anatomy. All I remember is how I withdrew in horror when my hand reached its unexpected target. I was paralyzed, speechless, stupefied. Somehow—I have no idea how—I threw on my clothes and ran into the street.

For weeks, I was in shock, hurt, betrayed, and clueless. I didn't know what to do or say or even think. I was so confused, and I had no one to talk to. I didn't know what it all meant. My sheltered upbringing hadn't exposed me to such things. They didn't exist in my world. My mind simply couldn't make sense of it.

"How is it possible for a woman to have a penis? Is it normal?" I questioned the invisible man in the sky. "Is this the way God created him, her, or it? Is Nora a man or a woman? Does the penis function like mine? Does she feel like a man or a woman, deep down inside?"

In my bewilderment, on some nights I laid awake, my mind in turmoil, seeking answers. Other nights found me hunched and weeping in my bed, overwhelmed with shame, guilt, and regret. If Nora was a man, my sin was far worse than fornication—I had committed the sin of Lot's people and the wrath of God would soon follow. I wanted so badly to put the whole episode out of my mind; I wanted to leave Egypt. It felt like a bizarre dream, one that stays with you every waking second. Yet, we had created so many happy memories together— so many sweet and innocent moments that had bound us together in tenderness before we surrendered to the hunger of the flesh and the trickery of Lucifer.

Unlike today, technology in the early and mid-1990s didn't provide a world of information in the palm of your hands. If you wanted to know something, you either asked those around you or sought the information from books. Who could I ask? Certainly not my mother. And which book would I look in? How on earth could I ask the sales assistant for advice? What about my friends? Could they slay the monster that was haunting my every waking moment? I tried them, but without success. They were as ignorant as I was, staring at me, uncomprehending:

"What do you mean a girl with male parts?"

"A girl with boobs and everything, but she has a penis between her legs," I weakly explained.

"Where have you heard about this?"

"From one of my friends in New York. We were on the phone last night and they told me about this friend of ours who we thought was a girl, but they'd accidentally found out the truth." I could only hope they would believe my nervously told story.

"I heard of hermaphrodites in biology class, but those were plants, not human beings," said Amr, the brainy one in the group.

"Do you think it's possible for people to be hermaphrodite?" I asked.

"I don't think so. I never heard of it. At least, there is no mention of it anywhere in school books or religious texts. If such a thing existed, God would have mentioned it in the Quran," Amr answered.

"There's no mention of any other genders, just males and females. Then there are the people of Lot, but those are men who desire other men. And there is mention of a woman who desires other women, too, but a woman with a prick, that's unheard of," he continued.

"Are you sure it's not a fat guy with breasts like Baba's man boobs?" asked Sameh, who was the group clown.

"No, Sameh—I forgot to ask that, but I will ask the next time I talk to my friends back home," I answered, trying to speak in the same lighthearted tone.

"So, what happened to her—or is it him or it?—once your friends found out? And how did they find out?" Mahmoud asked.

"One of our friends tried to sleep with her, thinking she was a girl ...."

"No fucking way," said Sameh, as a wave of laughter engulfed the group.

"That's bicycle behavior all the way."

"Bicycle?"

"Yes, bicycle—he was a *khawal*, a faggot."

Sameh's words pierced me like a bullet through the heart. This was getting worse rather than better.

"He can't be a *khawal*. He didn't know. He thought it was a girl!" I exclaimed.

"Dude, there is no way he didn't know. How could he not notice or see a penis? You know what? Both of them are homos."

"Next time you talk to your friend, you tell him what we say here in Egypt: fuck a rock and don't fuck anything with a cock," Sameh added. We all laughed some more, but my questions remained unanswered.

"Seriously though, guys, that doesn't make him homosexual, does it?" I asked.

"I don't know what it would make him, but based on the facts, he is gay. He banged a man in the ass. Shit like that only happens in the west. It's all the fucking they do out of wedlock. They're doomed. I'm not surprised something like that happens there."

"You know, we're all doomed because of those *kufar,* those infidels and their sins. I heard the sheikh say once that whenever two men are together and doing it, the seven heavens and the throne of God shake," Amr said.

"Your friend should be thankful he is not in Saudi. I hear they stick a burning iron rod up your *teez* or even kill you if they find out you're a homo," Sameh added.

As the conversation went on, images of my death, and that of Nora's, flooded my mind. My confusion and ignorance led me to a very dark place. The discussion with the guys kept on echoing in every part of my soul. It hadn't helped me in the least; it had only made matters worse. I was lost and I didn't know what to do. I couldn't shake off the sense of shame and guilt that crept into every nook of my being.

Did what happened with Nora make me gay?

Did I actually notice that she was different?

What will happen to me if anyone finds out?

What will Baba do if he finds out?

I am definitely going to hell.

Will God forgive me?

Why did God allow such a thing to happen to me?

Was it a test? And if he was testing me, what was the point of such a test?

There were many questions and no answers. There was no one to talk to and there was no way to get to the truth, bar one. Some of the guys knew all about the pleasures of being in the arms of a real woman. Some of them knew what it felt like to penetrate a real woman, and I was about to find out for myself.

Sameh knew a couple of girls that he used to bring around for the guys to feast on every once in a while. The guys used to tell many tales of their adventures with those girls. In the past they had often invited me to join them, but I had turned them down so often that they stopped asking. Sameh was the one to approach to make it happen. Making this first move wasn't easy, but it had to be done.

"When are you guys next getting together at your place?" I asked.

"I'm not sure—you know how these things happen, whenever I can get away with it."

"You should let me know next time."

"Why? Did you finally decide we were cool enough to feast with us? Or did your lady let you off the leash?"

"Come on, you know it is nothing like that. I just want to try something different and new. Plus, I am single now."

"Don't worry, we'll turn you into a man."

He kept his word. A couple of weeks later, he invited me to join him and a couple of our friends at his family's villa. His family was very well-off. His father had worked for an oil company in the Gulf for fifteen years.

He provided for the family, living in Saudi and visiting them whenever he could.

Sameh had an older brother who was living abroad to get his college education. It was just Sameh and his mom living in their oversized villa. The mother herself wasn't home much. She was a socialite who was always at events with her friends. Lack of supervision and an endless supply of funds turned Sameh into a wild and reckless teen.

It was my first visit to Sameh's gated villa in Heliopolis. The villa had a little garden, which wasn't well kept at all, giving a deceptive impression of the villa. The inside of the villa was definitely luxurious—crystal chandeliers were in every room, paintings were on every wall. The furniture was both modern and expensive.

I was beyond nervous that day as I walked through the gates of the villa. Among the many firsts that year, it was the first time I'd skipped school. I was anxious, even frightened, but I was determined.

Sameh was already home with two other friends from school. One was this skinny tall kid, Michael, and the other was Amr.

"Look who finally made it! I thought you were going to chicken out! You just made me lose a bet with Amr," Sameh said.

I laughed nervously. "I told you I was coming, no matter what."

"I didn't believe it then, and I'm still in shock that you're here."

"Stop busting his chops and tell us where the girls are," Michael complained.

"Yeah, where are the girls?" Amr echoed.

"Don't worry, guys, she is coming now."

"*She*! Didn't you say two were coming?" Michael asked.

"Yes, I did say that, but only one is coming. The other one couldn't skip school today because of a test but, don't worry, fellas, she can handle it all."

We waited for over an hour in the living room, watching porn and playing cards until the doorbell rang. The girl finally arrived. As Sameh headed to the door, each guy yelled out a number.

"First!" Amr yelled.

"Second!" Michael followed.

Sameh laughed at their attempt. "You guys know I always go first. My house—my rules. And since we have a new member, he will go second, before you two animals tire her out."

I was totally lost. I didn't understand a thing, but I said nothing, pretending I knew what was going on around me. My train of thought was interrupted by the laugh of the female arriving. She was about 5'3," a heavy-boned girl with a long face. She was wearing a grey skirt, a button-down shirt, and a school tie. As she greeted the guys, I tried to read the name of her school on her tie but couldn't.

As she turned to me, Sameh cried, "This is the one and only Donia, and she will turn your *donia*, your world, upside down. Donia, this is my good friend Osama. I want you to go easy on him today—this is his first time with us."

"Don't worry; I will take extra care of him. I like him. He's cute," Donia laughingly answered, giving me a squeeze.

Soon, Sameh disappeared with her into one of the five bedrooms. We sat watching porn, waiting our turn. The guys made comments about every scene, every position. It seemed to be an ongoing competition between them, as they listed all the positions they'd tried before, or boasted of how long they could last.

I waited quietly, amused by their bickering, and fascinated by the soundtrack of moans and screams.

Sameh strolled back into the room wearing the wide grin of a victorious king, a conqueror of new lands in a faraway country. The guys cheered him raucously as he took his seat, then the cheering voices were chanting my name. It was my turn to explore the body of a real woman for the very first time.

"*Yalla ya* Osama, it's your turn. Make us proud," Sameh instructed, as the chanting continued.

Getting to my feet, I asked Sameh if he had any condoms. The guys were totally bemused by my inquiry. They didn't know what on earth I was talking about. My attempts to explain to them what a condom is were in vain and were met with laughter.

"Why would you want to put something on it? That sounds like an instrument of torture, not protection!" Michael roared.

"Just go in and enjoy it. Feel the warmth of her thighs wrapped around you," Sameh added, laughing, as I hesitated.

"Osama, if you're not going in there, I'll go myself. Stop wasting time, we're paying for this," Amr grumbled.

I headed for the bedroom with a rising sense of panic. Knowing the risks of sleeping with a prostitute without any protection didn't make things any easier.

How is it possible that not one of the guys knows a thing about condoms?

What if she has AIDS?

What if she gets pregnant by one of us?

My thoughts were interrupted by her shriek of laughter as I walked in. She was sitting on the bed naked, inspecting and cleaning herself.

"So, you're the American. Are you going to show me some new moves? Or are you the same as those guys?"

My bewilderment was probably all too obvious. Before I could string together an answer, she quickly added, "Don't worry, sugar, I'll take care of you like no American woman could. Nothing beats a homebred woman, honey." She was still laughing as she made her bold claim, caressing her thighs all the while.

"Come closer, don't worry. I don't bite. Or are you going to stand there by the door the whole day?"

I stood there motionless for a few minutes, not knowing what to do. For a moment I wondered what I was doing there at all. She had the body of a woman. All her womanly parts were in place. There was nothing missing, nothing added on. She had an amazingly curvy figure that would turn on any hot-blooded male. There were others a few steps away who wanted her. They were hungry for her flesh and for her touch. Yet I had no desire to touch her; I had no desire to be anywhere near her. I wasn't aroused by her nakedness. Her seductive ways—her sugar-coated words—left me cold.

As I stood there, images of Nora and the events of that day flooded my mind. I remembered her deceit. I remembered the love we'd shared—the love I could not get out of my mind. The burning desire and raging hormones of a teenage boy ceased to exist. The hunger that led me into Nora's arms was gone without a trace. Shame, guilt, insecurity, fear, confusion—a maelstrom of emotions had taken its place. Donia's naked body was replaced by an image of my flesh burning in eternal hell. Her touch did nothing for me as her hands explored my body the way a snake wraps itself around its prey. I was immune to her venom.

"What's wrong, sugar? Don't you want me?"

"No, no, it's not that."

"Do you have a problem getting it up?"

"No, it's not that."

"So, what is it? Are you just going to sit there like a kid in a classroom?"

"I don't know."

"Do you want me to do anything specific? Or wear something you like? I have a bag full of goodies here."

"No, it is not that, but I don't think I can do this."

"Why not, *ya* Samsoma?"

"I never did anything like this before, and I have someone that I really love. I think I should leave."

As I headed for the door, she called my name softly and said, "You should just stay. We don't have to do anything. If you go out now, the guys will never stop teasing you about this."

"What do you mean?"

"Well, you've been in here for five minutes and you're still fully dressed. They'll know that nothing happened and they'll tease you about it forever. I've seen it happen many times before and it's never pretty. You seem like a sweet guy, and I like you. You should stay longer and don't worry; I will have them believe that you were a lion."

Her words made sense, and I stayed.

"Just sit down, I could really use a rest myself before the next one walks in."

She stretched her naked body on the bed as I lowered myself into a chair, my thoughts in turmoil.

My inability to do anything with Donia pointed to just one conclusion. The guys' comments about the "bicycle" echoed loudly in my mind. Twenty minutes passed, seeming to last an eternity. This experience was meant to have a different outcome; it was meant to put an end to my doubts. But it did not. It added more, and the doubts were turning into certainties. I was on the brink of tears. A scream struggled to escape my throat. I wanted to run as far away as possible. My thoughts were as noisy as

Times Square on New Year's Eve. I was glad when a loud moan from Donia brought the silence to an end.

"We have to make it believable, don't we?" she whispered, with a wink. "You should try to look the part. Take your shirt out of your pants and mess your hair a little. Here, come closer so I can imprint my lips on your face. And don't worry, your secret is safe with me."

"Thank you so much," I muttered, truly grateful.

"Feel free to brag all you want about this," she added, laughing. "They will believe anything you say."

Acts of kindness from complete and unexpected strangers are forever memorable.

1/11/2017

I wish I had listened to this one therapist who recommended writing down my thoughts and feelings. It feels great to finally let everything out on paper. I'll be honest with you, this has been therapeutic, and it has, in many ways, helped me cope with Baba's death, and it is still helping me with the mourning. I am exploring areas of my past that I, for years, blocked out.

Also, I can't believe that I just admitted going to therapy. Over the years, I have visited a few therapists for various reasons and certainly when images of Nora haunted me to a crippling point. There were times when images, so real and vivid, jumped out at me from nowhere. When I had them, it felt as if I was pulled into a different realm, lost in a maze of bloody images of her saying, "You did this to me." And guess what? I never shared the truth with any of the therapists; they never knew the true reason for my visits. I was there to talk to someone, and I was there for the prescribed medication, which was the only path to Lala Land. In fact, if it weren't for September 11, 2001, with everyone talking of mental health and trauma then, I wouldn't have gone to therapy. I was kind of forced into it.

I didn't want anything on my records. "It is not a secret if two people know of it," Baba always told us. I didn't want anyone knowing my source of shame; I didn't want anyone to know how I gave her looks of disgust, or how I tore up her letters right in front of her, or how I cursed her out on the staircase when she tried to talk to me, many times. I treated her in ways no human should tolerate. I was heartbroken; I was betrayed; I had no will to listen to anything she had to say. I was starting to change. I was becoming angrier. I didn't have much tolerance for anything. I was having these weird dreams of Nora. I started dreaming of her trying to take advantage of me; I was repulsed by her in every way, and in turn, I was repulsed by being in Egypt.

Baba and Mama thought that by sending us to Egypt, we would be saved. And that was not the case at all. In early 1994, there was a sudden, drastic change. It was Asmaa's second year in college, and she was beginning to spend more time on campus, without any explanation. This change had Mama in panic mode for a while, as she feared that Asmaa had reverted to her old rebellious self, and she was anxious about what might happen. In a way, I don't think Mama minded the change too much, because she was getting her daughter back. She felt that Asmaa was finally lifting herself out of her constant state of depression.

We knew little of what was going on in her head or in her life in general. We knew that she was actually going to her lectures and that she was among the top students in her class. All became clear when she walked in one evening wearing a *hijab* covering her head. It was a shock to Mama and to me, and to Baba, when we passed on the news later. That evening was a very emotional one in our household. Asmaa walked in, ran into Mom's arms, crying, and began kissing her hands and asking her for forgiveness for every wrongdoing she ever did. She begged for help to get Baba to forgive her too, tears covering both of their faces as Mom held her, soothing her gently.

Asmaa had been staying on after her lectures to attend religious lessons with some of her classmates. She had been doing this for months and hadn't wanted us to know. She was also spending a lot of time reading books about Islam to learn more about her faith and to help her repent and overcome her overwhelming feelings of guilt. By the fall of 1995, Asmaa was pretty much Sister Asmaa; she put on the *niqab*. No one ever saw that one coming. Asmaa, the diva, decided to become ultra-religious and fully cover up. I think that was when they decided that after five long years in Egypt it was time for us to return home. Baba was becoming more concerned about our well-being because of the terror and turmoil rocking the country, while Mama was worried that she was losing the two of us in Egypt. They each had their reasons.

My feelings were similar to those I had when we moved to Egypt—both sad and excited. But this time, the sadness was overwhelming. I didn't want to leave my friends and the way of life I'd experienced those years. I had learned how a country can possess a person entirely. The city that never sleeps is Cairo, really. I had learned that everything in Egypt is done in a way that feels so different. I had seen how people support one another and experienced the generosity of Egyptian hospitality. I had learned and seen things that both surprised and shocked me. I understood why Baba, Mama, and the twins loved it; I had become part of their clique.

In New York, kids wanted to party and get wasted drinking booze they had bought using a fake ID or through an older, cool sibling or friend. In Cairo, it was very different. Kids wanted to smoke and get high but needed no ID to get their kicks. I saw kids as young as six years old smoking on the streets of Cairo. In New York, teenagers fantasized about the day they'd lose their virginity and who they'd lose it with—and how—or simply brag about their sexual escapades and their victims. Egyptian teenagers fantasized about getting a hold of a picture of a naked woman or a pornographic film. They fantasized about the simple, innocent pleasure of falling in love. And I got to experience the latter, but with the thumbprint of the devil; an encounter with love that left me traumatized.

Didn't I tell you? She was my lighthouse and storm. She broke me down and left me in ruins on a deserted beach. The news of going back home came just at the right time; I wanted to be as far away as possible. I wished to forget her and everything we shared. Alas, some things can't be erased from our memories the way we do a digital file. It takes a lot more than a click. I thought the move back home would help. I was the victim of Nora's lies and deception, which was how I saw it then. The trip home was to be my rescue mission.

And I was so wrong. Nora haunted me the second I fastened my seat belt. The flight back to New York was the longest flight ever. My mind was in a tumult for the entire eleven hours we flew through the clouds and over the Atlantic Ocean. I mulled over the memories and mysteries. It was the first time I thought of the concept of unconditional love that your gedo referred to in his letter. That flight home was the spark to my insanity.

Seek help when you need it; don't be too proud!
Love and respect everyone equally; however, your trust should be awarded to those who are worthy.

1/12/2017

Dear Journal,

I really don't like you. I stopped writing last night because I couldn't stop myself from crying. I had to get up and pray to calm myself. It felt like everything came back at once, and I ended up wishing for Baba's arms around me to hold me safely, the same as he did in so many of our pictures. He held me as his most precious possession. I am realizing the depth of my own wounds as I try to tell Adam the whole story. I can give him a sugar-coated version of life where I am always the hero. People comply with those versions of the stories. Or I can tell him the truth.

The idea of me, of all people, being responsible for the well-being of another human gives me endless anxiety. I haven't been truly engaged with anyone since Nora. I haven't felt my heart beat this way since her and since that flight home. I tried to leave our memories up there in the skies thinking that home would be a safe shelter from her. It took me that many years to find some solace, and it is Adam.

Now, let me get back to addressing my son.

Hello, my dear son,

Before you, Nora was my greatest love story. Most will say that young people don't understand love because of their age and lack of experience when, in fact, those who love most and purest are the young. The absence of experience makes them fearless of risks that others would deem reckless. Wise, seasoned lovers are finally able to manage their fears and understand that it shouldn't stop you from giving your all. With Nora I felt love, I felt free, it was pure happiness. I didn't want the day to end whenever we were together. She was my sun, my moon, and everything else.

"I will always love you no matter what."

I said it to Nora, Nora said it to me. I know we both meant it, and yet there was no love left.

The love was replaced with sheer hate and disgust. But how can a love so strong be broken so easily? My young mind tried to make sense of it all but couldn't. I contemplated love and its fragile nature throughout the flight back to NYC, and I have pondered those things since.

Can anyone really love you regardless of what you do or believe in?

While in the air, quietly looking at my mother's face from a distance, I thought of all the possible ways I could tell her about what happened with Nora. I thought, no one but Mama would be able to understand and soothe the guilt I feel. There is a special bond that only exists between a mother and her child, a bond of unconditional love, and it has healing powers.

But the questions kept floating in my mind as the plane floated through the night skies. "Is my mother capable of such a love? Is my father capable of such a love? Is any parent capable of such a love?"

My mind continued to wonder as I looked at Mama. What if I was homosexual? How accepting would she be? Would she still love me the way she does today? Would she support me? Or what if I chose a different religion than hers? What if I became a Buddhist? Would she still love me then?

The one definite answer was that, in fact, unconditional love had no place in our culture. I didn't see many examples. Parents can easily disown their children for simply choosing their own career or partner, or for choosing to stray from the path they had in mind for them. It happened to Baba with my gedo. It happens to many people throughout the Arab world on a daily basis. Do I want to suffer the same fate? We were shipped off like cattle to another country because of Asmaa's mistake. I pondered the future, then: What if one day I become a father and my kids want to do things differently by rejecting my choices in life?

What if they find new ways to their true happiness?

What if you, my son, turn out to be gay?

Will I disown you because my culture and religion view homosexuals as sinners and outcasts of society? What if you denounce religion and the existence of God altogether?

What if you do all of the above and become a good and well-mannered human being, without ever disrespecting others or me?

Will I be so stubborn and stuck in my own values and beliefs that I will be unable to love you?

Or will I embrace you and love you, because you are my child?

Am I capable of providing such a love? Or can we only win love by abiding by some unspoken moral code and the ideals of others? Must we sell our souls and conform to certain standards to be loved?

You see, I have been thinking of you since I was a teen, and I haven't stopped since. I think it was Baba's "if you will be ashamed to share it with your kids, don't do it," that always made me think that far ahead.

And now that you are here and I am a father, it is nothing like I imagined it to be. I want to tell you everything and tell you all the stories like Baba did with us, but I have done a lot more than him. I have mummies, not skeletons, in my closet; they are very much preserved and untouched by other humans. I wonder if giving you access to all the information is a good idea—and when is a good age to do so? I think I will give you this journal when you can ask yourself these questions and possess enough knowledge to comprehend them and to answer them as honestly as you can. I couldn't do it. I was plagued with fears, ignorance, and insecurities. I couldn't figure out if Nora was the victim or if I was the victim.

As you read this journal, ask yourself these questions:

Does anyone really love you unconditionally?

Did anyone ever love you unconditionally and actually understand the true meaning of such love? Are your mind, heart, and soul open enough and large enough to provide this type of love to others?

Consider different scenarios with people you think you love, or could love, unconditionally.

What if they did something unspeakable? Would you still love them?

What if they betrayed you? Would you still love them?

What if they hurt you or someone you love physically and/or emotionally? Would you still love them? What if they deserted you? Would you still love them?

What if they hated you? Would you still love them?

I hope you are able to answer these questions whenever you are asked, because there will come a time in your life when you must.

I couldn't answer my own questions.

I knew one thing for sure—my family must not know a thing about Nora and what unfolded between us. I brushed it under the rug, thinking it was God's punishment for losing my virginity before my wedding night, but I still couldn't shake the doubt about my own sexuality. The experience, or the lack of experience, with Donia didn't make things easier. I was convinced that no one else had gone through what I experienced. There was no way of knowing what others went through unless you read it somewhere. That was before the Internet occupied our minds and injected them with new realities we didn't know existed.

How did we live before the Internet and Google? I always think back to that time of my life—what if Google had been available then? I would have had somewhere to turn; I would have made educated decisions, although the Internet is flooded with false information as well.

If I had known more about Nora and her condition then, if I had been equipped to handle such a situation, the outcome would have been totally different. She was perfect as she was, and I didn't know how to handle such a gem who radiated life. Everything she did, she did with love. She was about the only person who was capable of such love. Aside from the very few months of silent treatment, once she opened up, she was so warm. She had no option but to lie to me. She was born into an ignorant world and at the wrong time. Even now would be the wrong time. She understood the ugly reality of our world way before I did, and I did nothing but confirm the injustice of it. I'd be lying if I told you that was something I realized right away. It took me two decades to recognize it. I remember thinking that *she* was the one who broke *my* heart. I hated her. It was blind, ignorant hate.

Baba always said, "Knowledge empowers the mind; the mind empowers the heart. Your mind sets your heart free."

You can love anyone unconditionally: parents, grandparents, children, siblings, aunts, uncles, cousins, spouses, and friends. But the most important unconditional love of all is the love that a parent gives a child. I believed that Baba couldn't love me unconditionally if he knew the truth about me.

Imagine. If I believed the adult with the medical degree couldn't accept me, then how was I supposed to accept and love Nora, not knowing anything? I couldn't even accept myself. The guilt turned me into a scared little boy lost in a big mall with foreign signs. I probably missed any attempts others made to help me; there are a lot of things that I am not remembering.

However, I do remember thinking that Amo Mohamed and Tant Shadia loved Nora unconditionally. They were her support system when she needed them most; they were willing to move for her and give her all that she needed for her changing body. I was the only one, in her new reality, who failed her.

And even in loving someone unconditionally, you don't necessarily need to engage. Sometimes, giving the person the space and time to grow on their own is an act of love. Just like Gedo said in his letter, animals allow their young to be, and that is pure love.

Baba did love me.

Adam, I love you, and please know, I am always here for you, no matter what.

1/13/2017

I was thinking of how New York changed while I was living in Egypt, but I didn't have much of New York memorized when I left for Cairo. My Cairo memories were much more vivid and alive. On the other hand, New York was starting to feel like a new experience.

By the time you are old enough to read any of this, the city will look completely different than what it was when I was a kid. Everything looks so different already; they are changing it all, from roads to buildings, and there's the complete gentrification of neighborhoods. One thing that continues to be true about this city, it is continuously changing. The buildings and trains are not covered in graffiti like they once were. There are no prostitutes on corners trying to solicit business, and there aren't sex shops on every other block. Giuliani got rid of all that back in the 1990s, but it came with a high price—Abner Louima and Amadou Diallo paid a hefty price. New York was becoming notorious for police brutality, like Los Angeles and its police department. I can't believe I still remember those two names. I remember these random facts, but I am glad that I remember both the good and the bad. I wonder if the victims prefer to be forgotten. Well, Amadou doesn't have that option; he was shot dead.

As crooked politicians would say, "change comes with a price tag," or is it "collateral damage." And Baba was getting ready to pay a heftier price for all the changes he made. He made unnecessary trips to Egypt to visit us. He bought me all these gifts, hush gifts for me to quietly accept my circumstances; he bought them out of guilt. And back in New York, that guilt came in handy. I was getting ready to use it to my advantage. I became intolerable, and I knew he would do whatever I wished. I just felt it, and I was right.

Home didn't feel like much of a home. My room was very much intact—everything was where I left it—but I returned not the same kid who left it. I was suddenly aware that I was back in a place where not every household owns a *shataf*, a bidet. The bidet was the reason Baba always made sure we used the bathroom before we left the house. I had forgotten all about that part of America, and it was the one thing the boys talked about in grade school after their first sleepover: "Osama has a butt shower in his bathroom."

I didn't know it then, but those first few weeks were the calm before my many storms. The calm was a simple act of being in my childhood room searching for the pieces I lost while away. Yet the room was that of a child. It wasn't mine—it wasn't a reflection of me. The toys on the shelves didn't bring any joy. I emptied the contents of the room within the first week. I couldn't stand the sight of my younger and happier self. I wasn't that kid anymore.

"Baba, we need to do some furniture shopping." That was my first real interaction with Baba, then.

"Go with your mom this weekend. I totally overlooked the fact that you outgrew the bed."

"I will also need some boxes to throw away some things."

"I will get you some boxes on my way home tomorrow. You should sort through it all, and figure out what you can donate."

"I doubt anyone will make use of any of this. It's old clothes, toys, and whatever else that doesn't fit."

"Someone is in a hurry to get rid of their childhood," he murmured. "Put it all in boxes, and we will go through it later. I will make some space in the attic to store a couple of boxes. Make sure you save the photos on your walls."

The photos were of me with my childhood friends. The same friends I had to say goodbye to years ago. Those were young bonds that were never rooted in anything solid.

My only real bond had been with Nora, but she was no longer in my life, and I didn't know what direction to take.

Was my whole experience with Nora a mistake? And if what we did was as wrong as it seemed, why did it happen in the first place? Why did God allow it to happen? What did it all mean?

I had many unanswered questions and no one to talk to. My feelings of guilt, shame, and confusion remained, and there was no Nora to talk me through it. The emotional turmoil made my last semester of high school a dark and lonely time. During my senior year, I became a loner with no wish to mingle with others. I wanted to be left alone. I kept a safe distance between myself and most of my old friends. It was the same at home—I followed a similar pattern as that of Asmaa when we first moved to Egypt, I kept to myself. Plus, living out east on Long Island didn't make the move back any easier on me. It didn't feel like home, my friendships weren't what I remembered them to be, I felt estranged. I felt it on the very first day of class when Mr. Peterson, the English teacher, couldn't pronounce my first name as I had gotten used to teachers in Egypt saying it; in Egypt they enunciated each syllable in its native tongue.

It was roll call all over again, but this time the laughs weren't so innocent; they were tinged with a hint of suspicion. Things weren't as I left them; they were no longer simple. I believe that feeling hit me when we landed at JFK; the way the border patrol officer greeted us wasn't welcoming. He didn't say, "Welcome home" like he said it to others before us. I felt something then but couldn't identify it. Even pop culture was singling me out as the late, great Notorious B.I.G. was dominating the NYC airwaves: *Time to get paid, blow up like the World Trade*. Little did I know it at the time, but that particular lyric would be of particular significance in my life.

I think that was the reason I tried to go away right after graduation. When it was time to apply to college, I attempted to apply to a few schools out of state to be as far away as possible from the family. Still, Baba objected to the idea. It was the first time he and I had a serious disagreement. It was the first time he had objected to a request of mine.

We had many fights and arguments about it. He wanted me to be as close as possible to him. I, on the other hand, wanted nothing more than to get as far as I could from him and the whole household. I wanted to be where I knew no one and no one knew me. I wanted to find my own truth—to find myself without fear of discovery. I respected their truth—limitations to some—and I didn't wish to disturb the family's balance. I was certain that I needed to be as far away as possible.

You know, I really tried to enjoy my return. I had repented for all my sins—I did it while we were high in the skies, closer to the heavens. I had promised God to do better and to never have sex again till marriage. I had really thought I was going to marry Nora, and that was why I gave in to temptation.

Egypt was a closed chapter, and I wanted to start a new one. Yet I was faced with questions that took me aback. I tried to have fun when people asked, "What kind of name is this?" or "Where are you originally from?" but I felt an overwhelming sense of otherness. And the butchering of the name verified it as their eyes scanned me to make sure I was bomb-free, thanks to Omar Abdul Rahman and Arnold Schwarzenegger. It got under my skin; it made me long for Egypt, tremendously. It made me want to escape and find a place of my own. The twins were finishing up their medical school residencies, and Asmaa was being herself, distant.

It was around that time that the ideas of nationality and loyalty entered my mind. I began to wonder if I should join the American military or its Egyptian counterpart. The idea of the military and mandatory draft was very present, as I had just returned from a country where it is a common practice to join, and every male has to calculate the service into his plans. I was suddenly aware of the complex idea of national identity. It kept me busy; it allowed me to shelf Nora for a few months. And my fights with Baba for my educational freedom kept my mind from returning to my sinful action, regrets, and confusion. I had repented, and God accepts repentance when you do it from the heart and stop doing wrong. I was clear of Nora, and I had a minor victory against Baba.

I gave in to Baba's wishes, agreeing to go to a local school where I could dorm during the week and return home every weekend. I got accepted to New York University—Baba did help; he knew a board member—so I was moving to New York City, returning to Manhattan, my birthplace. The idea of moving to Manhattan and getting lost in its sea of people was my thread of hope. Once again, I was reliving Baba's life, especially when he insisted on getting me an apartment downtown. It was as if we were repeating what he had gone through with his baba. I don't know if it was his way of showing that he could do better, or if that was when he learned about Nora. Or was it his guilt for sending us to Egypt? Was that why I thought running away was the only solution?

1/14/2017

Dear Journal,

Life is cruel. It is playing a painful game with me. I found Baba's phone in the jacket I wore to the hospital. Mama had given it to me, saying, "Give it to him in the morning when he wakes up, and tell him to call me." I never got to give it to him, and I never gave it back. It has been in my pocket this whole time. I am scared to turn it on.

Why am I finding it now? Am I supposed to turn it on? Or should I just give it to Mama?

Is it Baba's way of sending me a message from the afterlife? Is there another message that I will find in there? I have been looking at the phone all day, and I can't seem to make a decision. It is as if the dead refuse to leave me alone. They must linger around and fuck with my head. I don't want to open it, but to have a piece of him in my hands, it feels like he is still with us. It also triggered memories that I had buried not long ago. The worms didn't get to feast on those buried memories, not just yet; it was a recent burial. The phone brought me back to one of the worst days in my life. I remember the phone ringing, and almost missing Asmaa's call.

"Did you hear?" Asmaa asked.

"Hear what?"

"Nora." She paused. Upon hearing the name, I froze in my place. What was she going to say? Did she know anything? Did the family find out? A million thoughts went through my mind before I answered. "What about her?" I asked in a manner that reflected that I didn't care, or at least that was my intention.

"She is dead. Baba was telling Mama earlier today."

I don't know what my facial expression looked like, but I was torn. I didn't know how to react. A part of me wanted to break down in tears. Nora was a major part of

141

my life and my first love. I loved her and there were no doubts about that. Yet another part of me was suddenly happy. My secret was finally safe. I didn't have to worry about anyone finding out about us. I didn't have to worry about it anymore after that day.

"I am gonna guess by the sound of your voice that you knew nothing. I am sorry, *habibi*, I know the two of you were close."

I was confused. I didn't know if I should celebrate or mourn. I didn't know if I should jump for joy or cry. I was in an emotional maze, going around in circles. "Do you know what happened? How did she die?"

"They found her body in front of the apartment building. I heard Baba say that she jumped off the roof."

Those words felt like a knife cutting through my being. I suddenly felt her pain. I had contemplated suicide a few times myself.

I couldn't stop myself from picturing her body in blood on a sidewalk. I saw it clearly, and I saw her hand pointing at the letter she had handed me a week before our departure from Egypt. I saw that look of defeat and hurt on her motionless face.

I put the phone down and rushed to the Quran, where I had that piece of Nora hidden. I had never opened it.

"Nora, how could you be so fucking weak?" I thought to myself. "Why do this to yourself? And why did Asmaa tell me? She was finally out of sight, and I was figuring out the heart and mind parts. Did she kill herself because of me? Did her family kill her? Did they find out what we did? But she is really a he."

I couldn't focus. My thoughts were all over the place. I was slowly shattering.

My Love Osama,
I have waited months now for you to calm down; I
have been waiting for a chance to explain myself to you,
but nothing has changed. You still avoid me as if I were
some dangerous disease. You still look at me with disgust
and hate every time we run into each other. I know you
think that I lied and deceived you. I know you probably
hate me so much right now. But the coldness and
distance between us kills me every day. The look in your
eyes every time I see you makes me wish I was dead.
That look alone makes me hate my own existence for
ever hurting you. It makes me wish that I was never born.
I am sorry, I am so sorry. I don't think I can ever say it
enough times for you to forgive me, but I am really sorry.
I know I should have told you the truth and I wanted to
tell you so many times about my condition, but I just
couldn't and didn't think you would understand it. I
don't even understand it myself. I don't understand why
God brought me into the world this way—I don't
understand why He would torture me in such a way. I
don't know if I should blame God for it. I don't know if I
should blame the Zionists who destroyed everything
beautiful in our lands, including hospitals, whose doctors
couldn't detect my condition at birth, or if I should blame
tradition that allowed cousins to marry.
I don't expect you to believe me, but Osama, I am a
woman. I swear to you on everything dear that I am a
woman. I was born a woman but with some genetic birth
defect. It is a condition called Female
pseudohermaphroditism. From birth, they thought I was
a boy, and it wasn't until I reached puberty that things
started to add up. Everyone treated me like a boy.
Everyone thought I was a boy, but deep down inside, I
knew there was something different. I couldn't identify
with boys, I didn't feel like one of the boys. I can't even

explain to you the amount of confusion and pain this whole thing caused me. I can't even begin to tell you how embarrassed I was once my breasts started growing. I didn't know what was happening to me and I didn't have anyone to turn to. I couldn't even speak to my parents, because I didn't know how to explain to them what was happening to me. I felt so abnormal. I felt things that no words in any language can ever explain. I used to go to bed every night silently crying, praying to God that I was normal, and whatever was happening to me happens to everyone else. Even when I told my parents, they didn't know how to handle it themselves. They were ashamed of me, and they treated me like an outcast. They fought every day with each other because they simply didn't know. If it wasn't for a doctor who was familiar with cases like mine and explained to them that I am actually a girl, and that I needed to undergo a surgery to correct the defect I was born with, I think they were about ready to kill me.

My parents didn't think they could face people in our village once we decided to go through with the change, so we moved to Egypt where I could have the surgery and start a new life away from everyone. I was allowed to act as a girl here, but all my official documents stated that I am a boy. And that is the reason I am being home schooled for now.

I have been ready to have the surgery for a while now, but my parents can't afford it just yet. And I was even more ready once I fell in love with you. I wanted to be the woman you could love forever and ever. I wanted to tell you the truth so many times—I wanted to be free of all doubts and pain with you. Your presence in my life made me feel like a woman. It made the wait bearable, it made everything that much better. I didn't want to risk losing you if I told you the truth. Our love gave me hope for a better future. You were the cure to every moment of

*pain, torment, and confusion. You were the light that
brightened up my dark and damned existence. You were
the only hope I had in normalcy.*

*Osama, before I met you, all I thought about was
ending my miserable life. My pain and the cruelty of
those around me defeated me. My wounds were
becoming permanent scars. I needed comforting arms, I
needed love and acceptance, but I didn't find them
anywhere. I didn't find them in my parents' bewildered
eyes—I didn't find anything there but shame and fear.
Do you know what it feels like when you know that your
parents are ashamed of you? Do you know what it feels
like when you know for sure that your parents fear you?
Do you know what it feels like to be so young and
innocent, but you can't find someone to hold you and tell
you things will be okay?*

*Before I met you, I went to sleep every night wishing
that I wouldn't wake the next morning. I didn't want this
life; I didn't want to live it. I really had lost faith in
everything and everyone. I had no patience. And deep
down, I felt like a total freak who didn't belong
anywhere.*

*Habibi, I felt alive because of the love you gave me. I
felt like a human once again because of the way you
looked at me. I felt like I belonged somewhere for the
first time in so many years. And now that you have taken
that away from me, life is once again unbearable. Now,
everything is darker and gloomier than ever before. I
have no desire to live another day knowing that I have
caused you pain. I don't want to live another day
knowing that I have hurt the one person who brought so
much beauty and happiness to my life. I will not and do
not want to draw another breath if you are not a part of
my life. I will wait for your forgiveness, I will pray for
your understanding. I will beg and plead for your love,*

but if I can't have your love and understanding, then I don't want this life.

Nora

My hands fell limp as the letter dropped to the ground. I killed her. I pushed her off the ledge. My negligence was the poison, it was the knife, it was the cold concrete where her body lay. The letter from Nora was the spark that set my conscience on fire. I pushed her off that ledge every time I gave her a dirty look when she tried to approach me to explain herself. I killed her when I looked at her with disgust and spat. My hands were stained with her blood. On the other hand, her suicide note was the knife that would kill me every day for years. It was the rock that dragged me down into hell's fire. It was the beginning of my downward spiral.

Staring at Baba's phone all day sent me back to dig out that grave. I think I am going to return the phone to where I found it. I will pretend as if I never found it.

I miss Baba; I miss Nora.

This is enough for tonight.

1/15/2017

Steve Jobs gave a speech once, about connecting the dots. The big lesson that stuck with me from that speech is that it is always easier to make sense of the big picture looking backward. And now that I am looking back at my own life with a new set of eyes thanks to you, I am able to see things a lot clearer.

Adam, this is the very first time I am sharing this with anyone out loud, or on paper, in this case. A lot of the events that unfolded from that point on remained prisoners in the jail cells of my brain. I am forced to step out of my comfort zone to become a better version of me to give you the best of me as a father. I can't carry the heaviness within my heart for long, it will crush every bit of my soul until there is nothing left. I wish there was a way to describe how I feel right now as I jot down these words. My soul is rattling with fear, and every fiber of my being is revolting and demanding that I stop this madness. My defense mechanism is simply saying, "Don't do it. Some things are meant to remain secret."

But there is a sense of excitement and lightness lurking around the corner. And I want these feelings to enter our lives as family, and I am choosing to free the words into the wilderness of this journal.

Maybe I didn't fully understand it then, but I do believe that it was Baba's past that influenced the way he handled his family life. It was the source of his weakness and of his strength. I was ten years old when Baba's father passed away. It was my first close encounter with death. It was also the first time I saw Baba's tears. I didn't know, then, if they were tears of grief, or the realization that he would never have closure. Now that I am looking back, I see it could have been both. I do wish Baba had the chance to say his peace to my grandfather, just as I wish I had it with Nora. I wish there was a way for me to go back in time and treat her with the love and respect she deserved. I can always blame her omission of the truth as the action that triggered my ugly reaction, but I should have known better; I should have done better. Baba taught us to be forgiving, to not harbor anger for long. "It is bad for your soul; it eats you up, and it is bad for your heart. A lot of people end up in the surgery room because of their anger." Baba used to always tell us that when mediating our sibling conflicts. In my case, my anger and unforgiving ways led to my greatest loss. I lost the only human I loved with every cell of my being, and I lost myself in the process of seeking to understand.

When Nora passed, I had no one to talk to about her and our relationship. Even if there were someone, I doubt that I would have divulged much. My sense of shame and guilt overshadowed all. And as great as my parents were, they weren't equipped to handle the situation; many parents of the same generation wouldn't be able either. Yesteryear's parenting was totally different from today's. There weren't as many books, blogs, and shows that focused on the mental, emotional, and physical well-being of children. The older generations were more focused on providing the essentials—that was their way of expressing love. There was no emphasis on telling the kids how special or beautiful they were; there was no one telling their kids "I love you" daily, and if there was, they were the exception rather than the rule. It's one of those patterns I noticed when people my age talk of their folks, and I attribute it to the two world wars. Both my parents were born into families that lived through and survived two major wars. In times of war, survival becomes the number one objective. If a mother and a father managed to keep their children safe and alive, that was their expression of love. I doubt my grandparents read a parenting book as I did when we were expecting;

the books didn't exist then. And I am quite positive that my parents didn't either, because I asked.

I do wish Baba had talked to me then. He could have saved me a lot of unnecessary struggle. He knew that Nora and I were close, and it seems like he knew much more than I thought. It still irks me that I don't know how he found out. Is it possible that Mama told him something? And if so, how did she find out? I would have loved for him to say something like, "Osama, everything will be all right. It is not your fault."

"It is my fault. I made her feel unwanted and undesired; I hurt her." Most likely that would have been my answer.

"It is not your hurt to bear. Nora was a special being, and we humans don't know how to handle special beings. Her hurt stemmed from a much deeper place; she had her own struggles."

"Why couldn't she just tell me the truth?" I would have yelled back.

"It was not easy to walk in her shoes. You don't know how hard it was for her. The internal jihad she had to endure was greater than she could handle on her own."

"She could have told me."

"She couldn't. She was in a new country and was trying to build a new life with a new identity. She had to adjust to her new skin and play the role. She couldn't be Nour anymore. Think of how it felt every time her mom yelled out Nour stead of Nora. It is a constant painful reminder for someone her age."

"I was right there with her. We talked about everything. I know she said I wouldn't understand certain things."

"And it was her choice to keep it to herself. It was her right to hold on to her truth until she felt safe. We all do it in every relationship. And Nora understood her reality;

she knew she was too much for most, and you had to earn her trust."

I would have loved to have someone explain to me how Nora was a twin flame or some other mystical creature who didn't belong among us humans. She was a powerful force of nature that couldn't be contained by our male and female limited capacities. Ancient civilizations created those fables to explain everything in a way that made sense to all. Now, we need a scientific degree to understand our own workings.

But I doubt that any of that would have helped much. I felt like a killer, and here I am finally opening up about it thirty years later. I served my sentence. I grew up believing that suicide is punishable by an eternity in hell; I also grew up believing that God is just and merciful. I couldn't shake the image of Nora burning in hell for the rest of time because of me. There was no justice or fairness in being judged for eternity based on the small amount of time we spend alive on earth. Things didn't make sense to my young and traumatized mind—the whole system seemed flawed. I was given a scrambled puzzle and I had to find the pieces that made sense for me.

There were times when I didn't wish to look for my pieces. I wanted to give in and do what Nora did. I contemplated suicide every time I stood on those yellow lines waiting for the subway. "Just end the misery, and do it right now," the voice in my head screamed. "*End it*." There were times when I held a knife to my wrist as if I was threatening the voice in my head to go away "or else." It was a tempting exit, but my anchors to this life were much stronger. I think I was discouraged when I found out that Nora's family didn't have a funeral for her—Islamic funerals are not held for those who commit suicide. I also couldn't shake the picture of Baba and Mama crying. I couldn't be their source of pain and shame; they never wronged me. And I knew I couldn't face God. "Yes, God, I am here looking for Nora, who jumped off a building not too long ago, in Cairo, Egypt." Nora had her own reasons that were more than enough to ruin anyone for life. I soothed my anxieties because I saw Nora in a better place as long as she wasn't among the cruel humans.

So, before I tell you all about my torment and hell, I have to first tell you about one of the main reasons my crash was far more devastating than I could've ever imagined.

Growing up with your grandfather, who was very religious, affected me in many ways. I grew up loving my religion, mainly because Baba had presented it so engagingly. He didn't force me to learn anything. "Osama, Allah is far more merciful on you than you are on yourself, and me." Baba said it quite often. Religion was part of the unspoken bond between the two of us. He loved Islam, and I loved him deeply. So, I loved almost everything he loved. At least that was the case for a large part of my childhood and teenage years. Other kids wanted to be like Mike; I wanted to be like Issa.

Many of the conversations we had remained with me, as did the few lectures I attended. But there was one lecture in particular, which I attended with Baba when I was about nine or ten years old, which lingered and impacted my life more than most. It was the one lecture that haunts me, to this day, as I navigate life to find my own answers and inner peace. In many ways, it has been subconsciously my moral compass as I have trodden my path through life, but it has also been the main source of my torment and guilt whenever I have strayed.

I think that one stood out because of its simplicity and the fact that the imam spoke comprehensible English. Every other imam was the butt of our mockery at some point for the way they pronounced certain words or letters.

We didn't have that many religious lectures then, and whatever we had, they were few and far between. There were not as many mosques and imams as we have now in New York. Most of the imams didn't bother giving their lectures in any language except Arabic; they hardly spoke any English and, when they did, we never understood them. Our parents were immigrants who spoke Arabic much better than we did. They had command of the language of the Quran, and they had received some formal education in their home countries. For us, it was different. Our English was much better than our Arabic, and some kids didn't even know how to read or write their name in Arabic.

Let me stop my rant here and tell you about this one lecture. The imam started with a very bold statement.

"We must be honest with ourselves and attempt to understand where we stand in life, how we can lead better lives and, more importantly, show the rest of the world what Islam is really about. If you present yourself to the world as a Muslim, I hope you know that you are choosing to be a representative of the greatest thing that ever happened to the human race. So, now, I would like you to evaluate every aspect of your life and be your own judge."

For some reason or another, I took the representative thing to heart. I didn't want to give my religion a bad name. I didn't want others to judge the religion based on my own actions. That statement was engraved onto my young and impressionable brain, and I think it is still somewhere there as I write these words. He then posed some questions, which made everyone question their own understanding of the religion.

"What do you know about the religion beside the Five Pillars, the name of the prophet, and the word Islam?

"What aspects of the religion have you been applying to your life?

"Have you attempted to learn more about Islam? Or are you just getting by with the little you know from your parents and peers?

"Do you know your obligations as a Muslim toward your creator, yourself, your family, friends, the earth, the environment, and in everything you do in life? Or do you think you already know it all, that you don't need to do any more research? Or have you been meaning to acquire that knowledge but have been so busy with everything else in your life that you have no time for God?

"Have you been looking at life through the glasses of Islam? Yes, the glasses of Islam. It is a concept that I once heard of, which is very useful when you apply it to your life. To illustrate, if you are wearing black glasses, suddenly everything around you will get darker, and if you are wearing red ones, everything will turn red. So, if you are wearing the glasses of Islam, you will start seeing life through the teachings of Islam. Everything in your life, and I do mean everything, could either count for you, or count against you, on the day of judgment. Once you start seeing life through those glasses, many of the things which could count against you, things which have become a part of your routine, things you think are trivial and can be overlooked, will change."

When you are as young and impressionable as I was, these things stay with you. He was talking about sunglasses. I understood that; I knew their function. His sermon made sense to me. It helped cement my Muslim identity, especially as I pondered other parts of my identity and labels.

"I know it's not an easy thing to do, to see everything from an Islamic perspective, especially since most of us have been brought up in the wrong environment, one that fails to provide us with the true food for our souls. In addition, it takes some time to get to the point where everything in your life matters. This is not because Islam is a harsh religion; it has to do more with the struggle we have to go through within ourselves in order to first take the initiative to learn and to alter our lives.

"It's very sad that most of us are only Muslims by name, because we were born into it, and we eventually follow in the footsteps of the devil. I don't mean that literally, because the devil could be anyone in your life; it could be the person closest to you, and you don't even know it.

"Yes, it could be anyone and anything that diverts you from performing your duties as a Muslim. That person or that thing is an associate of the devil and sometimes they don't even know it themselves, because that is the way they have been all their lives and were never taught any better. And that is when your role as a Muslim representative comes in. If you are true to God and the teachings of Islam, God will keep you away from such a person. If you truly care for that person, you will attempt to give a helping hand and bring light into their lives. But if you can't, make sure that you keep away for your own sake, before they drown you along with them."

This part of his sermon was echoed in our household. Both my parents repeatedly lectured us on picking our friends wisely. We heard things like "You are the company you keep" or—Baba's favorite thing to say— "Disease is contagious, but good health isn't. Even a doctor like me treats disease with caution."

I still hear the imam speaking, "Submit to the will of God. After all, the word Islam in Arabic means submission. I know many people who aren't willing to break the rules of their families, managers, teachers, and so on, yet they break the commands of God and his prophet on a daily basis, because it's not a big deal to them. How could you call yourself a Muslim then? How could you venture to sit with a complete stranger to explain the beauty of Islam and all it has to offer, when you yourself can't even give it the respect and love it deserves? How do you expect the whole world to give Islam and Muslims the respect they deserve when you can't do so yourself?"

I vividly remember wanting to submit to the God's will then; I remember wondering how to do it. How do I meet this God he speaks of? I was so eager to submit and be a good Muslim. He even made it easier; he gave us the answer, which made praying something I enjoyed doing for years.

"Every time you perform salat, you are standing in front of God. Every time you perform salat, you are meeting your creator. Every time you perform salat, He boasts of you to all his angels, especially if you are doing it out of love for him. Every time you perform salat, heaven opens its gates for you," the imam said.

For a ten-year-old kid who was fascinated by the stories his dad shared, I loved the idea of standing on a prayer rug to meet my maker. I wanted nothing more than to enter through heaven's gates. If that lecture alone wasn't enough to torment me, Baba had his way of emphasizing the points the imam made in his lecture. The lecture was pretty much etched into my brain.

"Osama, Islam isn't only a religion, it is a way of life," my Baba always said.

"I know, Baba, I hear the imam saying so all the time in Sunday school."

"Being a Muslim in a non-Muslim country is a great experience, yet a difficult one."

"Why is it difficult, Baba?"

"We are the minority here, which means everything we do is scrutinized. People here are very ignorant of what it is we believe in and what our world stands for. They think we believe in a different God because we say Allah instead of God."

"But why does it matter, Baba? We live in America and there is a place for everyone. That is what my history teacher told us in class."

"*Habibi*, everything sounds good on paper, but in the real world, it is different. People will pretend to like you to be politically correct, but behind your back, it is a different matter."

"I don't understand what you mean, Baba. I have friends from all over the world and I don't know what you are talking about."

"You are still young and innocent. You and your friends remain uncorrupted by social expectations and society as a whole. One day, when you are much older, you will understand what I mean."

"But what shall I do then, once I understand?"

I remember Baba's smirk of satisfaction; I knew that smirk because it was my favorite. I knew that I had asked the right question, which was part of another lesson he had taught me. To him, the wording of a question mattered more than the answer.

"Osama, promise me that, once you understand it all, you will be tolerant, loving, and accepting of everyone, because it is the right thing to do; it is the Muslim way to do things. I want you to be the best representative of Islam you can be. It is God's orders." Then he would do his usual and follow it with a Quranic verse, (49:11) "O you who have believed, let not a people ridicule another people; perhaps they may be better than them; nor let women ridicule other women; perhaps they may be better than them. And do not insult one another and do not call each other by offensive nicknames. Wretched is the name of disobedience after one's faith. And whoever does not repent—then it is those who are the wrongdoers."

"*Hader*, yes, Baba, I promise."

1/16/2017

Often in my adult life when people asked about my religious background, I did not, and I could not, say "Muslim." I did not want to disgrace the religion I love and respect so highly. I did not want others to judge Islam by my actions. It was my constant struggle trying to define and find myself as a Muslim. It was another label given to me at birth, and I didn't comprehend how people projected their skewed understanding of Islam. Seriously, a lot of Muslim-Americans are Muslim because of their name or by affiliation to a certain family, and most of those Muslims were forced to understand or pretend to understand the religion to defend it against the constant attack in the last few decades. Imagine a *Mohamed* in any city—he just stands out with that name, and he must answer questions; it is our nature.

Baba understood that, and he wanted to teach us as much as he could to make sure we were ready to face the outside world. And one of those oft-repeated lessons was the one about jihad, and what it meant.

"Great Jihad is simply a struggle that each and every one of us goes through—not only Muslims—as we all experience the same sorts of life events. It's the struggle we go through with ourselves to hold on to the innocence that we all were born with. It's the struggle to do right when presented with wrong, especially when the wrong road could be more expedient. It's about striving to be the best you could be without hurting anyone else and without any deception. It's basically about earning all that you get in life. It's taking control of our animal instincts and acting in a way that is civilized, acceptable, and aligned with the universal truth. It's succeeding in life and acquiring the sort of knowledge that could be useful to humanity. The struggle with oneself is much harder than any other, because the enemy is unseen. The enemy lies deep within you, your evil-inclined self. To defeat such an enemy is a very difficult task," Baba would say. "The decisions you make throughout your life reflect your own inner strength and all that you stand for, so be wise and smart about each of those decisions. If you are that one person who refuses to do wrong, then that makes you the stronger person, and you didn't let circumstances or your needs shape you. If everyone were to do the right thing, this world would be a much better place. Start with yourself, and start your own Great Jihad, because that is the real meaning of jihad. Don't worry about what the next person will or will not do.

"After one of the wars led by Prophet Muhammed, one of his companions said, 'Finally the jihad is over.' The Prophet shook his head and said, 'But now we are going back to the much greater jihad.'

"We strive to be the best versions of ourselves by doing the right thing, the right way." That was the usual ending to his lesson.

That lesson was the one that stuck with me the most. It was as if Baba knew that I would have my own jihad to deal with, throughout my entire life, and he made sure he repeated that lesson often enough for me to memorize it. It was almost impossible not to; he lived by his own words.

I remember Baba making a phone call from a pay phone on the street. I think I was about seven then. The call didn't go through, so he hung up to retrieve his quarter. Instead of just his quarter coming out, three additional quarters flew down into that little cup. Baba then called the operator and told her, "I tried to make a call and it didn't go through, and seventy-five extra cents came out of the phone when I hung up. I am going to reinsert them and would like you to accept them."

When I asked him why he didn't keep the extra money, he said it was because it did not belong to him. "This is a test. And since there was a way to return the money to its owner, it would be wrong to keep it."

It was one of those incidents that didn't make sense at all until I was in the same situation myself ten years or so later. I was at the airport with my friend and his cousin. I needed to make a phone call to my mother. I put in the quarter and the call didn't go through. I hung up and retrieved my quarter to try again. Lo and behold, three extra quarters came out. My companions said, "Wow! That's so cool!! You just got some extra change!" I didn't answer them. I didn't even need to think about it. I dialed the operator, told her what happened, and said I would insert the seventy-five cents and would like her to accept them. The operator was shocked at my honesty; my friend and his cousin were confused as to why I would even bother to do such a thing. It was the right thing to do. It was what Baba taught me. It was a test. It was a jihad. Maybe not that great of a test, but the lesson was that I should always do the right thing in life, no matter how great or how small it may seem.

I love Baba for teaching me this. I don't even know if he realized how that one experience had such a great impact on me. It's something that seemed quite insignificant, but it was a life lesson that he instilled in me, knowingly or unknowingly. I have him to thank for teaching me right from wrong. Jihad was my moral compass; it wasn't what FOX News had the rest of America and the world believe.

There is no point doing the right thing, if you are not doing it the right way! Keep trying till you get it right!

1/17/2017

You know, at some point in my life, I was in love with the name and word jihad. When I was young, and before I met Nora, I always thought that if I had a son or daughter, Jihad would be the name to go for. Now the word is worse than a curse—flights are delayed if someone utters it. Let me go back to where I left off before I go off on another rant about words and their original meaning.

With the sermon I mentioned earlier in mind, along with everything your gedo taught me, it was no surprise that my second reaction to Nora's letter was praying. At first, I cried; I cried for hours. I dropped to my knees, my forehead and nose pressed against the ground, and I cried. I didn't know what else to do but weep. I squeezed my eyelids shut and I saw Nora; I opened them and there she was again.

The letter was crumpled and so was I. I saw the letter transform into Nora's face. Her face was soaked in blood and tears; her lips were sealed, but her eyes spoke volumes.

"You did this to me, Osama. It was you who pushed me. You killed me," her eyes cried. "Why couldn't you love me? Why couldn't you accept me for who I was? I loved you; I gave you everything."

I felt like a criminal on the run, but there was nowhere to hide from the self-loathing and guilt. There was nowhere to escape that overwhelming feeling of regret. If I had been nicer to her—if I had been more considerate—she wouldn't be lying on the ground lifeless. If I had swallowed my pride the times she approached me, my hands wouldn't be covered in blood. If I hadn't ripped up the first three letters she gave me right in front of her eyes, she would have been among the living still. If I hadn't spit in disgust every time our paths crossed. If I hadn't ignored that last letter.

Hell itself would have been a better place than where I was. Nora was probably in a much better place than me. I crossed the borders and I entered the land of no return and the letter was my key. As much as I resisted entering such a place, I couldn't stop myself.

My soul slowly crumbled. It didn't matter how many times I cried. Praying didn't change things. I remember standing there on the prayer rug many nights and begging God for forgiveness. I wanted God to reach down from the heavens above and pluck the pain out of my aching heart. But my prayers and pleas were unheard and unanswered. It didn't matter what I offered in return. It didn't matter what kind of bargain I worked out in my head, I still got nothing.

I was left there all alone to suffer the pain of losing someone who was once so close and dear. I carried the burden of guilt everywhere; there was no escape. And I couldn't tell anyone a thing. Nora's suicide note was the source of my anguish, and it was also as classified as it gets. It was the only thing that tied me to Nora, it was the one thing I had of hers. It was the reminder of what once was. I thought of destroying the letter numerous times, but I was never able to do it. It had a very powerful hold on me. Every time I took it out of its hiding place to tear it into pieces, I broke down into pieces myself. I cried every time I held it between my fingers; I cried myself to sleep many nights with that letter lying next to me, only to wake up the next morning to fold it neatly and place it back where it belonged.

I don't know why I kept it all those years. I know we are sentimental creatures, but I have yet to figure out why anyone would hold on to something that shattered his being.

A soldier returns home after serving two tours overseas, and he is never the same after everything he witnessed firsthand. The images of those who died in front of his eyes never depart; the images of those he shot haunt him for the rest of his life. That soldier will spend hundreds of sleepless nights. He will have nothing but nightmares when he shuts his eyes. Flashbacks will creep up on him unannounced. He will stop at nothing to detach from anything that reminds him of those experiences, and he will lose interest in most things, including life. The effects of PTSD go on and on.

Those effects bring a trained solider to his knees; they break his spirit, regardless of how many medals of honor are pinned on his chest or hang from his uniform. A traumatic experience can easily break the strongest of men. Now imagine what it could do to a spoiled teenager who never had to deal with life's hardships firsthand. It killed the remaining pieces of my youth.

1/18/2017

I prayed and I prayed some more, but nothing changed. I made deals with God, but nothing changed. The pain didn't subside at all—it kept getting worse. I did my best to maintain an external form that didn't reflect the internal torment. I went to my classes. I visited the family every weekend or every other weekend. I disguised the pain with a very phony and calm smile when I was around others. Yet there was always a volcano of horror, guilt, and regret that was ready to erupt any second. Nora's face was always present—it was engraved in both my conscious and subconscious— there was no way of escaping her.

The emotional volcano erupted whenever I was alone in my West Village studio, and religion wasn't of much help. I accepted my reality as the punishment for sinning.

Desperation for a numbing agent led me to the only logical solution for a college student who lived alone in New York City's hippest neighborhood and attended one of its most prestigious schools. Yes, I found my relief in alcohol. I drank anything and everything. I was at every house party on or off campus. I showed up to drink, I didn't show up to party.

The drinking and partying led me to the next numbing agent—I experimented with drugs too. My pain was a ticking bomb and I was running around hoping that someone would know how to defuse it, but in my case, it wasn't someone. It had to be something. I couldn't talk to anyone.

How do you tell people that you pushed your loved one off a building and killed her?

My partying days with the classmates lasted for the duration of my freshman year. Then I moved on to the bigger party scene. I frequented local bars and clubs, and whenever one of the regulars attempted to make my acquaintance, I moved on to another place. I didn't want to make new friends. I didn't want anyone to know my story and I didn't want to know anyone else's story. I wanted to be in a crowded room, but I wanted to be left alone. I was there to numb the pain and not to socialize. The dark, crowded clubs of the city provided the best hideouts. The bodies moving to the music, trying to shake the core to feel something—we were meat packed into smoky rooms, bumping against one another to some loud beat.

And no, I wasn't trying to date. I had no interest in dating at all. I couldn't even get myself to like anyone.

My bar and club hopping led me one day to Krash—a club in Astoria, Queens. With its blue and mysterious exterior, it looked like the perfect place to hide from my pain. It was away from my classmates in Manhattan and away from my family in Long Island. This was way before Steinway Street and Astoria turned into little Egypt; this was way before all the hookah shops invaded the streets of Astoria. This was when we were still mysterious and exotic, and way before we turned our culture into nothing but a belly dancer and a puff of a flavored hookah.

Krash wasn't like most other clubs in the city. It was a gay club—though I didn't know that going in there. We didn't have Yelp or Google Maps to provide such information. We didn't have online reviews, and the Internet wasn't a big part of our lives yet. In comparison to the world you are born into, we lived in the Stone Age. We relied on word of mouth, newspaper advertisement, and basically stumbling onto things, just like I did with Krash. That club became my safe haven— I was never bothered there. Everyone was there to either enjoy themselves or to hide away like me.

It was where I met Steven, or Stephanie, as she liked to be called. Stephanie worked at Lucky Cheng's Drag

Cabaret. She reminded me so much of Nora, with the long dark hair and the wide eyes. I met her there on my second month of frequenting the club, and we instantly hit it off. We became drinking buddies for a while, until things suddenly progressed, thanks to the influence of alcohol. Something about Stephanie's company soothed my pain. Accepting her for who she was made me feel like I was accepting of Nora. I was making it up to Nora somehow and it seemed to be working, because Nora's face was no longer bloody and sad as it used to be. She was still haunting me, but she wasn't as angry with me anymore. I was finally able to find the right drug; it was a mix of alcohol and Steven/Stephanie. However, that drug only lasted me a few months before it got a bit more complicated.

Stephanie demanded more and more of my time and feelings, as well as my story. Those are the kinds of things you share when you are dating someone. She asked for things that I wasn't comfortable sharing, and I had to do what I did best then and throughout my twenties—I dug a big, black hole and hid away.

"What is 'nora'?" they'd ask.

"It is an Arabic word," I'd answer.

"What does it mean?"

"It means light."

"You were so drunk last night, you kept saying it over and over again."

"It is just a word—I am not sure why I would say that."

I had that conversation many times, and it was always a sign that the end was near. I never told anyone the truth; I never saw the need to do so. I wasn't there to share my story with them. I was there to feel their pain; I was there to get lost in their pain; I was there to take away that pain. Over the years, I heard hundreds of stories that could pretty much fill volumes of books.

There was Monica who was once Moneer. She was abused and disowned by the family at a very young age for being different. There was Patrick from a small town in the Midwest, who was beaten up by his homophobic classmates and left to die in a ditch. Patrick's family didn't file any case against the attackers; they were too ashamed of their gay son. "You had it coming to you," his father told him.

I heard some heartbreaking stories. Some ran away from home to escape the cruel looks from their own families and friends who saw them as beasts. Others were still trying to make sense of who they were and what they were.

The ones who accepted their reality—they were such beautiful beings, so full of life and love for everyone. Each one of those pained souls I met along my journey lacked the love and acceptance of their own families and friends; therefore, they didn't hold back their own love. They opened their hearts and arms and took in all of life. On the other hand, there were also the angry ones who never made peace with their past or accepted themselves. They damaged themselves more than the others would ever do; they were a hair away from jumping off a bridge or cutting their own veins in a moment of drunken rage or depression.

The beauty of a city like New York is, people are so self-involved, they don't have it in them to pry into others' business. You can live next to someone for twenty or thirty years and know nothing about them. You don't have to exchange anything but the courteous hello every now and then if you cross each other's path on the stairs or in an elevator. It is a totally different culture than that of Egypt or other parts of the United States.

Millions call New York City home, and millions more across the globe wish to do so. It is the Big Apple; it is the one place on earth of which you can't get enough. It resembles the finest of women who lure you with beauty so radiant it can be seen from miles away. Her exterior beauty is rough at times, but deep down, she is full of all the beautiful things that make life, life. She calls you to her like the Statue of Liberty herself. It is the place where millions first experienced the presence of freedom. It is the place where many dreams flourish and many others die. Like the dreams of all lovers who pursue the beauty in her soirée dress—only the worthy win her over. As Jay-Z and Alicia Keys sang, and Frank Sinatra before them, if you can make it in New York, you can make it anywhere—though I don't fully agree. I got to see a different side of the city. NYC is a place where many come to run after their dreams or run away from something.

And since there were millions of us, it was easy for me to hide when I wished. There were times when I locked myself in. I didn't want to see anyone; I didn't want to speak to anyone. I didn't know what to do with my feelings of regret and guilt. I am glad cell phones, texting, and Facebook weren't a thing back then. Or maybe it was a bad thing that we didn't have those things then. Maybe someone could have snatched me out of the darkness; maybe I wouldn't have gone as far as I did. Their absence, then, made it so much easier to totally disappear and dive into my own sadness. I confined myself within the walls of my place in total darkness. It was the only way I felt safe. Thieves, killers, and criminals lurk in the darkness, and I was one of them.

1/19/2017

Tonight, I am going to do some venting. We have a chat group on this application, WhatsApp. It's a group that was started for the whole family to communicate important messages. Yet your uncle Hasan keeps sending these annoying, silly videos.

Hasan is my brother-in-law who is married to your aunt Fatma, and he is Egyptian. You know, I just realized that I haven't mentioned any of the other family members this whole time. I made no mention of your cousins, or my other brothers-in-law, Arif and Bilal. I wonder if, in a way, I want to see things as they once were when we were kids. Anyway, I am conscious of it now, and I will try to step out of my own shell and see more of everyone.

So, Hasan sent this long message to the group, and I made the mistake of reading it. It was some rant about the torturous punishments that await those who don't pray. I absolutely hate it when he sends these long-ass religious messages in Arabic. It is as if forwarding a thread will grant him heaven. He never dared to do that when Baba was alive; he knew Baba didn't like it and didn't approve of such terrorizing approaches to religion.

I don't remember if I mentioned this earlier, but your gedo went to Azhar schools growing up, and he had the Quran memorized by the time he was fifteen. Nothing shook his faith in Islam or God. It is something I wish I had inherited from him.

"The first step is recognizing God, and the rest will follow," Baba used to say. "I can attest to God's existence; I know God exists everywhere. I see God in almost everything. I wouldn't be able to explain it to you if I tried. I see God every time a sedated patient is laid motionless and chest opened in the operation room. I see the complexity of His creation; I see the human insides as a mesmerizing world that I refuse to see as an accident. We are masterpieces."

Thanks to Baba and his many lessons, I grew up knowing and believing in a merciful and loving God. Yet I was not feeling his love or mercy. My college years and the years after were a fog.

Was that very numbness an act of love and mercy?

Hasan's message took me back to those college years when I began to question everything. I was not questioning my sexuality alone—I was questioning my religious and cultural identities; I was deciding on my labels and how others viewed them. I didn't feel like I belonged anywhere, and nothing was taking away the pain. I didn't know if people were looking at me because I am Osama, the Egyptian, the Arab, the Muslim or because I am Osama, the one they saw at the club moving, drinking, and dancing without a care.

Before Egypt, I was an American boy who traveled to Egypt, and after Egypt, I was the Egyptian Muslim boy who moved here from Egypt and didn't fit in anywhere. I was suddenly aware of all the forces working around me. I was feeling what Nora felt; I was starting to see what she saw—an ugly hateful world for anyone who didn't fit into our boxes.

As I got older, I found myself in more doubt. I deconstructed everything. I had to start from scratch, so I denounced God and religions in a similar fashion to Abraham when he questioned the status of the sun, the moon, and the stars. He didn't recognize a God in any of them. I wasn't recognizing God in anything else, except Baba. Yet his version of God and religion weren't welcoming of me, Nora, or anyone else who is different. The God I believed in was merciful and just. To my teenage self, I couldn't make sense of that and what happened to Nora and many others like her. I couldn't understand how a merciful God would allow anyone, myself included, to inflict such pain and suffering on anyone else.

I treated everything as a scientist would. It was all about data, evidence, and logic. And the first conclusion was: There is no proof that God exists. There is no tangible evidence, which is required by any scientific experiment.

I think it was around that time that I denounced God and the existence of a divine being, since nothing made sense. I pondered the idea of free will—it was the one logical step in my soul-searching journey.

Are we really free? Or are we just acting out our scripted parts? Do we choose the roles we play in life? Or are the roles preselected?

Why is there heaven and hell?

Why is there a judgment day?

Will I go to hell for the things I have done?

Will someone like Nora go to hell for taking her own life?

Again, that didn't make any sense. My mind failed to comprehend it all. Nora suffered. She suffered because of something she didn't choose. She was born that way. Her suffering was caused by those around her. It wasn't her choice, it wasn't her doing. It was the doing of her family, friends, loved ones; it was my doing. It was the doing of God. He is the creator of all; he is the all-knowing. Isn't he?

He created a flawed system where we fail to accept one another. Nora was a victim of an ignorant, judgmental system. But is it fair to attack God based on humans' actions?

I remember the heaviness I felt every time I thought of telling my family the truth about me and Nora. I thought things could maybe, just maybe, be different for me. I foolishly hoped that those around me could see me for me, and not for my labels, preferences, and lifestyle.

There were times when I would randomly banter with the family at dinner and ask bizarre questions about life in general to steer the conversation toward the topic of my choice.

One evening, as the whole family gathered to enjoy Mama's cooking, and while everyone was tucking into their *macaroni béchamel,* I threw a question at Fatma, who had just had a baby girl.

"Fatma, how much do you love Jamila?

"I love her to death, she is the apple of my eye."

"How about you, Hasan?"

"She and her mother are the two best things in my life."

"Do you guys ever think of her future?"

"All the time!" They both answered in the same breath, as if they had been rehearsing a script.

"We are always discussing the future of our family and our little princess," Fatma added.

"What if she grows up to really despise your way of life and wants to do things differently?"

"There is nothing wrong with wanting to be different and being whoever she wants to be. After all, that is the way Baba and Mama raised us."

"Yeah, that is the way they raised us, but we still conform to the social norms. Now let's say that Jamila decided one day to come home in a Goth outfit, what would you do?" I asked.

"I really don't know what I would do then, but I would probably hope it was nothing but her being a teenager, going through a passing rebellious phase," Fatma said, sounding nervous and unsure.

"How about if it is not a phase? How about if that is the lifestyle she wants for herself?"

"Osama, what's the point of these questions? When was the last time you met an Arab-Muslim Goth?" my brother-in-law Hasan asked.

"There are many of them, but you don't see them. I doubt that your worlds would cross, anyway."

"Maybe, but I would have heard something about them from family or friends."

"Really? Do you think an Arab parent would admit such a thing openly? Do you live in this world?"

"Osama is right. We are all about the illusion we create for others—the perfect family, the perfect kids, the perfect everything—it is appearances for us," Asmaa affirmed.

"All right, forget the Goth thing, imagine having a gay kid. Imagine your daughter comes home one day and introduces you to her girlfriend, who is also her lover," I said.

"These things don't happen to us. They don't exist in our world," Hasan quickly exclaimed.

No one in the room cared to answer him. Silence descended on the table for a few seconds. From the looks on everyone's face, it seemed they all agreed with his ignorant comment.

"I am sad to disappoint you once again, but there are gay Arabs and lesbian Arabs here and throughout the Arab world. As always, we prefer to deny things and brush them under the rug."

"Osama *habibi*, these things do happen and exist everywhere in the world, but it is rare in Muslim and Arab societies. We are people who know and fear God. We are not part of a society that revolves around sex and drugs. When we get depressed, we pray and read the Quran, and things get better by the will of God, but in those societies, everyone is on antidepressants or is in therapy," my other brother-in-law Arif said in his usual calm voice.

"Again, that is there, and we are here. If you choose to ignore the fact that these things do exist, and they have been a part of human history for centuries, but people are frightened of what will happen to them, that is totally fine. I call it denial. You have to realize that we are not in Egypt. We are here in New York and your kids will grow up exposed to many things you consider dangerous, harmful, or forbidden. The fact that they are of Arab or Muslim origin won't make them immune to any of it." Their passive attitude irked me; I always felt like it was the reason behind our misery. I was pushing their buttons hoping for someone to take the lead and say something different.

To my surprise, when I finished speaking, Baba spoke up.

"Osama is right, those things can happen to anyone, but the only thing you can do is teach your kids and give them the tools to make the right decisions in life."

I felt I had won the argument, but I knew by the looks on everyone's faces that nothing had changed. It was very apparent that the conversation didn't really mean much to any of them, and even Baba's agreement was his way of shutting me up. He knew that I would keep on going until I had annoyed everyone.

For the rest of the evening, I sat there quietly observing each one of them. In my mind, I pictured the different scenarios regarding what would happen if any of my hypothetical situations were true. I pictured their reactions if I were to tell them the truth. At that moment, as I watched everyone sipping their tea, I felt so distant from my family, an outsider amid my own kind. I didn't feel like an Arab, an Egyptian, or a Muslim. I felt nothing but their judgments of my labels rather than of me as a person.

Our judgments start with the misuse and misinterpretations of words. It's not that we are judgmental of one another; our default is to connect with each other. However, we are judgmental when it comes to words and our perceptions of them. The words "homosexual," "bisexual," "Arab," and "Muslim" don't sit well together. Actually, anything that has to do with sex and Islam is a big no-no. Sighting a unicorn would be a lot easier than finding an Arab-Muslim family who is accepting of any form of sexual preference other than what is considered the norm.

I was no longer Arab; I didn't accept my Arab identity. I rejected the family's way of thinking, but I had nothing to present as an alternative.

1/20/2017

Dear Journal,

Today was the inauguration of our forty-fifth president, Donald Trump. I wonder if people will move out of the country like they said they would. I don't think I can ever say his name and not think of the day Baba passed. Asmaa was right; Trump killed Baba, and someone should impeach him already before he does any more damage. No, I am just kidding, we are not there yet.

People have been falling for the president's distraction tactics. He has successfully created a culture of hate and fear, and he keeps feeding the fire with his tweets and outrageous pronouncements. He did it throughout the election, and he will continue to do it for the next four years. Many see him as the fall of the Republic, but for some reason I don't see it this way. I think he is exactly what our country needs if we wish to have any forward progress. For years, people talked of the racism, discrimination, and ignorance that plagued this great country of ours, and those claims were met with denial. Throughout his campaign, 45 has exposed many of the ailments that have been infecting our core.

Trump will soon end up in history's forgotten pages along with Obama, Bush Jr., Clinton, and Bush Sr. I can't think of something that any of them did to be considered a legacy by any respectful historian. Obama may have the upper hand, because he was the first African American president, but he too waged unlawful wars, killed innocent civilians all over the world, illegally spied on millions of Americans and non-Americans. I never understood how he won the Nobel Peace Prize.

I fear for Adam's well-being and safety in a world that has no mercy or compassion. Cruelty rules this world;

mercy is the exception. People are eager to hate because someone told them to do so. Humanity forgets what Hitler once did because of his own personal hate; they forgot about the genocide in Rwanda and the ethnic cleansing in Bosnia.

....

Adam, don't fall for politicians' fear and dividing tactics. They are doing it to break us apart. It is a bit too late for us with the current 45 and others around the world. I fear that one day, people will attack you because you have an Arabic, Muslim name. They will hate you not because you are an evil man. They will despise you because you say Allah instead of God. They will fear you; they will see you as a terrorist. Yet they are the ones terrorizing our lives with their constant questioning, their random screening. I have dealt with it all since my return from Cairo. I have felt the mistrust in everyone's eyes push me away. America has never embraced its Muslim identity and its Muslim citizens. We were never welcomed from the very beginning because Muslims confuse America. Citizenship court rulings throughout American history reflect this. Judges in the early twentieth century didn't think Muslim values and beliefs were befitting of America; they denied citizenship to Muslim Arabs but not Christian Arabs.

"It is a matter of finances. Muslims don't believe in usury; interest is forbidden for a Muslim, and capitalism operates on nothing but interest." That was your Tant Asmaa's professional opinion when she was all about her not-for-profit work. "America never acknowledged the Muslim slaves brought from African cities. To America, Africa is one country, not fifty-six countries with all shades and colors."

I have met so many people who told me to my face, "Muslim values don't align with American ones." And no one was ever able to explain this to me, especially when none of them have read the Quran or anything on Islam. They were parrots who repeated what they heard in movies and the news.

It worries me when a black man with African roots like ours, who heard the word Nigga and revolted against it, is the one calling me Sand Nigga or Camel Jockey. And if I was to say Nigga to him to prove a point, jokingly, then I am racist. It worries me when someone who is Semitic just like me and suffered at the hands of the Germans for similar reasons is part of the cruelty. Trump is not the source of the hate, but he is a clear reflection of our country. I have seen it all over the past twenty years as I hid in the darkest parts of the city and dwelled in its ugliest places where people take off their masks. Trump didn't birth this hate; he has simply brought it out of hiding, and we can't escape or deny it. It has been our reality for a while—we have been hiding behind masks of political correctness.

Political correctness has been the Band-Aid to this sickening social stigma. People have been pretending to know one another, but in reality, they know nothing at all, because if they don't pretend, they are not "progressive" enough.

Who managed to plant such hate in the hearts of so many? History books are full of hateful and racist examples, which we vowed to combat. We swore never again. Did anyone really mean it then? Or was it another theoretical act put together by politicians and the media to pacify their guilt?

We will survive Trump like we survived Bush—for two terms!

World War III may start because of a tweet!

Remind me to tell you about your Tant Asmaa next time.

1/27/2017

Your mama didn't come home tonight. She
volunteered to spend the night at JFK to help anyone
who may face a problem entering the country because of
a new executive order by the president. I have so many
other names that I'd like to use, but we wouldn't want
this notebook to fall in the wrong hands. Next thing you
know, I will be on trial for treason under some article of
Bush's PATRIOT ACT.

They are calling the executive order the Muslim Ban,
because it is targeting people specifically from Muslim
countries. The irony of it all is that the order is
supposedly a cautionary move in the best interest of our
national security, and it is targeting citizens of countries
we screwed over in the name of spreading democracy. I
really don't get it. We have so many problems at home,
and we keep sending our troops and money overseas.
Why can't we focus on our infrastructure? The streets of
New York City are worse than those of a less-developed
nation.

You know the most disturbing thing about all of this?
The rule is applying to people who are green card
holders and people have acquired an entry visa. There
were no warnings that such order would come to life a
week after Trump took office. It caught everyone by
surprise, and the scarier part is the fact that people are
cheering for it.

America has a funny way of embracing its diversity.
First, she lures you in with big ideas, freedom and
democracy, and juggernauts of pop culture. Then she
welcomes you with open arms if you meet the
requirements of the visa application, and if the
interviewer behind the glass window in some American
embassy labels you a fit match. She will give you enough
of a taste of whatever you craved all these years. She will

promise you more if you choose to chase her dream. And once you sign up for that dream, you are pretty much trapped into her cleverly woven web.

Once you are established as a community, you are automatically under attack, and the scriptwriters of Hollywood will find a fitting stereotype that will surely stick. Italians were nothing but Mafia and members of some family mob. African Americans or blacks are nothing but drug-abusing criminals. Mexicans are drug-trafficking rapists. Muslims are terrorists. Only in America will you find a thriving stereotype backed by movies.

Anyway, let's talk about something more cheerful for a bit. I told you that I made quite a few friends when I lived in Egypt, but only one of them became a friend for life; that one friend is your uncle Mahmoud, whom you will meet one day in the future. Mahmoud and I managed to maintain a strong bond despite the distance and time difference. Mahmoud was very much my friend, bodyguard, advisor, and anything else a friend can be. Throughout my stay there, he took it upon himself to look after me and show me the different aspects of life in his country.

Before I returned to NYC, Mahmoud and I promised each other that we would stay in touch; he also promised that he would come to visit me if he ever got the chance. He kept this promise during the summer of 2000. Mahmoud managed to get a tourist visa to enter the United States, which was not that easy then, and it is definitely getting harder, given the number of hurdles the American Embassy puts in the way of an applicant. Mahmoud and one of his college buddies were both able to get visas. They came to visit that summer to experience New York life and to pay their way by working here.

Mahmoud came from a well-to-do family, and his English was good. On the other hand, his friend, Ahmed, was the total opposite when it came to language skills. It was very apparent when I met him at the airport the day they arrived. He had both the strongest and funniest accent I had heard. I kept having to ask him to repeat himself when he spoke to me in English.

During the first two weeks of their stay, I accompanied them everywhere they went. I played the tour guide; I showed them all the famous attractions in the city. Mahmoud and I were very much alike, which was one of the main reasons we stayed friends for so long. We were both very laid back and we were both night people. Ahmed, though, was hyperactive, always on the go. He used to wake up early and wander off on his own. Usually, he would somehow end up getting lost somewhere in the city. Then he would call me from a payphone to ask for directions, and each time was funnier than the last.

One time, he wandered off downtown to the financial district. In that area of the city, the streets have names rather than numbers, which confused the hell out of him.

"Osama, I have no idea where I am," he moaned over the phone, panic in his voice.

"Are you still in the city or did you wander into one of the boroughs?"

"I have no idea, but the streets don't have numbers anymore."

"How did you get there? What train or bus did you take?"

"I took the 6 train and I got out at the last stop."

"Okay, so you are still in the city. Tell me the name of the street you are on."

"I am on One Way Street."

"What?" I asked.

"The street's name is One Way Street. There is a black and white sign with an arrow on it and that is what it says," he explained to me in Arabic.

I fell to the floor laughing when I heard his explanation. It was one of the unforgettable moments from their trip; I always remember it whenever I see one of those street signs. Thankfully, Ahmed made it back safely that day once I gave him directions. However, he didn't learn his lesson but kept on exploring on his own and getting lost until he had the city memorized better than a cab driver. But he still carried on, providing us with material to laugh about.

"I want to go the bitch tomorrow," he demanded once, as we were making plans for the weekend.

"Bitch, what bitch are you talking about?"

"And when and where did you meet her?" Mahmoud and I asked, exchanging bewildered looks.

"I want to go to the bitch to swim and see girls in bikini."

"Oh! The *beach*!"

"Yes, yes, the beach." He quickly brushed off the whole thing to make us forget about it, but we kept on teasing him about it throughout that summer.

Having the two of them in the city gave me the chance to explore it all over again and visit parts that most New Yorkers don't frequent. Like most residents of any city, my own city didn't appeal to me the way it did to outsiders. Most tourists come to NYC and they are mesmerized by its skyline, its nightlife, its diversity, and its museums. As a New Yorker who grew up in the city, none of that really impressed me, but I knew that I couldn't live in another city.

However, that wasn't the only thing I explored during their summer stay. After the first couple of weeks of fun, the two of them had to find work and an affordable place to live. They made some calls to friends of friends who were in New York to work through the summer and earn enough money to last them all year long once they returned to Egypt.

Ahmed and Mahmoud moved into a two-bedroom apartment in Brooklyn, near Atlantic Avenue, with six other guys. One of the guys they called introduced them to the group who lived in that apartment. It worked more or less as an hourly hotel and was a bit like a train station. The roommates came and went based on their work shifts. One group came in and another went out. It was their way of saving every penny possible to live on when they went back to Egypt.

Through Ahmed and Mahmoud, I was introduced to another side of New York life—to the reality of the American Dream pursued by so many. Most of the guys in that apartment came from the lower-middle social class in Egypt. Most were still in college, and some were recent graduates, yet all were trying to find their place in the world. That summer, I met doctors who worked on hot dog stands; I met engineers who worked in delis; I met scientists who drove yellow cabs.

That summer, I learned not to judge people based on appearances or jobs; I learned that New York is full of talents waiting to be discovered on every corner.

But one thing I always failed to understand was this— why would a doctor, an engineer, all these professional people, leave their home country and travel halfway across the world to work in a deli or on a hot dog stand?

Everyone blamed it on the high unemployment and lack of real opportunities back home, but most of those people wouldn't accept those same jobs in their home countries; they would consider such jobs demeaning or even degrading. I can never understand the logic, but I always believe that the reason our great nation has been so successful in marketing the American Dream is the billions of dollars spent on movies and media propaganda. A marketing campaign that has been so successful, it has people flocking in, in huge numbers, hoping to achieve the American Dream at any price.

Not everything is what it appears to be.

1/28/2017

At the very end of Ahmed and Mahmoud's stay, something major took place on the other side of the world—the second *intifada*. The Middle East was in total chaos because of the violence in Palestine. The images of a young boy dying in the arms of his father fueled the anger of millions across the region and the world. The anger made its way to New York City.

The fall of 2000 was the first and last time I was a part of any such thing. Asmaa—she was on her new, extreme activism—convinced Mahmoud, Ahmed, and me to join her in Times Square along with tens of thousands of others who were there to express their anger, dissatisfaction, and disappointment in faulty US foreign policies. It was a beautiful sight at first to see Arabs from all walks of life and all different countries rally for one cause. I saw Jews walk side by side with us in support of our cause. However, the beauty of this harmonious moment didn't last for long. The peaceful chants weren't enough for some; they turned angry.

A group of young men who were a few feet away from us decided to burn both the American and Israeli flags while dancing around the fire in a very barbaric manner.

"You shouldn't do this, it doesn't reflect well on the rest of us," Asmaa bravely yelled out, attempting to put out the fire. "You can get yourselves arrested."

In a matter of seconds, Asmaa was surrounded by those hoodlums. She was beaten by one of our own. It wasn't an Israeli soldier who knocked her off her feet. It wasn't anyone else but our own kind—it was another Muslim. We jumped in quickly to save her, and we got her out safely. Asmaa cried hysterically that night, and I felt helpless.

After that incident, I made up my mind. I was never to attend another protest or rally for any cause. Even in a protest for peace, we couldn't be peaceful. It was one of those encounters that made me want to crawl back into my darkness as soon as my friends went back to Egypt.

It was also around that time that your Tant Asmaa began to explore a new venture. She was studying for the GRE; she was set on getting her graduate degree in Women's studies. Her niqab days hadn't lasted long once we were back in NY, but she did keep a hijab.

I do admire Asmaa in a way—she was never shy about her trials and errors and was always willing to try something new, even if it meant making a fool of herself. She was definitely the extremist in the family. She had to stand out in whatever she did. Even in marriage, she didn't go traditional like Aisha and Fatma, who married doctors like themselves. Asmaa found herself a convert, John, or as he likes to be called, Bilal, while following one of her imams. She was an imam groupie at some point.

Asmaa and I had been close, but we drifted apart over the years. We were once best friends, but we just stopped talking to one another like we used to. I think we both felt naked in front of each other. I never asked about her secret again; I never asked her how she felt when we returned, and she never asked me about Nora. It was mutual silence. I felt Asmaa's loneliness; it reflected mine. I believe it was your uncle John who added some stability to her life, and it showed when they had their twins, Omar and Kareem. They are about four now. Yes, we have another set of twins in the family, and it was your aunt Asmaa who carried on that twin gene, or whatever you call it.

It must be both amazing and annoying to have another you. It is like Fatma and Aisha. I never really thought of them as lost or confused in any way like me and Asmaa. They were always doing their own thing. They were lucky; they always had one another from the very first moment of their creation. But still, with almost zero privacy.

Isn't it weird how we can admire something and recoil from it at the same time? I would have loved to have my own twin, but I don't think I would have liked the constant presence from the womb all the way into adulthood. I would have had to share pretty much everything with that other person who looks just like me.

We are so full of contradictions.

I am not sure if it was always the case, but I just noticed recently that most of us live by one of two mottos:

1-Don't put all your eggs in one basket
2-Give it your all (or something along those lines)
We are also told:
1-A bird in the hand is worth two in the bush
2-Don't settle for less than what you want

There is a saying, a proverb, a quote, a verse, or a divine revelation that fits almost every situation in life, even if they contradict one another. My point is, there are so many contradictions in things we believe in. These contradictions often cause much deeper psychological damage.

2/4/2017

Like Baba and Mama, I have attempted to create some kind of family routine here in our own home. Your mama and I have a biweekly movie night, and we usually do it on a Wednesday. We take turns picking the movie. Your mama loves her independent films; she's all about the underdog. I, on the other hand, am the total opposite—I'm more into blockbuster movies. I'm pretty sure I've watched all the superhero movies within their release week.

I remember in one of our earliest conversations when we met, your mama admitted to never having seen movies like *Titanic*, *The Notebook*, or *Braveheart*. I thought she was kidding, but with time I learned that she wasn't. I was fascinated by the fact that she had been able to escape the craze. The reason I am sharing this with you tonight is that your mama surprised me and opted for a non-indie movie. She picked *Along Came Polly*, a romantic comedy. I had never seen the movie before, and in one of the scenes the main character, Ben Stiller, eats Indian food to impress his date, but his body doesn't react well to the spices. He ends up shitting his brains out and clogging the toilet at his date's apartment.

It took me back to a childhood memory, hanging out at Peter Ruffus's house. His father was always running to the bathroom, saying, "When you gotta go, you gotta go." And he would always walk out with a smile on his face. He asked us once, "Boys, what is the best feeling in the world?" At nine years old, our minds limited us to simple pleasures like food and girl crushes. He rejected all our answers. "Kaka! It is the best feeling in the world. Boys, you will learn to appreciate a good kaka when you are my age. You will leave everything else for that porcelain throne, and when you are in there, you won't leave it for anything else."

Mr. Ruffus was right in more ways than one. There were things, as kids, we took for granted, and we never thought of the day when we would appreciate a good kaka or any of the simple functions of the body. Our ancestors said, "The body is the house of god." That is why it is said, "Man, know yourself." It also makes sense that bathrooms have been given the name, "house of rest" in Arabic. Bathrooms themselves are something we take for granted. I can't even fathom the fact that there are 892 million people, worldwide, who defecate outside. My childhood and many others would have been so different without the privacy of a bathroom.

2/5/2017

I know that the Quran talks of how each one of us has a book where everything is written down. "If IKEA can provide us with such detailed manuals, surely we can seek to understand the meaning of the precise, exact words God has provided us with." The precision that Baba spoke of scared me at times. I knew what I did, and I pondered the methodology used to collect the data.

Is it written down in words? Or is it put together as a scorecard? I hope it is more words than numbers. Words will tell more of a story, but numbers are very cutthroat. Numbers are simple. You don't second guess them. Repetition leads to perfection when it comes to numbers. Numbers don't turn on you. The equations are always the same; the rules don't change. Three will never come before one. It is the only constant in this chaos we call life. Everything else transforms without warning—men are becoming women, women becoming men. The old is now vintage. The unfit is now hip, winners and losers receive trophies. Thugs and drug dealers are becoming role models, while teachers are struggling to pay their rent. Porn stars are reality stars adored and followed by millions, and they are setting trends. The unacceptable has become fashionable. The world continues to change, but three plus four will always add up to seven.

I think that was the reason I chose a career with numbers.

Life stole away my peace of mind. Everything in my life was a constant battle from the moment I learned of Nora's secret. My life was never the same. It made sense to choose a career that I was innately good at; it made sense to pick the easy route. Plus, the world is in constant need of accountants and number geeks. Someone convinced us that we are not to be trusted with our own money and that we must pay someone a fee to keep it safe for us.

Don't worry, I don't expect you to follow in my footsteps. I brought it up because a day will come when you will have to make similar decisions. You will have to decide on a major that you may use to obtain a job or not. And when that day comes, you will have to choose between the practical and the passionate. I chose the practical. Your gedo used to always say, "The world needs doctors because there is always someone who is ill and needs fixing, and we will always need pharmacists to give us the fix to our ailment. We will always need builders and engineers to build and put things together—we hire people to put IKEA products together, for God's sake." An IKEA joke was always Baba's favorite engineers and architects cliché joke. "One day IKEA will make a house in a box to assemble ourselves."

I come from a long line of people who didn't set out to explore their passions. I am sure my own decisions were influenced by the Arab way of thinking drilled into my subconscious at a young age. Actually, I don't think I ever gave much of myself to anything, before or after Nora. I never had a passion of my own; my *raison d'être* was finding a cure from Nora and my haunting guilt. I had no time for passion—I was learning to adjust to life and its constant changes. I was learning to be an Egyptian when I was forced to move there, and I had to learn to be an American when I returned to New York. Both moves weren't by choice, and both brought on their own challenges.

Adam, this is the first time I am realizing this: I had been living and just getting by up till your birth. *You* are my passion! It makes sense that I am writing to you and opening up. I want you to be my friend and accept me for me; I will always accept you for you, I promise.

So, since I mentioned work and career choices, I should tell you a bit about what it is I do for a living and how I got there. I currently own two accounting offices, one in Brooklyn and the other in Long Island. Most of the business is done out of the Brooklyn office, the headquarters where it all started. But before that I worked for a finance firm in downtown Manhattan.

It was weird that I ended up working on Wall Street of all places, and if I had continued working there, I would have become an investment banker. I wonder if I did it to rebel against Baba in a way. I knew he wasn't a fan of anything that had to do with the stock market. I knew that from a very young age—I was about nine then.

"Osama, why are you smiling?" Baba asked while we were riding the number 1 train

"This man looks and smells funny." I pointed at the homeless man walking through the subway car.

"Take this dollar, go give it to him, and say you're sorry."

"Why?"

"Because it is the right thing to do. You don't laugh at others' misery," he firmly replied.

"But Baba, isn't cleanliness next to godliness?" I had my witty moments at nine; I had learned from Asmaa and her fast mouth.

Baba had this side look that was more disciplining than any whip his father had used on him. If he gave any of us that look, we just did what we were asked. I think we knew that he knew better, and that look was never followed with anything but a life lecture. So, I complied and handed the man the dollar. I also apologized, though I am pretty sure the homeless man didn't care. A dollar was a lot then, at least to me. I walked back to my seat next to Baba.

"This man is here because we failed him as a society. Wall Street broke everyone with their greed. A grown man doesn't choose to live this way. And we shouldn't add to his misery."

"What's Wall Street, Baba?" I asked.

"A place where people sell you dreams for nothing and make profit off hard-working people." Baba shook his head. "I will tell you all about Wall Street when you are a bit older. Osama, respect all people. We are all equal in God's eyes."

Guess what! We never did have that discussion about Wall Street, and I ended up working there right after college. I had a cubicle in the Twin Towers in 2001. My name was one of the names in its directory until September 11, 2001.

I wish there was a way to erase the memories of that day, like in that Jim Carrey movie, *The Eternal Sunshine of the Spotless Mind.* I want to forget the chaos, the destruction, the bodies flying out of windows, and the image of the towers falling to their demise.

It was another day that changed the course of my life, just like the day I learned of Nora's death. It was another Tuesday, but that time, it was morning, and I walked into work early to finish some reports I had been working on the night before. I perched on my desk and gazed out of the window upon the beautiful view of downtown Manhattan and the clear blue skies of this gorgeous late-summer day. I sat there dreaming of being anywhere else but the office, a daydream that was probably shared by many other New Yorkers. The summer was drawing to a close and the changing leaves of autumn would soon be buffeted along on the cool breezes.

I had twenty minutes or so to spare since I was there early—I got there before the rest of my team. I decided to take the time to appreciate the beauty of the river, the sky, and the warm sun through my window. I drifted into a trance of joy and ecstasy. A trance that didn't last long, a trance abruptly interrupted as I felt the ground beneath my feet shake. I jerked violently back to reality and stood at the window watching the whole thing unfold. It was unreal. Time froze. My body was paralyzed. Had my vivid imagination conjured this vision as I daydreamed? But it was really happening. The boom of impact. Explosion. Fire. Human beings leaping from windows. Was my mind playing tricks on me? Was it an illusion?

I took a step back from the window and stood there in a state of disbelief. Was it an accident? Did someone do this on purpose? Did I really see what I thought I'd seen?

"Osama, the North Tower was hit!" A colleague ran into my office, screaming.

"Osama, stay away from the window. Come on, let's get out of here!" He practically dragged me out into the hallway.

A crowd of people were fighting their way through to the exits, making their way to the streets, while others stayed in their offices, thinking they were safe in the South Tower. I was one of those who made it down to the streets of lower Manhattan before the second plane flew into the South Tower. Both towers were hit in a span of fifteen minutes. There were no more clear blue skies; there was no more sun; there was no longer any beauty left to appreciate. It was all replaced by a surge of debris, smoke, fire, and death. The rest of the day was nothing but a haze. Every time I remember that morning, I think of The Doors' lyrics: *This is the end, my only friend, the end.*

I was there. I witnessed the whole thing. I helped those who were injured. I helped the cops. I helped the firefighters. I lost friends. I lost colleagues. I was one of the fortunate ones who experienced it and survived. Yet my world was transformed that day into a much darker one, and not solely because of what I experienced or what I saw.

My life became a living hell because of my name. We later learned that Osama bin Laden was the mastermind of the attacks and he and I shared this first name. We also shared the same faith. All of a sudden, people had no difficulty pronouncing my name—it was the one name the whole world knew and hated. People looked and stared at me strangely as if they feared me. People judged me based on my name and hated me more for being a Muslim. I was no longer an American to them; I was the evil "other."

As if the trauma of September 11th wasn't enough, the FBI felt the need to worsen it, and the whole family was placed under arrest for interrogation. It was one of the most humiliating experiences for all of us. I never understood why the arrest took place, considering how none of us was ever involved in any suspicious political or religious activities. The only explanation that made sense was that someone who hated or envied our family reported us to the authorities. Yes, sadly, after September 11th, many Arabs and Muslims were reported by another member of their own community or someone who hated Muslims.

"Mr. Mohamed, what's your relation to Al Qaeda?"

"What is that?" I answered.

"How long have you worked at the World Trade Center?"

"This was my second year there."

"Were you or anyone in your family alerted to the attacks beforehand?"

"Are you kidding? No, I have nothing to do with this."

"So how do you explain the fact that you are the only one on your floor that survived?"

"I ran down to the streets when I saw the first plane go through the other tower. It was my initial reaction. Call it my survival instinct. These questions are ridiculous."

A long list of ridiculous questions was asked, which only implied that I, or someone in the family, was connected to the bloodiest attack on the U.S. I am sure it was someone who called the Feds thinking it was funny to do that to an entire family. I am also sure that the Feds pricked up their ears upon hearing the name Osama.

I always had mixed feelings about my name. Throughout my childhood, I hated it when people couldn't pronounce it correctly. It was a foreign name to them, and if you weren't an Arab, or someone who was familiar with Arab names, no one was ever able to say it right from the first try—there was always a second of hesitation.

Consequently, I hated my own name at times, but there were other times when I loved it. I loved it because it was different; it gave me character and a unique story—it meant *the lion*. Who wouldn't want to be a lion?

And now the lion was in a cage. I was being questioned about something I had nothing to do with. The victim was being questioned and the criminal was free to roam the earth. I remember wanting to yell at the officer during the interrogation and tell him, "Look, I am not your guy. You are holding the most Americanized Arab. You are holding a gay Arab." I was so tempted to scream it out, but I didn't do it. I didn't want to have it written down in a legal document that could haunt me or the family later on.

Sometimes, people don't have to utter a word to express their opinions; sometimes, you have to pay close attention to their eyes. The blank expression of hate that stares you down whenever you pass one another. Going back to work reminded me very much of the way I treated Nora in the last few months of her life. People looked at me with what I imagined to be the same hateful looks; they pierced right through me. I gave her those same looks whenever we passed each other on the staircase. Coworkers silently blamed me for an act of war that impacted my life as much as theirs, if not more. I blamed Nora for who she was; I blamed her for the way she was born. I judged her out of fear and ignorance, and it was time for payback.

My name went from one of the most unknown names in the western hemisphere to one of the most known and notorious names on the face of the planet. It was second to the anti-Christ on the list of evil names.

It was around that time that I couldn't focus on a thing. Nora haunted me. I was becoming her—I was the outcast, I was the damaged one who didn't belong in this world. The bodies I saw fly out of buildings were her. I couldn't shake the guilt of killing Nora, and I couldn't shake the guilt of being alive out of thousands dead. I surely didn't deserve to be alive. I didn't feel alive. Numb is an understatement. There are not enough words in a dictionary that can describe the pain I felt then. The world showed me its ugliest face, the same one I unmasked to Nora. I triggered hate with my name, not for what I did with Nora, not for what I did to Nora, not for the bodies I used in order to get over Nora, and not for surviving when thousands died. Nora was appearing more often; she was violent and aggressive. And nothing worked on her this time.

Drugs didn't work, and neither did alcohol. The random hook-ups did nothing. I needed a stronger numbing agent, something stronger than all three together. Nora kept on appearing and suggesting an eternal solution: "They will never accept you. No one else will love you as I do. Come to me."

The family came to my rescue. The impact of the traumas was becoming more obvious—locking myself in my apartment for weeks was a major red flag—and it is not like they didn't know that I survived one of my childhood fears, falling victim to a terror attack.

Actually, the whole country tried to come to my rescue and those like me who were traumatized for life. It was the first time in my adult life that the collective was aware of the trauma and of the word itself. We New Yorkers were finally familiar with PTSD and its venomous control over the mind. All the signs led to a couch in a therapist's office—well, a few of them.

I am having a really hard time admitting going to therapy. I am noticing that I keep dancing around it like I am ashamed of it or something. I wonder if it has anything to do with growing up as part of a generation or raised by a generation that looked down on seeking help from a therapist or a psychiatrist. Nevertheless, I ended up going to a few therapists. They didn't really help much, and it is not because they were bad. They didn't have my cure—or at least, that was how I felt then. I sat in their offices telling lies, and the biggest of them all was the omission of Nora and her haunting ghostly images. I told them of the ghostly images, but I lied; I told them what they expected me to say. They weren't those of Nora, they were of deceased co-workers and complete strangers. I couldn't trust anyone with Nora; I was a killer, not an easy thing to admit or share.

Do you think they would have been able to help me then? Do you think they had the capacity to understand what I was going through? I don't think they did. They couldn't even help me with my own identity issues; they couldn't help me get over the anxieties I had whenever I had to fill out a form with my name on it. I hated the looks I got. They were looks of hate, pity, coldness, and terror. Talking about it makes the blood in my veins churn. It was so easy to see through their fake smiles— they were doing it for the money, and I was there for the drugs. They helped me reach a deeper level of numbness. Pharmaceutical drugs are heavenly in comparison to street drugs. Street drugs are meant to entertain, but big pharma knows how to get you to comply with the hidden social code. We all must feel, think, speak, and look alike. I will have to save one of these anti-depressant commercials for you, in case we decide to outlaw them by the time you are old enough to see them.

Eventually, I came to terms with tragedy and the pain of loss. I numbed it all. I placed it in the same mental compartment where I kept Nora hidden for years. Yet I was never able to recover from the ignorance and blind hate of my fellow New Yorkers and everyone else. The looks that pierced me like daggers when I entered a room, even from coworkers and neighbors who knew me well and knew I had nothing to do with it. Hatred, fear, and suspicion were seen in the eyes of total strangers who judged me by my looks and name—even in the eyes of people who barely spoke English and were living in the country illegally. Hating an Arab or a Muslim was the American and patriotic thing to do, even if you weren't an American. This was perhaps what hurt and amazed me the most—people who weren't even born on American soil felt they had the right to look at me like that. Handing my ID over to anyone gave me anxiety.

Although most dared not say it to my face—so ingrained is the habit of political correctness—I saw it in their eyes. In their eyes, I was guilty of this horrendous crime. In the years following the attacks on the Twin Towers, I lived in a constant state of fear, bewilderment, and loneliness—not from the trauma of witnessing the tragedy firsthand, alone, but because I had lost people who were once my friends. I finally saw what it looked like when Nora jumped off the roof.

Thanks to 9/11, I had become too much of a liability— too much of an Arab for any American friend. I found myself an outcast, beyond the pale in the one place that would allow me to be anything or anyone I wished to be.

I lost my Americanism; I was no longer Arab, I'm no longer American.

2/6/2017

I told you how it was Baba who picked my name, and he picked it because of his fondness of Osama Ibn Zayed's history. It was right around early 2002 that he approached me and told me to change my name if I wanted to.

"It is just a name," he said, "You can change it to whatever you want. I don't want you to feel like it is permanent."

"I love my name."

"Osama, I know the looks you get. I feel like I plagued you with that name."

I will share another secret with you: I didn't mind the looks after a while. They were my escape from Nora. I finally had a place to hang all blame. My weird behavior was no longer weird. Everyone accepted that I was traumatized enough and that I should be handled with special care. They didn't think I noticed, and when I say *they*, I mean everyone around me. It took the fall of a few towers for anyone to notice my pain. They hadn't noticed it before. They didn't think much of the impact of their sudden move to Cairo; they didn't notice or investigate Nora's death and how it affected me; they didn't notice me at all. Or was I that good at hiding it all?

Karma is fair and just, and I was paying for my sins and crimes. I should have never walked out on Nora. I should have never walked out on my coworkers and friends. I accepted my punishment and I was serving my sentence without any protesting. I wasn't going to change anything for anyone; I enjoyed my suffering and I enjoyed watching the worst of humanity reveal itself to me. It fueled my engines to build higher walls.

I wasn't the only one suffering the consequences of ignorance, and I wasn't the only one who thought of change. A year or so after September 11th, the family was rocked by another dreadful experience: My older sister Fatma was attacked on the platform of the subway as she waited for her train one evening. A woman attacked her from behind, pulled her hijab off her head, and cursed at her with a stream of insults and invective, using every possible swear word in the English language.

The attacker had a deep well of anger and hatred toward Muslims and directed all of it toward Fatma, who just happened to be in the wrong place at the wrong time. However, the woman's attack was not the worst part of her ordeal, as Fatma explained.

"I had no problem fighting this ignorant bitch, I had no problem with her cussing me. I am so used to the looks and whispers wherever I go now. But the worst of it all was that other people stood there watching, almost as if they wanted to applaud. I saw it in their eyes as she kept swearing and kicking at me with all her might. Even when the cops showed up, they were looking at me as if I was the criminal. Thank God, *Alhamdulillah*, there was one good person who saw the whole thing unfold and stepped forward to tell them what really happened. Can you believe that the woman was trying to make out that I was the attacker and she the victim? She told the cops that I tried to push her onto the tracks, and they were actually listening to her nonsense. She told them, and I quote, "This towel head, camel-jockey terrorist came from behind and tried to shove me! I was just trying to protect myself.""

"She had an imagination and a mouth on her!" Asmaa commented

"She even went on to say that my husband probably beats me and forces me to wear the hijab and that was probably why I snapped as I did, trying to kill her. Then she said they should send me back into whichever hole I'd crawled out of."

Fatma and the woman were both taken to the police station to verify their statements, along with the testimony of the witness. Luckily, the woman's story fell apart once the police obtained a copy of the surveillance tapes from the station. Fatma was released and sent to the hospital for examination and then sent home. That night we all gathered at Fatma's place in Brooklyn to show our support and offer our sympathy. But the incident triggered major debates. There was talk of moving to Egypt or another Muslim country where it would be safer for family members and a healthier environment for the kids—certainly much better than living in a state of fear as the majority of America's Muslim community now did. That camp was led by my brother-in-law Hasan. That discussion trailed off as the women in the family began discussing whether or not it was safe for Fatma and Asmaa to continue wearing the hijab. They discussed the pros and cons of it, but the two refused to change anything just because of this one display of ignorance. And that discussion led to a much bigger issue: women's rights in Islam.

"You know what is sad about this whole thing? It is that all of these people, especially the women, are so ignorant and don't know the facts. Islam was the first organized religion and institution to respect women's rights and their roles in society, recognizing them as equal to men in all spheres of life. Women were granted their rights and roles in life fourteen hundred years ago, way before any other nation, religion, or body put such laws in place," Asmaa said. "The Prophet was actually the first feminist and the first person to fight for our rights. Women's status changed dramatically from how it used to be. The rights and dignity of women became as sacred as any other tenet in Islam."

Asmaa continued. "In a true Islamic society, men and women are equals. Did any other religion let women

203

enjoy their own legal identity and independence? Islam recognized women's individual rights in society and granted them the right to own property and manage businesses, centuries ago. Khadija, the Prophet's first wife, was a businesswoman and owned a trading business. The Prophet himself worked for her and managed her business before she proposed to him."

"You know, the problem is not that non-Muslims have a poor opinion of Islam and Muslim women. The problem lies within the Muslim world itself. Muslim countries restrict women's freedom and rights, which ultimately makes everyone believe that such ignorant rules are derived from the religion itself," Aisha added.

"But still, the western media seems to have it in for Muslims. They are always coming after us in one way or another. How come they are not saying anything about Jewish women who shave their heads for marriage? Or nuns who cover up just as we do? This is not fair to those of us who choose to adhere to God's commands. I want to be a good Muslim woman without having to justify myself to every ignorant person in the world who looks at me as though I am an alien for covering up my hair and dressing modestly," Asmaa said.

"You shouldn't let what others say or do bother you. At the end of the day, this is part of your struggle and God will reward you for holding firmly to your beliefs," Hasan said.

"That's easier said than done. You are a man. You don't have to deal with any of these things. No one looks at you like you have two heads or something," Asmaa interrupted.

"I know it is not an easy thing and all I am saying is that you are rewarded for every hardship you endure," he replied.

"Still, you don't get my point."

Baba interjected. "Look, girls, you don't need to argue or prove your point to anyone, especially not to those ignorant people who know nothing about Islam or even about their own religion. If they really want to know, most of the ignorant practices found in Muslim societies stem from the Judeo-Christian tradition and *their* attitudes toward women. They should read their own holy books before pointing the fingers at us."

"What do you mean?" I asked. "Non-Muslims treat their women much better than most of us do."

My question and comment were met with complete silence. No one saw this coming. But the question had to be asked. I knew that Muslims, and Islam as a religion, are always under attack in the media, and I also knew that Islam respects the rights of women and their role in society, but I didn't know where the ignorant practices they were talking about had come from.

"Osama, first you have to differentiate between religious teachings and customs, and the way people actually behave. As your sister said earlier, we are to blame because we fell into the trap ages ago. Islam is a great religion, especially for women, but there are ignorant individuals who force women to cover up completely, or refuse to let a woman drive, or treat women as objects. Those practices have no foundation whatsoever in Islam; they stem from other religious beliefs that preceded Islam. Take the story of Adam and Eve, in the Bible. The blame is placed on Eve alone and she is the cause of man's fall. The whole concept of original sin involves attaching the blame to women and devaluing their place in society. That was how it was for many years before Prophet Muhammed changed things. But, somehow, Muslims have adopted the old attitudes instead of those that the prophet taught and practiced." Baba paused. "Listen to what God has to say about this in the Quran. The Quran says it is both, rather than just

one. God said, 'O Adam! You and your wife dwell in the
Garden, and enjoy its good things as you wish, but do not
approach this tree, or you will run into harm and
transgression.' Then Satan began to whisper suggestions
to them, bringing openly before their minds all their
shame that was hidden from them before. He said, 'Your
Lord only forbade you this tree lest you should become
angels or such beings as live forever.' And he swore to
them both that he was their sincere adviser. So, by deceit
he brought about their fall. When they tasted of the tree,
their shame became manifest to them, and they began to
sew together the leaves of the Garden over their bodies.
And their Lord called to them, 'Did I not forbid you that
tree, and tell you that Satan was an avowed enemy to
you?' They said, 'Our Lord! We have wronged our own
souls: If you do not forgive us and do not bestow upon us
Your Mercy, we shall certainly be lost.'

"You know, the sad part is that if you ask most
Muslims nowadays, including the women, they will tell
you the same story but based on the biblical version that
places the blame on Eve."

"You tell them, Baba!" My brother-in-law Arif
cheered him on as his wife nudged him to keep quiet.

"Now you want to have your say—you've been quiet
until now," Aisha said, with a playful grin on her face.

Baba continued. "Polygamy is not an Islamic
invention; it existed before Islam in almost every faith,
and still does today. But non-Muslims love to pin it on
us. And who do you think started the whole practice of
female infanticide? The sense of shame that most
families felt when they had a daughter originated from
the teachings of the Church, which pretty much favored
the birth of a male over a female."

Mom chuckled at Baba's last comment, and my sister
and I joined in the laughter.

"Don't give me that look, you know I love all of you equally, and I never felt ashamed having any of you girls."

"We know, we know," Mama said.

"But we all know that Osama is your favorite child," Asmaa added, laughing.

We were all different and unique, but we came to each other's aid in an instant. All it took was a phone call and we were gathered. Baba always said, "You are all exceptional when you are together, as a whole," and we listened.

In the background of it all, I was walking farther away from the world. America, my home, didn't want us anymore. I didn't belong anywhere. I had no options really. Muslims were hunted down by everyone, and randomly selected at airports, and men with alternative life choices like mine weren't welcomed in most countries. But I wasn't ready to make changes; I wasn't about to face the world, and I hid some more.

2/7/2017

Earlier today, we were having our usual Sunday gathering at the family home in Long Island. After dinner, Mama was talking about some Egyptian movie, *Sorry for the Disturbance*. She insisted we watch it, and we did. The movie was about this engineer who lost his father and developed a mental condition because of it. He saw his father; he had conversations with him; he had a functional relationship with his deceased father who continued to appear to him. He lived in two different worlds. The movie pulled on the chords of my being. I excused myself and cried my eyes out in the upstairs bathroom. I don't know if I cried over the loss of Baba, or because I related the film to the conversations I had with Nora whenever she appeared in my dreams or waking moments. In a way, I was envious of how peaceful the man's hallucinations were.

Why didn't Nora appear to me as the calm and beautiful person she had been? Why didn't she talk to me? Why didn't Baba appear to me as a guide? He knew what I went through; he knew I needed his guidance in life.

We created a lot of great memories together. He was my father, my role model, my teacher, and most importantly, my friend. You know, we always thought that the coolest dads and moms were the ones who splurged and got us the latest Nintendo game or toy, but all that is easily forgotten with time. It is the sweet, personal memories that linger with us, though life has its own ironic way of highlighting the least favorite ones as well. Ever since Gedo's passing, I have been dreaming the same dream. He keeps appearing dressed in all white and smiling. It was the same look he had on his face when he completed the Hajj. I can't believe that my dream world chooses this one life event over all others; it is one of those occurrences in life that I placed in the far corner of my mind, as if it never happened.

In 2008, when I was in my early thirties, my parents were determined to go to Hajj and asked me to join them. At first, I refused to go because I didn't think I was ready for such a life-changing trip. I didn't think I was good enough to be in the holiest city, performing a religious pilgrimage. I grew up in a household that emphasized the holiness of the pilgrimage to Makkah, one of the Five Pillars of Islam. I understood that Hajj required a complete transformation—I couldn't sin anymore. It was something, realistically speaking, impossible to do. I didn't think I had it in me to fight the temptations, Nora, and the many other ghosts that didn't care to leave me alone. To me, Hajj was only for the older folks who were getting ready to meet their creator and were fixing the books.

I tried to convince my parents that it wasn't my time to go, and to take one of my older sisters, or any of their husbands, in my place. However, all of my attempts failed miserably, and I was left with no choice. In the weeks prior to the trip, I was so nervous I actually hoped the plans would fall through; I hoped the visa application would be refused by the Saudi consulate or an illness would prevent me from going. I wasn't ready to go, and I don't think I would have ever gone if it wasn't for my parents.

I even refused to give Baba my passport, which he needed to mail to the travel agency a couple of months before the departure date. My excuse was that I might need it to travel for work. Then I pretended I couldn't find it. I must have caused the family so much anxiety.

But my parents had me figured out and found a way around every obstacle I put in their path. I thought of taking an impromptu trip to Israel for a vacation, just to have my passport stamped with the Israeli entry visa, as this would surely mean my visa request would be refused.

I knew how important this once-in-a-lifetime trip was for my parents. My father had been saving his vacation days and rearranging his surgery schedules to make sure he could visit Makkah that year. He wanted to cleanse himself of all sins; he wanted to do all that God required of him while he was still on this earth. He had tried before, but something had always got in the way. This time he was going no matter what, and he was taking me with him.

For weeks, he couldn't stop talking about it and would call me up at odd moments to pass on any new information he had learned from seminars or from friends who had performed Hajj before him. A couple of weeks before our departure date, the package arrived with our passports, tickets, identification cards, informational booklets, DVDs, and the towels. Baba asked me to be there during the weekend to go through everything. We all sat in the living room in a semicircle, serious and focused as though for a major conference, and began to look at the contents of the package. The bag containing two towels puzzled me. "What are these for? I can supply my own towels!"

"Osama, this isn't the time for your silly jokes," replied Baba. "These towels are your ihram cloth, which you are supposed to wear during the Hajj."

"What? Are you kidding me? This is what I will wear for three weeks in Saudi?"

Baba wasn't at all pleased. "Have you forgotten everything I once taught you?" he cried. "Have you forgotten everything you learned at the mosque all these years?" He went on to explain the meaning of the ihram and the symbolism behind it.

"These two pieces of cloth represent your *kafan*, your burial shroud. You are simply ridding yourself of all your worldly and materialistic possessions. You wear your ihram as a symbol of humility and submission to God. It is also a symbol of your unity with the millions of others who are there for the same reason. And don't worry—you won't wear them for weeks, just three or four days."

There was something taunting about Baba in that dream. It had me think over the whole Hajj experience, trying to find some kind of hidden message. I did always wish I had the kind of faith Baba had in religion and God. I understood his faith in God. "It is personal," he said. "God reveals the *ayat* (signs) to us; there is a sign for each one of us. We can't treat religion as a wholesale store. You may see God in a mathematical equation, a scientific experiment, a random act of kindness, an interaction with another human, a line in a poem, or a sudden realization in a moment of clarity." I always envied the solidness of his belief; it showed in his action and it was reflected in his words. Baba was no novice surgeon—he was a master of his craft. He lived and breathed science, yet he was still a believer. It was the strength of his belief that was my anchor. I couldn't fathom that someone like him would fall for fables and antics. And whenever I thought I had cornered him with a good argument, he would find a way to show me otherwise.

"Baba, we don't even know if it is Ishmael or Isaac who was offered as a gift to God."

"*Habibi*, you are going about it the wrong way." He sat back in his seat. "First, you need to accept the idea of God, and go from there to inspect the information you are trying to contest."

"And what does that have to do with what I am saying?" I asked

"Because you are asking the wrong questions."

"How do I surrender to God? And why is it the wrong question?"

"That is why there are religions; they teach us how to surrender. And you are asking the wrong question, because both Isaac and Ishmael were the sons of Ibrahim, and both preached the same religion, the religion of God."

"Baba, stop with the puzzle talk, please."

"What is your definition of a healthy human?"

"Someone who has all the functioning body parts and organs, and those parts are doing what they are meant to do. Plus, working out, eating healthy, and maintaining a healthy lifestyle."

"Good and precise definition. Now, if one of those body organs was to stop working, we are no longer deemed healthy, wouldn't you say?"

"Yes, Baba." I remember wanting to yell out, "But what does that have to do with anything?"

"Religion is the one thing that teaches you to look within and ascend. Think of it as your manual to a better spiritual journey, or a navigation system. Whether it was Isaac, Ishmael, Peter, or whomever, it was always the same navigation system emitting a different voice." He leaned forward. "All these prophets preached Islam from the time of Ibrahim. Think of every one of them as a body part, and if we don't have all the body parts present, we are never healthy."

I mocked his argument. "I guess I will never be a healthy body."

"Baba, you know that Osama is just riling you up and joking around as usual," Mama interrupted.

I nodded in agreement to placate him but was still wondering about how I would wear these two pieces of cloth for days. One wrapped around my waist and the other over my shoulder? What if they come undone? I imagined what would happen if I accidentally displayed my "goods." Would people laugh? Would they stone me? Oh my God, what am I getting myself into?

My thoughts were interrupted by the arrival of Aisha and her husband. Baba invited them to this holy meeting because they were such holy rollers. They had performed Umrah a few times (this being a mini-version of the Hajj).

After all the *salams*, kisses, hugs, and small talk, we went back to our task. At Baba's request, I played the DVD. My mind drifted back to thinking about how I could get out of the trip without hurting my parents.

My thoughts were interrupted by my brother-in-law's heavy Egyptian accent as he explained to Baba the three different types of Hajj and the pros and cons of each one. Baba hung on to his every word and asked many questions. He was like a little kid arriving at a candy factory, and my brother-in-law was Willy Wonka.

He started telling him the story behind the Kaaba, which Baba already knew, but he was still mesmerized as though he was hearing it for the first time.

Although I was bored out of my mind, something about this whole thing made me happy. Maybe it was seeing Baba's joy suffusing his face, but all my doubts about the trip vanished. I had to do it for him. He had done so much for me and for us all. It was payback time.

"But how on earth will this towel stay on?" I blurted out. There was a moment of awkward silence followed by a burst of laughter.

My brother-in-law grabbed the towels and stood in the middle of the living room to demonstrate the different ways to do it.

"Look, you wrap it around your waist as you do when you walk out of the shower, and then you roll the top part twice." He did it with such ease, then challenged me to try to pull it down to test its durability.

"Look, Osama, it won't easily fall off. If you don't feel secure, you can always buy a belt when you get there for extra safety, but you won't really need it. I never used one myself. Here. You try."

I stood next to him, trying to follow what he did, but I just couldn't stop laughing. The room was now filled with laughter at my attempts to tie a simple towel around my waist. After many failed attempts I managed it, and I wore it for the rest of the evening to test it for myself.

Throughout my life until then, I had had this image of Makkah etched in my mind. It was an image of the old times— the times of the Prophet and his companions. I guess it was from all the old Arabic movies my parents had us watch growing up. The whole idea of Hajj was intimidating. I grew up listening to Baba and the imam at the mosque speaking of it so reverentially.

"Going to Hajj is like getting invited by the Most High to his house," Baba would say, or something along the lines of: "To go to Hajj, you have to be ready for a life-changing trip to the house of God. If you enter it with pure intentions, you exit it as innocent and free of sin as the day you were born."

These childhood memories, together with the pressure-cooker atmosphere created by the importance of this to my parents, gave me severe anxiety attacks during the lead-up until I actually arrived in Saudi Arabia. We arrived at the city of Medina, which is the place the prophet found refuge after many years of fighting as well as the humiliation and torture that he and his new Muslim followers suffered at the hands of the Makkahns.

2/8/2017

After arriving at Medina, an overwhelming sense of comfort erased my anxieties. It was both intoxicating and soothing. As the crowds answered the calls to the five daily prayers, you could see this shared feeling on all their faces. And yes, I was there with them, taking part in it all. My parents would wake me up for *Fajr* prayer at daybreak after going to sleep late the night before.

Every night after the night prayer, we had to attend a lecture about the rituals of Hajj. During one of those lectures, I ran into an old friend of mine from Sunday school at the mosque. He was there for work. It had been so long since we last met that we didn't really recognize each other at first, but he did recognize Baba.

"*Salam Alikoum*, Dr. Issa."

"*Alikoum Al Salam*."

"You don't remember me, do you? I am Mohanad Soliman. I knew Osama at the New York Islamic Center Sunday classes. You sometimes drove us home after class."

"*SubhanAllah*, I do remember! It has been at least twenty years or so, hasn't it?"

"Yes, Doctor. Are you here alone or with the family?"

"I am here with Osama and his mother. How about you, who did you come with?"

"I am actually here for work. I am one of the program managers for this Hajj trip."

"*Masha'allah*, which program are you managing?"

"Yours."

"You should stop by our table after dinner and say hello."

"I will definitely do that once the lecture is over."

Mohanad, who was few years my junior, took over the podium and began speaking to the crowd, welcoming everyone. He began his talk with an apology for delaying his appearance until the second day.

He went over everything in detail, from lecture schedules, buses, luggage handling, traveling to other cities, sightseeing, and visits to the burial site of the prophet. During his talk, Baba leaned over to tell me that he knew him, which wasn't a surprise to me; Baba knew many people from all walks of life. But I was surprised when he added that I knew him, too. I tried to remember who he was, but somehow my memory had skipped that part of my childhood.

After the talk was over, Mohanad stood answering everyone's questions and concerns. He then came over to say hello to us as he had earlier promised Baba. As he walked over to our table, Baba said, "You guys went to Sunday school together." And he shared how the two of them ran into each other earlier. But I really couldn't remember him. I went along with the formalities of saying hello and asking the usual questions people tend to ask each other in such situations. Thank God there was a sea of people wanting to ask him questions; he eventually had to excuse himself. Baba noticed the look of bewilderment on my face and decided to jog my memory.

"Do you remember him, Osama?"

"Vaguely, the name doesn't ring any bells."

"Remember the kid who was always asking weird questions during class, annoying all of you, but was always quiet on the ride home?"

"Not really."

"One day he asked the teacher about *jinn* and ghosts, and if they really existed?"

"Oh, yes! How can I ever forget that day? It scared all of us when the teacher said, yes, they exist. I couldn't sleep in my room alone for days. I was scared to even go to the bathroom by myself."

I recalled him as the awkward kid we avoided as much as possible, but it seemed he had turned out to be not so awkward and was now someone people turned to for answers. I am now the awkward one in the room and I pray to be unnoticed. It is funny how life works out sometimes. Once I was the cool kid and the center of attention because of all my cool toys and fancy clothes; now he is the cool one, but because of his knowledge and leadership ability.

A day or two went by before our second encounter, which was a little easier on my side. We talked of events from our childhood and of mutual friends.

"Do you still talk to anyone who went to Sunday school?" I asked.

"Yeah. I'm still in touch with a couple of people I see once in a while in the mosque."

"Wow! You still go to the same mosque after all these years?"

"I go there whenever I am in the neighborhood on a Friday. It's good to see some familiar faces." He paused for a second and asked, "How about you, do you still talk to anyone?"

"Not really. I hardly mix with any Arabs outside the family and family friends. That's more than enough of my quota of Arabs."

He answered with a laugh and a nod. He understood what I meant. It is a small community and everyone seems to know everyone else. That makes it tough when they all know about, and gossip about, every aspect of your life. We moved on to a more personal conversation about where we both were in life, as people do after a long gap in communication. I learned that he had married but that it didn't last long.

"Marriage is a failed social institution," he claimed, "but it's a necessary evil, isn't it?"

I couldn't have agreed more, and the grin on my face spoke louder than words.

"Why did you get divorced? Did you love each other?" I asked.

"Did you ever watch that Arabic movie about mothers-in-law and how crazy they can get?"

"No, I don't think so."

"Well, let's just say that my mother-in-law was the devil, the woman that every man fears, and somehow it was my bad luck to land on her doorstep."

"She couldn't have been that bad!"

"Osama, bad doesn't even begin to describe her. That woman turned our lives into a living hell. You know, at first, I thought, 'I can marry her daughter and do all I can to keep her out of our lives afterwards.' But she was like a poisonous canker that you couldn't get rid of."

"How about her daughter, your ex-wife?"

"Sadly, she was too weak when it came to her mother. She was Mama's little girl. If she told her to jump off a bridge, she would have done it. As much as I loved and cared for her, there is only so much a man can take." He paused.

"You know, I've heard about how in-laws can turn your life upside down, but I never knew it was real. I'd never met anyone who'd been through it."

"Now you have. At first, I thought she was being over-protective of her only daughter before marriage, especially since she raised her as a single mother. I figured that after we were married things would change, but I was so wrong. She became worse."

"What do you mean?"

"Well, before we got married, she was so demanding, controlling, and too damn materialistic. I figured I'd put up with it to win the girl of my dreams, the one I loved. And I thought she was being a typical Arab mother, trying to secure her daughter's future," Mohanad explained. "You know, Osama—Arab marriages are like financial transactions. The man must keep on paying the bill for the rest of his life."

"I don't know about that. I have three sisters; two of them are married, and Baba didn't make a big deal of any of the financial arrangements. He actually helped them out."

"Your Baba is a good man—and he is one of the few."

"I hope you don't mind my curiosity. I'm trying to get my head around it and understand the whole reason for the divorce."

"Let's just say that, before we got married, her mother demanded that we have a place in the States and another in Egypt. Then when it came to the *mahr*, the dowry, and the ring, I had to get her the most expensive ring there is, and a hefty amount of money for the *mahr*."

"Are you serious? How much did you pay for the dowry?"

"Yes, I am. She asked for fifty thousand dollars. The things we do for love. I should have known better. Her mother saw dollar signs written all over my forehead."

"But what happened once you guys got married?" I asked.

"She wanted to be the sole decision-maker in my household. She meddled in everything: little things, big things, you name it. My ex-wife's every sentence started with, 'Mama said this or that ....'"

He went on for a while about his struggles with his ex-wife and her mother and the lessons he had learned from it all. He explained to me how he thought love is very important, but it is other things that make a relationship or a marriage work. To him, it was about team work, communication, and trust. At the end of the conversation, he admitted one thing.

"It wasn't all because of the mother-in-law and her ways. It was also my wife and *her* ways. Before marriage, I felt like we were one team, but afterwards, we were on different pages. She wasn't the person I'd fallen in love with, and it was chaos."

While we were in Medina, Mohanad and I spent more time together. We had many talks, on a daily basis. Our talks made it a lot easier for me to tolerate the trip, and it didn't feel like a burden anymore. In a way, I felt like we both needed a friend to make our stay in Saudi a more enjoyable one. Although we didn't see eye to eye on some things, we had some things in common, and we had a lot to vent about.

During one of the religious lectures at the hotel, I noticed that many people approached him while he sat quietly in the far corner attempting to eat his dinner. He was constantly bombarded with questions, so often he could not eat until the lecture began. On one occasion, the questions kept coming, but he patiently answered every one, and didn't get to finish his meal.

I watched him leave the lecture area when he felt that all questions were answered. I waited a few minutes before I joined him to smoke a cigarette outside the hotel.

Although smoking was allowed indoors everywhere in Medina, Mohanad always smoked outside and away from the people. He had his smoking hide-out—his cigarette break was really the only time he had for himself. He showed me his smoking spot on our second day in Medina and even made me promise not to tell anyone about it for the sake of his peace of mind. I totally understood the need.

"Every year I come to this same spot to hide away from the people and my colleagues, to enjoy a moment of silence and a cigarette or two. I really don't understand some of these people. They have all the information in the booklets and on the bulletin board, and I update them every morning, yet they still ask the same questions over and over again."

"Please don't tell me that Baba is one of these people," I said jokingly.

"Actually, I love your dad. He comes up to me every morning to say his *salam* and to ask if I need any help, which is rare."

"Yup, that is Baba. I thought he was asking you about the rituals."

"Not at all. It's people like your father who make this trip worth every minute."

"How so?" I asked.

"There is no nice way to say this, but not everyone in our group is here for the sake of Allah or their own salvation. Some are here just to get the *Hajji* title; some do it because others made them tag along and they would much rather be elsewhere; others do it because of a sense of obligation as they are doing well physically and financially; others come to Hajj because they are getting old and feel that if they do it, they will part this world in peace. Very few actually come to answer God's calling and understand the true purpose of Hajj. Those who do are the ones I love serving—you can tell right away by their sense of gratitude and appreciation for the little things you do. They don't worry about trivialities such as food or which rooms they get."

"But why shouldn't they concern themselves with those so-called trivial things since they paid for them?" The devil's advocate in me had to enquire.

"That's fine and it is their right, but when these things become the main concern of the trip, then there is something amiss with that person."

He continued telling me about the differences and his experiences on previous trips, including some of the complaints pilgrims had made. His points were valid; some people treated Hajj as a vacation rather than as an act of worship. I saw it for myself when I was with him, people approaching him to ask about places to shop for jewelry and gifts. It saddened him. They were more focused on shopping than on what they had come to do.

2/9/2017

From leaving the hotel in Medina it took about six hours to get to the one in Makkah, including transfers, the flight to Jeddah, and a long wait in the hotel lobby to get our room key.

I was impatient to get out of my ihram—we had to put it on before leaving the hotel in Medina— and take a shower. Under Islamic rules, the ihram must be worn at the *Miqats*, the departure points. In addition, men must shave their pubic hair and armpits, which makes the whole ihram experience more difficult. I didn't mind any of this, but I was suffering from an unbearably painful rash between my inner thighs, which were now very hot and bright red, and made me very irritable.

"I wish I'd listened to Baba when he advised me to apply Vaseline before wearing the ihram," I moaned. A cold shower was very much needed to ease the discomfort. I then rested for a bit while my parents freshened up to get ready for the welcome Umrah. I was exhausted, but the sooner I performed the welcome Umrah, the sooner I could wear my regular clothes and, most importantly, underwear.

Despite applying the Vaseline, I was still in pain. My anxiety kicked in, too, as we got closer to the Grand Mosque. I was totally unaware of my surroundings as I tried to remember everything I was supposed to do and say upon entering. I really didn't want to mess this up. I didn't want to anger God or displease him, especially while I was a guest in his house.

Certainly, I hadn't wanted to be there in the first place, and not because I hated God or didn't want to visit his house. I didn't want to be there because I didn't think I was a good enough Muslim. I didn't think I deserved such an honor. But I was already there, and I wanted to show God that I was a good person, a good human being, capable of doing the right thing.

Upon entering the Grand Mosque and seeing the square-shaped structure covered in all black cloth and gold writing, I saw the Kaaba for the first time, and my anxiety gradually faded. I honestly didn't feel much at that moment. I didn't feel any of the overwhelming emotions others had told me of before and since. I saw a sea of people circling the Kaaba; I saw people pushing and shoving to make their way through. I did what I was supposed to do. I circled the Kaaba seven times, I prayed next to Maqam Ibrahim, and I walked between Al Safa and Al Marwa mountains right after, as Hager once did while looking for water and food for herself and her baby Ismail. I drank water from the ZamZam well, which was considered to be heavenly water as it quenched the thirst of Hager and her son. I did all of that, and I felt nothing.

Once we came out from El Haram, I was beyond exhausted and the rash was getting worse. I was walking oddly, and I was the only one who did. However, I couldn't go back to the hotel without finding a barber to cut my hair, which is mandatory if I wished to take off my ihram. By then, we had lost more than half of the group in the crowds, but thankfully, I didn't lose my parents or Mohanad. We seemed to be the first ones out, as there was no one at the meeting point we'd agreed to use if we had split up.

I was running out of patience and was desperate to get out of my ihram and sprinkle my thighs with ice cold water. All I could think of was how I missed wearing normal underwear, and how something so simple could be taken for granted. That first shower provided the form or relief that leaves you thinking about the simplicity of life and its pleasures. I didn't want to get out of the tub.

Once the first day in Makkah was over, I felt relieved. It wasn't as bad as I expected it to be and it wasn't as

grand as people made it out to be. The exhaustion of
traveling and performing Umrah sent most of us into a
deep sleep. My parents and I missed the Fajr prayer for
the first time since we arrived in Saudi. We missed
breakfast with the group, too. We had three days left in
Makkah before heading over to the camp cities of Mena
and Arafat. I decided to use my free time to explore the
city on my own. After each prayer, I chose a different
exit to wander into the streets of Makkah.

Makkah was nothing like Medina. There was no
serenity, no calm. It was an overcrowded city, very busy,
harsh, and loud. There were hotels everywhere, crowded
with people who were there for the same reason as us.
There was a state of constant movement in Makkah,
similar to New York City at rush hour, but Makkah was
far more crowded. One of the first things I noticed about
the area surrounding El Haram was how luxurious the
chain hotels were. Once I turned my back on El Haram
and looked at the strip of hotels near the King Abdul
Aziz gate, I felt like I was in Vegas or on Fifth Avenue.
Western brand names and chains pervaded the area. I
was happy to see them in one way, but deep down I felt
disappointment. I would never claim to be a religious
person, but the sight of those crowds rushing to the malls
to shop, or to schmooze at a nearby Starbucks, reminded
me of Christmas. Christmas was no longer a religious
festival; it was a commercialized holiday, and that was
exactly what was happening to Hajj. It was no longer a
journey of endurance and hardship, it was no longer a
journey to the house of God. It is now a business—it's
all about making as much money as possible from those
who have traveled thousands of miles to receive the
blessings of the almighty.

It was also hard to ignore the number of beggars
around El Haram. Most were of African descent, but they
were locals. I asked Mohanad about them one day, and

he told me that they lived on the outskirts of Makkah in a very poor area. My curiosity led me one day to take a cab and head to that part of town. The area was rife with poverty and drugs. It reminded me very much of the Brazilian *favelas* you see in the news—only language separated them. This was yet another shocking experience during this journey. I no longer viewed Saudi as a rich oil country. On the contrary, poverty was part of the country's social makeup and there were large numbers of poor, totally ignored by the government, like the homeless population of the United States

Our stay in Makkah finally came to an end and we had to take the next step. Buses transported the whole group to the camp city of Mena. Mena is a city on the outskirts of Makkah and it is full of tents to accommodate pilgrims during the Hajj season. We arrived there on the eighth day of the Zulhijja, which is the twelfth month on the Arabic lunar calendar. The stay in Mena lasts until either the 12th or 13th of the month.

At first, I didn't mind the long stay in Mena, and I didn't understand why everyone used to say it was the hardest part of the Hajj. However, upon arriving there in my ihram cloth, I came to understand the reason. The tents are erected in the middle of the desert and each tent is made to accommodate twenty to thirty people and their belongings. And although the tents were air conditioned, they felt unsanitary in many ways. It didn't help that we had to be in our ihram for two full days, until we finished all of the rituals needed to get out of the ihram state.

The first day was spent doing nothing but schmoozing with others. We spent the entire day in Mena and were advised to go to bed early and get a restful night of sleep because we had two long days ahead of us. And they certainly were both long and exhausting. On the morning of the ninth day, we were transported to the city of Arafat, which is home to the mountain of *Elrahma*

(Mercy). That day is the most important day of Hajj. As the Prophet once said: Hajj is Arafat. We spent the day reading the Quran and praying, until sunset. We were then transported to Muzdalifa, where we spent the entire night in the open desert. That night was one of the most difficult, as we were in our ihrams in the cold desert. Nor did it help that fumes from the buses were the only thing we breathed in during that night. We also collected the seventy pebbles we would use over the next three days in Mena.

We boarded our buses after the dawn prayer to head back to Mena. The drive took a couple of hours because of the traffic and the crowds of people heading in the same direction.

The five days in Mena are really the only days when all three to four million pilgrims are present in the same city. Moreover, the morning of the tenth day is the only time you can see these millions of people, all in white, heading in the same direction at the same time. I sat by the window of the bus in total awe, watching this truly beautiful sight for the entire journey back to the camp. Having reached it, we quickly crossed the Jamarat Bridge to perform the act of throwing of the pebbles onto the walls. The three walls represent the different locations where the devil—who tried to persuade Prophet Abraham to slay his son Ishmael—appeared to him. Each time the devil appeared, Abraham threw pebbles at him. At the end of the story, God orders Abraham to slaughter a sheep instead of his son. The two acts of throwing the pebbles and the slaughter of the sheep are reenacted in Hajj, during the stay in Mena. There are four things in all, which must be done to end the state of Ihram. The other two are shaving off the hair from the head, or cutting it, and circling the Kaaba in Makkah.

As bizarre as it may seem for men and women to throw pebbles at a wall in the middle of the desert, it is nothing in comparison to those who take it too literally, thinking that it is the devil in front of them, thus throwing huge rocks and anything they can get their hands on. The safety of others is certainly at risk—I had to dodge a few of those flying rocks and bags. However, the worst was yet to come. There was a sudden commotion and a heaving of the crowd, but at the time we had no idea what was actually happening. We later learned that there had been a stampede, and a couple of hundred people died just yards away from us.

This incident was, naturally, the main topic of conversation once we got back to the camp, with many different opinions being voiced. Some envied those who died there, because they would supposedly go straight to heaven. Others disagreed, saying that those who died had caused the death of others by their pushing and shoving.

"How could they go to heaven if they were the ones who pushed their Muslim brothers and sisters who were in front of them right to their death?" A Pakistani doctor in our tent threw that question out of left field, leading to total silence for a moment, before another broke it.

"But how can we blame those people? According to what I heard, the royal guards had blocked the road to the Jamarat Bridge for a prince or a princess to perform his or her ritual of throwing the pebbles, and instead of opening the road in an organized fashion, they let people in through a small gap, which led to this bloody accident. I blame it on the host government being disorganized and showing favoritism at a time when we should all be treated equally."

The Pakistani doctor asked another question. "I will agree with you that the government shouldn't play favorites and they could be far more organized, but if we should all be equal, then why are we here in this huge air-conditioned tent and not sleeping alongside those who have only a small tent on the streets? And if we won't blame these people for their own death and the deaths of others, then explain to me why people push one another in the Grand Mosque, right in front of the Kaaba? Why aren't they careful as they perform one of the holiest of religious rites? They are there pushing old men and women by the Kaaba as if they are about to win a grand prize. I am sorry to say it, but I blame both the people *and* the host country for their ignorance of the basic teachings of Islam about how to treat others, and I fear for their well-being as well as our own."

Most agreed with the doctor, and they began to share similar strange experiences they'd had during the trip. I was in agreement too, but I had a lot more to say about the experience. I witnessed the ignorance, arrogance, corruption, and dehumanization of others in the name of God. I didn't feel the presence of God in much of the process. I think the only time I felt anything was the day we did the farewell *Tawaf.* I almost forgot about that day and the incident with the old lady. It is a very important moment, and I will have to tell you about that another time. My hand is killing me.

2/10/2017

I didn't realize that I wrote so much about Hajj; I guess you can't say that I didn't teach you how to perform Hajj or Umrah. I'm kidding—you don't have to do it if you don't want to. I guess in a way my subconscious was trying to lead me back to that moment with the old lady.

On my last day in Makkah, I was more than ready to go back home. If only the Prophet was still around to see what those people had done to his birth city. I had gone to Makkah expecting to feel an overwhelming sense of spirituality. I was expecting to see and feel God in everything and everyone, but now I was ready to leave and I felt nothing but disappointment and disillusion. These feelings increased further when Baba asked me to join him as he attempted to touch the black stone after the Maghreb prayer. The pushing and shoving a person must endure to reach the stone cannot be described in the words of any language. I couldn't believe I was among other believers in the house of God; I couldn't believe any of it. It was similar to a crowd rushing the doors of a mall on Black Friday, when everyone in town and the adjacent towns shows up at the same exact moment to purchase one specific item.

"Do these people know anything about the teachings of Islam? Do they know nothing of manners?" I wondered to myself. I was very tempted to scream and yell at everyone for their shameful behavior. "No wonder all the gods have ascended to heaven over the centuries."

Finished with my Hajj rites and free of sin, I left the mosque, angrily heading back to the hotel. I noticed an old woman in her late sixties fall to the ground because of all the pushing. I ran to her aid without thinking. It seemed nobody else noticed this frail old woman fall. I helped her up and she held my arm as we made our way toward the exit. Once we were outside, she stopped and muttered something in my ear in an unknown language, which I assumed was a thank you. But she didn't stop there—she raised her arms in prayer, looking directly at me. I didn't understand a word of what she said, but the look on her face spoke volumes. At that moment I was overwhelmed by an immense emotion. I felt God's presence. Her prayers came from the heart; they were sincere. I looked up, and I felt and saw the gates of heaven open. I saw a full moon, the biggest I have ever seen, fill the skies of Makkah. If I hadn't experienced it myself, I would have said it was a scene out of a cheesy movie.

Believe it or not, that was one of the most defining encounters in my adult life. It was my sign that God was present everywhere. God didn't live in houses, God didn't favor any race over the other, God didn't speak one language, God didn't punish anyone or annihilate anyone. God exists in beauty. God exists in the moments we decide to stop and acknowledge others and work together. God exists in our random good acts that don't fall under our human calculations. I didn't look to gain a thing for offering the old lady a hand. I did it because it was the only logical and right thing to do, and for doing it, God allowed me to see the world through the divine's eyes, the way it was always intended to be. It was then that I was reminded of a younger version of myself, a version that believed in God and the magic of the world. I remembered Nora and her smile. It was the first time I remembered her and saw her smiling. My moments with Nora were always divine—her smile lit up the world. She laughed with her soul. I gave her what no one else gave her, normalcy. Our moments together were nothing short of the way God intended for us to be. We were made to love and love was made for us, which in turn made us exceptional together. Those were my best years.

I think it was then, because of that old lady, that my belief in God was cemented. I didn't care to know if it was a big bang, an atom, or an Adam. I just knew that God exists, and everything else was up for questioning. It was then, on the flight back home, that I made my second attempt to repent while high up in the sky.

It had to be something about having Mama around and being closer to the heavens. This time around, I had a lot of things that I wanted to make amends for. I thought of walking over to my parents' seats and having a talk with them. It was the first time in my adult life when I had a nagging need to divulge all to others. I kept looking at my parents, and I pictured their faces upon hearing, "Mama, Baba, I have had a problem with drugs and alcohol for the last ten years, and I have been sleeping with transsexuals, transgender, intersex, cross dressers, and anyone whose eyes sought my acceptance in random New York clubs."

That was when Nora popped up out of nowhere. She had been gone for the whole duration of our stay in Saudi except for that fleeting moment after helping the old lady. It was the calmest I had seen her, ever. She was observing; she talked me out of it; she walked me off the ledge.

It was Nora, it was always Nora who was meant to lead me into the light from the darkness. I tried to follow her lead once I was back in New York. My repentance was solid; I was willing to do whatever it took to get better. It was a groundswell that overwhelmed me, and the country was going through it too. Obama was president, with his promises of hope and change. I pushed myself to find out more about everything. And at that point of my life, I was already nothing but a broken man who believed he was gay. I come from a generation that defined any form of sex other than vaginal as gay. Since I had never had sex with a woman, I actually believed I was still a virgin, just like Bill believed he'd had no sexual relations with Monica.

It was then that I made a conscious decision not to open the matter with the family. I realized that I must respect their traditions and life style, and not necessarily impose my own views. The family and I didn't have to be in conflict, because both of us were right. So I chose to focus on the commonalities.

We think and believe that we are exceptional. We have created so many stories around how exceptional humans are. We were created by the hands of the divine, and the universe is our gift. We believe that it was all created to serve us. But the reality of the matter is, we are not exceptional. There is nothing about us that's exceptional except for our ability to kill beauty and destroy. We are not as fast as a gazelle or a cheetah; we can't fly like birds; we don't have fur to protect us in the cold; we don't have the natural strength to lift heavy objects like a gorilla or an elephant. We created fables to explain our presence, even scientific ones that we can't prove. It is all unproven theories, on all sides. We are not exceptional; we are only exceptional when we work together and in sync with nature like every other creature.

2/11/2017

It's concerning how much of a person's life falls through the cracks. There is so much that I can't remember from my own life. Things and people that I cared for are nothing but ghosts. I wonder if it was my decision to forget them, or I am forgetting them due to old age. Is it something we all do to deal with our traumas?

Is forgetfulness a blessing?

I have been having these thoughts all day long, and I haven't been able to shake them. The rush of my recent awakening is violent at times; it shakes my core every time I realize that I haven't been that present for most of my life. I want to ask someone to help me find the missing pieces, but there is no one to ask. No one was there to witness me unravel.

It was the sobering impact of the Hajj experiences and the reintroduction to the idea of faith that allowed me the clarity to ask myself some serious questions that I had never asked before, and they were all about her. I wanted to know more about Nora's condition. I read all I could about it, and one thing that stood out was the fact that Nora's parents were related. Those findings always led me to a very blasphemous conclusion. God created Adam, and then Eve was created out of Adam, or at least that is what I understood from all the religious teachings as a kid. In that case, Adam and Eve are much closer to one another than two cousins, which was the case in Nora's situation. Someone like Nora was physically born the way she was. It has nothing to do with preferences. So the whole thing makes it seem like God wanted us to be that way. We can't blame it on brothers and sisters or cousins who reproduce together. It started from the very beginning; it started from day one. Unless Adam was not supposed to sleep with Eve—but he committed the ultimate sin, and someone like Nora paid the price for his horniness.

Are we flawed by grand design? Was it an unintentional fuck-up? Or is there a different version of the truth?

I started my search from the very beginning of time, and something was off. If cousins produced Nora, Adam and Eve produced much more over the centuries. It was time to inspect the world and its creations. In Islam, we are taught the devil was damned because he refused to bow down to Adam, the first human, with the rest of the angels as per God's orders.

What if the devil was the good guy all along? What if the devil was the only one to pass the test? After all, he was the only one to refuse bowing down to anyone else but his creator.

God, the creator, could have taken away his free will, but God gave him a choice. The devil chose to bow down to no one else.

What if the devil is the angel that tests our faith? What if the devil is the angel to lead us to the Almighty? But the devil was never an angel; he is *jinn*, made of fire.

Nora was there through it all. She had a devilish smile on her face every time I did my homework and researched things online and everywhere else. She knew, then, what took me forever to understand. She knew that I had begun shedding all my labels and all the ancient idols instilled in me by my family, teachers, friends, and society.

Speaking of the Internet, my generation was the guinea pig of the Internet industry. We survived AOL, ICQ, MSN, HI5, Yahoo, Myspace, all the way to Facebook, Twitter, and Instagram. We were the pioneers; we were the first generation to use them all. Now, we are watching the abuses of the younger generations, and the older ones too—you know, the aunt that keeps posting embarrassing family photos, publicly. And we are shaking our heads. I truly believe that most people around my age suffered some form of PTSD because of all the information available on the Internet.

We started life with things like landline telephones, cassette tapes, analog televisions, VHS tapes, and writing actual letters. And within the span of our very short lives, all of that changed on us.

Previous generations passed information down in small increments, but in our case, it was an overload to the system. We were suddenly connected to everyone in the world; we were discovering all the lies that kept us apart. We learned that not every Russian is a spy, and not every German is a Nazi. We were suddenly exposed to the instant reality of the other. It does explain the sudden rise in travelers and the desire to travel. I guess I can't deny how beneficial it has been for someone like me. Without the Internet, I wouldn't have been able to do a lot of the things I have done. I wouldn't have lasted long with all the hiding and secrets kept from everyone else. It was also the main tool I used to dig for my own definitions, among other things.

It was a lot to sort through. The World Wide Web provided way too much information, and there was no easy way to handle it, so read it all. I read entire websites, forums, books, and whatever else I was able to get my hands on. I sat there mulling over every possible piece of information trying to find the one for me, the one to save me. We were almost done with the first decade in the twenty-first century, and I was reading similar arguments to the ones made by the guys in Egypt in our teen years. But there was nothing about the world that was attractive enough, for me, to do more than exist.

For the longest time, I lived a life that wasn't really deserving of the label "human." It was a mere existence. I was just a kid when Nora and I fell in love; I was too ignorant to understand her or my own circumstances. I opted for limited engagement from the moment I learned of her suicide. I too died that day—a big part of me. My inner child ran away from the shock. I doubt the child knew that he was capable of killing another human, or being the cause of someone's hurt. I still have a hard time convincing myself otherwise, and the thought scares the life out of me. What if I hurt more people I love? I lived a prisoner to the what-if and my own fears. I almost called off so many things—you were one of them, because I didn't want to bring you into this cruel world where I could end up hurting you myself.

I lived in the shadows of people's expectations. I was the son who was there for his parents when they needed, but otherwise, I didn't care to engage. I was the brother, the youngest, who lived up to the stereotypes: I was unreliable and spoiled in my own ways. I was the student who did the work but never participated in class. I was the token Arab or Muslim friend. I was the casual encounter that never emerged from the darkness. I questioned things but never dared to state my opinion; it was all conflicting information.

I questioned my own cultural and religious identities, because others constantly wanted to have these debates. They had to make a comment or two; I had to defend a billion and a half Muslims whenever one made it on the news. "Why are your people killing again? Is he your cousin?" I didn't care to engage, but it did hurt.

There was an ongoing war on terror, but in reality, I was the one living in terror. I was terrified to take my ID out of my wallet, and I still feel my soul shake at times, till this day.

2/12/2017

At that point of my life, I had denounced many of my labels. I didn't see myself as an Arab or an Egyptian, because of my sexual orientation, and I didn't see myself as an American because of a name given to me. The only labels that I had accepted for myself were Muslim and gay. Muslim was by default because of the name and the constant defense of Islam whenever someone felt the need to learn their Islam 101 upon meeting me, and the gay part was also by default since I never really confronted my experience with Nora head-on. It was also her ghostly image that kept me from uttering a word. It was her constant presence in my dreams and everyday life that led me into the arms and beds of many like her. She impeded my ability to love, because she was always there. I couldn't love another. I used their bodies to channel her into this world. I didn't care for anything else but her. And pleasing her ghost. I didn't question my own sexuality like I questioned everything else; I accepted it all.

I did everything to bury her in the back of my mind. She was the monster that I didn't care to awaken. It was time for me to figure out my other labels. And since my relationship with God was intact, thanks to Hajj, I started with my gayness.

First, we will go into a bit of the history of gayness. The term "gay" was formerly used to describe a happy person, and over the years it made a transition into what it is today. I wonder what Shakespeare would say if he were to return today; he has the word throughout his writings. However, I like to think of more historical roots to the word and its current meaning. I think it happened this way.

Once upon a time, many moons ago, a rabbi and a priest laid together in a faraway cave, away from all prying eyes. The two men found joy in something, which couldn't be explained to the rest. They found joy in one another, and the following dialogue was discovered in an ancient scroll.

"This sodomy lifestyle is making me very gay. You bring gayness into my heart," the priest said as he let out a releasing sigh.

"Me too, I feel the same exact way," the rabbi replied, looking up to the heavens. "I am very gay when I am with you."

"We must tell everyone that we have discovered the path to gayness." The priest spoke enthusiastically. "We must share this with the world."

"Do you think they can handle such a peak experience? Do you think they are ready?" the rabbi asked. "Think about it, they still believe the earth is flat. I think we need to keep them as far away as possible from all of this. Humans do nothing but tarnish and destroy all they touch."

"What do you suggest we do then?" the priest asked.

"I think we keep it a secret from all."

"But how?"

After a few moments of silence and pondering, the rabbi jumped to his feet. "I got it!" he cried. "Remember the story of Lot?"

"Come on, man, I am a man of God. Of course I know the story of Lot."

"Let's interpret it in a way that the destruction and the horrible ending is all blamed on sodomy. You speak to your people, I speak to my people, and before you know it, it will be the only acceptable truth."

"That sounds so devious. I love it. This way, no one can ever find the source of gayness but the enlightened, and it shall remain an exclusive practice," the priest exclaimed.

"We should also change its name and the name of its followers. We shall call them gay."

Words change their meaning. More accurately, we changed their meaning over the years. And just like many other labels, I learned from my research that I didn't have to choose anything. My findings always backed up my decision to keep my sexual life a private matter. My research was showing a different reality. The history of homosexuality and human sexuality were far more intricate than they appeared. Arabic poetry is full of homo-erotica, and many Arab poets were open about their sexuality through their writings. Sexuality wasn't a matter of label in many cultures; it was an intimate matter. No one was violating my right to sleep with whomever I wished, and I didn't care for anyone else to know.

There was no need to announce it and do what everyone else was doing. It wasn't a matter of pride; it was a matter of diplomacy and maintaining the peace. I also knew from others who have sought help that it wasn't a good idea to choose one label over the others. I remember the one time I spoke to someone at a gay center. "You should just come out to your family. You aren't living in the nineteenth century, and we are in America, Mohamed." The counselor said, "We fought for too long to continue living in the darkness." Coming out and adding a new label to myself was the solution many saw feasible. Coming-out parties were encouraged—they were the New York thing to do. They were everywhere, ever since Ellen came out on her show in 1997. But I never found myself in any kind of community, especially not the LGBTQ community. Everyone was pushing for a very specific agenda, and there was no room for someone like me, a traumatized and confused Muslim man. The advice offered never applied to me; I didn't want to come out of any closet, not for the price of losing the family. It seemed like no one understood me, and I was fine with that.

You know, what really bothers me is that there are a lot of people out there who need help and support, but cultural limitations and guilt have forced them to stay in darkness a lot longer than any human should have to stay.

It is like this gay Muslim who entered a club in Florida and started shooting everyone. As soon as they found he was Muslim, the media labeled it an act of terror. I remember watching the news with your mom, and feeling an overwhelming sense of sadness followed by frustration. The sadness was there for many reasons. I was sad for all the innocent souls that died that night. I was also sad because of how quickly the perpetrator was labeled a terrorist—in a matter of seconds, as soon as his origins were discovered.

"Something tells me that man was gay," your mother remarked. "They're saying he was a frequent patron at the club."

"Maybe he was inspecting it and familiarizing himself with the location," I contested. "Didn't they say he was married?"

"Osama, we are married."

"So, what's your theory, Sherlock Holmes?"

"It's simple. This man was gay and never came to terms with it. It killed him to pretend to be something he is not. He did his research, hoping to consolidate both his beliefs and orientation, but he found nothing but hate and death for homosexuality in holy books. This was an act of redemption for him."

"Are you turning him into a hero now?"

"No, I am not." She followed with a piercing side look and said, "I am simply saying he killed because he thought himself worthless. He knew if he was found out, he would be killed for being gay. He believed that gays should be killed, and he killed others and himself for it."

"I can see that," I replied. "I wonder how the Muslim world will react to this crime that it is labeled terrorism."

Thankfully, we didn't have to wonder for long. A hashtag, #PrayForOrlando, was initiated on social media. Everyone and their mother were using it. It fascinated us how many of our Muslim friends who opposed homosexuality used the hashtag in support of the LGBTQ community. Supporters crawled out of their closets. Hateful people from all sides, races, and religions made appearances too. They saw the shooting as the act of a God who didn't permit homosexuality. The sides fought with one another for the duration of the media coverage hype. The fact that he was a Muslim made everyone overlook the hardships a gay person goes through. The internal and external struggles in a homophobic environment can drive a person mad. I felt that we failed ourselves, the victims and humanity at large, because we didn't care enough to dig deeper.

It all reminded me of how the position of women in Middle Eastern societies stood in comparison to their counterparts in other parts of the world, and how the region regressed and attempted to define women's roles in a new light. Unfortunately, their foundation wasn't built on any real Islamic principles. In the same manner, the region regressed when it came to LGBTQ rights and attitudes toward members of the LGBTQ community. A quick glimpse through the sexual history of the region and I learned that sexual orientation categories never existed, and in comparison to its counterparts in other regions, tolerance was present. Europeans used to travel to the Middle East to live freely without the constraints of the conservative and intolerant European societies. Again, we didn't hear of the persecution and violation of rights until external forces attempted to impose their own social definitions onto those societies.

And just as I discovered that there was once an attitude of tolerance and openness in both Arab and Muslim history, I also learned of today's reality for gay Middle Eastern kids. They are watching as other kids in different parts of the world come out to their parents and are met with acceptance. Those kids in the Middle East want the same thing as their counterparts in more "liberal" societies, and some of them dare to ask. They don't have many happy endings. They are beaten; they are disowned—a disgrace to the family.

It is exactly the way it is handled by Arabic media. Some do it blatantly, and others are more covert, but it's almost the rule that the homosexual character ends up either dead, imprisoned, repentant, or going through conversion therapy. It is an ending that most Arab viewers and readers find justified for such blasphemous characters.

It is similar to the attitude you would have gotten from an American family during the 1980s' AIDS crisis. "They deserve that ending"—that was the collective approach. They did that in this big hit movie that was released in 2006, *The Yacoubian Building*. The one gay character, Hatim, was portrayed as a rich man who was once molested by the house servant growing up, which was the reason for his gayness. He spends his time hunting for straight poor men and seducing them with money and alcohol. As with most gay characters in Arab literature and films, Hatim was killed, and justice was not demanded.

Nevertheless, the one thing I found most troubling and yet entertaining was that as the Middle East regressed once again to fight external pressures, the region found ways to revive old practices, which were applied by the west against homosexuality and so on.

In no way is this is an attempt to blame Christianity or Judaism for the retardation of a whole region, because they are woven in the fabric of the region and its history. All three religions originated in the region. Don't let anyone fool you—Jesus was a Middle Eastern man and so was Moses, but no one is trying to cover that up. However, religious institutions—all religious institutions—have played a role in diverting the collective attitudes toward many issues without any basis in religious texts, just like that story of the priest and the rabbi. It could have been an imam and a monk.

African, Asian, Arab, and European history are full of women leadership, yet they are all criticized for their cultures and traditions just because the US hasn't joined the bandwagon. We haven't had a woman president here, ever. We should skip everyone and go for a gay president—now that is progressive. I'd vote for him or her.

Your life is the alternate reality of another person, and some other person's life is your alternate reality. Very few are content with the lives they pretend to live.

2/13/2017

Your facial features keep changing every day. One day you are looking like me, the next you look like Laila, and another, you look like Baba. I wonder how much of you will remain intact by the time you get to my age. I wonder if any of my own infancy or childhood traits lingered. I should ask Mama about this. Watching you eat, play, and interact with everything around you with such curiosity is inspiring me to follow your lead. The looks of excitement and your eyes widening when you hear the sound of the candy shaking in its box—it is as if you had that sound pre-installed in your audio memory. We tried tricking you with another kind, but you are surely addicted to your very healthy, organic, and non-GMO-gluten-free candy.

You know, my favorite part of the day is when I get home, change, get comfy, and play with you and your toys. I love being around you; your presence fends off all my demons. You are my refuge—you are sanity. I leave the insanity of the world right outside the door of our home, and I pack it back on the next morning on the way to work.

It is the one thing Baba always did right: He always made time for us. I miss him so much, it hurts so much, still. He was there for all of our big and small moments. He was there to watch cartoons with us on the couch (he loved Tom, and I loved Jerry). I remember sitting next to him watching cartoons on a TV without a remote control. In those days we had to walk up to the TV to change the channel. I always wondered, did the remote control come first or was it a consequence of the explosion of channels that overcrowded the airways?

I would think it is the latter. Necessity is the mother of all inventions. I can probably google this and find the correct answer and the history of the remote control.

Hell, I may find a documentary about it all. But I like thinking of the infinite possibilities allowing some brain cells to escape the mundane boundaries. You will grow up utilizing different tools to inspire creativity; you already have your own tablet. And I'm overjoyed watching Barney with you on your little tablet—there is nothing else in the world I'd rather do. I want to be here for you through it all; I want you to feel safe and secure enough to come back home anytime you wish. I want to give you everything Baba gave to us, especially a moral foundation.

I find myself wondering about when and how we should teach you about religion. It is said that learning at a young age is like inscribing on stones; it's permanent. I don't know if it is something I want to do to you. I don't want to teach you a thing about religions until you are old enough to comprehend the messages. Prophet Muhammed was forty when received the revelation; he wasn't preaching God in his infancy like Jesus did. Most of the prophets and messengers didn't get into religion until much later in their lives. Yet I know that you will face the same kind of struggles I had to deal with, in your unique way. You will be asked, "What are you?" "What do you believe in?" "What god do you believe in?" or "Why don't you believe in God?"

At the moment, as I write this journal entry to you, I like to think of myself as a Muslim, and I choose Muslim because it is more of an adjective rather than anything else. It literally means a person who surrenders, and I decided to surrender the minute you were placed in my arms. I saw a chance to do better, a chance to start all over again. Hence, I was adamant about naming you Adam. Your arrival marked my greatest jihad in life; it was the kick in the ass that I needed to get back to answering all my unanswered questions, to dot the *i*'s and cross the *t*'s.

So remember how I told you that Tayta Hannan is the human I aspire to be? Well, in case you missed it, she had converted. YAY, ISLAM WINS!! I am just kidding, I swear. Mama's conversion made her approachable; she was someone I knew how to seek out and speak to. She wasn't as firm and absolute as Baba.

She was always the most sensible one in our household. I viewed her as the glue holding our family together. She had an incredible ability to put the needs of others ahead of her own. She also had the wisdom to keep us all in order, including Baba. She was the one we would run to at the worst times; she was the loving presence that made everything go away. Her kindness and sensible ways made her the one person I wanted to talk to. I wanted to know what made her abandon the religion of her forefathers. I couldn't even imagine myself doing the same thing—my name wouldn't let me. Mama was braver than any of us. Therefore, the next logical step was to ask your Tayta everything. She gave me much more than I had hoped for.

"When I married your father, I had no one else but him, and I was willing to convert for him not to lose his family. He refused," Mama told me. "He wanted me as I was and told me to convert if I feel like it is the right thing for me, and not for anyone else."

"How come I didn't know about that?"

"There are some things that we like to keep to ourselves—they are our little oasis of that love we shared all those years. Some of the things you do for one another don't need to be mentioned, you simply appreciate them knowing they happened."

"But there was no harm in that to anyone. If anything, you would have a support system around you," I protested.

"Issa was adamant about starting a life together that wasn't based on lies or half-truths. He was always a man of principles, and I loved that about him." Mama was not as sharing as Baba. She didn't volunteer much information unless she was asked. "*Habibi*, I think I was Muslim way before we made a production of it."

"What made you do it?" I asked.

"Look, it comes down to the interpretation of the texts," Mama said. "Our problem in the Muslim world was that we followed the same interpretations set forth by our Christian and Jewish predecessors. We didn't care to pay attention to the differences in the stories told, and most people who studied theology opted to copy and paste those generic stories in their commentaries."

"And what's wrong with that? They are the people of the book, and we believe in the same prophets and messengers."

"We do believe in the same people, but there is a reason God sent new books, and it was the same reason new books were sent in the past." She pulled her chair closer to the dining table. "Abraham was sent to ratify whatever was left of the original teachings of his forefathers, and so was everyone after him. Someone was sent whenever we strayed from the original message. The Jews denounce Ishmael and his birth, claiming that he is an illegitimate child; they are pretty much accusing him, the patriarch of all religions, of committing adultery. And once you do that, our collective conscience accepted the act of adultery. The Christians told us that Jesus was crucified and ascended to heaven to elevate him to a God, when in reality, he didn't die on the cross, but it looked like it as the Quran tells us."

"But how is that changing the story?"

"Well, we adapted the Church's belief when the Quran clearly states that he didn't die on the cross. To be crucified is to actually die on the cross. Placing someone on the cross doesn't mean that person was crucified. It *looked* like he died on the cross and they took him down after a few hours, but crucifixion takes more than a day. In every account, Jesus was taken down and placed in a cave where his wounds were attended to. He was a man with a message from God to the tribes of Israel, and the first two of those tribes refused to heed to his words, and he went on to search for the other ten tribes."

"So how come no Muslim imam talks of this version of the story? Is there proof of that theory?"

"There is a tomb in India with Jesus's name on it." She paused. "Let me ask you this—where are the most Muslims in the world today?"

"East Asia, I think."

"You are right!" Her eyes widened. "And East Asia is where most Sons of Israel took refuge in the past to escape persecution, and most of them still hold on to their original Jewish tribal names till this day. I do believe that Jesus made it out to East Asia and delivered the message to other people of the book who accepted him as the messenger of God, which explains their smooth conversion to Islam. I believe that East Asia is where we can find purer versions of religions and spirituality."

"But why would no Muslim imam talk of this? This makes more sense than God placing the likeness of Jesus on someone else on the cross; it makes a lot of sense."

"Those religious institutions probably have enough dirt on one another to destroy each other's creed and fan base. They probably have back deals to let each other survive and to continue to profit." She gave a lopsided smile. "Even the story of Solomon, we interpret it as him stealing the Queen's throne to show off his ability instead of him commissioning someone to replicate it, and that would have been far more impressive and logical."

"Seriously though, how come no one talks of these versions of the stories?" I asked.

"Because they would have to expose many of the lies they have been feeding us for centuries." She paused. "Remember years ago when you had a conversation with Baba about the different religions, and he spoke of the three main religions as being one, and said that religions are like a tree?"

"Yes, that was years ago. What about it?"

"So I didn't want to say anything then; I wanted you and your father to have that moment for yourselves. But I wanted to tell you then that religion extends way beyond Judaism, Christianity, and Islam. We are programmed to look at all others as pagan religions, but if we choose to look beyond the ignorant stereotypes and our biases, we would find more pieces to our own puzzles."

"I have believed that for a long time, but I never really heard anyone say it like this before, with such conviction."

"Look, if it is a tree, you can remove a branch or leaves, and it doesn't take away from the tree itself. But in religions, they are all part of our collective psyche. A cat is not a cat until it's a kitten first, and it's not a kitten until a mother has given her birth; for this to happen, the mother first has to become pregnant. A tree isn't a tree out of nowhere; it was a seed, which was sowed and watered for a specific period of time. The tree will not bear fruit unless it receives all it needs from nature or from a farmer. You can't take a newborn baby and enroll it in college; the baby has to go through stages of development. The baby has to learn to talk, walk, and develop the capacity to learn; the child has to go to preschool, elementary school, junior high, high school, and then college. And you can't give a newlywed couple a grown man or woman as a son or a daughter, because they have to learn to develop and adjust to a new member of their family. Imagine if you were born in the same form you are in right now. Now look down at your feet and imagine if they didn't grow as your body grew. Look at your own baby pictures and compare them to what you see in the mirror.

"Even an idea or a thought isn't fully developed without giving it time to grow and mature; when it's fully developed, you act on it."

"I get the idea."

"Everything, and I do mean everything, has to go through different stages of development to get to where it needs to be. Now apply this development theory to religion. Perhaps all of the religions are meant to lead to one end—meaning one religion. Perhaps they are just different stages of development toward one religion, but some of us happen to be left behind or, as Freud would say, are still stuck in the oral or anal stages of psychological growth."

"But how are we left behind? Who gets to decide which stage is the final one? I think this is why people get tired of religion and everything that is associated with it. There is always some kind of hierarchy to it."

"For centuries, the nobles, kings, queens, presidents, prime ministers, and many others used their power to manipulate religion to enslave the common man and woman to ensure that their hunger for power was satisfied. They knew that we had a soft spot when it came to religion; they milked it to the very last drop and they still do." She sipped on her coffee.

"That would raise the question, is religion a manmade concept?"

"Parts of it are man-made, and that takes us back to my original point. The stories go back to as far as the Sumerians, way before Moses or any of the biblical prophets, and we kept transmitting these stories as we moved around the world. The stories changed as we encountered more of our kind who didn't speak the same language. Imagine how people interacted back then, in the context of their time."

"Now we are roleplaying." I laughed. "What languages do we speak?"

"No languages. Let's say you called your god Amun, and I called mine Brahman."

"I have heard of Amun before, but who is Brahman? It sounds very close to Al Rahman."

"Doesn't it? You should look it up; Brahman is the highest manifestation of God in Hinduism."

"I will. I am intrigued." I moved closer to her and grabbed her hand playfully. "What's next?"

"How would you explain your God to me if this was your first visit outside your tribe?"

"Pump my chest and yell out *Amun*." And I did act it out. "What would you do, Mama?"

"I would draw a circle in the sand, or point to the sky and everything around us. I would also keep saying the name."

"I doubt that would accomplish much."

"My point exactly. We choose to believe that God selected a favorite group, and that group is always our own. As part of our belief system, we—all—tend to believe that our version of God is the purest of all, and we forget to apply the same measurements of criticism to our own belief system. We are not honest with ourselves, and I wish we lived our truth."

I said, "It's like we are all stuck in a loop; it is the same story repeating itself. We rewrite the chapters, reorganize them, reshuffle them, remove some characters, and add new ones. The new ones will be a better version of the older ones, you know, to fit into the loop."

"You are so right. That makes so much sense, and it fits perfectly with a thought I have been having." She surveyed her mind. "Serpents, snakes, cobras, and anything that looked like one, were once considered holy. They were the protectors. Look at ancient crowns and antiquities; they were highly revered. Somewhere along the line, a serpent became the source of temptation and sin, and the reason humanity was damned out of heaven. We changed our attitudes toward snakes; we suddenly feared them. We were no longer fascinated by their ability to shed and renew their skin. They became of the devil. We did the same thing to women over the centuries—we were queens and goddesses. There was a time when we women, too, embraced our transformations and coming of age as we did that of snakes. We celebrated every boy and girl; we celebrated the milestones in life, and we rejoiced at those crossroads. Now, we denounce the older versions of ourselves and run away, as we do from snakes. We run away, leaving behind a hollowed-out shell; we abandon the past as if it was never a part of us."

"Then we are doomed."

"No, we are not. I still have hope." She sighed.

"What? How? And why?" I asked.

"It seems like everyone is spiritual nowadays. Everyone, especially those in big metropolitan cities, is trying to establish a sense of some kind of spirituality. Religious institutions failed humanity— they couldn't connect the dots. People of different faiths would find out if they interacted and compared notes; they are putting in serious efforts to connect."

"Really? You are truly an eternal optimist, Mama." I patted her hand.

"Spiritualism is today's version of religion. Yoga studios are becoming the structures where followers congregate." Her mouth curved into a smile. "I see yoga mats as the prayer rugs Muslims carry around when they are going for prayer. The yoga poses are very similar to the mechanism of the Muslim prayer."

"Mama, but that is our prayer. How does that relate to others? That doesn't make sense. You are truly becoming one with Islam."

"Son of a—" she stopped herself. "I will have you know that almost every other religion had similar mechanisms for prayer, but that was changed over the years."

"No way," I exclaimed.

"Yes way. Remember, I was one with another religion." She laughed. "*Shoft ya homar*, do you see, donkey? That is the problem with everyone today; no one looks deeper into things, not even journalists."

"But I don't think people are going to yoga for religious reasons. And how does that relate to what we were saying?"

"You insist to be a *homar*, donkey. Yoga is really praying; it is part of Hinduism. It is not just another gym exercise. It is about focus and looking inward to connect with the source."

"And what is that source?"

"That source is God. People are getting rid of labels that tarnished religions for centuries. They are going for the very core of every religion, the connection with the creator, the source, the divine, Jesus, Allah, Yahweh, or Horus." She paused. "Aren't people today doing intermittent fasting because science says it's good for them?"

"How did you know about that, Mama?

"It is all over the Internet in every language. Every Muslim on Facebook has shared it to prove a point about fasting Ramadan. It is like they are trying to prove to others, and themselves, that fasting isn't an outdated practice."

"It makes sense. People ask a million and one questions about Ramadan. And the looks of shock on their faces say it all. If we were aliens doing cartwheels in the middle of Times Square, we wouldn't get the same looks."

"It breaks my heart when I hear you kids talk about the looks and stares you get. I will tell you one more thing that I didn't share before. You know why I finally decided to convert in 2004?"

"Baba asked you to."

"No." She gave me a playful evil look and paused. "I wanted you kids to know that I relate to your pain. I hated hearing stories from the girls, and their kids. Most importantly, it was the look on your face. And I knew you were suffering the most after everything you had gone through."

Her hands reached for one of mine and hugged it. It was good knowing that Mama understood some of my pain, but I wasn't ready to share with her just yet. I was at the very beginning of my climb.

Parents are full of surprises!

All religions are one: God became energy, or the universe to some. Prayers became meditations and yoga poses. Yoga instructors are the spiritual advisors. Fasting is part of a healthy lifestyle rather than a religious obligation.

2/15/2017

Tayta Hannan is the cutest, most adorable, and most sentimental being I know. We were the first ones to arrive at her house. We found her listening to a mix tape, which Baba had made for her for Valentine's Day of 1992. I couldn't believe that she held on to that cassette tape all those years, and I couldn't believe that she had a functioning cassette player.

"Mama, what are you listening to? The music sounds familiar."

"It should. I am listening to the tape Issa sent me when we were in Egypt."

"I can't believe you held on to that tape. I remember you used to play it every time you got off the phone with Baba and whenever you missed him."

"Were you spying on me?" Mama blushed.

"It was that obvious, and you played it a lot. Asmaa and I used to joke about it every time we heard one of the songs. We had the whole thing memorized. Those were the best times to ask you for anything—we knew you were in a good mood. Plus, Baba used to have me record those tapes for you."

"He was always thoughtful like that."

As we talked, Nagat's song ended, and it was followed by Mama's favorite song, *Ana lak Alatool* (I Am Yours Forever), echoing in the background. It was also my favorite Abd El Halim Hafez song. It was the song I dedicated to Nora on our first anniversary.

I am forever yours, be mine
Take one of my eyes, and look at me
Take both eyes, and ask about me

My parents were unlike most other married couples. Their love for each other never wavered for a second. They were the envy of many who saw them together. I often heard Mama's friends asking her for advice on how she and Baba didn't fall into the trap of boredom after so many years of marriage and how they managed to keep their marriage full of life and joy.

"You have to grow together. You have to push yourselves to do things together, otherwise love can't catch up. If one of you is constantly learning, and the other has no interest in it, you will have a growing gap between you." I still remember that answer; it made a lot of sense.

For some reason, Arabs tend to fall into the trap of routine and responsibility a year or two after marriage. The love slowly dies away, and so many other things die along with it. A permanent cloud of dreariness replaces the love and joy that once existed. The husband takes on his role as the breadwinner who does nothing but work, while the wife plays her role as the housewife or the baby-making machine. It is rare that you find an Arab couple who don't fall into that same trap. I think it is a generational thing, though. I hope my sisters are following in our parents' footsteps.

My parents never did live by any code but their very own; they always managed to make the time to keep each other happy. They always danced together at weddings and every other chance they had. They were truly in love, they were truly happy. Mama always told her friends, "Marriage is like a company and, for the company to remain successful, you have to keep on working hard. Otherwise, it will go bankrupt and you are out of business. You have to always find new ways and new places to build up this company and keep it at the top. You can't give in to routine, and you can't get too comfortable because you think it will last forever."

I don't even remember how old I was when I heard her say those words, but they were forever imprinted in my mind. I vowed that I would be the same as them, which in many ways explains my desire to fall in love with

Nora in the first place. I was imitating their love story. I still try to do that in my relationship with your mom, and our little family. I guess this is a good place to tell you about how our little family came to be. I promise to tell you all about it, but for now, I must go to sleep to be up early. Have a goodnight, *Habib Baba.*

3/5/2017

It has been very busy around here lately, and work has been crazy as we near the tax season. As I told you, we are always in need of people who can handle our money. Most of us are so inept with money matters. I want you to remember one thing: Don't fall for the credit card and debt scams; they lure you by seducing your senses and making you want more. They are always targeting the young.

Anyway, I did tell you that I would share how our family started. So, most marriages or families start something like this: In the beginning, there was a one who needed to be a two. The one searched for its one, and they found each other. The two needed to be three and four; they united. Their union is nothing short of a big bang. And out of their collision, millions of atoms are created, and an Adam or two.

However, you, Prince Adam, came into the world after much deliberation and debate. Many elements had to align for our prince to arrive and save this man from the darkness. I think the pressure that was put on me to get married and start a family were among the things that Baba apologized for in his letter.

If it wasn't for him and his wish, we wouldn't be here. And it started on January 27th, 2011, and it was all because of Egypt. You know, I had not gone back there since we returned. I didn't go back until your gedo decided to play hero and go that year. I never wanted to return to the place where Nora died; I never wanted to face that part of my past. It was better that way. I lost Nora in Egypt, and I almost lost Baba too.

"Osama, which do you love most? Is it Egypt or America?" Baba asked, instead of answering my question. I wanted to know his reasons for wanting to go to Egypt so badly when things weren't safe or stable there. I knew in my heart that he would have wanted me to say Egypt, but I couldn't lie to him.

"Honestly, Baba, I have a love-hate relationship with the two and I can't pick one over the other."

"Forget that question. What would you do if someone attacked your mother or if you saw her in pain?"

"I would rush to her and kick his ass or do whatever it takes to ease her suffering."

"There you go; you answered your own question then."

"What do you mean? I don't understand."

"After my own mother, *Masr,* Egypt is a second mother to me—she is my home; she is the womb that brought me into this world. And I won't stand around watching her in pain and agony from afar."

"But Baba, it is not safe there now. I think—we all think—you should wait. Plus, this is your home now; New York has been your home for over forty years."

"Osama, my mind is made up about this and no one will stop me from being there for my mother when she needs each and every one of us. New York is home, the home I chose for all of us, but nothing will be greater than my bond with my mother, and her blood runs through our veins."

Though he was a medical doctor, Baba always managed to use the weirdest and most creative metaphors—I guess that was where I got the beautiful woman metaphor from—to win any argument. Winning an argument with him was one of the most impossible things to do. There was no stopping him from going to Egypt—he wanted to witness what he called "history in the making." He was no longer able to sit still watching TV or reading online to learn what was going on in Tahrir Square and throughout the country. He wanted to be a part of it, he wanted to experience it, and he wanted to help. He saw the thousands and millions of Egyptians fill the streets of every Egyptian city demanding the fall of the military regime led by Mubarak. He repeated their chants to himself. The euphoric unity in Tahrir Square seduced his senses.

Despite all of our efforts and concerns, he booked his ticket, and flew out on the first of February, 2011.

For the following eight days, I was glued to the TV and computer, watching CNN, BBC, Al Jazeera, and every news outlet I could think of. Everything seemed so uncertain, confusing, misleading, and foggy. I was in a constant state of panic and fear. I feared for Baba and the lives of those who were once close and dear to me; I feared for the lives of those in Tahrir Square and for the future and stability of Egypt.

I wanted the so-called "Revolution" to end as soon as possible; I wanted things to go back to normal. I wanted it all to stop, just like a little kid watching his parents have a nasty and violent fight. I wanted Baba back.

I was furious. I was furious with the regime. I was furious with the protesters and the misleading and brainwashing media coverage. The reports on television and elsewhere conflicted with what I heard from those on the streets of Egypt as I frantically began calling old friends to ask them about the situation.

One day as I sat in the living room watching the events unfold with Mama, my sisters, their husbands, and a group of family friends, Hasan, my brother-in-law asked:

"If you were in Egypt right now, would you go to Tahrir Square?"

"It is time to get rid of this tyrant regime. I would definitely be there right next to your father doing whatever I can," Mama said.

"I would be the first one in there and I wouldn't leave until the people got what they want," Asmaa said.

As we all took turns, most said that they would be with everyone in Tahrir Square, or that in some way, they supported the protestors. However, when it was my turn, I answered without any hesitation and my answer was a simple "No." It was an answer that many of them found shocking because of my constant talks about the need to change our ways and the need to democratize and liberate the Middle East from its old ways.

"I am not saying *no* because I agree with the practices of the Mubarak regime; I am not saying no because I don't think Egyptians have the right to protest or revolt against the oppressions and injustices suffered for decades."

"Then why are you saying no?" Hasan asked.

"Because what I see on TV isn't a revolution—I see it more as a penis-measuring contest with Tunisia. It's an act of venting and releasing a massive amount of anger and disappointment that was embedded in the inner layers of many Egyptians for so long. I said no because there is no leadership, there are no obvious demands, there is no sense of direction."

"What are you talking about? People want to get rid of the regime and they want justice, democracy, and equality," Aisha said.

"That is not true. They don't know what they want. This whole thing started because of the abuses of the police. That is the reason it took place on January 25th— it is the anniversary of the police forces. It was never meant to be a cry against the regime itself as a whole. Plus, even if they were to take down the regime, who will replace Mubarak?"

"We will worry about that then, but for now, his reign must come to an end," Hasan said.

"Come on, you don't really believe that. You must have a plan for what is to come after, and if there is none, the whole thing will tumble. Anarchy and chaos will follow.

"The very sad fact that we must face and admit is that the majority of Egyptians are not ready for such a change. They never received the form of education that would prepare them to participate in the so-called democratic process," I added.

As I uttered those words, silence befell the room. Everyone looked at me and looked at one another. It was clear that no one knew what was coming next.

And before anyone could add a word, I received a phone call that added fear and worry to the silence.

"Hello," I said. The person on the other end began talking in such a sad tone, I was puzzled for a moment, not knowing who it was.

"Osama, this is your uncle Ibrahim. Your dad's older brother."

"Yes, sure, I have heard so much about you from Baba. How are you? And how is everyone in Egypt?"

"We are good, *alhamdulillah*. Osama, I know this is the first time we are talking, and I wish our first time to talk was under different circumstances, but I have some bad news."

"Is everyone okay? I am not sure if you know, but Baba is in Egypt. I can give you his number; you would probably reach him faster than I would."

"It is about your dad. He is here in the hospital in bad condition. Luckily, he was accompanied by someone from our village who reached out to us right away. I got your phone number out of his phone."

The doctor who traveled halfway across the globe to serve and assist his fellow countrymen and women, the doctor who wished to treat the fallen youthful heroes of Tahrir Square, became the patient himself. He fell victim to a stray bullet to the chest. The bullet had his name inscribed on it. Baba flew over the Atlantic to meet that one bullet. It traveled through the gun's chamber, through the crowds scanning each face, until it found its way into a medical tent and into Baba's right lung. Instead of helping the patient stand once again, Baba collapsed on top of him, and that was the end of his adventure in the Square.

Fortunately for Baba, he was surrounded by doctors, unlike many others who expired before reaching a doctor. In so many ways, he was so fortunate to fall when he did. The timing was perfect. He was there to meet his bullet; the bullet was there to greet him; but most importantly, there were doctors there who knew how to stop the bleeding and stabilize his condition. Outside of the tent, an ambulance stood waiting. In Egypt and under normal circumstances, ambulances are not always there when needed because of traffic or just bad services. In Baba's case, there was an ambulance right there.

My body froze, my heart was skipping beats, and my hands were shaking. In less than twenty-four hours I was at Kennedy airport and boarded a flight to Cairo. I got on a journalist-filled plane, and quietly drowned in my own thoughts, remembering every little thing from the second I received that call to how it was decided that I alone would go to Egypt to be next to Baba. I sat there scared and frightened of what could happen. I leaned my head back, closed my eyes, and watched the movie of my life.

The movie was all about Baba and me; it was about all the things that he has done for me. It was a movie of sweet, everlasting memories of growing up and learning from him. I saw the many nights he stayed up by my side when I was sick; I saw him teaching me biology, chemistry, math, and science. I saw him buying me my first bike when I was five.

I couldn't help it, I began to cry. The movie was soon over, and I began to think of how the hours had flown by since the moment I received that call. I wasn't ready to lose him; we are never ready to lose anyone. I was ready to make a deal with God, the Devil, or anyone who would have handed me a deal not to lose Baba.

I arrived in Egypt the morning of February ninth. I took a cab to the hospital, which was conveniently located in Nasr City, not too far from the airport. That part of Cairo didn't look that affected by what was going on in Tahrir Square, or so it seemed during the day hours.

"Where are you flying from, sir?" the cab driver asked, looking in his mirror.

"New York," I reluctantly answered.

"Why would you even come at this time? If I could, I wouldn't be here at all."

"I have some family matters to take care of. But why wouldn't you be here?"

"I have not had any business for weeks now and I can't even work once it is dark out. Bandits come out and will steal your car. They will make you sign a sales contract at gunpoint."

"I didn't hear anything about that on the news."

"That is the problem. The whole world is watching Tahrir, but no one is focusing on the real problems this whole revolution bullshit is causing for regular folks like us," the driver said.

"But don't you want change?"

"What change, sir? They will bring someone who is even worse than Mubarak and his gang. I'd rather stick to the crook I know. Look at it this way— he has been milking the country and its resources for thirty years now, he doesn't need anything at this point. If you bring in someone new, we will start from scratch."

"Still, though, change is needed, don't you think?"

"*Ya basha*, we don't change. We just need them to treat us like human beings," the driver said, taking a long pull of his cigarette.

"I am with you on that one. That should be the demand in Tahrir."

We arrived at the hospital within ten minutes.

"Be careful when you are out at night, thugs come out at night," the cab driver said.

Once in the hospital, I walked to the room where my father lay. The closer I got to the door, the slower my feet moved. I felt weak, helpless, paralyzed, and fatherless. I opened the door and there he was, lying peacefully in a white hospital gown. It was just the two of us in the room. He looked like an angel. I sat by his side, clueless of what to do. I put my hands on his head, kissed his forehead, and looked at his frail face. I was shortly joined by my uncles. That was a very cold meeting. I am glad Baba always made sure we stuck together as a family.

I always knew that I had a big family in Egypt on my father's side, but I had never met any of them before. I did see old pictures of my uncles in Baba's photo albums. He always made sure that we were aware of their existence in the hope that one day things would work themselves out and he would reunite with his siblings. Somehow Baba knew that such a day would come, and so it did. It came as his life was hanging on to this world by a thread; it came as he was ready to leave, and the only thing keeping him alive were those beeping machines he was hooked up to.

As we sat around Baba's hospital bed, I made polite conversation with the family, and my uncles were impressed with how much I knew about them. And they were far more impressed by the fact that I was able to identify each one of them without ever meeting them before.

"Issa did a great job raising a man," Uncle Ibrahim said.

"Baba always told us stories of growing up in the countryside with all of you. We had this photo album of the whole family. I grew up, we all grew up, knowing everything about all of you."

"We wish we could say the same thing, but the minute your dad married your mother, we lost touch with him. Your grandfather issued a decree that no one could talk to him in any form possible, and we all gave in," Uncle Saleh said.

"I know, but I will never understand it. Baba always spoke of the importance of family and family ties. The way he spoke of all of you was one of respect and admiration, as if you were a part of his life still."

"Blood can never turn into water," Uncle Saleh commented. "You never met your grandfather. The man was tough and whatever he said had to be. No one was ever able to break free of any of his rules, but your father did when he chose to marry your mother. The saddest part of this whole story is, your father was his favorite. He was the spoiled one and always got his way. It broke your grandfather's heart when it happened, but I am sure he did it for a reason. He had to set an example for all of us," Uncle Ibrahim said.

"And the fact that your dad left the country and you guys were out of reach all this time made it even harder to reach him, even if we wanted to," Uncle Saleh added.

"It is all in the past now. I really can't wait till I see his face when he wakes up to see all of you around him, *Inshallah*, God willing. I am sure that will make him so happy," I said, as tears soaked my face, thinking of the possibility that he may not get up and see his brothers once again, as he always wished.

I spent hours by his bedside, praying that he would wake healthy and sound. It was hard to sit there watching him lie helpless. That was the first time he had ended up in a hospital, and he managed to hang on to life a few years longer. I was there for both times, and I hope you never have to see me in such state. I wish we had had more time to do it right; I wish I could have gotten one last chance to say goodbye properly and thank him for it all. I hate that I still feel the pain of his loss this much— it is as if it happened yesterday.

Time is a slow fucking healer sometimes.
How much time do I need to give time to heal me?

3/11/2017

I never realized how much Baba meant to me, or the kind of support his existence provided. Actually, that is a lie—I always knew it and that was why I kept that distance between us. I knew that we often couldn't see eye to eye, but I also knew that I could count on him for almost anything.

Fuck, we missed out on so much time together.

I am relieved that Baba never approached me about Nora; I am glad it is you I am having this talk with. I imagine anyone else to be a quick judge—we don't listen to full stories anymore—who would minimize it all to a simple traumatic experience. No one knew Nora like I did; no one could fathom the love we shared— they would only fathom my hate and confusion.

Where were Siri and Google in the 1990s?

I think by the time the Internet was a necessity in every household, I was long gone into the darkness of my own mind. I didn't question much of who I was or any of my labels unless I had to. I accepted my lifestyle and choices to be a matter of fact; there was no time for questioning who I slept with or how we got there. They were there to play one specific role: Nora. They were there to recreate a failed love story. They were there for normalcy. We used each other.

If Baba had confronted me, I would have been forced to make choices and limit myself to one box or one label. I was lost, but in being lost, I was found by Adam. I am loving walking back into the light, following Adam's baby steps. It is not traumatic. It is easing me into accepting things, which therapists failed in showing me.

As great as Baba was and as much as he taught us, he never taught us how to handle those political and religious conversations outside of the house. He followed the herd on that one ("Don't discuss politics or religions") and didn't teach us how to fight off the suspicious stares, or the prepackaged hate. But there was one time he did open his heart to the world. He participated in a *New York Times* article that raved about the surgeon who played tapes of the Quran in the surgery room because of one particular Quranic verse: "Unquestionably, by the remembrance of Allah, hearts are assured."

Yes, Adam! Your gedo asked the patients for their permission to listen to Quran. He explained to them that he was just a tool in the equation, and matters of life and death are left to God. I don't think many patients declined his request, and enough people talked about it that they had to write about it. He was so proud of that article. It told of his journey from Upper Egypt all the way to becoming the head surgeon at New York Presbyterian in 2000. They listed his academic achievements, which are formidable, and listed some of his prominent patients who come from all over the world. He never discriminated against anyone, but he had preferences. He favored those who were similar to him. Maybe the similarities gave him a sense of comfort and belonging.

Unlike him, I surrounded myself with all that was unfamiliar; I looked for differences. I waited patiently like a fisherman for others to reveal their oddness. It comforted me. My twenties and thirties were all about stripping away layers and removing the masks I was somehow forced to wear. I got to learn some great lessons about our diversity.

Baba had planted a seed of tolerance when he demanded we respect all, and that was a lesson that was cemented with Nora's death. My reaction can kill someone; my disrespect can push someone to a dark place. I learned that lesson so damn well that I accepted everyone else. I always focused on the good qualities in all people. I recognized the spirited and soulful roots in the African culture where it all started. I saw the zest of life in the Latin culture and its dances. I respected the stubbornness of Arabs. I appreciated the calmness in the spirituality of the East Asian sphere. I fell in love with Eastern European classical history with a modern twist, and the pragmatism of the Western half. As for America, it was where all of those realities met, and they met daily on the streets of New York and in its subway cars. I don't think it was something that Baba allowed himself to enjoy fully. I doubt he ever gave up on the idea of returning home. He held onto his roots, tightly.

I guess this is when I confess: I ended up turning on Baba's phone. I missed him so much, and I couldn't stop thinking of the possibility of another message somehow waiting for me. In a way, I was hoping that he had planned for me to find his phone all along and left tons of messages behind on there—for me.

Maybe I should do something like that with this journal, as I mentioned earlier. What about a treasure map?

I was really nervous pressing the power button. I turned on the phone quickly (it had a password, and it was the date he first met Mama, 2211) allowing it to load the messages, and I took the sim card out of the phone to make sure that no one knew it was on. I didn't want anyone to see that the phone was turned on through any of the applications—I didn't want to freak anyone out. Imagine the look on Mama's face if Facebook Messenger informed her that Baba was online!

So the first thing that I can tell you is that your gedo used an Arabic operating system, and that didn't make it easy to navigate. It was a good reminder that I need to work on my Arabic skills—they are not as good as they used to be. There was a time when we spoke nothing but Arabic at the dinner table; it was a strict house rule that we followed until your cousin, Jamila, was old enough to speak. Your mom and I rarely communicate in Arabic—we are more comfortable conversing in English, and so is the rest of the family. I want you to learn Arabic though, and as many languages as you can learn.

I went through some of Baba's text messages, and I know that I am going to burn in hell for this, but I had to do it; it is a piece of him. There is so much of us in our phones, and I found something interesting. Mama knew about the letter that Baba left behind.

Baba: I gave the letter to the lawyer.

Mama: How are you feeling?

Baba: I am not sure. I am relieved, yet worried.

Mama: Do you want to talk about it?

Baba: You know that I talk to no one else but you. I am worried he won't understand why I couldn't do it now. I am worried he won't forgive the things I have done. I was my father.

Mama: Issa, you are not your father. And you have done a great job with all the kids, they all love you. You are our rock. And Osama loves you more than anything in the world. Adam will help him understand.

Baba: I want to talk to him face to face. I should tell him these things myself.

Mama: We agreed that your heart may not handle the confrontation. Osama was never responsive to those. You know how he gets.

That last message had me second guessing everything. What on earth have I done for Mama to fear for Baba's life around me? And now I am really curious—how much does Mama know? Was that how Baba found out? And how did Mama find out? As much as I love the fact that their bond is unbreakable, it can be really annoying. We were never able to break their defenses. It always felt like they controlled everything from behind the scenes. I think that was how they lured me into marriage and made me stick to my deal with Baba. I can see the two of them scheming behind my back, and Baba telling Mama to remind me somehow of the promise I made him.

Although my parents were already grandparents, as my older sisters had given them grandchildren—seven of them—they were set on the idea of having one to carry on the family name. It was more Baba than Mama; it was his Arab tribal mentality, which I always considered to be one of his few flaws. My mother never wanted to upset him, so she agreed with him to have a fourth child to fulfill his wish to have a son. And I think she would have had a fifth if I had been a girl.

I was a few months shy of turning thirty when the pressure intensified. I was still single and no one in the family knew much about my dating or personal life. The only thing that they knew was my workaholic nature, as I was supposedly working whenever they asked me to join them at some family function.

I was part of the family, but I did the minimum required of me, and work was my usual excuse. No other excuse would have been sufficient for my parents. Throughout the second half of my twenties, whenever a family friend got married or had kids, my parents would hint at the idea of marriage and starting a family of my own.

"We're going to Mona's wedding next weekend. Are you coming with us?" my mom would ask.

"No, I am busy that weekend, Mama," I would answer.

"You should try to come. Mona has a lot of beautiful friends and they are going to be at the wedding," my mom would add, trying to sell me the idea of joining them. I always had a very diplomatic answer ready to soothe her worrying mind.

"I wish I could come, but I have this really important report to finish for work. Make sure you take pictures of the girls you like."

"*Habibi*, try to come this time. You didn't come with us to the last couple of weddings. Try to finish your report early and join us."

"Mama, if I can, I will."

"*Inshallah*, it will be your wedding next." Mama could never resist adding this comment.

"*Inshallah*, Mama."

Oh, I loved that word, *Inshallah*, "God willing." It was always my get-out-of-jail card. It is very comforting and reassuring, yet, for us Egyptians, it was a way to leave things hanging in the air, without committing yourself. Baba always insisted that I use *Inshallah* whenever I'd say I would do something tomorrow or at a later time.

"Osama, say '*Inshallah*.' You can't take tomorrow for granted," he would insist.

However, it annoyed him how other Egyptians used and abused it. And I rarely used it with him if I knew that I wouldn't do something that he had asked of me. But Mama wasn't as strict as Baba, and I used it with her quite often. I am pretty sure she knew when I didn't mean it.

To my parents, every social gathering within their circle of Arab friends was a chance for me to meet Miss Right—my future Mrs. Right—but I didn't share their sentiments, for obvious reasons. My interests lay elsewhere and there was no way to tell them. I spent years excusing myself from attending these events—to dodge the issue of marriage—but she would then bring the issue home. I'd often come home to find small gatherings of Mama's female friends and their daughters, especially those whom my mom thought would be good candidates. She really thought she had me figured out;

she really believed that she knew my taste in women. If she only knew the truth.

Sometimes, I went along with it to keep her happy, but it wasn't always fun sitting in a room full of Arab women who have the same intentions for their daughters as my mom had for me.

Arabs are so funny when it comes to the issue of marriage. Once their kids reach a certain age, marriage becomes the main focus, as if they were breeding dogs or horses. But it is a lot worse for the girls, and I am glad I am not one—although sometimes I felt like one, the way they were trying to force the idea on me. I believe girls begin to hear about the idea of marriage, and finding a good man, once the first period arrives. On the other hand, most Arab men don't hear much about it until they graduate college and get their first paycheck.

"*Mabrook*, Osama, now it is time to find yourself a good woman to have a family of your own and enjoy the blessings of Allah together." Those were Mama's first words when I told her of my new post–graduation job. At times, it was beyond annoying to listen to their nonstop attempts to persuade me to marry. It was as if the survival of mankind depended on my sperm uniting with an egg to populate the earth. I did my best to escape those conversations, arguments, and sometimes fights. I didn't give in for years, not until Baba became more involved.

Baba was getting older and starting to feel that he didn't have much time left. They became a hunting party—Mama would corner me and Baba would move in for the kill.

"Osama, what are you waiting for? *Alhamdulillah*, thank God, you have a great job, great education; you have your own place, and you make enough money to support a family."

"Baba, so what if I have these things?"

"Say *Alhamdulillah*; others don't have even half the things you have."

"I know Baba, *Alhamdulillah*. But having all of these things doesn't automatically mean I have to get married. There is so much that I want to do before I settle down. I want to enjoy life first."

"You've not had enough time to enjoy yourself? You must be kidding me! I don't know anyone who travels and goes away on luxurious vacations as much as you do."

"So what, Baba? I want to do and see more."

"You can do and see more with your wife. Life isn't always about doing things for yourself and by yourself."

"I know, but Baba, marriage is such a huge step and I will be doing it for myself, not for anyone else. With all due respect, I don't see why you and Mama concern yourselves so much with it."

"We want to see you happy and we want to see you settled in your own home with your own family before we leave this life."

Somehow, Egyptian parents feel fulfilled and accomplished when they have married off all of their children. They make it seem as if it is their only goal, or their greatest accomplishment in life, and they don't rest until it's done. I would always jokingly reply to my Baba's hints about him dying of old age, "Baba, God forbid, you will live to see one thousand. You are a healthier and fitter man than I am." It always seemed to work, and it was always a great diversion to start asking him some health-related questions. It always worked except for that night at the hospital in Egypt. I couldn't joke about his health, and I couldn't evade his request. Baba used his time on that Egyptian hospital bed well.

"Osama, I want you to make me happy soon."

"How, Baba?"

"You know exactly how."

"But Baba, I am waiting for the right moment."

"And what right moment is that? You have everything, and I will provide you with anything else you need."

"Wouldn't you be happier if you saw me marrying someone I truly love, the way you and Mama love each other?"

"Yes, I would, and I wish nothing less than that for you. But your mom and I come from a different time and a different world. People believed in the idea of a soulmate; people knew what they wanted from their lives. When you met 'the one,' there were no distractions. But now, it seems everyone enjoys the confusion of window-shopping more than anything else."

"But Baba, that doesn't mean I should give up on finding my one true love."

"I'll be in my grave way before you even attempt to find out what you want or you think of making a move."

"Come on, Baba, stop this talk. I know exactly what I want from my life."

"Do you really?"

"Yes, I do."

"Okay, so go ahead, tell me," he ordered, challenge in his voice.

"I want …" I froze as I almost told Baba everything, but I couldn't risk losing him to a heart attack in his condition.

"You see, Osama, you don't know, you are over thirty, and you don't know."

"But, Baba ,..." I really wanted to finally confess everything to him. I wanted to rid myself of the constant feeling of guilt, but I couldn't bring myself to do it.

"There are no ifs, ands, or buts. I want to see you married with kids; I want to see my own grandkids. I want someone in the family who will continue to carry our name. And we both know that if we leave it up to you to do it, it will never happen." The way he said it made it sound as if he knew something. In a very low and defeated voice, Baba went on, "Look, *Habibi*, you are my only son, and I am not getting any younger. I am getting older with every passing moment, and I would love to see your kids and play with them just as I do with your sisters' kids. I want to know them and I want them to know me."

It had been many years since I saw tears form in Baba's eyes, but I saw them then, as he continued. "I want to be here to welcome them into the world and teach them a thing or two of what I know. Osama, please make me and your mom happy in our last days. Consider it a dying man's wish."

I had flown to Egypt willing to give up life itself for Baba, and here I was sitting next to him in a hospital bed. It was a test I didn't expect. It truly sucked at being the only son who is supposed to carry on some legacy. I wonder if that was how Ismail felt when his father, Abraham, informed him of the divine orders. Ismail was willing, and he actually offered himself as some kind of sacrifice.

Did he feel pressured to comply because he was the only son?

Did he know that his dad was anxiously waiting for an heir to his heavenly kingdom?

Was his dad anything like my Baba?

Abraham had a falling out with his father because of religious beliefs. He was an outcast because of his beliefs, just like Baba, who was disowned for doing things differently and carving out his own destiny. Was Ismail aware of all the hardships his father endured? Did he agree out of devotion? Or did he agree to do it out of his sense of obligation?

Many times I played along out of my sense of duty to the family, but my love for Baba exceeded my love of self. I knew how much he sacrificed for the family; I knew that he did everything within his power to keep the family united. I knew we were his home, we were his happy place. He lost one family, and he did everything to keep this one intact.

I gave in to his pressure and persuasion, but I had a few conditions of my own. He had to agree that I would find my own bride without any meddling from the family, especially my mother. The other side of the agreement was that I had to find a Muslim woman. I am not sure why I agreed to the latter but, at that point, I was ready to do just about anything to keep Baba happy.

Marry for love!
And if you settle for less, make sure you both know it.

3/19/2017

Hi Adam,

I have been super busy with work, but I have also been spending some time browsing through Baba's phone, and thankfully, it reminded me that the upcoming Egyptian Mother's Day (I forget these things at times, yet I remember what day my parents first met) is in two days. And I don't know what to get Mama. I want to get her something that she will love—it is her first Mother's Day without Baba. Your aunts were of no help; they didn't know what to get her themselves. I find myself thinking of these little things that Baba did for Mama and wanting to fill that void for her. The two of them had no one else but one another; they did it all together ever since they left Egypt when one Egyptian pound equaled three American dollars. They drew their own plan and stuck to it. Mama made sacrifices—she gave up her medical career for years to raise the family. Baba made his own sacrifices as well—he gave up his whole family to be with Mama. They recognized and acknowledged those sacrifices every chance they got, and it is my turn to continue Baba's ways. The more involved I am with the family, the more of him I see in our daily lives. I am thinking of giving Mama the phone. I know it has been therapeutic for me having it around and seeing the notes he wrote in the phone with the stylus. I love the constant presence of his handwriting. And speaking of handwriting, I can't read his—doctors need to do something about their handwritings. I don't think I will tell anyone about the phone just yet.

Who gets the phone in these cases? Or do we just destroy it? Is it selfish that I want to keep it to myself?

With all the running I did from the family, I feel like everyone else got to have more of Baba than I did, and yet they say I was the one he loved most.

Back to my own sacrifice. Once I had agreed to what I thought was Baba's dying wish, for weeks I thought of nothing but where on earth I might find a Muslim bride who would understand the situation. How could I present it to her without her freaking out on me and me having to reveal the whole truth?

Do I marry just about anyone who seems like a suitable candidate for marriage and do the minimum required of me as a husband to live something close to a normal life? I thought of all possible ways to solve the predicament I found myself in, but each and every one of them could end badly. There was no way I was going to risk everything without considering the consequences of each possible solution. Meanwhile, I had joined several dating websites for Muslims and Arabs to show my parents that I was serious about the business of finding a bride, but none of my efforts yielded the desired results. I pretended I'd been on a few dates with some of these girls. I made up stories of disastrous dates and complained to my family about how bad the dating scene was at that point. I am not sure whether they believed me or not—some of the stories were too horrific, too extreme for anyone to believe. But they did the job and gave me the time I needed to think and draw up my master plan.

One day, while I was sitting at work, one of my coworkers sent an email to ask my opinion about an apartment he found on Craigslist. While I was on the site, I browsed around and landed on the personals section. I began reading some of the ads people posted there and their weird requests and fetishes. I spent hours on the site, not knowing what I was looking for, or what I was doing on it, but I clicked one link after the other. I spent about a month or so exploring the new world of Craigslist and people's posts. In a way, reading some of those posts made me feel normal. I no longer felt like a misfit who didn't belong. It was something that I had missed since AOL chatrooms and its many screen names became useless with the rise of Myspace and Facebook.

It finally dawned on me that I should look for my bride on Craigslist. Maybe I would find my answer there. It took me awhile to finally put up an honest ad. The first time I did it, I posted it under a different state. I couldn't risk anyone finding out it was me doing it; I had to be covert, and so did everyone else. After I posted my ad, I learned that many Arabs and Muslims, both men and women, use the personals section. I received a lot of hate email from other Arabs, and I also received a lot of emails from others who sympathized and encouraged me to tell my family the truth. Some of them went as far as telling me the details of their own stories and struggles with their families.

For days, I read both the hate and love emails I received. They were very entertaining at times. The hate emails made it seem a very good idea to find a wife, to try to appear normal in front of family and others in a culture that rejects people like me. To my surprise, and after weeks of posting ads on different sites, I learned that there were many others who were in the same predicament. I also found out that there are many Arab women in desperate need of a way to appear normal to their families, too. Although I didn't care about anything besides finding a woman to marry, I had to choose carefully to find someone I could bring home to meet the family. There also had to be some friendly chemistry with the woman for the plan to work.

Sometimes, I want to smack myself over the head for not opening up to others. I should have trusted one of my therapists with the whole story— someone could have made sense of it for me. Or, I could have trusted Nora; I could have given her a fair chance to explain herself. She could have been here with us if I had done that.

We are never alone; there are others who know exactly what it feels like.

3/27/2017

The title of her ad on Craigslist was: *Looking for a Muslim Hubby with a twist.*

I am a successful attorney. I work for a big law firm in Manhattan. I am looking to get married to someone who will understand my situation—in-the-closet lesbian, Arab, and Muslim. I need someone who understands what that entails: family visits, a facade of real marriage. I don't care to hear your views about lesbianism in Islam and how I am going to burn to hell. If you think that way, what are you doing here, you sick pervert? Please, no time wasters. I am looking for someone who is maybe in the same boat and looking for something similar.

I saved some of the emails we exchanged.

Hi,

How are you? So I came across your ad, and I am not sure how to go about this. It is the first time I am replying to someone, but I really liked what you wrote. I posted on here before looking for a "mustache," but I didn't have much luck. I really hope that you are real.

I am 34, Egyptian/American, native New Yorker. I am an accountant, and my family doesn't know anything about my other life.

O.

Hi "O"

I have to admit I am surprised anyone answered. Or at least answered with something other than insults. I posted this yesterday, after yet another family reunion where everyone was making a point of making me feel bad and unworthy to still be single and childless. My mother always comes up with those "great candidates" for me to consider; yesterday's new batch was the icing on the cake.

I simply am out of excuses for not getting married to whomever my family sees fit. I might as well take the bull by the horns and handle this myself. I don't know what I was thinking exactly, though. I hadn't quite anticipated getting an answer.

So yeah, I am quite real, and so is my problem. Looks like I'm not the only one having the same, and frankly, I'm not sure how that makes me feel. No wonder you didn't get an answer, if you specifically indicated you had a mustache, ha-ha. An accountant with a mustache. Very glamorous.

Sorry—I am straightforward. Hope I haven't hurt your feelings.
L.

Hi "L"
I am totally surprised myself; I didn't think you would reply. Thank you for overlooking the crippling mustache image.

I can only imagine the kind of pressure you have to go through—Arab families are all about mating and having a family with a single mate. Come on, we are not that foolish, and you are not that clever.

Guessing by the tone of your emails, you are the one to wear the pants in your relationships.

I hope I didn't hurt your feelings.
O
P.S. Why does one wear a mustache anyway in the twenty-first century?

Hi O,
I was feeling bad after hitting send. I figured you may be offended by the mustache joke ... looks like not so much.

No feelings hurt. An eye for an eye. I suppose I do wear the pants. Maybe that's why I can't bring myself to pick any of those candidates, because I know how it would eventually end up with those men trying to be the manliest and most macho, proud men. Not pretty.

The pressure is bad enough from my family. And it conflicts drastically with some of my (non-Muslim) friends' culture. It is sometimes maddening. Plus, at the law firm it is already hard enough to make my spot as a woman. A number of white conservative males in the firm, although they are not saying it out loud, believe a woman's place is barefoot and pregnant in the kitchen, not in court. Let's not even mention when that woman is Muslim and a lesbian. Better they don't know some of my private details, but there too it is getting hard to dodge the question.

Some of the younger ones have tried to hit on me. A good marriage alliance would help with that, in addition to the family pressure. No doubt.

L[osing her mind]

Hey Losing her mind,

Be careful there! Mustaches are making a comeback soon, very soon.

And no, I can def take a joke, and I am glad you can too. We are off to a good start (alhamdulillah -thank god) LOL.

Yes, there are people out there who still think a woman belongs in the kitchen, though I grew up in a household where my dad always helped around the house.

I can relate to your predicament, but I believe that gay Muslim/Arab men have it worse. I have to act macho all the time to live up to some social expectation.

Any Arab man would want to have a lesbian for a wife, she can be his wing woman.

So since you brought up the younger ones, and you haven't given me any information yet, I have to ask:

Are we age appropriate for one another? (You might be an 80-year-old Arab spinster.)

And what kind of Arab are you?

It is only fair—you know my answers already.

O

Laila's family came from south Lebanon to escape the war that broke the country apart. They, too, wanted a new life for themselves in the New World. She briefly told me of her family's history and explained that her family was very strict and religious. That was the main reason I had responded to her ad and agreed to meet, after many emails; she did get it.

We both had secrets to guard with our lives, secrets that could not be revealed to just anyone. We didn't want our personal choices to hurt those we loved and were loved by. Our loved ones had been unable to give us the kind of unconditional love and acceptance we longed for, but we both understood that it wasn't their fault. We defined things differently.

Every family has its own intricate reality!

3/28/2017

Your mom and I exchanged emails for a couple of months. We went through all the necessary steps to verify that we were both real individuals. We talked on the phone, we video chatted on skype, we became Facebook friends, and we finally met in person. She was petite with long brown hair, fair skin, and hazel eyes. Her professional demeanor made her look very serious and somewhat cold. I was totally intimidated at our first meeting, yet I found myself drawn to her. There was a sense of positive energy about her; she was different from all the other women I'd met during my quest. I felt comfortable talking to her and discussing openly with her many things I'd never dared to talk about openly to anyone before.

"So why are you really doing this?" She leaned her elbow on the table and moved closer.

"Doing what exactly?"

"You know, looking for a wife and trying to get married to appease others."

"You just answered your own question. I am doing it for the family and to make sure others are appeased."

"But why not tell them the truth considering we don't live in the Middle East? You can pretty much do whatever you want, be whomever you wish to be, and you don't have to be around the family."

"I can ask you the same question." I reclined in my seat, crossing my arms.

"That's fine, I will answer it first. I am really tired of lying to my family. I would love to tell them the truth, but that would be fruitless; our parents prefer the roles of judges and executioners much more than they do the parenting part." She sighed.

"So you do understand." I leaned over the table. "It's pretty much the same situation in my case. Plus, my dad made it his death wish; he's like every other man who wants to ensure the continuation of his own kind."

"This is so axiomatic; it sounds like an Arab man problem." She laughed.

"You would be surprised." I joined in on the laughter. "It is not just Arab men who want boys to carry their legacy and to keep the bloodline running. A lot of men still subscribe to that ancient tradition, but they are not as vocal about it as Arabs are—they will say it among other men, but never in the presence of a woman. Arab men don't care."

"Yea, it is that undersexed and underdeveloped brain fueled by hyper masculinity." She took another sip of her wine. "You're right. Arab men just don't give a fuck. They'll watch a scientific experiment unfold in front of their eyes demonstrating that water is made out of hydrogen and oxygen, but will insist that science is bogus because it doesn't match their perception of God's word."

"This conversation is getting too deep for dinner and wine."

"Man up, Osama; you have to learn how to roll with the punches if you want to get with this." She pointed at herself with both hands.

"I didn't know that lawyers had a sense of humor."

"We are humorous when we lose a case and must bring you the sad news," she giggled, "and when drunk."

"And other times?" I asked.

"We are just as miserable as doctors who see us at our weakest and how desperate we are to hold on to life, or cops who have to do deal with the worst of the worst in every community. We deal with corrupt politicians, thieves, killers, rapists, molesting priests, and tax evaders." Her facial features took on a gloomy form as she struggled to draw a smirk. "And at times, we have to fight for them because they have the money to fight it and we can find those loopholes to free them."

"So you are good at finding holes."

"That's what she said." She broke into a vigorous fit of laughter. "Seriously though, you are doing this because it is your dad's death wish."

"Yes, I am."

"But, why?"

"I really love my family. They are everything that means anything to me. I know there is nothing they wouldn't do for me, but I also know and understand their limitations. I don't think it is something they could handle. I know some of them might try to understand, but things would never be the same again."

"Are you doing it out of love for them? Or is it done out of fear?" she asked

"I believe it is both, but more love. I really want to give my father something I know he wants more than anything else. I see how he is with my nephews and nieces. I have never seen anyone give so much of himself, selflessly, and it is about the one thing he has ever asked me for."

"No need to be melodramatic; I get it."

Every time we met, we got closer. We opened up easily.

"I can't stand the thought of a man touching my body. I tried in the past, but I couldn't. I'd rather get hit by a speeding truck," Laila explained. "The things I went through still haunt me—I was a little girl."

"How old were you?" I hesitantly asked, not wanting to impose.

"I was about ten then."

"How is that possible? Did you tell anyone? Did you scream for help?"

"I did try, but no one believed me. Everyone loved my uncle and no one dared to think he did such things. My

own mother called me a liar when I mentioned it to her."
She put up her hands, making the quotation sign. "He
was a man of God."

"I am so sorry you had to go through that. I can't even
imagine that some people are capable of such things."

"Yeah, they are. Especially men—some of them are
monsters."

"Did this happen once? You don't have to answer if
you don't want to."

"No." She paused for a second. "It kept happening
randomly until I was fourteen. He would just walk into
my room while I was sleeping and no one was home. I
would feel his hands reaching up my pajamas and
scream. He silenced my screams with his hand. He used
to overpower me and take what he came in for."

"I really don't know what to say. I am so sorry you had
to endure that."

"You know, it took me forever to trust any other man,
but for some reason or another, men see me and they
want to fuck me."

"What do you mean?"

"In my freshman year in college, I started dating this
white guy. I didn't want to be near any Arabs and I
figured I'd be safer. But no, he too was the biggest
douchebag, he almost did the same thing to me; he tried
to force himself onto me when I had clearly told him I
didn't want to do anything. Then he had the balls to
blame it on me—he said the same thing as my uncle did
when I confronted him. I was supposedly the one
provoking them."

"What?! Are you serious? They are blaming you, the
victim. I am really speechless. I thought I had heard it
all."

"You know, as much as I love my family and all, I can
never trust them to this day. I sometimes catch myself
thinking that it was all their fault that any of it happened

to me. We are supposed to feel safe with our families, but I never felt that way with mine, and I didn't want to be around them."

"I know what you mean in a way. I keep my family at arm's length too but for a different reason. I do it to protect them and to protect myself."

"Now that sounds like a puzzle."

"Well, I know they wouldn't understand or accept who I am today. They love the version of me that I let them see, but if they were ever to find out the whole truth, I know it would break them, especially Baba."

"Did you ever think about telling them?"

"I tried to so many times, but I know how they are. I just learned to respect their traditions and lifestyles and not impose mine forcefully. We don't have to be in conflict. So we can focus on the commonality."

"I thought about telling mine, too, but I wanted to do it to hurt them. I wanted them to feel my pain, but I knew they wouldn't believe me. There were many times when I was drunk and I wanted to phone my mother and scream at her for not believing me then, but I was never ready to totally lose them. I guess in a way, I understand you." She then turned her whole body and moved closer. "Now it is your turn to tell me your story. When did you know? And when did you finally come to terms with it?"

"I knew when I was in high school, and then college was when I accepted it all." I lied; I told her about Nour rather than Nora. I shared a lot of what Nora and I did, but I used misleading pronouns. I didn't know how to tell her about Nora and how I was the cause of her death. I didn't know how to tell her that I never came to terms with that part of my life or anything else that had happened since.

As Laila and I continued to talk and meet on a regular basis, we soon became very good friends. We made sure to be seen out and about as a normal couple would. The friendly chemistry between us meant we enjoyed each other's company. We soon had our own private jokes and code words. Our strong bond was built on transparency, acceptance, honesty (though not when it came to Nora), and the thing we wanted most—a safe space to be ourselves.

One evening, over drinks, Laila took a deep breath. "So, on which side of the fence do you stand? Nature or nurture?"

I deflected her question with another. "Where do *you* stand?"

"Come on, I'm the one asking the questions here, you can't always do that. I'm not letting you get away with it this time."

"I really don't know."

She leaned over the table as she always did when she got serious. "How could you not know?"

"I just don't. I can see both sides of the argument. I can't come down on one side or the other. There's no real empirical evidence that one supersedes the other."

"I'm not buying that answer. You're being a politically correct asshole right now."

"What?" I shook my head. "If I really wanted to be politically correct, I'd have picked the nature side of the argument, but I didn't. I really don't know."

"Okay, fine."

"How about you? Which side are you on?" I asked again.

"*Hmmm*. I lean toward the nurture side."

"I didn't expect that answer."

"Why?"

"I don't have a reason, but I really thought you would have picked the nature argument."

Laila laughed. "I wonder why everyone seems to think so. You're not the first one to say that to me."

"It is the energy or the vibe you give off. You seem the type who is more about science than psychology."

"I guess you were wrong on that one."

"So why do you go with nurture over nature?"

"It's a matter of logic for me. I know in my case it was circumstances that brought me to where I am now. You know, with everything that happened in my childhood and all. I hate men because of the things that they did to me growing up as a little girl; I've never been able to get over that."

"Yeah, but that doesn't mean everyone is the same as you."

"I know, but that's my take on it. Anyway, I believe that there is the natural order of things, and then experiences and circumstances are added to it."

"How so?"

She waved her hand in front of her face. "Forget it—it's too long to explain."

"No way—you started this. You're not getting off that easily. You didn't let me get away with answering your question with another, so I'm definitely not letting this one go."

"I don't know, but to me it sounds very logical. In nature, a cat will always chase a mouse. A dog will always chase a cat. A lion will chase and eat a gazelle. That is the natural order of things, but nowadays you'll see a cat and a dog playing together in a household because they were domesticated, and somehow you think of it as normal, you accept it. Or you see a lion riding a unicycle at the circus and obeying the commands of his trainer. Those are not the animals' natural behaviors, yet most of us come to accept them and we forget all about the natural order of things."

"Does that make us abnormal or unnatural?" I asked.

She giggled loudly. "It makes us unique. I told you, it isn't easy to explain."

"I don't have anywhere to go. So, go ahead, give it another shot."

"Okay. Look, in life we are governed by different kinds of laws. We have the divine laws, the laws of nature, and manmade laws. Each law has its role and purpose, but some have precedence over others."

"You're starting to sound like my philosophy professor back in school."

"Osama. Stop being sarcastic. I'm trying to explain."

"Go ahead, I'm all ears. The stage is yours."

"Sex is fun and all, right?"

"Yeah."

"But most of the major religions forbid sex outside of the sacred union of marriage. That is, fornication between a man and a woman."

"And? What are you getting at?"

"Imagine if regular heterosexual sex is forbidden and classed as a sin."

"I'm not following your logic here. We already know that premarital sex is a sin and is frowned upon by God. Still though, what is your point?"

"When was the last time you heard someone talk of their sense of regret or shame about sex? And you know, and I know, that everyone in this city is fucking and people are cheating on each other."

"Quite often, actually."

"Osama, I am not talking about you or other Muslims. We were brainwashed to feel that guilt for the rest of our lives."

"Fine," I said. "You're right. I rarely hear anyone talk about it. At least not in the way you mean. People will regret it because it was bad sex or drunken sex or whatever, but never for religious reasons or fear of divine law."

"Now you're catching on. And now sex is the norm, including casual sex and one-night stands. People don't have a problem with those things anymore. Think of how things were twenty years ago or so." She made air quotations. "'Hooking up' wasn't the norm."

"Are you trying to say that some people choose to be gay or lesbian?"

"You don't really choose it, but circumstances and environment lead you to become that way. We tend to normalize things as we continue to grow."

"So how did we normalize it?"

"Let's say that homosexuality is a human behavior, which falls under the same category as manmade laws. Add to that the fact that homosexuality has existed for thousands of years. People did it all the time but, for the most part, they did it secretly."

"They weren't doing it so secretly in Sodom and Gomorrah or the Roman Empire."

"Focus on the rule, not the exception."

"I like that idea better."

"What idea?"

"The not discussing if it is natural or not. Let everyone be whoever and whatever they wish to be. In the end it will be only up to God to judge."

She sipped more of her wine. "If only it was that simple."

"It is simple, it is very simple. People should be able to respect one another simply as human beings. Why let orientation, skin color, religion, or anything like that be the deciding factor?"

"I just love how you simplify everything."

"Why couldn't it be this simple?"

"Because it isn't. Because there are civil rights and a welfare system."

"What does that have to do with anything?"

"That is everything; that is the main reason the whole argument of nature versus nurture is surfacing like never before. Homosexual couples can't claim their partners on tax forms, medical insurances, inheritance, and so on," she asserted.

"So, wait, if you're my gay partner, I can't claim for you on my health insurance?"

"Yes," she said. "And, by the way, if I were a gay guy, I would so not date you."

God is inclusive, the message was for all.
Human rights are inclusive!
We are all equal in the eyes of God, and we should be so in the eyes of our manmade law.

4/5/2017

I went into Barnes & Noble to purchase a finance book, and I noticed that self-help books are some of the best sellers. My curiosity was most certainly piqued; I did a google search, and it was true. For the last two decades or so, self-help books became a cornerstone in the publishing world.

The whole thing reminded me of a conversation I had with your gedo when one of his nurses recommended a book, *The Secret*, to him. Unlike myself, Baba was an avid reader and he welcomed book recommendations from everyone and anyone. Though he read the book and liked it, he wasn't so thrilled about the idea of it—it was the last self-help book he ever read. He viewed the spike in self-help book sales as a clear indication of the fall of religions.

"You know, people are looking for answers outside of religion, because no one is explaining it in a way people can relate to," he said. "All these religions and men of God complicate things. They try so hard to flaunt their knowledge; they reference all those dead people to solidify their arguments, and they lose us in the process. God's message is beyond simple and straightforward. God wants us to be good to one another. Most who criticize religion do so because of the people who call themselves religious yet don't adhere to the teachings. If you are teaching kids about religion and how great it is, and they grow up to find out that you were a hypocrite, they will hold you accountable. They should hold you accountable. The whole book can be summarized in one Quranic Aya, but there is no one to present it in simple terms."

"Which Aya is it, Baba?" I asked.

"'And when my servants ask you about me, I am near. I answer the call when called upon—so let them answer me, and have faith in me that they may be rightly guided.'" He reached for the Quran to verify what he recited.

I am starting to believe that your gedo was on to something. I know I do the same thing as most. I look for the quick fix; I google for answers to most of my questions, and my curiosity is usually pacified. It is very rare that I dig deeper for more answers. I never make it to the second search results page, and I doubt that many do. It is the dark abyss of the Internet where information dies.

Baba was a wise Arab Yoda. "People stopped believing. They believe in things they see, touch, hear; they believe with only their senses, and we are selective with our beliefs. We seek that which is familiar; we don't dare to challenge our belief system. Today's sense of belief is incomplete, it's disingenuous."

At some point in your life, you will hear people talk of how we don't appreciate things until they are gone, and they are correct. I do wish to have many days back with Baba, my wise Yoda. I wish life had given us a different path. I would have loved to spend more time with him; I wish I had appreciated his wisdom when he was around. He was not perfect, but he was a pretty damn good father.

Since we are on the topic of religion, it was one of the factors that I thought about when I met your mother. It was probably my way of trying to get out of marrying someone. I always found something negative about every prospective "mate." In case you haven't picked up on it yet, I was never that religious a person, and I had a closet full of skeletons that could lead to a public beheading in some parts of the world. I knew a lot based on my readings, upbringing, and travels, but there were things that I didn't have much exposure to. I knew little about Shi'a Muslims and their ways. It sounds so weird worded like this, "their ways." I didn't know how the family would take it once I announced my plans to marry Laila, with the religious differences. And guess what! Who was the person I went to then? *Mama.*

"Mama, what do you think of Shi'a Muslims?"

"I don't have any thoughts. I have some good Shi'a friends, and they are beautiful. Why do you ask?"

"I met someone."

"Do we like her?" She tried hard to control her excitement.

"Yes, she is really nice."

"Do you have a picture of her?" I showed her a picture of Laila on Facebook, and she was very pleased with the prospect of it all.

"If you like her, you know we all support you." She did her usual reassuring hands hugging my hands. "Religion is a personal and an intimate relationship with God; it is far more intimate than the relationship you will have with anyone else. It only aims to discipline you into becoming a better human. It has no place in matters of romance and love. I understand your concern about children and their future beliefs, assuming that's why you asked, but this is not a matter of romance or love anymore, it is a matter of tribal thinking and the survival of your tribe if you put the differences first." Mama paused. "Osama, you are a Jets fan, right?"

"Yes, Mama."

"Be a proud fan, don't look so defeated," she said, laughing. "They must be doing horribly."

"They are. How did you know?"

"The look on your face said it all." She continued to laugh. "I see defeat in your eyes."

"What does a football team have to do with any of this? We are talking about religion here."

"It is the same idea. You have been cheering for the Jets since you wore diapers, and you were fed religion when you wore diapers. The two are part of your story. Even when your team sucks, you still root for them on the sidelines. Most people continue to be loyal, or they outgrow the sport, or they develop an interest in something new, but they rarely cheer for another team.

"I think it has to do with the way most games are played today. Back in the day, the players had loyalty to the jersey they wore, and to the fans. Today, it is not so much the loyalty; it is all about money and endorsement deals. And that is the idea. A lot of people are disillusioned with religion because they are finally figuring out what the institutions did all those years. Religious figures and institutions treated religions as a money-producing cow; they reaped the benefits for years, and they said whatever they had to in order to keep their followers, and the flow of money."

"Is that why Baba is against the idea of people making money off religion?" I asked.

"Yes, and that is why we have tons of fabricated stories that defy logic in every sense of the word. When religion becomes your main source of income, people tend to get creative with their thoughts and opinions to maintain a following."

Conversations with your grandparents always had a life of their own, and they never ended where they started. And as I mentioned to you earlier in the journal, your grandmother truly believes that all religions are floors to one big building, and each prophet or messenger is the construction worker building each level, while God is the architect of this beautiful, magnificent edifice we call religion. It is a building, and each floor needs the support of the one below it. You can't get to the top without going through each of the other levels, and you also need a strong foundation before you can even start to build.

"If the foundation is fragile or tainted, it won't matter how beautiful and sturdy the structure looks from the outside to everyone else. A wind, strong enough, will knock it down sooner or later," Mama always said.

"How do you avoid making that mistake?"

"First, you deconstruct whatever building you have previously built, then inspect every brick, examine the foundation itself, and don't fear starting your own new foundation. Most of our foundations are based on our comfort zones—family, friends, lovers, local community, local church or mosque—and it is tough to recognize the fragility of our own foundation because it involves emotions more than anything else."

I interjected. "If one or all of these religions was the true one, why would each be so fragmented, divided into different sects?" Though I was the one who initiated the conversation, it sometimes got under my skin when Baba and Mama went off topic and got deep into religion. But knowing now, for sure, that they had their own team effort going, it makes a lot of sense that they always pushed these lessons.

"*Ya Allah*, I told you already. Religion, like everything else, had to go through stages of development. God could have given the first man a fully developed religion, but would it have made any sense to that first man? Would he have understood the meaning of any of it? The human race had to pass through many, many generations first to learn what everything means. We had to experience and explore, as a baby explores its world. History tells us that we have always had a sense of a higher being, as the creator of all; the human mind has always wondered about that being and searched for it. The ancient Egyptians worshipped a higher power and established their own religions, and the Indians did, too. Religions developed and evolved all over the world."

"Mama, that was before we had science to disprove a lot of those myths."

"Religions never got rid of the corrupted teachings or the corrupted institutions, which until this day still reap the benefits of serving those in power as a fee for brainwashing and the undernourishment of souls. If they told the stories the way they were meant to be told, we wouldn't have a constant clash between science and theology."

"I seriously find it impossible to find the balance between the two. Do I believe in the big bang theory and human evolution, which is very evident? Or do I believe that we were created from the union of one man and one woman?"

"Who said anything about one man and one woman?" Mama fired back.

"The Quran, the Bible, and the Torah."

"The Quran doesn't; it doesn't even mention Eve."

"*L'aa'aaaa*, Mama. No."

"*Wallahi*, I swear to God, Eve isn't mentioned at all in the Quran, and Adam is mentioned as someone who was selected from among others like him."

"Mama, are you serious?" I was intrigued.

"And the Quran talks about how we were all created from one single *nafs*, and the translation of nafs can mean a few things: the soul, the ego, or the self, but there are a few times when the Quran mentions the nafs as the very first thing created and it was split into pairs, and that applies to all that was created. Each of those pairs went on to be their own species. The nafs could have been an atom."

I paused to process this information. "How come no one told me these things before? Why am I always hearing things from you for the very first time?"

"This information has been available, and God, in the Quran, keeps on daring us to question things; he commands us to let our rational thought handle these stories. It is one of the reasons I fell in love with the book and the religion. Do you know that the first nafs is referred to with feminine pronouns? And God makes no mistakes in his book, *Habibi*."

Your Tayta went on to school me about the differences between the story of creation that we heard growing up and the one that aligned with the Quranic verses rather than the made-up Hadiths.

"First, God has no likeness and we weren't created in his likeness. We wouldn't be able to comprehend God if we tried; that is the reason most Jews won't write out the word, and they will spell it as G-d. There is nothing like God even in writing the name, and the Quran backs it up.

"'There is nothing like unto Him.'" She paused.

"Second, God's messages weren't just revealed in the Quran, the Bible, and the Torah; God sent others, and we don't always know where or how. It is part of our test to recognize God in all.

"'And We have already sent messengers before you. Among them are those whose stories We have related to you, and among them are those whose stories We have not related to you. And it was not for any messenger to bring a sign or verse except by permission of Allah. So, when the command of Allah comes, it will be concluded in truth, and the falsifiers will thereupon lose all.'"

"I knew that one," I commented

"Adam wasn't the first man, but he was the first human."

"And what is the difference?"

"Man is more the animal form, or us without cognition, just the id. And that was why the angels feared Adam to be a destructive force once he was elected; they didn't know the future of Adam, the human, but they knew the past of man." She took a sip of her tea. "Think of Adam as the first teacher of a language class. God says He taught Adam all names. Even scientists will tell you that we had a sudden change; we went from man to human."

"So, you are saying we went through an evolution?"

"Yes, and our beginning started with dust, water, and mud. It is always from the ground up." She smiled and recited some more verses. "'Who perfected everything which He created and began the creation of man from clay. Then He made His posterity out of the extract of a liquid disdained. Then He proportioned him and breathed into him from His created soul and made for you hearing and vision and hearts; little are you grateful.' Quran 32–7–9, and in another Surah, 'God says, "when He has created you in stages"' Quran 71–14."

I know Mama had a lot of years before me, but she wasn't born into Islam, and her knowledge of the Quran after converting intimidated me. She was becoming more scholarly than Baba, for sure, especially with her references. I think, in some way, she pushed Baba to be a better Muslim, and the whole family, too. She challenged the status quo with Quranic verses. "I didn't convert to just believe; I am doing it for me. It is my relationship with God." That was something that she definitely picked up from Baba—the two were uncompromising when it came to their relationship with the creator, and it was for their own personal sake. They shared with us, but they didn't impose, which was pretty obvious in our choices.

"I know you are trying to do right by us, and I know you will do what is right for you. Shi'a, Sunni, Sufi, atheist, agnostic, or whatever you choose for yourself, make sure you can build together for a very long time. It shouldn't matter that she is Shi'a. Your father and I worked out our differences early on, and we drew our very unique path. We both made sacrifices that never felt like such. We talked and created our own reality as a team. If you and Laila have that kind of openness, you are off to a great start. We want to see you happy, *Habibi*. That is all that matters."

We went on to talk about other things, and then your Tayta threw me a curveball: She mentioned Nora. It was the first time that anyone in the family had even acknowledged her existence in my life.

I wonder if that was Mama's way of hoping that I would open up about her then—you know, before I made such a big decision, marriage.

"I am sorry, *Habibi*. I didn't know how to pull you out of your darkness. You looked so in control of your emotions; I didn't want to disturb your balance. I thought I was doing the right thing, letting you be. I did it when Nora died. I did it after September 11."

I froze. It was the first time Mama mentioned Nora in a way that suggested she knew more. I guess everyone around us knew, and we thought we were so clever hiding our secret romance. Her words caught me completely by surprise and left me speechless; any words I had crowded my vocal cords and blocked the passageways. I was finally able to mourn Nora in Mama's arms. I cried; I cried in a way that we allow ourselves to experience only when our mothers are present.

"It was one of the saddest pieces of news I ever heard. I imagined her as one of my own, and it broke my heart. I couldn't even call Shadia to offer her my condolences." She was fighting back tears. "We used to laugh about being future in-laws whenever Nora left us to watch you play soccer at El Nadi. Her mom was happy to see her enjoy the transition."

After what seemed like eternity, and with absolute hesitation, I asked, "What transition?"

"The move to Egypt. Shadia told me all about Nora's troubles adapting to Cairo, and she hated everything about it at first."

Mama didn't know a thing about Nora's condition, and that was in 2012. I wondered if Baba told her anything since then, and if I should tell her the real reason for Nora's suicide. I did lead her to believe that Nora was troubled and suffered a lot of trauma back home, in Palestine. I told her half of the truth, and I didn't tell her the most important half. I left out the part that would have indicted me.

"Yea, remember how quiet she was when they first moved? She never uttered a word; we thought she was mute."

"Osama! Speak well of the dead," Mama demanded.

"She is someone who committed suicide. She is probably burning in hell." I didn't mean any of those words, but I had to say them to keep Mama's curiosity from asking me any question about our relationship. If she had asked the right question, I don't think lying would have been an option that night.

"It is not your place to judge. That is something left for the divine alone. You don't know what drove her to the ledge of the roof; she could have been dealing with issues that you and I could never understand. And get that idea of burning in hell out of your mind."

"Mama, it is what the Quran says."

"The Quran also says that the descriptions we have of heaven and hell are metaphors. No one knows what either one will be like. Fire is a simile because of its association with pain and destruction. The afterlife is a spiritual journey, and it will be the nafs, our original form, meeting its creator, and not for the first time."

Hidden within the folds of my own nafs, I was so proud of Mama. I was happy to see her come to Nora's defense. I was relieved to learn something new—Nora wasn't really burning in hell's fire like I saw her in my dreams hundreds, if not thousands, of times. Knowingly or unknowingly, Tayta gave one of the very first ropes to my uphill climb. There was a side to things that I wasn't aware of.

Nora was quietly sobbing in the corner; she was no longer covered in blood.

04/11/2017

Baba didn't have any secrets of his own, at least not the kind that can compromise a person's character, and if he did, he must have buried them deep into the past along with the family in Asyut. In contrast, I have lived a life full of secrets and hiding. My closet is full of skeletons, which would have given Baba a heart attack if he had ever found out the details of them all. It makes sense that Mama didn't want him confronting me. I am looking back and I see nothing but ugliness. I was not engaged fully; I opted out to be a watcher and a fearful participant.

I think it would have been easier to relate to him, or I would have felt safer going to him about things, if I knew that he was able to relate to my struggles. And it is not that he wasn't approachable, it's that his goodness was intimidating. The man did no wrong, and his phone is the best evidence of it. He truly lived by his word in all situations. Everything in the phone is organized, dated, and decluttered. He has a whole folder for you, Adam. There is a folder for every family member, and at the moment I am diving into my own folder. Baba has handwritten notes—there are drafts of the letter he left with the lawyer. I was ecstatic to find the folders. In a way, I am feeling like the universe, God, the source, or whatever, is out there is giving us a chance for closure here. It's as if the minute I started to engage myself or my nafs, as Mama would say, and I started introducing you to my own life in a way I never did before with another soul, the universe gave back.

Was that what Baba meant when he used to tell us this Quranic verse, "Indeed, Allah will not change the condition of a people until they change what is in themselves"?

I am finally getting a glimpse into Baba's mind when he wrote that letter. I found different drafts of the letter in the phone. He did it all out of a place of love. Read what he had to say about love in his phone: "True love means wanting the best in life for your beloved as much as you want it for yourself. Isn't that what every parent wants for his or her children? Isn't that what every brother and every sister wants for his or her siblings? Shouldn't that be what every lover wants for his or her beloved? Think really hard about what you consider to be the best out of life. In my opinion, the best thing that anyone could want or desire would be heaven. Heaven is the prize of life, and everything else in our lives is just the price we pay to earn that ticket to paradise. Is there anything better than heaven to want or aim for?"

Adam, he really thought it was his responsibility to get us all, his kids and family, to heaven. I am not sure if I should be mad at him, or cry for losing someone who really loved me this much. I am looking at you sleeping in your own bed, and I know that I want the same thing for you; I want all the best for you. I am doing all of this for you and with you. I am troubled that Baba thought it was his duty, and I am understanding his intentions when he coerced me into all those things. Was that why he ended up using the animal's metaphor to show me that he finally understood?

If anything, the final version shows that Baba did grow himself while writing my letter.

04/22/2017

Dear Journal,

Today is Earth Day. Yes, we do need a day to remind us to be good to Mother Earth. If anything, I should wish Adam a happy birthday too, since his name originates from the same word that means "earth" in many other languages.

I am not that big on science, but I am a numbers guy. Based on the numbers I heard lately, we are totally in for a big natural catastrophe with this whole climate change thing.

Is Adam going to be okay? Are we going to be fine? Are people in other parts of the world going to be safe? It is so hard to ignore it when neither our summers nor our winters are the same as they used to be. It feels like something is brewing here on Mother Earth. She is skewed and losing her balance.

We humans like to think that we are superior and unique in every way. We tend to view ourselves as the ones who broke the mold. On one hand, we believe ourselves to be at the very top of life's pyramid; we are the rulers. On the other hand, we are very insignificant, if you look at the numbers. Out of billions and billions of sperms a man ejaculates, only one makes it out to this side of the world. That sounds pretty damn awesome. The thought is somewhat empowering. We are all the chosen ones in some fashion. On the other hand, we are only one of billions and billions of possibilities who made it to this side of the world. And in the grand scheme of things, we are of little importance. The average human lives about seventy to eighty years, and in comparison to the age of the planet, we are insignificant.

We are consumers—gone are the days when we worked and created with our own hands. We try to minimize the use of our brains, as if that would cure all our problems. I remember the days when I had to do math equations in my head or using pen and paper, but now we rely on technology. Software can do my job. Sometimes I don't understand why millions of people pay someone else to handle all their financial matters.

We don't like to accept fault for our wrongdoing. We prefer delegating our duties to others. Our greed has led to many environmental problems that we will leave for Adam's generation to handle, if the planet survives that long. The hole in the ozone, it is our doing; the extinct animals, we hunted them for pleasure; the polluted water, we spilled the oil and threw our garbage into the oceans. The scars are very obvious, but we can't seem to unite to heal our planet.

There are two warring sides. One is based on science and facts, and the other is based on traditional religious beliefs. I like to call them the forefathers vs. the offspring; it is the repeated cycle we have been stuck in for centuries. One camp is begging the other side to become more conscious of the way we treat the planet, because we are killing it, while the other camp believes that the heavens will take care of it, because it is God's will. And it sure doesn't help that our dear president decided to withdraw from the Paris Agreement to fix the global issue of climate change.

I really don't know if we are we moving forward, or if there is any real progress at all. Or are we stuck in a vicious cycle? I think it's the latter. The ancient Egyptians used hieroglyphics, and we are now using emojis to express our emotions. Innocent people died in unjustified wars; we are now dying due to random acts of hate. Past trends are repackaged and reintroduced, be it fashion, politics, or theology. The fighting will continue between the new and old, the liberal and the conservative, the pious and the wicked, the religious and the secular, and Democrats and Republicans.

The one thing I do know—it is a problem that can't be solved unless we work together; it requires cooperation. And the one thing that's essential for such cooperation is respect. All sides need to learn to respect one another's belief system or point of view. An atheist shouldn't ridicule a man or a woman of faith for believing in an invisible divine being. A person of faith shouldn't mock an atheist for believing it is all an accident. At the end of the day, we weren't there to witness life and its first heartbeats, but we are here now, together.

. . . .

Adam,

Be good to Mother Earth!!

Don't be wasteful!! Gedo made sure we didn't leave the dinner table if we didn't finish. "Nothing is to go to waste. If you put it on your plate, you finish it."

Save water!! There are millions who shower a couple of times a year.

Spend time in nature!!

Travel to different parts of the earth and explore its magic.

Happy Birthday, Mother Earth!
Osama & Adam

4/25/2017

Tax season is officially over, and I can go back to my normal schedule. You would think as a business owner I would work less hours. "You can make your own hours," Baba said when he convinced me to start my own business. That was not cool Baba, not cool at all.

I am not sure how he got me to do it. Wait, I do know—I couldn't find a job for the longest time because of my name. That was why. That was his way of pushing me in the right direction, but according to him. I am also realizing that there is a lot of fog. I am not recollecting full stories; I am really remembering only the big transitional moments or my traumas.

Is it possible that Baba tried all those years to help me find my own way and I didn't let him? I absolutely hate it when I can't recall things and I start doubting my own memory. I don't care that he convinced me to have my own business; I had no better option, and who on earth would say no to being his own boss? It ensured my survival and independence. And having you here in my arms, I definitely don't hate him for wanting me to marry your mother—it was the greatest gift.

I want to live again; I want to make the world better for you, Adam, and everyone around us. I wish Baba was still here with us to be a part of our journey. He is the reason we are a family; he is the one who insisted on having me, and he insisted I have you. The man never stopped until he got what he wanted, and we all loved him so much, we just did it willingly and lovingly. It is what you do when you love; you just give. He gave us so much.

4/26/2017

Dear Journal,
The mention of Baba makes me realize how much love was there between us all along. That realization triggers waterfalls; I keep feeling the emptiness and realizing how big a hole his loss has punctured in my heart. There is no other surgeon in this world who could fix it but Baba.

Anyway, I promised myself not to get too emotional tonight, and continue telling Adam the story.

So, Adam,

Remember when I told you about the conversation with your Tayta, and what she had to say about your mom? That eased my anxious mind. And, after all, I knew Baba wouldn't mind having a Shi'a daughter-in-law—he had a Pakistani and a white American convert as sons-in-law. So, it was time to discuss it with Laila to find out if she was ready to take the next step.

Every Wednesday, Laila and I went out after work for dinner and a movie. It became our ritual, and has been so ever since. We always tried to pick a new restaurant in the city or the outer boroughs to enjoy a new adventure. In those days we tried to avoid big blockbuster movies, choosing foreign films and documentaries instead. Our family and friends would ask us for recommendations, calling us the Zagat couple. So, during one of those outings, I decided to bring up the topic of marriage. That was the idea all along. Things were going great between us—we seemed to have a level of understanding and comfort that led me to believe that we could work as a team.

On that particular day, we were at a cozy Moroccan restaurant on the Upper West Side. It was very low-key and the layout allowed us privacy. I had booked earlier that day, reserving a table in one of the private booths.

After we had ordered our meals, I leaned over the table and firmly told her, "I think we should get married."

With a look of surprise, she paused and asked, "Osama, are you serious?"

"Yes, I am. I know we are not in a rush to beat your biological clock or mine, but our intentions from the start were aimed at marriage. Six months have gone by. I am ready, and I think you are. We trust each other."

"I do trust you, but I need more time."

"I understand. Take your time. I just wanted to let you know what was going on with me, that I'm ready. The sooner we do it, the sooner we are both free from those around us and their nagging and expectations."

We continued our evening as planned, making small talk as I ate my lamb Tajin and she devoured her favorite dish of couscous. Although things seemed fine, Laila had a look of bewilderment on her face, which she insisted on blaming on tiredness. She was distant for a bit.

A month or so later, Laila decided to revisit the subject of marriage. She was the one who initiated the conversation as we boarded a fairly empty train, heading to Brooklyn for some Thai food.

"Osama, a month ago you said you were ready for marriage, and it startled me."

"Oh yeah, I remember that night clearly. You mean when you rejected me," I laughingly answered.

"Well, I am ready to discuss it once again if you still feel the same way."

"Go ahead, I'm all ears."

"You see, when you brought it up then, I wanted to say I was ready too, but I had to make sure that it could actually happen."

"What do you mean? Why wouldn't it happen?"

She let out a loud laugh and said, "I am Lebanese, from El Janoub, the south, and Shi'a. You are *Masry*, Egyptian, and Sunni. Hell would have to freeze over before a family from El Janoub agreed to something like that."

Laila's family comes from Yaroun, a small town in south Lebanon. The southern region is predominantly Shi'a, and they like to maintain their strength by keeping to their own kind.

Apparently, her family opposed the idea at first and didn't wish to discuss it any further once Laila approached her mother. However, she didn't give in and decided to go straight to her father.

"It wasn't an easy battle to undertake with my parents. I had to use every trick in the book to get them to hear my argument. They questioned my faith. They presented many other suitable suitors once I brought up the idea of marriage and the fact that I was finally open to it."

I guess it was my lack of involvement with other Arabs over a period of years that made me totally ignorant of how dogmatic and ethnocentric some can be. I was in total shock listening to Laila's story about her battle with the family. I knew that the whole Sunni and Shi'a thing can be something of a problem, but I didn't know it would be as bad as Laila described it.

"They gave up on me for a while when I kept turning down every suitor who came to our house, and believe me there were many. My mom was approached almost every other day. Even our relatives back in Lebanon would phone my mom about suitors from all corners of the world. This was happening from the day I turned eighteen. But I turned down every offer because of school times, then because of work, and lastly because I didn't want to marry just any suitable man. I told my family, 'When I'm ready, I'll let you know.'"

That part of the story didn't sound unfamiliar. It was the same approach Mama used with me at one point— Laila laughed when I told her that.

"So, how did you get them to finally agree?" I asked.

"It wasn't that hard once I reminded them that I am in my thirties, and I am not getting any younger. I told them you are the man I love and that I won't marry anyone else. And of course, I had to shed a few tears."

"What? You love me?" I asked, grinning.

"You know I do." She laughed and winked at me.

5/2/2017

Although we were getting married to please others, our hearts were mysteriously filled with joy and happiness. It was the happiness a prisoner feels when the time of his or her release nears. I wonder if they are really excited stepping out from behind those high walls into a society that most likely won't accept them for their criminal record. We kept our records on the hush- hush.

Our decision to get married was our rebirth into the world. Soon, we would be free of the nagging. Soon, we would give our families their sense of fulfillment and make them happy—and in return we would gain our freedom. Once married, we would no longer have to meet their expectations. It was about time we set our own expectations.

There weren't any fancy romantic proposals. Once Laila had persuaded her parents to agree to our marriage, I asked her to set a date for our parents to meet to discuss the details of our engagement, wedding, and everything else that needed to be agreed upon.

"It is nice to meet you, *amo*." Laila ushered us in.

"Finally, I get to meet the man who made Osama give in." Baba extended his arm.

"How did you know it was Laila?" Mama asked.

"Didn't he just finish telling us that she is an only child? Plus, who else is going to open the door with that much excitement but the bride herself?" Baba pointed out the obvious to Mama.

"*Mashallah*, Osama, you didn't tell me Laila was this beautiful."

"Thank you, *Tant*." Laila blushed.

Laila led us through the hallway of the house. The house had a lot of open space. The walls were covered with various Islamic art pieces: One wall had this framed Quranic aya, the second wall had a picture of the Ka'aba, and the third had a picture of Al Aqsa Mosque in Jerusalem.

"*Salam alikoum*, everyone," Laila's dad said as he entered the room. "You guys are on time—you are not Egyptian, are you?" His sense of humor and smile made the introduction a warm one.

We exchanged our *salams* as Laila introduced us to her dad.

"Baba, this is Dr. Issa, Tant Hannan, and Osama. Everyone, this is my dad, Hussien."

"Who doesn't know Dr. Issa? He is one of the few Muslims who have made us proud here in New York."

"You are too kind."

"You have to pardon me, I was getting ready as you came in. I took my time, thinking you would show up at seven o'clock, Egyptian standard time."

Laila's dad was a lot more hospitable than I had expected, considering the fact that the opposed the idea of marriage previously. For some reason, I expected him to be this rude, short, fat, and bald-headed Arab man who rocked a mean mug. However, he was nowhere near my expectations, except for the fact that he was bald. He had very thick hair on the sides of his head ,which was pretty shiny and smooth in between; he was thin and tall.

A few minutes later, Laila's mother walked in, greeting and kissing my mom, followed by handshakes to both Baba and me.

"Before anything, what would you like to drink or eat? I see Laila and her dad didn't offer you anything. Tea or coffee?"

Laila's mom, Mona, served everyone their choice of drinks along with a variety of Middle Eastern pastries, which Mama loved.

"Oh my god, where did you get this konafa and baklava? These are the best I ever tasted."

"I make them myself. I make everything from scratch," Mona answered.

"Hannan, you should learn how to make them just like that," Baba said.

"No, no!" Mona laughed. "This is a secret family recipe."

"I guess Osama is going to luck out in that department," said Baba, who was genuinely happy for me.

Laughter and small talk were the theme of the get-together. Everyone seemed to be getting along just fine. They talked about how and why each family had moved to the states. They talked of the Arab-American community and politics. After all, what is a congregation of Arabs without politics—they couldn't and wouldn't have it any other way. The fathers talked of the Arab spring, while the mothers talked of their different cooking recipes. Laila and I kept jumping between the mothers and fathers.

The different conversations were flowing freely for a couple of hours before an awkward silence took place for a minute or so. However, that minute felt like an eternity. It reminded me of those old Arabic movies I watched with my parents. Awkward silence seemed to be the common dominator in every marriage scene. I pictured my mom playing the tough mother-in-law role like Mary Monieb once did in one of those movies. I just pictured her pulling Laila's hair to make sure she was not wearing a wig, or giving her a hazelnut to crack with her teeth to test her teeth.

"It is not a secret why we are here," Baba said, clearing his throat. "The kids seem to know each other well and know what they want. So I am not going to give a long introduction or a speech. Our family would be honored to have your daughter, Laila, as a member of our family, and I am sure we won't find anyone better than her for our son, Osama."

As I heard Baba utter those words, I felt this overwhelming sense of both ease and bewilderment. It was really happening. Laila and I were looking at each other in a state of disbelief. Things were progressing; the two families got along just fine.

"Kind words from a kind man. And we won't find a better family or home for our daughter. She is your daughter from this moment and you can take her with you," Laila's dad said.

"Wow, Baba, you really want to get rid of me that quick, don't you?" said Laila, laughing.

"*Bint*, Laila, hush. Let the men finish talking."

"I am not sure how Lebanese people do things, but for us Egyptians, once we agree, we recite the *Fatiha,*" Baba said.

"We are not that different. It is pretty much the same."

"I am sure we won't disagree on anything, *inshallah*." Lifting his hands up closer to his face, Baba signaled everyone to start reciting, "*Yalla, Bismallah*. Let's do it, in the name of God."

As everyone said *amen*, deafening ululation from both mothers replaced the silence, and everyone was congratulating Laila and me. That was one of many gatherings between the two families. However, it took another one or two meetings to settle all the details concerning the marriage. The dowry was set based on the amount that was customary in Laila's village back home, and Baba almost doubled that amount. And by the third gathering, I got to meet most of Laila's family in the states and she got to meet the rest of my family. We all gathered at her parents' house to announce the engagement to everyone. A custom that had to be followed—the engagement is not considered final until the largest numbers from both families meet under the same roof and pretend to discuss and agree to the terms of the marriage. It did seem like we were asking for her hand all over again.

It was finally official. I had a woman in my life. The nagging stopped. I had an engagement band on my right hand with Laila's name engraved on the inside. The band was my access pass to freedom. Laila and I were invited to many functions, dinners, engagements, and weddings by both sides of the families and extended families. We were both happy to appear at such events and enjoy ourselves without worrying about who is trying to set up whom. We were able to be ourselves with each other and participate in the festiveness of it all. It felt great to reconnect with my Arab side once again without having to worry.

Once the wedding date was set, the excitement and chaos of wedding preparations took over our lives. It took over my parents' lives; it took over Laila's parents' lives as well as Laila's, to my surprise. Considering that the wedding was meant to be one of convenience and practicality to satisfy our families, I never thought that Laila would act like a bride-to-be. It was understandable why our parents were excited about the whole ordeal. Her parents were happy for their only child's marriage. My parents were also happy to see their last and only single child get married and carry on the family name. The letter that Baba left behind explains his great excitement; it also explains why he was so willing to double the amount of the dowry, and why he had no problem covering all expenses.

The rest was history from that point on. Your mother became Bridezilla.

"Osama, we need to figure out the seating arrangements, the centerpieces, the flowers, and the music," and so on and so forth.

As much as I tried to fight and no matter how much effort I put into not getting as involved as everyone else, I felt bad letting Baba do the running around alone with the women. I didn't want the exhaustion to cause any setbacks to his health. However, it seemed like he was enjoying it a lot more than any of us, as if he was the one about to get married. I was finally sucked into it myself once I had to go shopping with the mothers and Laila for the jewelry. These women were tireless when it came to both shopping and spending money.

"I don't understand why we can't just buy a ring and that is it, like everyone else does."

"Stop your griping, this is Laila's big night, and she will have the best of everything. She gets to have everything she wants," Baba said.

"Still though, why does the woman get a whole set of jewelry and the man only gets a wedding band, if he is lucky?"

"Do you want us to get you some earrings and necklaces too, or what?" Mama laughingly asked.

"Osama, here is a golden rule you should know. A wedding night is something every woman grows up dreaming about, it's her night to be a princess, to live out all her fantasies and dreams. It's her night to be in the spotlight. You should just go along with it, nod your head and agree to everything she asks for if you want to have a happy life," Baba said.

I went through the motions with everyone else as we booked the wedding hall, the mosque, and the band, as well as sending out invites and every other bit of detail. However, I was not enjoying any of it. The longer the process took, the closer I was to walking away. I had my moments of doubt, and I almost had a relapse like I did when, after Hajj, I thought I could face the outside world but I failed the first time life presented itself. Now I was about to live a big fat lie if I went through with the wedding, and marriage would include screwing up someone else's life as well. I didn't want to have anything to do with that. I didn't care to be responsible for another human's life. There were moments when I wanted to call off the whole circus, but seeing the happiness on everyone's face brought me back to the path I chose to take along with Laila; it was our decision.

"What's wrong, Osama?" Laila asked one day.

"What do you mean?"

"You look like you are on a different planet. You hardly said a word the whole time we were finalizing the details with the caterer."

"I am just tired, that's all. And I know you have everything under control."

"I think it is more than that. Tell me, what is wrong?"

"*Wallah*, there is nothing. There is a lot going on at work and I haven't had a chance to rest with all the running around for the wedding."

"Are you sure? Are you having second thoughts about any of this? If you are, you can tell me."

"No, not at all, I am actually excited about this as much as you are. I even had a fun idea for the wedding itself."

"Really? What is it?" Laila asked.

"I was thinking we should have a little bit of fun with the wedding and do something different. We should choreograph a dance for the entrance instead of the boring *zafa*."

"No way! I love that idea. I saw a few of those grand wedding entrances on YouTube and I loved them."

I should talk to Laila about some of the things I have unveiled here.

5/5/2017

In spring 2012, your mother and I were taking the steps needed to finalize the marriage escapade as we stepped into the mosque to do *Katb Al Kitab*. There is not much to remember about that day, except for a couple of things. The first was the fact that I was as nervous as everyone else who walked down this road before. I always made fun of others for getting so shaky once the imam talks them through the process—they end up messing up the few simple lines or simply forgetting the name of their wife-to-be or husband-to-be. I always felt that they were faking it and there was no reason to be so nervous. However, I learned that day how nerve-racking the whole process can be as you sit there, in the house of God, vowing to love and care for this person and protect this newly formed and sacred bond. So, yeah, I ended up giving your mother a different last name as I repeated the information behind the imam, which was surely the laugh of the evening.

The wedding was the most typical Arab wedding, yet it wasn't so typical. We organized it the same way most Arabs do: We had the *zafa* music; we had the belly dancer; we had the *halal* champagne for toasting, as no alcohol was served; we had the Arabic DJ; we had *dabka* music. We made sure our wedding was as Arabic as possible—no details were spared. On the other hand, we had the creative and choreographed grand entrance that surprised everyone and made its way onto YouTube. It was our night, and we decided to have fun with it in every way possible.

Along with practicing the grand entrance dance to Michael Jackson's *Thriller* with an Arabic twist, I had to learn how to dance to *dabka* music, which is very big on your mother's side of the family. We did a lot of dancing that night, more than I did my whole entire life. And the times we weren't dancing, we were sitting in our seats watching everyone as they watched us.

We couldn't help but make fun of all the married couples who were sitting there clapping without moving a muscle or coming near the dance floor. It was ridiculous how uptight some of those people were. Your mother and I had the best seats in the house. I am pretty sure people were sitting there criticizing us for one thing or another. Some were probably complaining about the music playlist or food. Others were probably gossiping about Laila's dress or hair. If they only knew that we were doing the same exact thing as we kept leaning toward each other, whispering and pointing out funny things to each other. The wedding served its purpose. And it was a great bonding experience for us.

The ones who stood out the most were my parents and the way they acted with each other, which was something that Laila herself noticed and pointed out once she saw them slow dancing with each other.

"Your parents are adorable, too cute for words." She smiled.

I love people who understand and know their own truth; however, I have more love for those who understand their own truth and the truth of others, and are able to balance the two. Baba and Mama, together, exemplified love; they found the right balance that worked for them. Your mother and I will hopefully find the right balance that will work for the family as a whole.

Love is not meant to be caged behind our ribs. Express it! Find a partner who will laugh, dance, cry, and build with you.

5/11/2017

Your mom and I have been talking about giving you a brother or sister. In a way, we've decided that we will go for it; we have been trying. She doesn't want to miss the window of opportunity before her eggs expire, and she doesn't want you to be an only child like her. We both think it is better to have more than one child. Don't worry, the second will be a spare in case anything happens to you. I am kidding. You better love your baby brother or sister and be good to them.

The discussions about having a second child led us to consider adopting a Syrian orphan. Sadly, there are many of them with all the chaos unfolding there.

Does it make us biased that we considered a Syrian child before any other nationality?

I guess it does in a way, but we are also concerned about the millions of orphaned children out there who don't get a chance in life. We figured a Syrian child would fit perfectly in our little family. He or she wouldn't have much to adjust to in terms of language and religion at home. Anyway, it was decided that we would adopt down the line, 5 or 6 years from now.

I know one day you will ask us about where babies come from, and I am curious as to whether we will tell you the actual mechanics of it or if we will make you watch the *Storks* movie.

And since I did mention my conversation with Laila, I did tell her about what I do in here every night. "I am proud of you," she said. I am slowly sharing things with her; I don't think I can just unload it all at once. We also talked about some of the things that I shouldn't share until we share them together, with you. We talked about creating some kind of a video diary for you, and we briefly discussed family therapy.

"There is a lot of junk in there, and I want to make sure it doesn't hurt Adam, or anyone else," I told your mama.

"I feel the same way, but it is not always the best option to provoke what needs not to be provoked."

"Mine was awakened the minute Baba passed and left me a letter."

"What letter?" Her eyes widened.

I showed her the letter, and it was a very tearful night for both of us. "I am thinking of going to a therapist," I said.

"That's a good idea." She repeated herself, "It's a good thing. I should do the same— or maybe we should do it together. We agreed to make it through together." I think it was the first time Laila allowed me to see her scared inner child. I recognized something in the way her eyes widened. They were the eyes of a child lost in the mall who just realized it. So, we will have more discussions about that, but for now, I can share with you how you were made, but nothing else about our married life; Judge Laila ruled it.

It was our first big decision as a married couple. After three years of marriage, Laila and I finally agreed to have a baby to keep the families happy. It wasn't enough that they pressured us into getting married and that we had to live this lie. As soon as we returned from our so-called honeymoon, everyone was asking if we were expecting. Every Arab couple must endure this question from family and friends as soon as they tie the knot. In the eyes of many Arabs, marriage is for baby making and nothing else.

Luckily, I had managed to marry my best friend, who had similar views. We had agreed from day one that we wouldn't bring any children into the world until we were both ready and sure that it was absolutely the right thing to do. We worked together as a team, battling against the mounting pressure from both families. We managed to silence their nonstop nagging. We made it very clear to everyone that it was none of their business and that it was our decision alone. But that didn't mean they stopped dropping hints altogether.

The decision to go ahead after three years wasn't difficult—not nearly as difficult as keeping up the lie and keeping our secrets safe. We needed to be sure we were in this for the long haul and that we could make this marriage work and appear normal to the outside world. We had to consider whether it was fair to bring another human being into our complex equation. It wasn't a normal family setting and we needed to be sure a baby would not suffer because of that. We both loved children very much, and we had to be sure that our decision was the right one for the child, as well as for us.

At that point in our marriage, Laila and I had everything figured out. We lived as happily-ever-after as any married couple could wish for. We were as close as it gets; we were best friends. We experienced an intimacy that many of our heterosexual married friends envied. We were totally naked and transparent in front of each other. Our home was our safe haven; we didn't have to hide anything from each other. The masks were off once we entered our home.

We talked often of how we had failed to establish such a bond of mental and emotional intimacy with past lovers, friends, and family members. We did everything together. We shopped together, we cooked and washed dishes together. We had fun times going on spur-of-the-moment trips. We had our weekly date night and we had our movie night at home. What we had was by far the healthiest relationship either of us ever had experienced.

"Osama, I think I am ready," she casually said as we were clearing the plates after dinner. Your mom has a knack for letting me know her decisions out of the blue.

"I know you are. It's been a while since you had any," I jokingly responded to her vague comment.

"I'm being serious now. I think I'm ready to be a mother," she said, looking surprised. "Oh my God, I can't believe I just said that out loud!"

"I believe you—you should see the look on your face! I can't believe you said it either."

"I know, I know, but I do think it is about time to add another person to our little family."

"But, Laila, we already did that quite a few times."

"Osama, stop being an ass. You know what I mean."

"I do. So, let me ask you this: Do you think that we are ready?" I asked the question with an emphasis on *we*.

"I think we are."

"We can't just *think* it. We have to be absolutely sure of this. We're no longer talking about just the two of us. We're talking about bringing a new life into the world."

"That's why I am bringing it up, for us to ponder together. Look, I'm not getting any younger, and my eggs will dry up one day soon. I would love to enjoy the gift of motherhood and I know in my heart that I wouldn't want to do this with anyone else. I know we will raise amazing kids together."

"Laila, I feel the same way as you do, but I'm just concerned that adding a child will complicate things for us in the long run. What will we tell him or her one day if the truth comes out? We can't be selfish about this; we have to be very careful making this decision."

"Hiding our secrets from one more person won't be that hard. We've done great so far, and we're great together."

"How about the religion issue?" I threw that question in sarcastically.

"You must be kidding me, aren't you?"

"It's a valid question, and you know people will ask it," I answered.

"Well, Mr. Smart-Ass, I don't care. Our kid will be Muslim and that is it."

"I don't care either, Mrs. Smart-Ass, but how about when the families ask?"

"I'll let you take care of it."

"Come on, that is just wrong."

"Hey, you are the one who asked."

"Fine."

Laila and I never had to argue much about religion. She is Shi'a and I am Sunni, but we had a similar attitude about it—we are a fusion, we are Sushi Muslims. We never felt comfortable with how others labeled themselves. In our world, there was one Islam, one Christianity, and one Judaism. There was no place for disunity or philosophical gaps in our home.

"So, Mrs. Smart-Ass, how do you propose we do this?"

"What do you mean?"

"You know, the whole business of getting pregnant and bringing a kid into the world," I answered, standing in imitation of a pregnant woman, hands on an imaginary bump.

"Oh shit, I totally forgot about that part. Now that is a real dilemma." She started laughing as she said it.

"Yeah, I'm not sure what you were smoking or drinking when you thought of this unless you can magically make a child appear."

"I don't know how, but I'm sure we'll figure something out."

Finally, we decided it was best to conceive a baby by natural means rather than using medical means. We trusted each other and it was for the greater good, or so we told ourselves.

"Osama, we don't really need to go anywhere to get this done. I don't think either of us has a problem making a baby. All of my organs are functioning and so are yours."

"What? How did you know? Have you been watching me or something?"

"Oh yeah, I'm always watching you while you sleep and in your shower. I know all about what you do in there," Laila added, with a mischievous smile.

"Okay then, now you are freaking me out. Have you given this a lot of thought?" I asked.

"Really, Osama, and yes, I've been thinking about it ever since we talked about it a few weeks ago."

We continued our discussion and Laila told me of her preferences and her reasoning.

"Although we're not a normal family, I would love everything about this baby to be normal and natural." She held both my hands in hers and looked me in the eye.

As with every other decision, it didn't take us long to come to an agreement. We would begin trying to conceive a baby when her next cycle approached. We also agreed on a couple of practice rounds to familiarize each other with things we liked and didn't like.

We had never done anything more than kiss on the lips and hug in front of others to maintain our façade.

On the designated day, we went out to dinner. We had a few drinks to loosen up. We weren't our usual selves that night. We were both very tense and nervous. We had seen each other naked before—we had lived under the same roof for three years. We shared so much with each other, but we had never shared the experience of physical intimacy.

Neither of us was a heavy drinker, so we had just a few glasses of wine to avoid getting really drunk. After dinner, we went out for a walk along the streets of the city to enjoy the beautiful fall weather. We made small talk along the way to avoid awkward silences. It felt like

I was on a first date with my wife. We joked about it on the way home.

"Tonight I will become Mrs. Osama; I'll no longer be the virgin bride."

But that night was not it. Laila remained the virgin bride. We were both so nervous and so tipsy that we kept on laughing every time our bodies touched. At one point, I grabbed her breasts and pretended I was honking a horn.

We made other drunken attempts to consummate our marriage physically and bring a baby into the world, but we kept on failing. Every time, we ended up laughing hysterically about one thing or another, or we just snuggled and fell asleep in the process.

Our failure frustrated us; we didn't know the reason for it, but it kept happening. We talked about it over and over again. We even considered bringing others to join us to make us both feel comfortable and get over the anxieties that were making us fail so miserably. We even discussed using ecstasy or other drugs to take the edge off, but we dismissed that idea. We wanted to bring a baby into the world as naturally as we could.

So, we decided that we wouldn't keep forcing things to happen, but we would start sleeping in the same room, in the same bed. We figured it was the best way to feel comfortable with each other physically. At first, the new sleeping arrangement was very awkward; I had never shared my bed with anyone for more than one night. It took some time to get used to, and I often wanted to give up on the new arrangement, but something always stopped me.

There was a small part of me that enjoyed the new level of intimacy and closeness between us. There were times when I woke in the middle of the night and found my arms around Laila, or hers around me.

Slowly but surely the awkwardness faded and, instead of falling asleep on opposite sides of the bed, we began to snuggle our way into sleep. It took us almost two months of the new regimen to get this close to each other, and it took another month or so until the first time we had sex. The credit for that first time all went to Laila, who took control over the whole thing. She just knew all the right things to say and do to have me completely submit to her. She did everything right to make me feel both completely comfortable and aroused. Or maybe I did want it to happen; maybe we both wanted it to happen since we were both deprived sexually. We had agreed to deny ourselves any form of sexual gratification until we had accomplished our mission. I lost my virginity, vaginal sex, to your mom.

That first time, and the many other times we had sex, confused me because I actually found myself enjoying it and looking forward to more of it. I found myself asking Laila what she liked. I found myself looking forward to pleasing her. It was no longer about sex alone; it was no longer about making a baby. There was more to it, and I didn't know what it was.

5/30/2017

Dear Journal,

Tomorrow is Baba's birthday; he turns 80.

I visited his grave earlier today. It was my first visit since he passed. I spent a few hours there talking to him. I had to catch him up on everything that has been going on, and I had to tell him that he was wrong.

Baba thought I was the one responsible for his understanding of unconditional love, and as much as I'd like to concur, I will not do so. Looking back at everything, I realize that it was he who taught me to be everything I am today. We had our disagreements, and we had our agreements, but he never stopped being there. He didn't disown me like his father did him for following his heart. He dealt with it the best way he knew how, and that is the funny thing about love—it manifests itself in many forms, and we all think our way is best. Every generation has its way of showing love. I will tell you this much: Most people in my generation didn't hear their parents say "I love you" enough. It was rare. And now, it is all about expressing your love to your children and telling them they are special. Back in my day, our parents loved strictly with one of many items—belts, hangers, flip flops, broom sticks, forks, spoons, or whatever item was within reach. We didn't have time-outs, we did hard time in the kitchen or the yard or any chore they invented right then and there. I am sure my grandparents' generation expressed itself by controlling every aspect of their children's lives. I know it is the easy thing to hate him for coercing me into marriage, and God knows what else. Yet, when I look back I see nothing but progress. I see one generation loving better than the one before it. I choose to see love and I choose to be a better person, a better father, a better son, a better brother. I shall love better and that is one thing I learned from Baba.

It's a lesson that I wish I had learned in his lifetime. Though he's gone, I feel a lot closer to him than I ever did. I feel his presence in my roots; he is present in my every thought. We have conversations before I go to sleep every night. He passes through my dreams every now and then. That letter he left behind melted away all my fears and worries and the walls I had up for years. It allowed me to embrace the pieces of Baba that he had entrusted me with. And this is why I am choosing to stop writing these journal entries for a while. I want to spend more time creating more memories with you and the rest of the family. We all remember Baba for his actions and the little things he did for each of us. It wasn't how much money he left behind, and it wasn't any medical degrees or research published—it was his efforts to be present and a part of our lives.

I had to let him know that he was truly missed, and I didn't want to leave him alone. I didn't leave the gravesite until it got dark and staying wasn't an option. I did, however, bury two notes next to his grave. I hope they do make their way to the other side.

Dear Baba,

I did get your letter, and if you are reading this, it means you got my letter too. As you can see, I am getting back some of my humor. It has been a while since I found joy in anything besides my dear boy. Life hasn't been the same without you at the head of our dinner table on Sundays, and without your random calls and requests to see Adam. He is getting big, and he is starting to look like you.

I have been following your advice, and I have been sharing with Adam all the things you taught me. I am also sharing all the things that I should have shared with you.

I understand and respect your decision to do things the way you did. I always understood your stance on exceptions and how they lead to disappointments. You always did tell us, "The second you make one exception, you will make another and another, and that will lead to the decay of our existence." I understood that you operated within the boundaries of divine law, and I knew that you would pick God over anyone else. I guess that was why I never came to you either. I have no doubt that we both did it out of love, and it was our jihad in this realm.

Baba, I hate that you are no longer a part of our world, but I do feel your presence every now and then, and I am also seeing you in my dreams. I know you are in a much better place, but I selfishly wish you were still around us. There is so much that I want to discuss with you; there is so much I want to share with you.

I am trying to re-learn it all for Adam's sake. I do plan to teach him about the homeless shelter or orphanage test. I don't think I ever shared this with you, but Laila did pass the test. She was super nice and sweet to everyone. You were right—there is so much you can see in a person's reaction around the less fortunate and babies; we are simply vulnerable. I bet you didn't think I was listening that night when we were watching *A Bronx Tale*, and the car test scene was on. It was then you told us of this timeless test to pick a good partner.

I don't know if I should be mad at you or thankful that you coerced me into marriage and having a child. I am definitely more thankful. Adam has been helping me see things through your eyes, the eyes of a father who loves his kids more than anything else.

Though you never explained what you meant by preferences in your letter, you sure had me dig deep to know what it is you know, but with no luck. During the digging, I came across some gems that I wrote for Adam in a journal which I plan to give him. I am practicing discussing the big issues with him, starting now.

I would share them with you, but they are our own family secrets and they don't leave our household—you taught me that too.

You have been my greatest teacher—well, a close second to Mama—and I would move mountains for you because I know you would do the same for me, over and over again.

I love you and I miss you.

Osama

Dear Nora,

I am not sure where to start or what to say to you. In all these years, I couldn't think of what I would say to you if I had a second chance. I know that I can't take back the things I said and did, and I can't go back and do things differently. You are gone, and that has been my terrifying reality.

You have been a part of my reality for the past two decades. You haven't left me in my drunken or sober moments; you have been constantly present. I have tried to run away from you—I have tried everything but confronting you.

I hated you for what you did to the two of us. You omitted the most important aspect of you; you didn't give me the chance to decide for myself. You wrecked me, and in the process you wrecked yourself too. I really didn't know what to do back then; I didn't know the right things to say. You were right—I didn't understand. I was just a fucking kid. I can make all the excuses in the world for my actions, and blame it on you, society, ignorance, and faulty educational systems that failed us both, but that doesn't take away from the guilt I've carried all these years. I've wished there was a way for us to trade places; I would have taken your place in an instant.

Now that this part is out of the way, I can tell you that I am truly sorry for not giving you the chance to explain yourself. I am sorry for all the times I cursed and spat at you, I am sorry for ripping up all those letters and cards in front of you. I truly regret that it was me who was the cause of your death. I don't think I will ever be able to forgive myself, but I do hope you can find it in your pure and beautiful heart to forgive me.

I wish there was a way for you to know that you were the one who always mattered to me. Since you, nothing about my life mattered. I saw you in everything and everyone. If reincarnation was a thing, I would have sworn that your soul had returned and took the form of many people.

You were the only true love in my life until my son, Adam, arrived. I was going to name him Nour as I had promised you, but I couldn't do it. I couldn't handle another reminder of you. However, I did tell him all about you, and all the good and bad we shared. He is the only human I have been able to share that with.

I am trying to educate him at a very young age, and teach him about all our differences as humans. I am hoping he will be a better man if he is ever in a similar situation. I am teaching him to embrace the commonalities of our humanity before anything else.

The world is not that much better since you left it. We are still struggling to define who is deserving of rights and who is not, and it is 2017. We have yet to learn that every human is deserving. I hate to admit this, but you wouldn't feel at home on our planet, you would have to be very selective, and you couldn't reside in many countries. They would kill you, and me too, if they were to know the truth. I am sorry we are not doing better.

I won't ask you to stop with your random appearances, because it is the only way I am able to see you. However, I do ask you to smile more; I miss that smile of yours. It was and will always be my lighthouse.

I miss you and I love you.

Osama

6/21/2017

Dear Journal,

I haven't done much writing as of late. I didn't want to share until the month was over, but I did fast the last few weeks. It is my first Ramadan in years to not fake fast. I decided to do it for Baba and for myself, too.

So, let me tell you this one thing first: Fasting Ramadan during the summer months is brutal, but God said things should be easy on us. I don't know why, but it feels like we are calculating something wrong. The lunar calendar months refer to the seasons of the year— two of the months are called spring, and other two refer to freezing.

What good is a system that farmers, merchants, and hunters can't follow?

Is that why we follow the Gregorian calendar for everything?

I read somewhere that Ramadan came around the same time of year throughout the life of Prophet Muhammed. Anyway, I am determined to fast the whole month. We are a few days away from Eid.

The past few weeks have been a great reminder that Baba still lives within all of us. I felt his presence as we worked together to prepare meals for *iftar* and when we broke our fast together every weekend. I felt him in the love we all share for one another as siblings. I saw him in the twins and their detail-oriented ways. His love and openness were present as our very mixed family reached over the table to fill their plates.

The time with the family made me realize how much I missed out on over the years. It is a realization that was made when I looked through Baba's phone, which I plan to keep as my guide or key to Baba's world, as this journal will be yours, one day, to mine. I did ask Mama if I could keep the phone.

As I look through Baba's phone, I realize that I didn't know the man as well as I thought. It made me wonder if people are seeing one another the way they wish others to see them. Like, how did Baba see himself? And how did he think we saw him?

I read his texts with friends, and I see his silly humor in the form of medical jokes. I read his texts to us, his kids, and there is an engaged parent who loved with all his heart, and the same thing when it comes to his texts with Mama. I was the one who put all our names into his first smart phone. When it came to Mama, he insisted on naming her Hayaty—"my life"— and he turned red when I teased him about it. The two of them had a layered bond, an unbreakable one.

Hayaty: What is the difference between *bashr* and *insan*?

Baba: Why are you asking?

Hayaty: The translation has them both as human.

Baba: What do you think is the difference?

Hayaty: Bashr is our form, human, and insan is the cognitive bashr.

Baba: I always thought it had something to do with the bashra, the outer skin.

Hayaty: You taught me to treat the word of God with close attention to details.

Baba: I didn't know I would have to meet higher standards.

It still amazes me how they kept the fire of their love going all those years. They also kept challenging one another up to the very last minute. They constantly pushed one another to do better as humans, individuals, parents, Muslims, and citizens. They were members of book clubs—I hadn't known that about them at all.

It is part of the reason I am reading the Quran and other books. I am attempting to be more than a pork-free-diet kind of Muslim, and to engage Mama a bit more.

She enjoyed doing so with Baba, and I am trying to give her all that he would have loved for her to have. It makes her happy, learning new things and sharing them with us all, and from the texts, I can tell that Baba was her copilot in that process.

I have been reading the Quran on his phone, and I am following all the verses that he marked. Those remind me of every time he quoted one of them. "Osama, whenever you find yourself in a bad place, search for God first; talk to God and ask for guidance, and if you can't hear the voice of God within, go help others. That's where you find goodness—go to an orphanage and spend a day around those kids, put a smile on their faces." He loved doing for others, and it was the words of God that made him see it that way. "Righteousness is not that you turn your face toward the east or the west, but true righteousness is in one who believes in Allah, the Last Day, the angels, the Book, and the prophets, and gives wealth (in spite of love for it) to relatives, orphans, the needy, the traveler, those who ask for help; and in freeing slaves; and who establishes prayer and gives *zakah*; those who fulfill their promise when they promise; and those who are patient in poverty and hardship and during battle. Those are the ones who have been true, and it is those who are the righteous." He used to point out how God placed all those factors ahead of praying and the pillars. "Believe in God and in judgment day, and be useful to yourself and others. That is the least God asks of us."

Baba never knew this about me, and no one else does but Laila, but I did follow his advice. I volunteered at orphanages, and I spent time with newborns at adoption agencies. It was my only refuge away from the world. Babies don't judge; they don't care for my name or religion; they don't ask questions. They did exactly what I needed—they restored bits of my humanity, enough to keep me going. It was my attempt to never lose sight of God and the beauty of life.

From Mama, I am learning that God is not a religion. God is not bound by structures and institutions; God is much more than that. "God is beyond our comprehension. Don't let the action of others be your guide to God. We are not reflections of God; we are reflections of ourselves. The misery of the world is our creation; the ruining of the planet is our fault. The suffering of men, women, and children, wars, droughts, hunger, and famine are our own doings. It is our politicians and leaders who are waging wars; it's our factories disposing of toxic waste in rivers and oceans. Humans did all of it, not God. You should remember that God is the creator of beauty, and it is we who ruin it. As to the way you treat people, be mindful of God, and when you are with God, don't worry about anyone else."

She is teaching me how to read the Quran with close attention to details. "Remember, those prophets and messengers knew God as fact, and no one would do wrong after learning such truth. Look at what Pharaoh's magicians did once Moses revealed the power of God; they surrendered right away. Imagine those who communicated with the divine. Whenever a story tells you otherwise, check your sources."

She is also teaching me to understand the meaning of words. The other day, she asked us all for the meaning of the word *Masakeen*, and we all got it wrong—we thought it was in reference to the poor, but we were far from the truth. She did a Dr. Issa move and schooled us on the root of the word. "Masakeen is inclusive of persons with limited means and it's inclusive of those with disabilities, and it comes from the word *Sekoun*, stillness."

I tried to challenge her with a modern-day concern and asked whether or not weed is forbidden. She shot me down with the most logical answer. "Osama, is it one of the items God declared forbidden?" And she went on to tell me how we can't forbid something as humans, but we can create laws that outlaw them if we collectively agree.

For now, Baba's legacy lives through all of us, and it will continue with Adam.

7/11/2017

Dear Adam,

Your mama and I decided to wait a bit on the baby brother or sister thing. Sorry, buddy. It is a decision we made once we agreed on going to therapy and booked our first few sessions. We figured it was best not to have the fetus growing during a very emotionally charged period of our lives. I guess it's a good thing I have been writing these things to you instead of saying them out loud. And that brings me to the next point.

I will stop writing the journal entries in your room. I am now aware that it is not best to expose you to my unstable energy. I can't stop thinking of the possibility that I am the reason you haven't talked yet. It is possible that we somehow did this to you. I want you exposed to only the best of me until you are old enough to handle it. This was meant to journal moments in our family history and to share Baba with you. Instead, it turned into much more than I ever anticipated. I loved every single second spent in your room watching you sleep peacefully. It was your peacefulness that triggered my war. A war waged with one goal in mind: the peace that will provide you with more peace.

Baba's death made me realize many things, but the most important lesson was the fact that he was our peace. He was *at* peace, and it gave us a sense of safety and security; he was our anchor. I know that if it weren't for him, I would have ended up dead from an overdose. His voice was always there to keep me within certain boundaries. It always pulled me back from jumping in front of a speeding subway.

I will continue this internal war to the very end, and fight every one of my demons to give you half the father I had. I look at you when you smile, and the whole world shimmers. You make me want to do and be better; you are making me better.

I wish I had a word other than war to describe everything I feel inside and all the things I wrote you about. However, I do promise this: It is a war of love and peace. My days of causing collateral damage through my actions are long gone. There are no causalities to this war; this is my holy war, my jihad. In my struggles to reach the holiest of holies, God, I will continue to search and fight for peace within, peacefully and mercifully.

Baba's passing was the big bang and the darkness. Your room became the womb where a new me found his way back into the world, and next to you, my inner child learned to dream and search for joy once more. It all happened right here on the pages of this journal, and I hope I get the chance to share it all with you one day.

Your presence makes me want to hold on to life. I want to be here to see you do it all—your first full sentence, your first day of school, your first soccer match, and whatever else you decide to get yourself into. I want to be here to celebrate you the way Baba celebrated us. You are making me think of my own mortality as I am coming full cycle in my grief.

So in case I am not the one to hand you this journal one day, and you found it on your own, know this! You will get an earful about taking something that is not yours. I would probably tell you all about the Straight Path like Baba did the first time I took a calculator from the twins' room without their permission. I'd probably tell you to never take things from others that they are not willingly giving to you, especially their hearts. If you don't recognize someone as your soulmate, don't try to steal their heart away. It can take a lifetime to recover from a heartache.

Learn to earn everything you have and to appreciate it, because I am not going to be here for you all time, nor will your mother. Work hard for your grades in school and do your best, and you are sure to attain what you deserve. If you think that you aren't getting what you deserve, look inside yourself first, and don't blame others for your failures, because you were probably the one who set yourself up for it. Learn to take responsibility for your own actions and don't blame others, even if they try to project some of their flaws onto you to make themselves feel better and to justify their wrongdoings. Stand on your own two feet. Don't wait for me or your mother or any other being on earth to do for you that which you can do for yourself. Create your own world by following your own dreams and goals. Move through life with purpose.

I do have a request to make—don't let money be the main focus of your life. I have seen many lose their integrity, pride, morals, values, families, and religion for the sake of money. People tend to lose sight of their true innocent nature once they are touched by lust for money. Money is a great tool to have when it is available, because, sadly, most things do require money, but remember that the best things in life are free, and all the money in the world can't buy them. Another thing you must remember: Money doesn't make *you*, you make *it*.

My dear child, life is like a big amusement park that you must learn to appreciate as you live and grow. If you step out of the picture and look at it from the outside as a whole, you will find out how amusing it all can be. One day, you will laugh with others or at them and the next day you will laugh at yourself. However, you must teach yourself to enjoy the simplicity of life, to find simplicity in every experience.

Do not judge others. Most people, if not all, are trying to hide their vulnerabilities in one way or another. People will hide their tears behind a phony smile. You will meet those whose smile will brighten your days, but behind that smile there is nothing but pain, which they hide away from others. So, to put it simply, don't judge a book by its cover, or, better yet, don't judge at all, because it is not your place to judge another man or woman. Learn to accept and respect all unconditionally; learn to be tolerant and loving. You must learn to keep an open mind to all in order to understand it all.

Don't worry about what other people think, be considerate of their feelings—you can argue ideas based on facts, but feelings are abstract facts that can only be acknowledged. Learn to speak your truth in a way that won't hurt others' feelings. Words can be a two-edged sword, and we don't all hear the same meaning in them.

You were lucky enough to be born into a well-to-do family and in New York City of all places. There are privileges available to you that aren't available to everyone else. Keep this fact in mind as you deal with others—know that there are people who haven't had a tenth of what you have. Be kind to others, and be mindful of our creator as you engage them. I hope you are never the type to blame the poor or victims for their misfortune, and definitely don't blame the Almighty. The blame falls on all of us collectively; it is our doing.

I want you to educate yourself as much as possible. Read and experience all that you can, but choose wisely. Education will one day be your main tool to advance in life and to understand life better. And I don't mean the kind of education that requires schooling alone. I am referring to your own curiosity, which will expose you to new adventures and to meeting interesting individuals in life. Ignorance is not a blessing; it is the scourge of humanity, especially if mixed with religion.

There is one fact that I want you to always remember. We, the human race, are the successors to the Creator to run the affairs of the planet and one another. You are never a minority, an immigrant, or a refugee anywhere you go. You are always home, and we should be good to our home and to our neighbors. We were wired to depend on one another, so work with others in harmony.

My dear son, I want you know that I have loved you with my whole being. You are a product of pure love, and if it were up to me, I would be here until we were ready to go to the next life together. You turned my world upside down. In my darkness, you are the light that keeps seeping through my walls and defeating my guards.

It is a scary feeling knowing the things I know now. I know that both my action and inaction can influence your outlook on life and experiences. I could easily pass down my fears and insecurities. I could also teach you my own understanding of the world, which in turn could limit yours. I know all of this because I am now aware of how my own experiences were shaped.

It's a huge responsibility, and I sometimes panic thinking about it. Just as I would want to live long for you, I would probably want to accompany you everywhere you go to make sure that you are safe. I wouldn't do it forever, but I would do it long enough for you to have learned the differences between the three types of nafs. I would stick around until you tamed your evil-inclined self and cemented the morals of your reprimanding self and added knowledge and faith to your assured self.

Teach yourself to tame that evil-inclined self. Even if you are doing wrong, don't lead anyone else into doing it. Always direct people down the right path, and there is no better way to do so than to lead by example. I believe that we are innately good, and we gravitate toward one another. However, hundreds of years of conditioning and pre-loaded applications of nationalism, religion, gender roles, and so on, can do so much damage to the human network. Regardless, learn to respect our differences and don't think you are better than anyone. Don't be their judge, because you will never be as fair and just as the Creator. Just give them the respect they deserve as humans, never take advantage of them, and don't try to force anything on them. And that doesn't mean that everyone gets the same kind of respect from you: Learn to differentiate between those who are real and those who are not, and always look people right in the eyes when you talk to them. We are accountable for our actions.

Those were the lessons I learned from Baba, and in his absence, I was tested. I allowed my lowest form of nafs to take over, and I barely paid attention to the other two. I blamed Nora; I reacted based on ignorance, and I never for a second took responsibility for my own part in it until she was no longer a part of our world. I also blamed Baba. I thought he couldn't love me for the things I had done, and I thought he didn't love me because he didn't confront me. Yet I am seeing it all now as the ultimate act of unconditional love. Love is freedom, and it is liberating; he made no threats, he made requests. He ended the previous cycle of his forefathers, and it is our turn to do the same. We will create our own cycle that won't be compared to the animal kingdom; we will create one based on our humanity and compassion.

I promise that I will always love you unconditionally and support you in every way I can. I promise to do my best to be there with you and for you every step of the way. I promise to always be the caring listener, comforting arms, watchful eyes, wise friend, and loving parent you may need throughout your journey.

Now go out and find your own truth. Don't believe a word of what I have written here, because I don't want you to believe everything you read or hear. I want you to always go and find the truth and compare your findings with what you have been taught. I want you to question every word I have written and test it for yourself, and then come back to me and let's talk about it. If you find that you were wrong, don't let your pride stand between us, and if you find that you were right, tell me about it, because you will teach me a new lesson. And do not fear me—I am your Baba and I am always in search of meaning as well.

Love you always,
Baba

Acknowledgment

I wouldn't have started writing if it was not for Daniel Kaplan encouraging me to do so back in high school. From there, I fell in love with poetry and storytelling through Michael Jackson's Dancing the Dream—it was magic. And without the challenging readings and ideas presented by Roy Mittleman and Beth Baron in my college years, I wouldn't have much of an intellectual foundation. I have been fortunate to have amazing teachers and professors who were passionate about their craft. My decade spent at the UN with beautiful people from every corner of the globe exposed me to the cores of our common humanity. To my former colleagues, the world still needs peace and security—keep at it.

Now, if you want to blame anyone for the fact that I pursued writing, you can point your finger to one of my dearest friends, Nicole Ergon. You convinced me that I had what it takes to be a writer, and for that I am forever thankful.

My cousin Simo was the first person to witness the inception of this story in writing and my obsession over the little details. Thank you for all the brainstorming sessions while hunting for the next great restaurant in Cairo. And if you don't like the novel, you can blame Siveem El Nashar. She was the first reader and editor, and it was her comments that made me believe I could do it. I am forever thankful for your time, thorough edits, and boost of confidence.

Caroline Denis, Heather DeViccaro, and Mahvash Javed, thank you for all the hours spent reading, editing, and discussing the many versions of this book, for so many years. El Kordy's, you two are forever inspirational; your input and thoughts were always unique and out of the box.

Jennifer Lopez, you captured the ideas for the cover in one sketch. Nasser Jaber, you were the secret weapon and joker behind the scenes. Perihan Abouzeid and team, I am grateful for all the hard work and effort before and during the crowdfunding campaign.

It was my good fortune that led me to a tough editor, Gina Heiserman. Your edits and comments were challenging and invaluable to this novel's maturity and birth. Ellen Peixoto, you were the perfect second set of eyes to put on the finishing touches.

Hosam El Khateeb and Michelle Collins, thank you for being there for the last stretch. My sanity is still somewhat intact because of you. And the same goes to the odd and long lifetime friendships that revolved around the simple concept of sharing ideas, which evolved into much more: Hosam Mekdad, Haythem Noor, Samer Ibrahim. The adventure continues.

To my lifelong and childhood friends, Mohamed, Mohamed, Mohamed, and Wael, thank you for being the anchors and constant family in this existence. Also, I am thankful for the Metwali crew and their extended families for all the amazing memories. We painted the town hunter green.

Ahmed El Masry, and Ahmad Ismail, the two of you have been the voice of reason and great older brothers in your own ways. Thank you for everything.

My gratitude, thanks, and love to the Abo Leila family, El Haddad family, Gafary family, Ismail family, Mohamed family, and Nasser family for being my big and long extended family.

To my family on all sides of the world, and to my siblings—Sam, Nancy, Nada, Sally, Adam—I love you all. And Sam, sorry you had to put up with my ongoing curiosity in the confines of a car stuck in NYC traffic.

Mom, Dad, thank you for always giving me the space and time to find my way, and loving me unconditionally. I love you.

This book has been a great journey. It has been a tiring, exciting, weakening, strengthening, and life-like journey. I have learned a great deal about life and myself throughout the writing process. I have learned things that I would had never thought about learning, if it wasn't for Osama and his nagging need to question and push boundaries.

Along the journey, I have met many who have been great guides. And to those great souls, I say thank you. I also extend my thanks to all the Kickstarter backers. There are many people to thank for their thoughtful discussions and lessons, so in one big, collective, and genuine gesture, I thank all of you from the very bottom of my heart.

Glossary of Arabic Words

Abu: father of
Alhamdulillah: Thank God, Praise be to God
Amo: Uncle
Athan: Call to prayer
Ayat: Signs
Azhar: The oldest degree granting university in Egypt.
Baba: Dad
Bashr: the Qu'an refers to human beings as 'Bashar', the mere appearance and physical aspects of human beings are the focal point.
Bent elkalb: daughter of a dog
Bint: girl
Bismallah: In the name of God
Dabka: A native Levantine folk dance performed by Lebanese, Syrians, Palestinians, and Jordanians. Dabke combines circle dance and line dancing and is widely performed at weddings and other joyous occasions.
Donya: life, world
El maktoob: that which was written
El Zamalek: A soccer team in Egypt
El-Ahly: A soccer team in Egypt.
Fajr: is the first of the five daily prayers (salat) performed daily by practicing Muslims. Fajr means dawn in the Arabic language.
Fatiha: The opening sura of the Quran, used by Muslims as an essential element of ritual prayer.
Galabia: a losse fitting gown or robe worn by men.
Gedo: Grandpa, informal
Habibi: my love, masculine
Habibti: My love, feminine
Hader: Yes, formal
Hadith: Sayings of Prophet Muhammed.
Hajj: Pilgrimage

Hajji: A person who has performed the pilgrimage
Halal: permissible
Hijab: Headscarf
Homar: Donkey
Ibn elkalb: son of a dog
Iftar: Dinner meal at sunset to break the fast.
Ihram: Clothing which is worn by Muslims during the Pilgrimage.
Imam: The person who leads prayers in a mosque
Insan: the Qur'an uses this word to refer to human beings, the personality, qualities and non-physical features of human beings are intended.
Inshallah: God willing
Intifada: uprising
Jihad: Strive, or struggle.
Kaaba: meaning cube in Arabic, is a square building elegantly draped in a silk and cotton veil. Located in Mecca, Saudi Arabia, it is the holiest shrine in Islam
Kafan: an Urdu word which refers to a length of cloth or an enveloping garment in which a dead body is wrapped for burial.
Katb al kitab: An Islamic marriage contract is an Islamic prenuptial agreement. It is a formal, binding contract. Its literal translation means writing the book.
Khalifa: Successor
Khawal: faggot, insulting
Kofta: ground beef and lamb mixed
Kufar: A term which is known to mean infidel. The literal meaning of the word at its root is to cover something.
Mabrook: congratulations
Masakeen: A needy person who has limited means for survival.
Mashallah: God willed" and used to express appreciation, joy, praise, or thankfulness for an event or person that was just mentioned.

Miqat: are the stations at which pilgrims on the Hajj, the pilgrimage to Mecca required of all able Muslims, put on ihrām, the pilgrim's garment.

Mufti: A Muslim legal expert who is empowered to give rulings on religious matters.

Niqab: a garment of clothing that covers the face, worn by some Muslim women as a part of a particular interpretation of hijab

Nour: light

Ramadan: The month of Ramadan when Muslims fast

Salam: Peace

Salat: Prayers

Sekoun: stillness

Shataf: Butt showering device/ Bidet

Suhoor: Meal in the middle of the night to prepare for fasting

Tant: Aunt

Tayta: Grandma, informal

Teez: butt

Umrah: the nonmandatory lesser pilgrimage made by Muslims to Mecca, which may be performed at any time of the year.

Wallah: By God, Swearing to God

Yalla: Let's go

Zafa: A wedding march, is a musical procession of bendir drums, bagpipes, horns, belly dancers

Zakah: is a form of alms-giving treated in Islam as a religious obligation or tax

Zulhijja: The 12th month in the Islamic lunar year.